The Marrow
from the Bone

Other Kelly Kane Publications

ORDERS FOR THE CAPTAIN
by James Kelly

A carefully documented account of the Dublin Arms conspiracy
trials of 1970
First published 1971
Reprinted 1986
Distributed by Well Red Distribution Co-op

THE GENESIS OF REVOLUTION
by James Kelly

Shows how the situation developed inexorably until the British
Army and the Provisional IRA confronted each other in February
1971.

The author also shows that by ignoring the basic causes of
violence in Northern Ireland, the British and Irish governments,
like the Koumintang in China, and the French and Americans in
Vietnam, are put in a position of escalating the level of repression,
thus continuing to force a guerrilla situation.

The Marrow from the Bone

JAMES KELLY

KELLY KANE LTD

First published in 1987
KELLY KANE LTD.
Bailieboro,
Co. Cavan.

© James Kelly

ISBN No. 1 870300 00 9

Typeset in 10pt Times
by Laserworks Co-op,
38 Clarendon St.,
Dublin 2.

Printed by:
Leinster Leader,
Naas

Cover Illustration: Peter Kelly

Distributed by:
Well Red Distribution Co-op
Tel: (01) 794793

"The artist has the liberty to exaggerate, to create in his novel a world more beautiful, more simple, more consoling than ours." - Guy de Maupassant

When I set out to write a story about Tunnygee, a mythical small town tucked away to the north of the Irish midlands, I did not follow Maupassant's advice. Instead, at the risk of sacrificing beauty, simplicity and consolation, I set out to make my story as realistic as possible.

Nevertheless, the majority of the characters are fictional, in that they do not relate to or are not based on any individual person. The exceptions to this are such as Ministers of State and one or two other State functionaries, who may be recognisable as real persons, despite the use of pseudonyms.

Because it covers a period of over thirty years, from the early fifties to the present day, it is practically inevitable that *"The Marrow from the Bone"* should, to all intents and purposes, be two books. This arises, because the cataclysmic events of 1969/70 in Northern Ireland affected people all over Ireland and, in particular, people in a border town like Tunnygee.

The second book could be said to start with Chapter 26 where Ian Paisley is to the forefront in a TV programme. This programme is viewed by a group of Tunnygee people in Tom Burke's pub.

In conclusion, I would claim that *"The Marrow from the Bone"* is an historically accurate interpretation of the Ireland of the period. As such I dedicate it to Suzanne, Jacqueline, Sylvia, Peter, Justin and Sheila Marie.

The Author,

Bailieboro, Co. Cavan.   April, 1987

1

Maisie was the eldest of the nine Dempsey children. In October 1952, she was sixteen years old. At that time, she was beautiful: short, yellow-red hair and big brown eyes looking out in wonder from a finely chiselled face, the contours of which were still rounded by the soft flesh of adolescence. With her nervous smile and ever ready blushes, it added up to an impression of appealing, childish defencelessness. Two weeks after her sixteenth birthday, she left home to work in the local town, Tunnygee.

The land to the north of Tunnygee was hilly and scraggy. It was here that Pat Dempsey scratched a living from a dozen infertile acres. A lifetime of hard work had left him bent and battered at sixty. In fact, all he knew was work and, if he had not the work, he would not have known what to do with his time. His day-to-day routine absorbed his all and his greatest pleasure was to sit by the fire at nightfall, sucking his short-stemmed pipe, spitting deliberately and regularly into the blazing turf.

Mary, his wife, was a shrewder, more intelligent, person and the management of affairs was left in her hands. When Pat sold a litter of *suckers** or one of the black polly bullocks on a fair day in Tunnygee, he strutted into the whitewashed kitchen. With a half dozen bottles of stout under his belt, he was the happiest of men as he counted out the dirty notes on the kitchen table.

"Mickey, the daler, didn't cod me the day," he told Mary, "He drives a hard bargain, yon fella, but he didn't get the better of Pat Dempsey. I got every penny of twenty-wan ten for that black divil of a bullock. A . . . A coorse, there was five bob luck, but there wasn't a man in the town got a better price for a baste the day."

* Young pigs

Mary counted the money again, carefully flattening each note, before placing it in the black box, which she kept under their bed in the room behind the fire. This money was used to pay the rates and the rent and to purchase the family clothing from the street traders on fair days. The other major source of income was the hens, a hundred or so of them, half-bred and half-wild. It was on their eggs that Mary depended to meet her obligations to *Tom the Shop*. Few of the eggs were eaten, but, most of them, washed and clean, neatly packed in the old wicker basket, found their way to Tom's ramshackle, corrugated-iron hut at the crossroads, where the six fly-blown soap cartons, lying haphazardly in the narrow, dusty window, were the only indication that inside could be had anything from a bag of meal to a card of pins.

When Maisie left school at thirteen, she became her mother's right hand, looking after the younger children and feeding suck calves, pigs and hens. Young Pat, the second member of the family, hired out to a local farmer at fourteen, while Tommy, the next in line, a month short of his thirteenth birthday, stood in the Tunnygee hiring fair in the Spring of fifty-two. Maisie walked the four miles into town with him that morning. They stood with their backs to the bank railings. Tommy was big for his age and soon a farmer approached.

"Are you for hire, gasson?"

"I am, surely."

"You'd want to ate a few more bags of male before you could plough, I'd say?"

"No better man to plough."

"Can you feed pigs?"

"Aye."

"Can you milk cows?"

"I can milk anything but a hen."

"If you're as lively with the spade as the tongue, you'll do rightly," the farmer said.

"That I am."

"Well, you're a brave wee maneen anyway."

Half an hour later, the bargain was sealed at £12 per half year. The farmer brought up his cart and Tommy hopped up on the seat beside him. He did not turn his head until the cart was rounding the courthouse corner. Maisie waved tentatively as he raised his hand in a half salute. She then began the walk home.

Her mother was sitting by the fire, with twelve-months-old baby Sean on her knee, when she entered the kitchen nearly two hours later.

"Is he gone?" her mother asked.

"He is."

"How much?"

"Twelve pound the half year."

"He did rightly. Was he lonely?"

"I don't know. Anyway, he had his usual smart answers. You'd nearly be ashamed of him."

"I bet you he was lonely all the same."

"If he was, he kept up a brave front," Maisie said.

"Didn't we all? I suppose you'll be the next to go, Maisie?"

"Aye, Betty will soon be able to take my place."

"She's only eleven, but she's a good capable wee lassie. And a mouth less to feed, and the few shillings extra, would be welcome."

"I know that, mama, but it will be hard on you."

"Never mind me, Maisie. I'm in the whole of my health, but your father's getting on a bit. Now, with the two lads gone, he'll get it tight. You better stop until the Summer work is over. Then we'll see about getting you placed in the town. I wouldn't like you to move too far away. After all, you're my first."

Impulsively, Maisie went over and kissed her mother on the forehead.

"That's the first time you've done that in years," Mary wiped a tear away, "but, come on, that's enough of that. Give me over that po'nger there till I get a sup of milk into this fella. Like the rest of them, he'll be a year older next year. John will be eleven then and Betty twelve, nearly thirteen. We'll be well able to manage."

Maisie lapped hay that Summer. In the Autumn, she tied the sheaves of oats after her father's scythe and, in October, as the evenings closed in fast, she picked an acre of potatoes after his spade. On the third day of November, she and her father finally closed the potato pit. The oil lamp was lit in the kitchen when they reached the house. They were several yards from the door when it swung open and Mary stood outlined.

"You'd never guess who was here today," she called, her voice high with excitement.

"No, but will you let us in first?" Pat answered quietly. "The night would freeze a brass monkey. The hands are falling off us."

He went straight to the fire, flopping down on a low stool the better to garner the heat. Maisie stood to one side, her hands held out to the blaze. The mother closed the door and took her stance in the centre of the floor.

"Peader Kennedy was here," she announced.

"What did he want?" Pat asked.

"Maisie, what do you think? He wants her to work in the house. He wants her to start on Saturday."

"Saturday?" Maisie blurted.

"Aye, Saturday, are you not glad?"

"I am, mama, of course, I am."

"It could be worse, girl," Pat assured her, "it's wan of the best houses in the town."

Later that evening when the younger children had gone to bed, Pat sat on the three-legged milking stool in under the chimney-breast, puffing steadily. Mary occupied an old wicker chair on the other side of the hearth. Maisie sat on another stool opposite the fire. She was half asleep, luxuriating in the warmth, when her mother suddenly announced:

"Once you can hold your head up in the world, that's what matters. Riches is not everything. There's manys with plenty of money that have a lot more to hide than the likes of us. At least, we've nothing to be ashamed of."

Vaguely, Maisie wondered what her mother was talking about. In her sleepy state, the message did not impinge, but Mary was intent on driving the lesson home.

"I only heard it the day," she spoke to her daughter, while looking at the print of the Sacred Heart that gazed down from above the fireplace, "Katie Maguire skipped to England the day before yesterday."

"Katie?" Maisie was wide awake now, "I was talking to her on Sunday at Mass and she said nothing about it."

"It's a scandal," her mother declared, "a scandal, a regular scandal, but, sure, what can you expect? She's not the first of her breed to go the same way."

Full realisation of Katie's crime struck Maisie. She found it hard to believe - Katie Maguire, who had been only a class in front of her at school, going to England to have a baby. She knew all about babies, but she did not associate them with Katie Maguire. Imagine her letting any man do that to her. She squirmed on the hard, wooden stool at the thought of it.

"It's a scandal," her mother persisted, "I only hope I never live to see the day the same thing happens to one of mine."

"It won't happen to me," Maisie assured her.

On the following Saturday, she presented herself at the Kennedy household, where she was greeted by Peadar.

"The missus is down with the vet," he explained. "One of the dogs is sick."

At that time, Peadar was a handsome, middle-sized man, with brushed-back, brown hair over a round face. Thirty years before, as a timid fourteen year old, he had come straight from a mountain farm to work for Mick Dancy as a grocer's assistant. Once in town, he shed his timidity so quickly and so effectively, that at the end of a year Dancy could refer to him as "an impertinent wee bucko". He had graduated from the dour isolation of the farmboy to the ranks of the cocky, young shop assistants, to each of whom the town's one straggling street was his own private dunghill. On each halfday and every summer evening after work, they strutted, skylarked and guffawed in their harsh, guttural voices from the Protestant Church at the western approach to the town to Tommy Mac's meadow on the Dublin road. In their gauche cameraderie they found an outlet for the tyranny of long hours behind a shop counter and, as they crowed, Peadar Kennedy crowed louder than the best of them. He was a better businessman than the best of them too, and, before he was twenty, he was Dancy's top assistant. From there, he made the step to ownership by the simple expedient of marrying the boss's daughter.

Tall and slim, blond hair pulled back severely into a bun at the nape of her neck, Suzanne Dancy was good-looking in a palefaced sort of way. She was twenty-five when her mother died and five years older when her hardy, old father - he was eighty five - bid his thriving business a grudging farewell. At thirty, she was the sole owner of the Dancy enterprises, but a convent schooling and over a decade of gentility, as befitted the daughter of the opulent Mick Dancy, had not fitted her for the rigours of business life. In the circumstances, it was inevitable that the capable Peadar Kennedy should adopt an increasing management role. Eventually, Suzanne handed over complete control to him and retired to the house on the hill - the house her father had built for his bride nearly forty years before - to train maids and to improve the strain of cocker spaniels, which her father had taken to breeding in the later stages of his life. It was a lonely, austere existence and when, two years after her father's death, Peadar proposed marriage, she accepted. A year later, they were married.

In 1952, after twelve years of marriage, they were childless. Peader knew that it was Suzanne's fault. He had fathered a son over twenty years earlier. It had been a minor scandal in the town at the time. Rosie Burke was eighteen and Peader was twenty-one. Rosie had died giving birth. Suzanne's father had been intent on sacking Peadar at the time, but her mother would not hear of it. Suzanne had overheard the argument.

"Anyway, why are you so sure he's responsible?" her mother asked.

"Sure, weren't the two of them making arrangements to go to America after the birth. James of the post office told me."

"All the more reason not to dismiss him. At least, he was going to stand by her."

As the childless years passed, Suzanne, aware that Peadar had already fathered a son, became more withdrawn. In the end, she seldom appeared in public, except to go to first Mass on Sunday morning. The cocker spaniels in the backyard became her all-consuming passion. In fact, she was rapidly becoming recognised as a breeder of some distinction.

In the house, Suzanne had become a martinet, with order and cleanliness practically a fetish. Meanwhile, Peadar went about his business activities with apparent unconcern, but there were girls in the town, and some older women too, who learned to avoid his lurching embrace if he came across them in a secluded corner. He largely ignored the succession of girls whom Suzanne hired to help her in the house; young, country girls whom she could mould and train to fit in with her finicky ways. As she retreated into herself, rejecting Peadar more and more, some of the girls, not averse to submitting him to a coy glance or a provocative wiggle, assumed the role of wily, teenage temptresses in his eyes. The hare sits and waits on the dog, because it knows that it has the legs to outrun it, but, when the stone-age damsel showed her matted locks around the base of the oak tree or over the top of the gorse bush, she had no intention of outrunning her club-wielding future mate. So it was with the buxom girl who preceded Maisie. One night Peadar grabbed her in the back hall and Suzanne heard the shriek of mock surprise. When she accused him of attacking the girl, he was crudely indignant.

"I don't believe in shitting on my own doorstep," he said viciously.

"That was not always the case," was her tart rejoinder.

She sacked the girl at the end of the week, informing Peadar that she was capable of managing on her own. A month later she announced that it was either the dogs or the house, that she could not manage both, and Peadar suggested employing another girl.

The break between the two of them was complete when Maisie arrived. Instinctively, Maisie was aware of the tension, just as she was aware of and slightly fearful of Peadar. He was always polite and, indeed, friendly, but she was not happy in his presence.

Each morning, it was part of Maisie's duties to bring the brasses on the Kennedy halldoor to the shimmering perfection demanded by Suzanne and, each morning, she was at the halldoor immediately after breakfast, for this ceremonial polishing was the part of her day's work that appealed to her most. The fresh air at the top of the windy steps exhilarated her and she was back again, carefree and happy, on the high hill behind her father's house, inhaling the gusty heather-scented breezes swirling up from the bogland below. On her day off, having cycled the four miles to her home, she invariably made her way to the top of that hill and for the rest of the week the trip to the Kennedy halldoor served to give to her the same spirit of freedom and adventure.

One morning, when she was about four months in Kennedy's, she breathed on the gleaming brasses of the front door and, gently, caressingly in fact, rubbed the smear away to be confronted once again by the contorted reflection of her face in the dogshead of the door knocker. The dogshead was spotless, but she gave it a final rub. She was loath to leave the wintry sunshine of the front door and resume her labours in the comparative darkness of the kitchen.

Maisie was admiring her handiwork, preparatory to moving into the house, when her reverie was interrupted by the slamming of the garden gate, followed by a quick step on the path. She started and dived at the knocker again, rubbing fiercely. All her senses were alert, as tense and agitated, her eyes burrowed into the blind, unwinking eyes of the brass dogshead. At the foot of the steps, Peadar stopped and she felt a shiver running down the flesh at the back of her neck. She rubbed with still greater vigour and her teeth were tight on her lower lip as she fought unavailingly against the violent blushes. The drops of sweat that sneaked from her armpits were cold as they careered down her body.

"If you're not careful, you'll rub it away," Peadar said casually, turning off towards the back of the house.

Maisie waited and when she could no longer hear his footsteps, grabbed her accoutrements and bolted for the kitchen.

It was the second time that Peadar had surprised her. One afternoon, a week previously, she had been in Suzanne's bedroom. As she folded Suzanne's nightgown, she decided to try it on. She took off her jumper and skirt and put on the nightgown. She was pirouetting and preening in the flimsy garment in front of the dressing-table mirror when Peadar burst into the room.

As in Mick Dancy's time, when the room was his, cash was kept in a safe in the corner of Suzanne's bedrom. Bursting into the room, Peadar stopped in his stride when he saw the firm, well-developed young body outlined through the pink clinging material. For a moment, Maisie stood like a terror-stricken, cornered animal before, in a frenzy of embarrassment, charging from the room and nearly knocking over the gaping Peadar in her wild flight. He regained his balance and, taking a key from his pants pocket, tossed it meditatively in his hand before putting it in the lock and swinging upon the heavy safe door. Meanwhiie, a horrified Maisie lay with her back against her own bedroom door and listened until she heard the front door bang after him, the nightgown, that had so captivated her a few moments before, crumpled in her hands.

A week later, when he came upon her at the front door, she was back again in Suzanne's bedroom, half-naked before his eyes.

2

S t. Patrick's Eve each year was to Suzanne Kennedy a red-letter day. On that day, months of grooming, preparation and loving care, culminated in the transportation of the best of her golden cockers to Dublin, for the dog show on the following day. She travelled in the front of Jimmy Devine's hackney, while the well-mannered dogs reclined on the back seat. Two days later, sometimes prizewinners and more often not, they returned in the same way, the dogs to the well-ordered regime of the backyard, and Suzanne just home.

On St. Patrick's Day, some weeks after Maisie had been surprised in the bedroom, Peadar sat by the fire idly contemplating the whiskey in the bottom of his glass. He should have been at Croke Park. His St. Patrick's Day visits to the Railway Cup finals in Dublin were as much a ritual as Suzanne's to the Ballsbridge dog show. It was the first time he had missed the big games in years, but he was not feeling well. When the boys had called after first Mass, he was dressed and ready, but the pain in his head was worse.

"Come in and have a wee drop before we go," he invited, "I think I have a touch of flu coming on."

"Croke Park's not the best cure for that sort of thing," one of his would-be companions said.

"Aye, I was thinking of staying at home with the old bottle and a good fire. I can always listen to the matches."

"Don't be letting us down like that," Johny McCaffrey said. "A flask of ten year old in your hip pocket will keep any flu at bay."

"I don't know about that, Johny. I'm not as young as I used to be. It's time I'd sense. I'll stay at home."

When the men departed, Peadar settled down with the bottle of whiskey on the mantel beside him and when Maisie served the midday meal a cosy warmth of intoxication had crept over him. He said nothing, but he watched her; watched her trim efficiency as she served and the lithe way she left the room, closing the door gently and unobtrusively.

Standing on the hearthrug, he filled a pipe and the match trembled in his fingers. The powerful attraction Maisie had aroused in him surprised him and frightened him also.

There was a gentle tap on the door.

"I'm finished now, Mr. Kennedy. I'm going out for a walk," Maisie said shyly.

"Aye...Aye...whatever you like, Maisie."

"Thank you, Mr. Kennedy."

"A minute...a minute before you go, Maisie."

Maisie hesitated in the doorway. Facing her, Kennedy pulled on his unlit pipe.

"Do you know something, Maisie, I think you're afraid of me," he said breezily, "I wonder why's that now? Sure, I wouldn't harm a fly."

"No...No, Mr. Kennedy, I'm not afraid of you."

"Well, that's good news anyway, but, just the same, I sort of think you keep out of my way."

From under his eyebrows he looked at the abashed and embarrassed girl.

"Close the door and come in...and sit down for a minute," he told her, "I haven't had a chance of having two words with you since you came to the place."

Maisie pushed the door closed and took two or three uncertain steps into the room.

"Come on. Don't be shy. Sit down on the chair there," he directed her to a seat with the stem of his pipe.

Nervously, Maisie obeyed and sat on the edge of the big, ornate, leather chair.

"That's it. Make yourself comfortable," Peadar emptied the end of the whiskey bottle into his glass.

He sat down opposite Maisie, and elbows on his knees, grinned forward into her face.

"I suppose you don't touch the hard stuff at all . . . No . . . No, you're a bit young for that yet. Still, an odd wee sup is good for anyone now and again."

He swallowed another mouthful and, then, to Maisie's surprise, he emptied the glass. Deliberately, he placed the empty glass on the mantel before playfully reaching out his hand to tousle her hair.

"You can't beat a ...a drop of the crathur to put a bit of...of...life in a fella," he said, the words thick in his mouth.

Maisie shrank back until her shoulder blades, in the thin housemaid's dress, touched the cold leather of the chair, and watch-ed, as he went to the sideboard and opened a fresh bottle. He put it to his head and, gulping at it, slopped whiskey down his shirtfront. Grinning drunkenly, he stood over the girl.

"I was right, you're...you're afraid of me...You're...you're afraid of Peadar Kennedy."

"No, Mr. Kennedy, I'm not...I'm not."

"No, Mr. Kennedy, I'm not...I'm not," he mimicked. "Sure, the way...the way you say that is...is enough. You're...you're afraid, that's what you are, but you needn't be afraid of Peadar Kennedy."

She cringed back further to avoid his hand.

"I'm frightening you. Tha...That's what I'm doing and...and I've no right to frighten a wee girl like you...Never mind me, **Maisie**. Never mind me...I'm...I'm only a harmless old eejit."

He sat down again.

"How long are you working here now, Maisie?"

"Nearly six months, Mr. Kennedy."

"Mr. Kennedy...Mr. Kennedy...I was christened, me girl. Peadar's my name...Peadar's my name...Call me Peadar."

"May...May I go now, Mr. Kennedy?"

"There's no one stopping you. Of course, you can go, but, for God's sake, stop Mr. Ken...Kennedying me."

"Yes, Mr. Ken...Yes...Yes, sir."

"Yes, Mr. Kennedy. No, Mr. Kennedy. Yes, sir. No, sir," he mimicked again, "Peadar's my name, is that not good enough for you? Am I not good enough for you, is that it?" his voice turned to a roar.

Suddenly, he leaned forward and grabbed the hem of her skirt, balling it around his fist.

"Women," he shouted, "you're all the same, all bitches. That woman of mine is a bitch too. I'm not good enough for her either. She thinks more of one of the old bloody mongrels in the backyard than she does of me."

Maisie attempted to stand up. Peadar fell to his knees, but with one hand on the floor, he held on to the skirt with drunken determination. It came down around her knees and she fell forward across his back. She managed to wriggle one leg free, but he grabbed it and threw her off her balance. Her head hit the heavy mahogany table as she fell. She lost consciousness for a moment. Vaguely, she became aware of him on top of her, pulling at her clothes. Saliva ran from his mouth on to her face and she lost consciousness again to the stink of whiskey from his breath. She regained her senses as Peadar staggered from the room muttering to himself. Instinctively, she reached down and pulled her partially removed knickers into position. She did not remember leaving the room or going upstairs, but she awoke at four in the morning stiff with cold, on top of the clothes in her own bed.

She lay, pondering, with increasing horror, the events of the night before. Then, she realised that her skirt was missing. She would have to get it. What would Suzanne think if she found it? Her body was sore when she stood up and she had a dull ache in the head. Gingerly, she felt the bump over the right ear.

Downstairs, she found the skirt under the table. She was relieved, when she got back to her room, but what was she going to do? She had to leave, but where was she going to go? She couldn't go home? She couldn't tell her mother. She would be too ashamed. How would she tell anyone about what had happened? She began to cry, quietly and hysterically. She fell asleep again to awake shortly after seven. It was the halfhour church bell for eight o'clock Mass that prompted a seeming solution to her problem.

"Calm, calm yourself now, child. I'll talk to your mother and everything will be alright. And I'll have a word with Mr. Kennedy too."

"But.... but supposing I have a baby, what'll my mother say. I couldn't face her."

"You can't. From what you told me, you weren't impregnated. I'm practically certain of that. Listen, you'll have to see Dr. Carroll. I'll make that arrangement."

"Will he know about the baby?"

"Of course, he will. Wait till you see, he'll confirm that you won't have a child, that you can't have a child. Wouldn't that be a big weight off your mind?"

"It would, Father."

"Leave it to me so. I'll have a chat with him first, but it'll probably be evening before he can see you. Today is his dispensary day. I'll make an appointment for you to see him in his private house after tea."

"Will I have to go back to Kennedys', Father?"

"You won't go home," the priest mused, "and maybe it's best until your mind is set at rest about the baby. It's a logical first step to see the doctor. Come to think of it, it might be as well if you went back to Kennedys' for today. Make no move till you see Carroll, that's probably best."

"But how will I face Mr. Kennedy, Father?"

"How will he face you might be a more pertinent question? But, never mind that for the moment. This thing will have to be kept quiet for everyone's sake. Consequently, it might be as well if you went back to Kennedys', for one day at least."

Maisie left the church unhappy and uncertain. Passing the convent, she stopped at the iron entrance gate. When she pushed it, it creaked slowly open, but her courage deserted her. She attempted to close it again, but the creaking unnerved her and she hurried away. Reluctantly, she went back to Kennedys'. She had nowhere else to go.

When she opened the Kennedy kitchen door, she was confronted by Peadar.

"God, Maisie, I'm shocking sorry about last night. Sure, I didn't know what I was doing, I was that drunk. I didn't do you any harm now, did I? I got a terrible fright when I saw you were gone. I didn't know what you had done. Where were you anyway?"

"I was at Mass, Mr. Kennedy."

"Did you tell anyone about last night?"

"No, except that I went to confessions. I...I had to tell the priest."

"Sure, you had nothing to tell him anyway?"

"I told him."

"Did you name me?"

"He asked me. I had to tell him."

"God, you were fairly quick about it," he paced across the floor. He stopped and looked at Maisie.

"Was it in confessions you told him? You weren't talking to him outside the box, were you?"

"No."

"That's not so bad. He can't use anything he hears in confessions. You're sure you told no one else?"

"No, I didn't."

"And what are you going to do with yourself now?"

"I'm going to join the convent."

"Ach, will you have a bit of sense, girl. You can't get in there that easy, but you could get to England very handy."

"Could I?" Maisie asked, hope suddenly stirring in her.

"No better man," Peadar was all bustle now, "the missus is still above in bed. She won't stir till dinner-time after yesterday. The only thing that might move her are the dogs. You feed them straightaway. I'll be off down the town for an hour."

At eleven, he was back.

"It's all fixed," he told Maisie, "I sent a telegram to a friend of mine in London. She has a café just beside the station where the boat train comes in. She'll get a job for you. Maybe, fix you up with one herself."

"But, my mother, who's going to tell her? I can't run away like that."

"Leave that to me, girl. I'll go out to see her the night. Tell her that a good job came up in London and that it couldn't be kept open. Leave it to me. I'll handle that."

Dazed and relieved, Maise packed her clothes and Peadar escorted her to the Dublin bus at midday, giving final instructions on how to get to the cafe from Euston station.

"Don't worry about a thing now, Maisie," he assured her, "Judy Duncan will look after you in London and... and here's a little present for yourself."

"Thank you, Mr. Kennedy," Maisie said, taking the proffered envelope.

At eight o'clock that night, she was on the Liverpool boat that sailed out from Dublin's Custom House quay.

3

Maisie walked past the cafe again, a small cardboard case in one hand and a brown-paper parcel under the other arm. On the boat, the laughing, singing, puking crowd had reverberated around her. She overheard a young couple with two children discuss living in London. She followed them from the boat and into the same carriage on the train. She followed them to the London street and watched them pile into a waiting car. She was alone in the rushing crowd, but she crossed through the traffic in the midst of a stream of people. Go down the street opposite and take the second turn to the left, Peadar had told her, it's the fourth or fifth house on the left with a Cafe sign on the window. *Cafe - Fish and Chips a Speciality,* the sign said, over a drooping white curtain. The mist on the glass, and the curtain, effectively combined to block her attempt to see inside. She glanced furtively around, but the hurrying crowd paid no attention. She walked to the door and pushed it open. A bell jangled above her head and the middle-aged woman, standing by the serving hatch at the other end of the empty room, turned her head. Maisie smiled tentatively and sidled to a table close by the window. Taking a chair, she carefully settled the parcel on her lap and placed the case on the floor beside her.

The woman walked down, snipped the lock on the door and pulled the window blind. She came and stood across the table from Maisie, one casual hand on the back of a chair, red-dyed quizzical head to one side.

"I stayed open specially for you," she said. "That's the type of miracle Peadar Kennedy can work. But you're probably famished after coming all the way from Ireland. What would you like to eat?"

"Could I have some tea and bread please?"

"And what about a nice plate of brown stew? I bet you'd enjoy that."

"Yes."

The woman served the meal and poured a cup of tea.

"I'll tidy up at the back while you eat that. Then, I'll bring you a nice little bit of apple tart to finish off properly."

Maisie buttered some bread and began to eat. It was over twenty-four hours since Peadar had put her on the bus and she had not eaten since lunchtime on the day before. The woman returned with the apple tart and sat down opposite her.

"Did you enjoy that, duckey?"

"Yes, thank you, ma'am."

"Did you travel over last night?"

"Yes."

"This is your first visit to London?"

"Yes."

"Eat up your apple tart. It's a recipe I brought from Ireland."

"Are you Irish?"

"Of course, I'm Irish. Not too far from Tunnygee either. How do you think I knew Peadar Kennedy? What's your name? Peadar didn't mention it in the telegram."

"Maisie... Maisie Dempsey."

"Glad to meet you, Maisie. Judy, Judy Duncan . . . Joe, that's my man, works on the railway there," nodding towards the street and the railway beyond. "And you're looking for a job?" Judy questioned.

"Yes, ma'am."

"Would you like to work here, Maisie?"

"I'd love to, ma'am."

"You have no experience of working in a cafe?"

"No, but I was a servant girl in Ireland and. . . . . and I know how to serve table."

"I don't know. The work's very hard."

"But I'm used to hard work, ma'am."

"I suppose you are," Judy, moved by the pathetic eagerness, placed her hand on Maisie's. "Sure, I was used to hard work myself when I first came through the station archway yonder. Straight from the heart of Ireland to the heart of London. I suppose I'd have been glad to meet a Judy Duncan then."

"I'd love to work here, ma'am."

"Okay, Maisie, but if you're going to work here, no more ma'aming. Judy is what all my friends call me. Now, first things first. You'll want somewhere to sleep. There's a vacant room upstairs. It's not much, but it's yours until maybe you get something better."

"Thank you very much, ma'am."

"You mightn't thank me when you're a few days in the place. It's no picnic."

Lying in the narrow, iron bed later, the noise of the city crowded in on Maisie and, at first, she thought that the big buses swishing past were going to burst in on top of her. The roofs of the double deckers were level with her bedroom window. Eventually, the street quietened and she went to sleep with the not too distant crash of engines, shunting in the railway sidings, the only major sounds disturbing the quiet.

The early morning breakfasts were finished when she came down to the cafe next morning.

"Did you sleep well?" Judy asked, pushing hair back from a red, hot face.

The first day's work was agony. The tempo of the place was completely at variance with anything Maisie had experienced previously. The customers were demanding and some of them were rude too.

"Get your finger out, doll," one of them told her when his soup did not arrive as quickly as expected.

She blushed and stuttered and went back for another order, but the other girls pushed before her at the hatch and shouted orders over her shoulder. Most of her orders were late and it was a relief when the midday rush came to an end. She and the four other waitresses, supervised by Judy, cleared, cleaned and set the tables again in preparation for the evening. Judy and two of the girls left then.

"Now, we can have a cup of tea and a natter," Jean, a blond girl not much older than herself, told Maisie.

Betty, only slightly older than either of them, brought out a pot of tea from the kitchen and the three of them sat down at the end table.

"When's old busybody Duncan coming back?" Betty asked.

"Never, I hope, the old skinflint," Jean said.

"And an Irish skinflint too, which is worse. Sorry, Maisie, you're Irish too, of course. No offence! We're just shooting our mouths off. In fact, some of us are very fond of the Irish," Betty winked at Maisie.

"Not any more, we're not. Not after last night, we're not," Jean declared.

"Oh, tell us all about it. We'd love to hear it all, every little detail. Wouldn't we, Maisie?" Betty winked again.

"My first Paddy and my last, a real dancing hands, that boy. I don't know what the picture was about, I was so busy beating him off. In the pub, he had three pints of Guinness and I had three gins and lime. He couldn't get me out fast enough. Oh my, my first Paddy and my last. Are they all such hot stuff back in Ireland, Maisie?" Jean laughed.

Maisie laughed also, a short, forced laugh to cover her embarrassment.

"He was in a hurry, Paddy was. A regular Walter Raleigh he was too. He spread his coat on the bombed site at the back of the church and he was in business in a flash. The gin didn't help me either. It always does that to me, but I pushed him off," Jean stopped to sip her tea. "Could I have one of your cigs, Betty?" she asked, taking one from the packet on the table.

Betty held out her butt to light it.

"Don't drag it out, Jean, what happened?"

"Oh, nothing much. We struggled for a while and he lost it. My, a regular wild bull of the pampas he was. Are they all like that in Ireland, Maisie?"

"No, I don't think so," Maisie murmured.

"My, but you are shy, Maisie, but when you're here a spell, you'll know a thing or two," Jean assured her.

"Don't worry, Maisie," Betty said, "Jean talks a lot. London is not such a terrible place."

In bed that night, Maisie was not so sure. If it was not a terrible place, it was certainly a strange place. It would be good to be back in Kennedys', if only Peadar wasn't there. She had been happy there, but Peadar spoiled everything. He was drunk. Drink brings out the beast in a man. Her mother often said that. Jean drank too. No woman should drink, or no man either. It brought out the beast in Jean's fella just the same as in Peadar. All day she had not time to think, but thinking now, she cried.

Next morning she awoke to the sound of the buses again. It was strange to sleep so close to the street. She could even hear the voices of people passing on the footpath. It was six on the alarm clock Judy had given her. It was set to go off at eight. There was no need to get up any earlier, Judy had told her. You need all the rest you can get, Judy said.

Judy was very kind, but it seemed that the girls did not like her. They said terrible things about her, but they said terrible things about everyone. Maybe, they said terrible things about me too, Maisie thought, but what would they say if they really knew why she was in London? But what if she had a baby? The priest had said it was an impossibility, but it could happen. Go to sleep, but she could not sleep. Get up, but it was too early. It was still only ten minutes past six. It was then that she noticed the bible. Casually, she thumbed through it, reading a paragraph or two, but she could not concentrate. That night she took it up again. It was next morning, again awake at six, when she read: "Now, Sarai, Abram's wife, bare him no children: and she had a handmaid, an Egyptian, whose name was Hagar . . . And Sarai, Abram's wife, took Hagar . . . and gave her to her husband Abram to be his wife . . .And he went into Hagar, and she conceived . . ."

A tremor of excitement ran through Maisie. She was Hagar and Peadar was Abram. The wife told Abram to do it, but Suzanne wouldn't do that. Still, she and Hagar were in the same boat. No one asked either of them. Hagar conceived, but she did not seem too worried. She looked down on Sarai when she knew she was going to have a baby. Things were queer then. Maisie would not look down on anyone. She just hoped and prayed that she would not have a baby. It would be better to be barren like Sarai or Suzanne. The jangle of the alarm cut across her thoughts. It was ten past eight. She jumped out of bed.

That evening, as she listened to Betty and Jean, she was reminded of Hagar. Both were proud of the attractions they had for men, and they boasted of the fellows they had. Jean said that she went out with married men sometimes and that they were the best, because they knew how to handle a woman. Betty said that she would not go out with married men, that they should stick to their wives. Jean laughed and said that when you looked at some of the wives they were stuck with, you would not blame them. It seemed that Jean despised wives, just like Hagar despised Sarai.

Maisie went back to the bible that night. She read that Hagar's son was called Ishmael and that when Hagar ran away from Sarai before the child was born, it was an angel of the Lord who told her to return. She knew that the Angel Gabriel had come to Mary to tell her she was going to have a son, but God had sent a message to Hagar too, who was going to have a baby by a married man. That could not be right. A girl should only have a baby by her husband. God would not bless her otherwise.

Abram was eighty-six when Ishmael was born. That was very old. Her father was only sixty-three and he was an old man. But then Abram was ninety-nine, when God told him to change his name to Abraham and Sarai's to Sarah and said that they would have a son. A year later they had a son, Isaac, and when she had her son, Sarah insisted that Abraham "cast out this bondwoman and her son: for the son of this bondwoman shall not be heir with my son . . ." Abraham did not want to let his son, Ishmael, go, but Sarah was adamant. Abraham got up early on the morning of their departure and gave Hagar and Ishmael bread and a bottle of water, before sending them to wander in the wilderness of Beersheba. Peadar Kennedy had been kinder. There was sixty pounds in the envelope he had handed Maisie. She was luckier than Hagar. She had not to wander in any wilderness. And, poor Hagar, her water ran out and she left Ishmael to die. She walked away, crying and weeping, but God came to her rescue. He showed to her a "well of water."

Twice, God had come to her assistance. He might be on Sarah's side, but he looked after Hagar too. When God, however, gave a son to Abraham and Sarah, Hagar and Ishmael had to take second place. Just like me, Maisie thought. Both of us had to run, Hagar to Beersheba and me to London.

In her third week in London, Maisie knew she was not going to have a baby. That morning, she got up and literally danced around the room. It was one of the happiest days of her life and she faced the cafe customers and the girls with a new confidence. At the teabreak that evening, Betty asked: "Tell us the good news, Maisie. You're like the cat that has lapped all the cream. What's the big secret?"

"I'm just happy, Betty."

"Did you win the Irish Sweep?"

"No, but I have some money. I'd like to treat both of you. Go out somewhere, you know?"

"Why not come to the Saturday night hop with us?" Jean suggested.

"Yes, and I'll pay," Maisie said.

4

On Saturday, Maisie spent three pounds ten shillings on a green dress. She had a half-day off and she spent most of it posing in front of her wardrobe mirror. Several times she combed the red-gold hair that was growing longer and beginning to curl at the ends. At eight, she was dressed and ready and sat down in a glow of excitement to await the arrival of the other girls.

"Wow, you're a smasher," Betty exclaimed. "Jean and I haven't a chance tonight."

It was Maisie's first dance and the alien atmosphere of the ballroom overwhelmed her: boys and girls locked tight in each other's arms shuffling around to the slow beat of the music. Within minutes, Betty and Jean were dancing and Maisie backed away to the end of the hall. Surrounded and smothered, as the new, pulsating life of the dancehall crowded in on her, she edged further back.

"Want to dance?" a squat man stood in front of her.

"No, thank you," she muttered.

"Come on, we'll shake a leg," he said.

"But I never danced."

"There's always a first time," he took her by the arm and pulled her on to the floor.

"Relax, baby, don't rush it. Just a one, two, three, a one, two, three," he advised.

"That's it, baby, you're doing fine," he assured her.

"How long are you across?" he asked.

"How did you know?"

"It was a good guess, wasn't it?" he laughed, "how long are you here anyway?"

"A few weeks."

"Where are you working?"

"Duncan's"

"Where's that?"

"Near the station, it's a cafe."

"Ach, I know it well. Not a bad place for a feed. What part of Ireland are you from?"

"Tunnygee."

"Ah. Holy God, you're not. Well, you must know Tom Burke then, he's from Tunnygee too."

"No, I don't. I come from a place four miles out. I don't know many in the town itself."

"You'll have to meet the bold Tom. You never told me your name?"

"Maisie Dempsey."

"Right, Maisie, we'll have to find Burke," he pulled her by the hand as the music ended.

"By the way, I'm Mick Dwyer, Butsy, my friends call me," he told her.

"Hey, Tom . . . over here. . . This way. There's someone to meet you here," he shouted, waving his hand in the air.

Burke came towards them. Maisie saw a dark, strong face under black curly hair, showing white teeth in a big grin.

"Here's a townie a yours, Tom. All the way from Tunnygee. Maisie Dempsey she calls herself," Butsy introduced Maisie.

"I'm glad to meet you, Maisie," Tom was about average height, light-boned but well built.

"I'm glad to meet you, Mr. Burke."

"I'm not called mister very often, Maisie. Tom will do me rightly. Will you dance, Maisie?"

"I'm not great," she said.

"So, you're from Tunnygee?"

"Not from the town. I live out in the country."

"Where?"

"Out the Cavan Road."

"Be God, I have you now. Your old Pat Dempsey's daughter from out at the Red Bog."

"That's right."

"I know your father well. I used to see him at Johny McCaffrey's."

"Johny McCaffrey's?"

"You must know Johny! He has a big slipe a land on the edge of the town. He keeps the boar."

"I know who you're talking about now."

"I met your father when he used to come with the sow."

The next dance was an "excuse me". On the last encore, a tall youth tapped Tom's shoulder and danced off with Maisie. Tom attempted to cut in the next time around, but he was shrugged off. When the dance ended the youth kept his arm firmly around Maisie's waist.

"We'll dance the next one," he said.

"But I'll have to get back to my friends."

"They won't miss one more dance."

Maisie glimpsed Tom looking round for her. He saw her, but, the music had started and he was cut off by dancers. Halfway down the hall, he was waiting.

"Excuse me," Tom attempted to tap in, but the youth ignored him, swinging Maisie away.

"Get him the next time around. Sink the bloody pick in his head," Butsy advised.

When they came round again, Tom tapped the youth on the shoulder.

"This is not a tap in," the youth said.

"Do you mind if I dance with my girl?" Tom gripped his arm above the elbow.

"Fuck off, mate," the youth shrugged him off.

Tom's left fist caught him high on the side of the head, staggering him away from Maisie.

"Up from the heels with her," Butsy's swing caught a man full in the face.

Several girls screamed. Butsy grabbed Maisie and shoved her out of the way.

A bouncer burst through the crowd, his fist raised to chop Tom down, but Butsy's charge deflected the blow and the bouncer went down beneath his flailing arms. Tom was fighting off two men.

"He'll be killed," Maisie said.

"Not at all," a voice behind assured her, "you don't swing a pick five days a week and double time on Sunday for nothing."

"I'm a friend of the boys", a tall man said, as Maisie glanced around.

Tom staggered back from a blow to the face, but he shook his head and gathered himself for another charge. Left, right, left, he rained blows on his assailants, but the two men were too much for him. The tall man stepped forward and put an armlock on one of them.

"Police!" someone screamed.

"Come on lads, get out of this. We don't want to end up in jail," the tall man shouted.

The three of them ran for the door. A policeman held out his arms to bring them to a halt, but they barged straight into him, bowling him over. Maisie found herself standing alone. The other dancers were looking at her, standing in a half-circle. Someone caught her elbow. Terrified, she jerked away, but it was Jean.

"Come on, quickly, before they start asking questions," Jean said. Jean collected their coats at the cloakroom and ushered her past a helmetless policeman who, hands brushing his uniform, was attempting to reassert his authority. Outside, Betty stood, arms interlocked with a man.

"Why are you leaving?" she asked.

"Did you see the fight?" Jean asked.

"No, we were at the pub, but we saw three men running away. They came bursting out, knocking the policeman for six."

"They were pretty cool about it," the man said, "one of them stopped to pick up the policeman's helmet. They ran off that way, one of them wearing the helmet. A crowd of crazy Irishmen."

"They're friends of Maisie's," Jean said.

"Oh, no," Betty looked at Maisie, "no wonder you look frightened."

There was the whine of a patrol car at the end of the street.

"Let's get out of here, Maisie," Jean laughed, pulling a dazed Maisie with her.

It was Butsy who grabbed the helmet and ran down the street wearing it.

"Get that bloody helmet off you, you mad lunatic. You'll have us arrested," Tom warned Butsy. "Throw it away, for jasus sake, or we'll get a month in the cooler."

"No, I'm bringing it home. I always wanted a peeler's helmet," Butsy half-concealed the helmet under the flap of his jacket.

Two streets away, he put the helmet on again and swaggered round a corner straight into the arms of a policeman. Following a few yards behind, Tom and his tall friend slowed down and walked casually past the policeman and a blustering Butsy.

5

Tom Burke was born on October 16, 1929. His mother, Rosie, was two months short of her eighteenth birthday at the time. She had been living with her Uncle Pakie in Screelahan lane for three months prior to the birth, her mother having thrown her out. Rosie's mother had been reluctant to turn her out at first, but there were four younger daughters in the house, and, when Rosie began to show, her mother made it clear that she could not stay.

"You brought scandal enough on us as it is," her mother told her, "I won't let you scandalise the young ones by having your bastard in the house."

The nuns ran a home for unmarried mothers in the next county, to which her mother made arrangements to have her admitted. At that stage, her Uncle Pakie stepped in.

"I'll take her," he said, "I'm on my own. If you are afraid of what people say, my place is backward enough."

The thatched three-roomed farmhouse was nearly a mile from the main road, with a small lake beneath it, and the rolling drumlin hills all around. Living there with her placid, easy-going uncle was a holiday for Rosie. Pakie slept in the settle-bed in the kitchen and, each morning, he had a boiled egg on the table and a mug of tea poured before he called her.

"You should let me make the breakfast," she told him, rubbing the sleep from her eyes.

"Don't worry about it," he told her, pointing to the hearth, "it never went out since your grandmother's time. All I have to do in the mornings is give a wee blast at the bellows and it's off again. Sure it's no trouble at all making a bit of breakfast."

On the day of the birth, Pakie came in from the potato field to find the fire burned down under an empty kettle and the kitchen in darkness. In the back room, he found Rosie semi-conscious, bleeding heavily, and with a new-born baby beside her. He ran out, grabbed his bicycle and tore into town, three and a half miles away. Dr. Ryan was at home. Pakie came back with him in the doctor's Model T. Ford, but they were too late. Rosie was dead when they arrived.

Dr. Ryan took the baby, christened Thomas a week later, to Rosie's mother's house, and he was reared there until he was six years old. Pakie took him back then, and the thatched farmhouse became his home.

He went to school across the fields, where the harsh discipline of Mrs. McCabe didn't bother him. He was clever and, when he left school at thirteen, he was at the top of his class. He spent the next three years helping Pakie on the land and went with him on *céilís* to the neighbours' houses at night. Here he listened to the arguments about football and politics. Everyone agreed that Jim Smith of Killinkere was the best footballer ever to play for the county and the best centrefield man in Ireland. That was until the Leitrim man arrived to build an extension to the local church. He claimed that there was a McGoldrick from Leitrim, who played for America in the Taillteann games, who would kick Smith off the field. That was the first time that Tom saw his granduncle get excited. Red in the face, he shouted back at the Leitrim man that he knew nothing about football and that he wouldn't know a footballer from a hole in the ground. But if Jim Smith was his uncle's footballing idol, Dev was his political hero. In 1939, at the April fair in Tunnygee, he struck a man who referred to Dev as a Spanish bastard. He was saved from a bad beating by two of his neighbours who dragged him into Jimmy Kelly's public house.

In the early days of the second world war, Pakie supported Germany. "England's difficulty is Ireland's opportunity," he told Tom. "It's a Hitler we want here. Look at the way he went into the Sudeten-land. The County Council sent him a telegram of congratulations. That was the October thirty-eight meeting below in Cavan. It was the only council in Ireland to do it too."

Pakie sympathised with the Finns. They were like terriers, he said, snapping at the bear, and they knew how to fight in the snow. There was an old newspaper photograph of a Finnish soldier attacking a Russian tank with a molotov cocktail. Tom studied it for hours, wondering if the Finn would escape. He imagined the tank exploding into flame and the flames engulfing the Finn too. He saw himself as the Finn and calculated the chances of getting back under cover in the bushes. When the Finns held the Russians for a while, both Tom and Pakie were delighted.

"And England was supposed to send them help, but who could depend on England?" Pakie asked, when the Finns were defeated.

Tom looked at the photograph again and pinned it to the report on the council meeting congratulating Hitler, before repinning both to the curtain on the kitchen window, where Pakie kept his meagre collection of cuttings.

When Germany invaded France in 1940, Pakie considered purchasing a radio. He went into town to Lynch's butcher shop in the square, where the son, Patsy, sold radios.

"Shake hands with Patsy Lynch," Pakie ordered Tom, "not alone was he the best full-back ever played for Cavan, but the best ever played for any other county either."

Tom looked in awe at the square, bulky figure in the white butcher's coat, but, to his disappointment, Pakie did not buy a radio. They were too dear, he told Patsy Lynch, who merely smiled and said that every man must be his own judge of that. As they were leaving, Patsy nudged Tom and said: "He's a fine, hardy gasson this minute, Pakie. He'll do you proud some of these days."

"Patsy was always a shocking nice fella, never got a swelled head or nothing," Pakie said as they walked down the street.

Rooney, the barber, was another great Dev man. For Pakie, a visit to town would not be complete without calling on Rooney. On this occasion, Tom and he found Rooney, hopping around on his stiff leg, attempting to pin a large map of Europe to the wall.

"Here, let me give you a hand with that, Hugh," Pakie said. Between them, they got the map in place.

"Now, I'll show you how the war is going," Rooney said, taking a handful of green-headed and red-headed pins from the pocket of his brown shop coat.

It took him some minutes to place the pins to his satisfaction. He then placed two arrows in position to show the lines of the German advances, before standing back and announcing: "There you have the situation as it is the day on the Western Front. The Germans are advancing on two fronts, one through Luxembourg, here," pointing with his finger, "through the southern corner of Belgium and into France. The other advance is through Holland," again pointing. "The idea is to trap the British and French forces in a pincer movement. The trap will be sprung somewhere around here," he placed his finger on the coast in the area of the French-Belgium border, "the French will be finished then and the British too."

"God, you're a genius, Hugh. I never saw anything as plain as that before," Pakie said.

Twice or three times a week during that May, uncle and nephew went into Rooney's to be brought up to date on the war news. As Rooney snipped away at hair, all the talk was of war. At intervals between customers, he took time off to give a little lecture with the aid of the map. When towards the end of the month, the order was given to evacuate the allied troops from Dunkirk, he exulted: "What did I tell you? I told you the trap would be sprung. Well, it's sprung now good and proper."

The trap was not sprung as tight as Hugh and his audience imagined, however, and, in late May and early June, over 300,000 Allied troops were ferried across the channel. In the July fair of Tunnygee, Tom met one of them.

Pakie had sold a heifer that day and the jobber arranged to pay him in Kelly's. Afterwards, Pakie stayed on to celebrate the sale with a few bottles of stout. Tom went out to get some sweets and when he came back, Pakie whispered to him: "See that tall fella at the bar there. He's after getting out of Dunkirk."

Everyone in the pub was shaking hands with the soldier, congratulating him on his escape. He was a tall, fair-skinned man with black hair.

"Who is he?" Tom asked.

"He's Bobby Johnston from out the road there, that's his brother Jackie, who's with him. We'll go over and have a word with him."

"I'm glad to see you home, Bobby," Pakie shook hands with the soldier.

"I know that, Pakie," Bobby said, "and is this Rosie's gasson?"

"That's right, Bobby."

"Your mother was one of the finest young lassies walked the street of Tunnygee. I remember her well," Bobby turned to Tom.

"What age are you now, son?" he asked.

"Eleven, I'll be eleven in October."

"Eleven years ago, it's hard to believe. I'd a sort of a half notion of her myself, even though I was only a snotty-nosed young lad with no arse to my trousers at the time," Bobby said, turning back to his drink.

"I suppose a good Republican like yourself would favour the Germans, eh, Pakie?" Jackie Johnston asked in a bantering tone.

"Well, you know, Jackie, that I'm not too fond of the English," Pakie answered.

"Sure, us Presbyterians have a terrible lot to answer for. When we went out from Corglass to Rebel Hill at the castle below in ninety-eight, we started the whole thing. And we were annihilated too, and there were a good few Catholics in the militia that time."

"I know that, Jackie. My own father often told me about it and about the blood colouring the river all the way down to Parker's Lake."

"And some of that blood belonged to a great granduncle of mine and of Bobby's too, and there's Bobby an English soldier now."

"Someone has to stop Hitler," Bobby said.

"Still, I find it hard to be sorry for the English," Pakie persisted, "but I'm glad to see you, Bobby, home safe and sound."

"I was lucky. Only for a couple of good English mates of mine I might never have seen the Emerald Isle again. See that there," he pulled up the leg of his trousers.

"God, you got a fair belt," Pakie said, looking at the still raw, half-healed wound in the calf of Bobby's leg.

"Is it sore, Mr. Johnston?" Tom asked, with new-found respect in his voice.

"Not any more, son," Bobby replied,"but that's what one of the German planes done to me, and only for my English mates dragged me with them, I'd still be lying on the sand at Dunkirk. The English are not all bad, you know. I found them the best mates in the world, anyway."

"You get the good and the bad everywhere," Pakie conceded.

"And yon Hitler fella is one of the bad ones, one of the worst. We might all learn that to our cost, one of these days," Jackie warned.

Pakie was quiet on the way home. At sixty, he was tired after a long day, that had begun at five in the morning, and he plodded along beside Tom. In the house, Tom blew the fire into life and hung the kettle on the crane. Pakie sat down at the table and went to sleep, his head resting on his arms on the tabletop.

Tom went out and brought in the three cows that were lowing at the field gate. When he returned with the milk, Pakie was still asleep. When Tom shook him awake, he stood and stretched himself.

"God, I was never as tired," he said, "and that kettle is jumping out of its skin. Do you want tea?"

"No, I'm going straight to bed," Tom yawned.

Pakie took off the kettle and began to rake down the fire.

"Do you know something, Tom," he said, "everyman has his own know. Even if them Johnstons are right about Hitler, he's the one man can teach the English a lesson."

Both of them continued to call to Rooney's, where the proprietor nightly gave his own particular interpretation of events. After Hitler invaded Russia in June, 1941, Pakie was disappointed. He saw England being let off the hook. On an evening in early July of that year, Rooney, having finished work for the day, sat in his barber's chair, his stiff leg on a stool in front of him.

"I agree with Pakie. England is off the hook," he announced, "Hitler's bitten off more than he can chew this time. Napoleon, the greatest military genius in history, failed in Russia, so will Hitler. That's why Dev, in his wisdom, is right to pursue a policy of neutrality . . ."

"But what about the Six Counties? We'll never get as good a chance again," Pakie protested.

"And walk us into a civil war," Rooney retorted, "and . . . and give Churchill his chance to invade. Didn't he already threaten and didn't you hear Dev's reply? Dev declared a policy of neutrality and stated that if any of the belligerents invaded or attempted to take the ports, or any part of our territory, that he would fight. What do you think would happen, if he let the I.R.A. have its head? It would give Churchill the excuse he's waiting for and then we'd be a battlefield for Germany and England to fight over. I thought you had a bit of sense, Pakie?"

"It's a pity," Pakie said, "but we always seem to get the short end of the stick. Tell me why did he have to shoot Paddy McGrath, a man who was badly wounded in the fight against the British?"

"You're an impossible man, Pakie. Paddy McGrath was shot, and Tom Harte too, and there's no man sorrier than me that it had to happen, but they were wrong, very wrong. I'm sure Dev is sorrier than either of us, but he can't let anyone walk us into a situation where thousands of Irishmen would die between German bombs and British . . . British tanks," Rooney's voice was raised in anger.

"And what if Germany wins the war?" Pakie asked quietly.

"Even if it did, we'd end up with a devastated country. Are you willing to pay that price?"

"Maybe you're right, but I always heard that England's difficulty is Ireland's opportunity," Pakie had the last word.

As the war progressed, Pakie's disillusionment with his two heroes, Hitler and Dev, increased. Tom was vaguely aware of this, but, with the simplicity of youth, his admiration for both men remained unshaken until the war's end. Pakie had indoctrinated him well. Tom's faith in Hitler was undermined first. In September 1945, a film show at the Excel Cinema in Tunnygee barred those under sixteen on the grounds that the horror of Hitler's concentration camps, which was the subject of one of the documentaries, was not suitable viewing for young people. One result of the barring order was that the cinema was packed with young people during a week-long run. Among them was Tom.

He was certainly horrified, but not in any detrimental fashion. In fact, the horror of the skeletal bodies of the dead, and the equally skeletal bodies of the living, brought home to him what the term concentration camp meant in Hitler's Germany. He left the cinema hating Hitler, but what upset him most was that Pakie, the man he admired most in the world, and his constant companion for nearly ten years, should have been so wrong. He intended going for chips to Bell's at the top of Australia Street, but, in his anxiety to talk to Pakie, he went straight home.

Usually, if out late, Tom came in to the house quietly, lifting and closing the latch gently, but, on that night, he burst through the door and went straight to where Pakie was asleep in the settle-bed along the kitchen wall. Pakie sat up with a start.

"I was at the pictures and I seen all about the concentration camps. Hitler was a bastard, that's what he was, a bloody bastard," Tom shouted.

"Calm yourself, gasson. Turn up the lamp for a minute."

"I'll turn up no lamp. I'm going to bed, but you're coming to the pictures with me the morrow night. You'll see it all for yourself then."

"It's a shocking waste of money dragging me here and you after seeing it last night," Pakie complained, as they took their seats in the cinema the next evening.

"Wait till it's over and then you'll know," Tom told him.

"Now, was Hitler a savage or wasn't he?" Tom asked after the show.

"He was a baste, no better than the brute animal, a baste entirely," Pakie admitted.

Pakie finally swung against Dev over the McCaughey affair. Sean McCaughey had spent over four and a half years in prison in April 1946. During that period he refused to wear convict clothes. He was also allowed no visitors. He went on hunger strike and later thirst strike, dying within seventeen days.

At the inquest, Sean McBride, cross-examined the prison doctor:

McBride: "Are you aware that during the four and a half years he was here he was never out in the fresh air or sunlight?"

Dr: "As far as I am aware he was not."

McBride: "Would I be right in saying that up to twelve or eighteen months ago he was kept in solitary confinement and not allowed to speak or associate with any other persons?"

Dr:"That is right."

McBride: "Would you treat a dog in that fashion?"

McBride (rephrases):"If you had a dog would you treat it in that fashion."

Dr: "No."

Tom was working for Johny McCaffrey for a few months at that time. He slept at home, cycling to and from McCaffrey's each day. He arrived home late one night. He was surprised to find Pakie still up. Pakie had taken the oil lamp from the wall and placed it on the table. He had a paper spread out in front of him.

"Here, listen to this," he said, "McBride asked, would you treat a dog in that fashion, and the doctor answered no. What . . . what do you think of Dev now?"

"What are you talking about?"

"What am I talking about? I'm talking about the McCaughey inquest. You'd want a read about it too. They let him die like a dog. It's all there in black and white," an agitated Pakie tapped the newspaper with his forefinger.

In the angle of the light, Pakie's head looked skull like, the bones etched in the tight-drawn skin. His forefinger continued to tap on the newspaper. He is getting old, Tom thought.

"Ach, sure it's all over now," he attempted to mollify him.

"Sure it's all over now, is that all you can say?" Pakie jumped up, "executing men for doing what he walked them into and now letting McCaughey die like that. Over four years with not a stitch on him. Dev shouldn't have done it."

"I know that. Don't we all know that? But he kept us out of the war and you said yourself that he was right about that. You said yourself Hitler was a baste and some of them fellas would have had us fighting side by side with him."

"It's Rooney, that's what it is. You're listening to him, him spouting away in that old barber shop of his."

"But he's right this time. We'd have been ruined if we joined Hitler."

"You support the executions then and you'd support treating McCaughey like a dog, worse than a dog. I never thought I'd hear you saying that, Tom."

"I never said any such thing. I'm against the executions as much as you and I'm against what was done to McCaughey. Dev went too far. There was no need to execute anyone and he could have let McCaughey wear any clothes he liked, and he could have still kept us out of the war."

"I'll never forgive him for what he done. Would you treat a dog in that fashion, he asked the doctor and the answer was no."

"Don't worry about it, Pakie," Tom put his arms around his uncle's boney shoulder, "the way I see it, you reared me up to think of Hitler and Dev as heroes. I got my eyes opened about Hitler and so did you. He was a madman. Dev is no madman. He played his cards well to keep us out of the war, but he shouldn't have executed the lads, and he went too far with McCaughey. I'll never look on any man as a hero again."

"You're right, son. Hitler was a wrong wan, as wrong as be damned, but . . . Dev let me down too."

"Remember what Johny McCaffrey said the last fairday, Pakie, the only safe hero is a dead one?"

"I hate to admit that an old blueshirt like McCaffrey is right about anything, but he's right about that. Come on, we'll get to bed."

"Aye, Dev won't mould McCaffrey's potatoes for him the morrow."

Tom got fifteen shillings a week from McCaffrey for what was a twelve-hour-day for most of the year. Even in winter, McCaffrey kept him busy. He had four swampy fields at the lower end of the farm, and from November to January, Tom worked clearing drains, pulling weeds and shovelling mud. Invariably, the pungent smelling, dead water oozed over the top of his boots and he often came home wet to his stomach.

One January morning, his wellington slipped on a root and he sprawled full-length in the slimey water. He went home to change his clothes and didn't return that day.

"Where were you yesterday?" McCaffrey demanded next morning.

"I fell. I went home to change my clothes."

"You could have told me."

"What do you expect for your fifteen bob a week?"

"A day's work every day, that's all I expect."

"For a half-crown a day. It would barely keep a fella in fags."

"It's the going rate, and what about your grub? Aren't you fed like a fighting cock?"

"It's the least you might do."

"And what about the free milk, since your Uncle Pakie got rid of the cows?"

"A thimbleful!"

"That quart can you have on the front of the bike is a quare old thimble."

"Ach!"

"And who did the bit of ploughing for Pakie last year? I suppose he'll expect it this year too."

"You have all the answers, Johny."

"Aye, lad, maybe I have."

The harvest came late that year, and the wind-lashed rain flattened Johny's three fields of oats. Tom and he stood on a headland one evening.

"It looks like another black forty - seven," Johny said.

"It's in a bad way," Tom agreed, "There's nothing for it only the scythe."

"Aye, Owney Smith's coming the morrow. He's an acre a day man. And you're fairly handy with the scythe too, and there's myself."

"Pakie might give us a hand," Tom suggested.

"Is he fit? He's shocking failed looking this last while, not a bit on him."

"He might surprise you. He has our acre and a half saved, and he mowed every bit of it himself."

"Fair enough. There's seven or eight lads coming out from the town too, teachers and bankclerks and the like. They'll do rightly for the tying."

Next morning, Owney Smith took charge of the townsmen.

"There's four of you there never tied oats before. Now, if you just stand back, I'll mow a bit at the corner here and show you what's to be done."

He mowed for about fifteen minutes, then handed his scythe to Sean Cosgrave, the school teacher.

"Here, Master, you take charge of that and I'll soon show these lads how to tie."

He scooped up an armful of oats and pulled a handful from it.

"Now, watch," he said.

He wrapped the handful of stalks around the sheaf, caught the two ends of the handful and twisted them smartly. He then shoved the loose ends up under the new band.

"Now, you try it," he ordered.

They all tried and Owney rejected three sheaves.

"See that," he took one of them up and it fell apart. "I'll show you once more. The whole secret is in the first twist of the band. Get that tight and firm and you can't go wrong."

"Right, Owney, we'll get started. They'll learn as they go along," Johny said.

The rain held up work for two half days, but in a little over a week Johny had his seven acres of oats in stooks.

The tea arrived out on the last evening. Although the ground was wet, a watery sun appeared, as sitting on sheaves, they dipped their mugs in the bucket of tea and gulped down Mrs. McCaffrey's sandwiches. When they were finished, they sat around smoking.

"I'm not much good at making speeches," Johny said, standing up, "you'd want someone like the Master there for that, but I want to thank you all. You did great work. Little did myself and Tom here think when we stood on the headland over a week ago that we'd see the three fields stooked this evening. Now, I'll be in Jimmy Kelly's on the Fairgreen tonight at nine o'clock and I want to see you all there."

"Now, Master, what about a few words from yourself," Owney Smith suggested.

"It seems I'm appointed to speak on behalf of the non-farmers, the townies," Sean Cosgrave began. "We are delighted to be here and to help in the great work of saving the harvest. We are especially delighted to be here with Johny McCaffrey and for one good reason, the meals that Mrs. McCaffrey sent out to the field. I was never better fed than I was for the last week, and as sure as my name is Sean Cosgrave, Mrs McCaffrey's culinary skills will be remembered long after the bad weather that brought us here is forgotten. As far as I am concerned, my friends and I are on call to Johny McCaffrey at any time. And, yes, Johny, we'll be in Jimmy Kelly's tonight."

The following year, the weather came bad again and Johnny had to call in Owney Smith and his scythe once more. Pakie came the first day, but he had to give up after a few hours. He seemed to go downhill quickly afterwards, spending a lot of time asleep by the fire. He was not obviously sick, but he was thinner than ever and Tom noticed that he had stopped smoking his pipe. One morning in early November, Tom found him dead in the settle-bed.

Tom's world fell apart. The main prop in his life was gone. Suddenly he realised how deeply they depended on each other and the depth of friendship that bound them.

His grandmother and his Aunt Bernadette came to organise the wake. They laid the corpse out on his bed. As chief mourner, Tom greeted the neighbours who came and went.

He watched a fly crawl across the bridge of his uncle's nose and up onto the forehead, as the rosary was said. He was glad when his grandmother got up and brushed it away. He sat by the bed all night and most of the next day, and when they coffined him he watched as they kissed his forehead. He merely put his hand on the cold head and held it there for a moment. He couldn't bring himself to kiss goodbye to the man he loved. It seemed too final.

With three cousins, he carried the coffin from the church to the adjoining graveyard. When the prayers were said, he took a shovel from one of the neighbours who was filling in the grave.

"You needn't do that," the man said.

"I want to. I want to help bury the best friend a man ever had," he said, throwing in a shovel of clay.

He went back to McCaffrey for a while, but, shortly after Christmas, he told him that he was going to join the army.

"I'm surprised at a good Republican like you joining the Free Staters," McCaffrey joked.

"Who's a Republican now?" Tom asked, "Didn't McBride and the rest of them join your crowd?"

"And wasn't it one of our crowd, McKeown, that released the prisoners?" Johny replied.

"Aye, and Costello declared the Republic, even if he went to Canada to do it, but, seriously, Johny, I'm going because with Pakie gone, there's nothing to keep me around here now."

"I know that, Tom."

"Anyway, the army pays better than you," Tom laughed. "A recruit gets twenty-eight bob a week, plus his keep and clothing."

"It's as good an excuse as the next," Johny said.

6

The slim, prematurely-grey recruiting Sergeant in Cathal Brugha Barracks, Dublin was gentlemanly and polite, possibly because Tom was the only potential recruit to present himself that February day. It was after lunch when an officer arrived to swear him in.

"Have you any friends in Dublin?" the Sergeant asked.

"No."

"I better get a bed for you so. I'll fix up this one," he pointed to the bed in the corner.

At twenty past four, the Sergeant handed Tom a tin plate, an enamel mug and a knife and fork.

"Come on," he said, "I'll bring you to the cookhouse".

An orderly was quartering loaves of bread and slamming pats of butter on each in the dining hall.

"Another bloody redarse," he grunted, when he saw Tom.

"Never mind that, just make sure he's fed," the Sergeant ordered.

"Sure, Sarge."

"Take one of those lumps of bread," the Sergeant told Tom, "and go and sit at one of the tables."

There was a rush of heavy boots and the first group of soldiers appeared. They formed a rough line, as two cooks came in with tin trays containing bacon and black pudding. The orderly beckoned Tom and one of the cooks put a slice of bacon and pudding on his plate. A soldier came in with two steaming buckets of tea and went round the tables filling the mugs. Three young soldiers sat across the table from Tom. They ignored him, but he realised by their conversation that they had just finished their recruit training in the Curragh. Eventually, one of them turned to Tom.

"Off to the Curragh, nothing there only the three Ss," he said.

"What's that?" Tom asked.

"Sheep, shit and soldiers," the soldier laughed.

The plains were sprinkled with snow when Tom arrived at the Curragh next day. At McDonagh Barracks, a soldier brought him to his billet. He saw his first Curragh sheep when he went to the lavatory that night. He fell across one of three in the passageway. They charged out, jamming in the doorway. The lavatory was outside, and when he came back, the sheep were in again. He chased them out and closed the door. Then he opened it again. The sheep might as well be in out of the snow too, he thought.

He and fourteen other newcomers were issued with kit next morning. Afterwards, a Corporal lined them up and marched them to the showers.

"Strip off," the Corporal ordered when they reached the bathhouse.

Tom had never been in a bathroom before, much less a communal bathhouse. A tin basin had sufficed for his ablutions at home, with an odd dip in the lake in good weather. He hesitated in removing his trousers.

"Get them off you," the Corporal shouted, "you're in the army now. There's no one going to bite you."

Afterwards, most of them knotted a towel around their waists and quickly pulled on their first army greyback, a fibrous wool mixture shirt. One lad, however, came prancing out of the shower, with a towel pulled tightly around his hips, but with his penis jutting out over the top of it. He jumped up and down on the tiled floor, shouting:

"Johny Whelan, the man with the dancing mickey."

"Cut it out," the Corporal roared, "a few bollocks naked laps of the square might settle you. It would soon shrink that weapon of yours."

There was a general laugh, raucous, yet embarrassed.

"A bloody exhibitionist," the tall man beside Tom said,"I wouldn't mind if he had anything to show."

"Aye," Tom agreed.

In stiff, brown fatigues, awkward in new army boots, they were marched back to the lines in straggling formation.

"Right, dump your stuff in the billet and get back down here on the double," the Corporal ordered.

"And bring your plate and mug with you, and your knife, fork and spoon. Grub's up," he shouted after them.

In the dining hall, they queued for the main course and queued again for the sweet. When Tom came back to the table with his sweet, his new mug was gone and in its place was a chipped and dented model, with food encrusted under its rim. He looked around the table. There was one new mug there. Its owner stood up to shout at a friend of his. As he half-turned away, Tom took the mug and replaced it with the old, chipped one. He noticed a small piece of string tied to the handle of the new mug. He pulled it off. The soldier sat down and saw the chipped mug.

"What lousy bastard stole my mug," he exploded, "I'll fuckin' debolicate the fucker, that's what I'll do. That's mine, you fucker you," he made a grab at the mug in front of Tom, but Tom grabbed it away.

"It's mine," Tom said.

"It's fuckin' well not. It's mine. Hand it back and stop acting the bollocks."

"How do you know it's yours?" Tom asked.

"I know, there's a bit a string on the handle of that mug."

"There's not," Tom held the mug up.

The soldier banged the chipped mug down on the table-top.

"There's some fellas too smart for their own good," he warned, before standing up and strutting up the room.

Within minutes he was back with a brand new mug.

"There," he said triumphantly, "and it's a better mug than the last one."

That evening the Corporal moved into the billet. He brought his own bed with him. One of the concessions of rank, it had a wire base and was bigger and higher than the other beds. The latter were small and narrow, with metal slats for a base and thin, biscuit-type mattresses. The Corporal took the best place in the room, a corner near the fire, having ordered the original occupant to move himself and his bed to a spot near the door. When he had his bed laid down and his kit-box installed, he gave a short speech:

"I'm your Section Corporal, Corporal Duggan. I'll be with you until your recruit training ends. We'll be a sort of married to each other, but there'll be only one boss in this marriage and that's me. When I say jump, you jump," he glared round him for a moment, "if you get that into your thick skulls, we'll get on well together."

About thirty, the Corporal was blue-jowled, with small eyes and crew-cut black hair. Less than five six, he was a bantamcock of a man, chest stuck out in a tight uniform. He strutted on short, stiff legs, with his surprisingly big boots shooting out at a seemingly permanent angle of forty five degrees.

At reveille the morning after the Corporal's arrival, no one moved to get out of bed. The Corporal waited a moment before erupting.

"Hit the floor boards, you shower of gits. This is no bloody holiday camp," he shouted from the bed.

With one exception all jumped out on the floor, looking in-congruous in greybacks and drooping longjohns. The tall man, who had spoken to Tom in the bathhouse the day before, was still in bed. At twenty, Mike Houlihan, was the oldest of the group. It was rumoured that he was a good hurler who had played for the Dublin senior team on a few occasions. The Corporal bounded across the room and whipped the clothes from Houlihan's bed. With slow deliberation, Mike put his feet on the floor and sat on the side of the bed.

"You shouldn't have done that, Corporal," he said quietly.

"Get up, get up, stand to attention," Duggan ordered.

"I'm putting on my socks," Mike pulled a sock on.

"Stand up."

Mike stood up, one sock on and the other in his hand.

"Stand to attention," Duggan shouted.

Mike brought his heels together and stood looking down on the Corporal from his six feet one inch. Lithe and muscular, with dark good looks, even the longjohns seemed to fit him, while the Corporal's drooped badly. Mike half smiled.

"I'll wipe that grin off your face, just as soon as we come off parade, "Duggan threatened and, with a final glare, turned away.

The half seven check parade was held on the main square. As befitted the lowly station of troops not yet in formal training, Tom's group marched on last. They stood shivering in their fatigues, as the parade was handed over to the orderly officer. Back at the lines, Duggan ordered Houlihan to stand fast and dismissed the others.

On the way to breakfast, Tom could hear the Corporal roaring at the corner of the block. He walked up and peeped around. Duggan was standing grimly to attention in the middle of the frosty roadway, his big boots exaggerating the regulation forty-five degrees, a swagger stick under his arm.

"About turn...About turn...About turn," he bawled at the jogging Houlihan.

"At the double, at the double," he screamed.

"Get them knees up, elbows into the sides. Left, right, left...left, right,left..." he speeded up the tempo.

Ten minutes later, Houlihan strolled into the dining hall, picked up his rations, and shoved in beside Tom.

"He's a right hoor, that fella," Tom said.

"There'll be another day. Beidh lá eile leis an bpaorach, mar deirtear," Mike said quietly.

"Do you speak Irish, Mike?" Tom asked.

"I have a few words. I got a bit a schooling. My parents throught they'd make a doctor of me."

"And you joined the army?"

"I might never have had the pleasure of meeting Corporal Duggan if I didn't."

"God, you're a gas man, Mike," Tom said.

The Corporal and Mike had another run-in the following week. More recruits had arrived from various parts of the country, but there still weren't enough to form a training platoon. Consequently, between bouts of footdrill, the section spent considerable time on fatigues. One day Tom, Mike and seven or eight others were in the turfyard, shovelling mould and sorting out bits of turf. Corporal Duggan was supervising. In the afternoon, he was missing and some horseplay ensued. Mike threw a clod at Tom as he dashed behind the turfstack. He missed, but the clod knocked the cap of the returning Duggan.

The Corporal caught the cap in his hand and put it back on his head, straightening the ever-present swagger stick under his arm, before marching up to Mike, scattering turf mould with every stride.

"You did that on purpose, Houlihan," he accused.

"No, honest to God, Corporal, it was an accident."

"It was an accident, was it? We'll soon see about that. Get out on the road."

"The rest of you get back to work," he ordered, "and if there's any more acting the jinnet, you will all be in the guardroom."

He marched Mike up and down for half an hour before dismissing him. Next morning, Mike was before the Company Captain charged with assaulting Duggan. Beltless and capless, with a cookhouse orderly acting as escort, he stood to attention as the Corporal barked out his evidence:

"At approximately three p.m., March 3, yesterday, sir, I was supervising in the turfyards, sir..... Private Houlihan assaulted me, sir, he threw a sod of turf at me, sir, hitting me on the head and knocking off my cap, sir... That concludes my evidence, sir."

"What have you to say for yourself, Houlihan?" the Captain asked.

"It was an accident, sir...."

After some further perfunctory questioning, the Captain accepted Mike's explanation.

"If it wasn't an accident, it would have been a serious offence, Houlihan, assaulting a superior officer," he announced, "I accept your explanation this time. But you still threw the turf. Three days CB. March him out, Corporal."

The Captain followed them out.

"I want to talk to Houlihan, Corporal," he called.

"Halt. Fallout. Report to the Captain, Houlihan," Duggan ordered.

"I understand you hurl for Dublin," the Captain said.

"I played full forward in a few league games, sir."

"You should be up to inter-barrack standard so. I'll get Lieutenant Kelly to have a word with you. He's in charge of hurling".

"Yes, sir."

The platoon filled up that week and, on Friday, it was announced that full-scale platoon training would start on Monday.

Corporal Duggan was designated as company orderly sergeant that week. One of his duties was to wake the company each morning. He did it in his own inimitable fashion, kicking the door of the billet and charging in with the handle of a sweeping brush, which he pounded on the floor for the length of the room. He then thumped it along the legs of the beds, shouting: "Arise and shine, you shower a gits, arise and shine".

That night, he did his rounds at "Lights Out". He again carried the brush handle and he again pounded the floor. Tired, after the first full day's training, all the recruits were in bed and most of them asleep.

"Stand to your beds. Stand to your beds," he roared, till all were standing at the ends of their beds.

He then walked slowly up and down the room, insolently inspecting each man. On the way out, he beat a tattoo on the door with the brush handle. He left the door swinging open. Later in the night, Tom woke up. There was some one beside him. He felt a cold hand on his lower stomach. He jumped out of bed and the figure of a man jumped out the far side. Tom lunged across the bed at him, but the man backed away against the wall. Someone switched on the light. The man was Duggan. He grabbed the brush handle and swung it viciously. Tom dived under it and scrambled across the bed. The handle hit him on the shoulder as he closed with Duggan. He hit the Corporal with his elbow on the face. The Corporal tried to stamp on his bare feet. Tom didn't even notice. He was throwing punches as fast as he could. The Corporal went down and Tom was astride him pounding the already bloodied face. Mike and another lad pulled Tom away and he stood panting in the centre of the billet. The Corporal lay groaning on the floor, between the bed and the wall. The orderly officer and the orderly sergeant arrived. The Corporal went to the hospital and Tom to the guardroom. One of the privates suggested that maybe Duggan got into the wrong bed by mistake, or that maybe he was drunk.

"If he was, he won't make the same mistake again in a hurry," another chortled. "Did you see the way Tom tore into him. He bet him good-looking in about two minutes".

When Tom returned next morning, he was a hero. He and the others in the billet were questioned by two officers and that ended the affair as far as they were concerned. Word filtered through that Duggan was not coming back. He was replaced that evening by another Corporal. He was a raw-boned Galwayman with a shock of red hair. Big and easygoing, he commanded respect by his calm confidence. Pat Layde was his name and he was a hurler. He was on first name terms with Mike within half-an-hour. With Tom, he was more reserved.

"You did a fair job on Duggan. He deserved it. It wasn't the first time," he said cryptically.

On the following Wednesday, Layde and Mike were on the McDonagh hurling team, the Corporal at left full back and Mike full foward. They beat Kent Barracks by two goals and a point, Mike scoring the two goals. The teams were entertained in the Corporals' Mess and when a bleary-eyed Mike returned to the billet, there was a general cheer. The platoon had its second hero.

At Easter, Mike and Tom went to Dublin for the long weekend, arriving in the city on Good Friday evening.

"We'll go straight home," Mike suggested, as he led the way on to a bus in O'Connell Street. "The sooner I dump this bullswool and get into a suit again the better."

At the bungalow on the Templeogue Road, Mrs. Houlihan opened the door.

"Well, aren't you the stranger?" she half-accusingly greeted Mike. "You disappear seven weeks ago and then a note to say you're in the army and not a word since."

"Here I am safe and sound now, ma'am," Mike winked at Tom.

"Do you have to wear that uniform and...and the big soldier's boots?"

"They don't trust us recruits with civvies yet, ma'am," Mike grinned.

"Come in, come in," she said.

"Who's your friend?" she half smiled at Tom.

"Tom Burke. We joined the same week. My mother, Tom."

"Glad to meet you, ma'am," Tom stuck out his hand.

She took it, but Tom did not feel he was very welcome.

"Your father had another small stroke," she whispered to Mike as she opened the sitting room door.

Mike's father sat stiffly upright in the armchair, peering ahead through round, silvery spectacles.

"I thought it was your voice I heard, Mike," he said, enunciating each word slowly.

His suit was too large for him and his neck was shrunken in the shirt collar. Tom thought he was an old man, but Mike told him later that he was only fifty-five. He got slowly to his feet, pushing himself up with the arms of the chair. He was about Tom's height, five feet nine. Standing beside his wife, stout and equally tall, in the bloom of middle aged health, he looked particularly frail.

"You brought a friend, Mike," he held out his hand to Tom.

"I'm Tom Burke," Tom took the proffered hand.

"How are you feeling, dad?" an obviously shocked Mike asked hesitantly.

"Not great, not great, son," he replied, easing himself back into the chair.

"You should have told me. You could have written," Mike accused his mother in the kitchen later.

"Well, the way you ran off. Anyway, I thought we could have managed. Mr. McElwaine is very good in the shop, you know."

"I could always leave the army, mam."

"I thought you hated the shop."

"But it's a different situation now."

"Oh, Mike, could you leave? It would take a load off my mind. Mr. McElwaine is not as young as he was. Oh, Mike, it would be great if you could get out," she placed her hand on Mike's arm, the facade of her middle-class reserve crumbling.

"He could always get out on compassionate grounds," Tom said from the background.

"Yes, mam," Mike put his arms around his mother,"I'll apply for my discharge on compassionate grounds first thing on Tuesday morning."

"I'm glad, Mike, but will you get it, will you get it?" she asked anxiously.

"Of course, he will," Tom assured her.

"Oh, Tom, that's the best news I've had in years," she kissed the embarrassed Tom on the cheek.

Next day, both men went downtown shortly after lunch, Mike in civilians, and Tom wearing a pair of Mike's father's shoes in place of his boots and leggings. Mike wanted him to take one of his father's suits too, but Tom refused.

They walked down Rathmines Road to Quinn's pub at the entrance to Cathal Brugha Barracks. It was full of soldiers and a sergeant, flushed with drink, recognised Mike.

"I was in Croker the day you scored the two goals against Kilkenny. It was the first Sunday in November, amn't I right? You banged them in in the last fifteen minutes, amn't I right?"

"That's right, Sergeant."

"I played a bit myself, you know. I was handy enough before I was carrying this cag around," he prodded his stomach.

"You have the cut of a hurler despite the gut," Mike said absently.

"What do you mean by that crack?" the Sergeant was uncertain.

"Nothing, nothing at all, Sergeant, except that I'd know by the cut of your jib that you hurled a bit."

"Are you a smart alick or something?" the Sergeant got heavily off the bar stool.

"Forget it, Sergeant. We didn't ask for your company," Tom butted in.

"And who the hell's blazes are you anyway?"

"Tom Burke."

"And not a wet week in the army either."

"Forget it," Tom turned and put his elbows on the counter.

"Don't turn your back on me, soldier boy, and...and stand to attention when you're speaking to a superior officer."

Tom spun round so quickly that the Sergeant took a half-step backwards.

"Yes, Sergeant, sir," Tom stood stiffly to attention.

"A bloody redarse, the lowest form of army life," the Sergeant spluttered.

"Hold on a minute, It was all my fault," Mike put his hand on the Sergeant's shoulder.

"Take your hand off me," the Sergeant ordered, spitting out

each word. "Just remember this - no redarse is going to get up on my back. I'm too old a cat to be bucked by a kitten."

Bald-headed, and straightening his stout-stained apron, Batty Quinn had come out from behind the counter.

"God, that's a good one, Mick, too old a cat to be bucked by a kitten. It's a new one on me. Maybe we can settle this argument the easy way," Batty shoved between Tom and the Sergeant.

"You stay out of this, Batty. I'll deal with it in my own way," the Sergeant told him.

"Listen, Mr. Quinn, maybe I was a bit short with the Sergeant, but I came home for the weekend to find my father sick," Mike explained.

"Aye, half-dying and the Sergeant here called him a smart-alick," Tom cut in.

"So, it's all a mistake. We'll leave it like that," Quinn addressed the Sergeant.

"Maybe we will and maybe we won't, but I'll have a piss first," the Sergeant shoved past Quinn.

"Mike's father is sick," Quinn assured him on his return.

"Right, shove up three drinks there," the Sergeant ordered.

Tom staggered a little on leaving the pub later that night.

"Drinking glasses of stout and you're showing the effects," Mike laughed. "All you had were four or five pints altogether."

They walked to Grafton Street, turning right into Anne Street.

"You better straighten yourself up now, or we won't get into the dance," Mike advised.

Tom stood inside the glass doors in the foyer. As the ballroom door opened and closed, he could see the dancers, dark shadows under intermittently flashing beams of light. There was an air of sophistication about the scene far removed from the hall in Tunnygee. Subconsciously, his foot tapped in time to a quickstep.

As Mike approached the ticket hatch, a tall blond man in a dinner jacket and bow tie tapped him on the shoulder and beckoned him aside. Mike followed him to where Tom was standing.

"I'm very sorry," the man said, "but soldiers are not admitted."

"He's wearing shoes," Mike said.

"I see that, but the house rule doesn't permit us to admit soldiers."

"What's wrong with soldiers?" Tom demanded.

"I'm sorry, sir, but there's a house rule."

"Why?"

"We don't allow in soldiers in uniform, sir."

"So you object to the uniform."

"Don't be awkward, sir. I don't make the rules."

"It's a quare sort of rule," Tom persisted, "I suppose we're only good enough to fight for you."

"I don't agree with the rule myself, pal," there was an edge to the manager's voice, "I was in the army myself, you know."

"What about the soldier in uniform who went in ahead of us?" Mike asked quietly.

"No soldier went in, I assure you. I've been at the door all evening."

"The Yank with the two girls, did you see him?"

"But he's an American."

"He's a soldier in uniform, isn't he?" Tom asked. "Why's a Yank in uniform better than an Irishman in uniform?"

"It's the rule. The argument is getting you nowhere. You must move," the manager jerked his head slightly, and two burly men, also in dinner jackets, joined him.

"I'm going. You can call the dogs off," Tom turned away.

"But it's still a bloody disgrace," he called back over his shoulder.

7

Mike got his compassionate discharge within a fortnight of his return from the Easter weekend and went off to manage his father's bookshop on the Dublin quays. Tom passed out as the best soldier in his platoon in July and was posted to the the 5th Infantry Battalion in Cathal Brugha Barracks. The army was run down after the war years and Tom joined a company with less than twenty privates, a handful of N.C.Os and two officers. It was a let down after the sense of soldiering inculcated during his recruit training, but he soon fell into the routine of fatigues and constant guard duties. In May of the following year, he was glad to be selected for a N.C.O course, even if it meant going back to the Curragh for a further six months. Once again, he passed out at the head of his class and returned to his unit, proudly wearing his new stripes, two weeks before Christmas, 1950.

In the New Year, he supervised fatigues, which was more boring than performing them, and was detailed for guard duty only slightly less often. He met Mike about once a week, when they had a few drinks, generally in Guiney's pub on the quays. Butsy Dwyer, another Corporal, often accompanied him to Guiney's and, regularly, the three of them went dancing to the Anne Street ballroom, where the manager and they had become very friendly, even to the extent of one or other of them being let in free on occasions.

Tom and Butsy were selected for the Easter guard-of-honour at the G.P.O. that year. Soldiers were drafted into Cathal Brugha Barracks from the various Dublin units and from the Curragh for a fortnight's special training - concentrated arms and foot drill, all day, every day. On Easter Saturday, the final rehearsal took place. The Officer Commanding, Eastern Command, was present. Afterwards, he expressed himself as satisifed with the turn-out, assuring the troops that he had never seen a finer guard-of-honour in thirty years of soldiering.

On Easter Sunday morning, the soldiers of the guard stood around under the canopy of the Adelphi Cinema in Abbey Street. Self-consciously and stiffly, they stood proudly erect with webbing blancoed and brasses shining, smoking nervously. At half past eleven, they formed up on the roadway and marched out on to O'Connell Street to the cheers of the still assembling crowd. Halt, Left Turn, they faced the G.P.O. Having dressed by the right, the two lines stood motionless, bayonet scabbards in line and creased trousers bloused over short leggings. Not a muscle stirred, it seemed, but each man could feel leg muscles twitching, while toes moved spasmodically beneath shining, brown toecaps.

"Sure, they're a fine body of men, a credit to the country. My brother's in the army too," Tom heard the Dublin woman in the shuffling, restless crowd behind, exclaim.

Looking straight ahead, Tom's eyes probed the gloom behind the garlanded stand and the grey pillars of the General Post Office. In under the portico was a knot of black coated figures, ministers of state, and higher officials, with the beribboned green of the Chief-of-Staff in their midst. They seemed uneasy, moving around stiffly and talking occasionally in self-conscious asides. Padraig Pearse had come out from the portico to read the Proclamation in 1916. If only Uncle Pakie was here now, he would be a proud man. I wonder what would he think of Dev now, still out of power. He would have something caustic to say, but the framed photo of Dev remained on the wall above the settle until the day he died. It was still there in the empty house, showing Dev on parade before the '32 election. He looked like Mr. Sandeman in it, black coat flapping below his knees and the wide-brimmed black hat to top him off.

"The chisseler, where's he gone? Come back, come back, Dessie, come back out of that," the Dublin woman's voice again, more high-pitched this time.

Tom felt a pull at his scabbard. There it was again, someone pulling at him. Look to the front, Don't move. He felt the cold sweat under the band of his cap. Another tug and a small boy's voice at his hip: "Are you a soldier, mister? I'm going to be a soldier."

"Come away out of that, Dessie. Leave the soldier alone. Don't mind him, mister. He's only a chisseler," the woman's voice was at his elbow.

"He's mad on soldiers, mad on soldiers," Tom was glad to hear the voice fading back into the murmur of the crowd.

"Any sign of the lad in the park yet?" a man's voice called in the singsong of West Cork.

Cork was playing in Croke Park that evening. Probably up to see the match, or maybe he was one of the players, red-faced over a white shirt and long, swinging tie. He might swing a hurley later, dancing on dainty feet, sleeves rolled back over bulging, unweathered biceps. Tom was going to the game. Mike was a substitute on the Dublin team. He might be playing. There was a roar down to the right and the crowd was clapping. The band on the left burst into a crescendo of music and, out in front, the officer's heels lifted fractionally as he shouted the commands. The guard presented arms and the Presidential Salute rang out. Out of the corner of his eye, Tom could see the President. White face and white hair, under a grey topper, Sean T. was a jaunty little man. One of the old guard, he was close to Dev. He was fond of a drop of whiskey, they said, and Dev never touched the stuff. Sean T. did not look much like an old revolutionary as, with quiet dignity, he walked along the line of soldiers. He mounted the platform and stood bareheaded on the dais, as the jets hurled overhead.

"Janey, they'll take the roof off the post office," the Dublin woman announced.

"So them's the jets. They're like forked lightning," the Corkman marvelled.

The first troops marched past, six abreast, arms shoulder high in unison.

"God bless them, but they're only boys. Our own lads marching through Dublin. See them, Dessie, not one of them out of step," the Dublin woman enthused.

"I can't see them, mammy," her son complained.

"Can't you see, son. Move over there. Excuse me, sir. Can you see better now, son?"

"Your grandfather would be a proud man if he was alive today, Dessie," she declared. "He was in Flanders in the first world war and he never lost his taste for soldiering after, God rest him. Your other grandfather, God rest him too, was a Sinn Feiner, one of the boys. Maybe, he even fought in the post office there. Anyway, I remember the two of them, a lily at Easter for one and a poppy in November for the other."

Artillery, all new paint and glittering brass. Sean McEoin, the Minister for Defence, stood foursquare at the President's shoulder. White hair, brushed straight back, untamed over an open countryman's face, he had made it hot for the Black and Tans in Longford. An old soldier and a gallant fighter, the Blacksmith of Ballinalee had the bullet wounds to prove it. Pakie had a soft spot for him. He could never understand why he took the wrong side at the

Treaty and "him the man that got the young Sheridan fellow to hospital after the ambush below in Ballinagh".

Armour rumbled past and, then, the crowd's applause swelled to a roar. A naval detachment had swung into view and the confident sailor's tread had an electrifying effect. There was a certain swagger to them in the blue and white uniforms. The tail-end of the parade went past and the guard-of-honour marched off, turning left into Prince's Street. It was into trucks and back to barracks the long way round, down the quays and up the South Circular. A few girls waved and were answered with catcalls and whistles. Back at Cathal Brugha Barracks they tumbled from the trucks and were dismissed.

"A pint before dinner!" Butsy suggested.

"We'll get into civvies first if we're going to Croker," Tom said.

Legs still stiff and shakey after the long stand, it felt good to stand up to the counter. Tight uniform discarded, the loose civilian attire gave a sense of freedom. The barmen were up to their eyes in quick-filled sudsy pints, but there was no one objecting. Tom got his hands around the cold glass and lowered his pint quickly.

"Two more," he called.

They got two chairs in a corner. Cigarettes going and glasses on the floor, they sprawled contentedly.

"The parade went off well, Butsy," Tom said.

"All the bloody same, Tom. Spit and polish for weeks for less than an hour of glory in O'Connell Street, with old one-eyed Nelson looking down on you."

"He shouldn't be there at all."

"It's Nelson's pillar, isn't it?"

"Still, a British Admiral . . . . . . !"

"Isn't he as good a target as any for the seagulls?" Butsy laughed.

"But he's an Englishman."

"What's the differ? He doesn't bother me anyway."

"Still, an Englishman up there lording it over Dublin."

"Listen, Tom, if he stood on his hands and pissed through his toes over Dublin, it wouldn't worry me. Come on, get that drink into you. We want to get to the match."

They left the bus in O'Connell Street and joined the crowd trekking towards Croke Park.

"Get your colours here for the big game. Sixpence each, colours of the teams. Dublin and Cork colours, sixpence each," the street traders hawked their wares.

In the park, the blue and red jacketed boys of the Artane Band worked intricate patterns to the strain of the music. Small boys, and some not so small, perched precariously high up on the Railway Wall, while at the other end, the terraces were packed right back to the Canal Bank. The dark, cavernous stands towered along the pitch on either side.

The teams trotted out onto the green grass, the blue and white clad Dubliners first, followed momentarily by the red jerseyed Corkmen. The thirty athletes lined up and the pre-match parade was on, strong-muscled, heavy-shouldered men highstepping behind the shortstriding youngsters of the band.

"He's not playing," Tom said.

"Sure the bastard's drinking too much. Probably had a skinful last night again," Butsy shrugged.

The ball was thrown in and the game was on. The small leather ball sailed from end to end, bone crunched against bone and, sometimes, stick against bone and flesh in the fast, fiery action of the game. The ball came up the field and a Corkman had it. His stroke was straight and true and the ball sailed high between the posts. First blood to Cork and a thousand throats distended in a wild, partisan roar.

Cork came under pressure and the goalkeeper grabbed the ball from the air. He swung hard and, at centrefield, a teammate took the ball on his stick. He flicked it to a waiting forward. Nearly bald, head small on a sturdy body, with short legs and powerful arms, the forward twisted, turned and attempted to strike, but a burly Dublin back laid him low. He bounded to his feet and, when the ball was placed for the free, he sent it over the bar.

"Oh, Ringey, Ringey, Ringey," a fat girl in front of Burke screamed.

"Up Cork," Butsy shouted over her shoulder.

"Up Cork," she turned her head, two round blue eyes in a round face, framed in a halo of frizzy blonde hair.

"I'd say you could milk cows, girl," Butsy laughed.

"That I can, boy," she grinned up into his face.

"What about seeing you home, girl?"

"But I have to be back at work at half-six.

"No matter, we can have a jorrum first."

"I don't drink. I was never in a pub in my life."

"You're joking, girl."

"No, honest to God, I have the pledge."

"You've no badge."

"It's at home in my everyday clothes."

Dublin fought back, but Cork were still two points ahead at halftime. For the first ten minutes of the second half Dublin had the edge and went two points in front. Then, the Cork centre-back pointed from eighty yards. The battle was now desperately joined and the ball sailed from end to end. Two hurleys splintered like matchsticks as the Dublinmen held on grimly to the one point lead. A Cork puck was going wide, but the lazy, loping gait of the tall corner forward was deceptive. Reaching out a long arm, he kept the ball in play and the balding Ringey had it.

"The maestro has it. The maestro has it," the fat girl screeched, jumping up and down on springloaded heels.

On the field, the ball seemed glued to the end of the Ringey's stick. Like a trout in a stream, he darted hither and thither, swerving past a chopping hurley and diving beneath the swing of another. Fourteen yards from goal, four Dublin backs hemmed him in. Suddenly, an eel-like twist of his body, a flick of the wrists and the Cork cheers coincided with the bulge of the ball in the back of the net.

"Oh, maestro, maestro," the girl shrieked and flung her arms around Butsy's neck.

"You've a fair hoult there," Tom said sourly to the grinning Butsy.

"Hey, Houlihan's coming on," he shouted at Butsy.

"Good old Mike," Butsy turned away from the girl, "he'll soon show the Corkies how to hurl."

"Come on Cork, Come on the rebel county," the girl shouted.

Trailing his stick, Mike trotted to the corner-forward position. From the puck-out, Cork regained possession. Dublin fouled and the resultant free went narrowly wide. Cork were in the ascendant now and the Dublin goal had two further lucky escapes. Mike had moved out towards centrefield. The ball came loose, rolling along the ground. He did not pick it up, but ran with it like a hockey player. He weaved his way down the wing, beating three Cork men in succession, before cutting in towards the centre. The full back dived at him, but Mike left him sprawling. He attempted to tap the ball past the goalkeeper, but he mishit it and it rolled harmlessly past the right post. The Dublin roar died to a collective *ah* as Mike fell flat on his face. The trainer rushed on and Mike was half-dragged, half-carried to the end line. A substitute ran on. From the puck out, Dublin gained possession, but were stymied by the shrill blast of the final whistle.

"He's drunk," Tom declared, "look at him sitting there with his head in his hands."

"Up the rebel county," the girl called back, making her way down the terrace steps.

They waited for Mike at the back of the Cusack Stand. He was one of the last players to leave the dressing room."

"No, I wasn't drunk," he told an accusing Tom, "I only had a few last night."

"What did they say to you in there?"

"Nothing much. Just that if I didn't train, I'd lose my place. I said fair enough. What do you mean by fair enough, one of them asked. If I don't train I lose my place, that's fair enough, I said. Are you going to train, he shouted, losing the rag a bit. He ranted about drinking for a while. I said nothing, just stood looking at him."

"That's all?"

"That's all, Tom. Why? Are you worried?"

"Why the hell should I worry?"

"Exactly, Tom, why should you?" Mike moved towards an exit.

"Where are we going now?" Tom asked.

"For a drink, what else?" Mike grinned.

8

Tom's three years of army service officially came to an end in February 1952, but between pre-discharge leave, annual leave and the Christmas holidays, he was effectively discharged the previous Christmas week. Next day, he took the bus to Tunnygee. He called first to Johny McCaffrey, where he got a great welcome. Johny brought a bottle of whiskey and two glasses from the parlour and poured two substantial measures.

"Here's to the prodigal son," he held up his glass, "we're more than delighted to see you home, Tom amhic."

Johny's wife insisted that he stay for tea and opened one of the Christmas puddings in his honour.

"Is Edward still in Maynooth, Mrs. McCaffrey?" Tom enquired.

"He is, indeed, Tom. We're expecting him home the morrow."

"How many years has he done now?"

"Five. God willing, he'll be a priest two summers from now."

"That's great news, ma'am. Edward done you proud."

"Maybe, it's the other way round, that we done him proud. Isn't that right, Alice?" Johny laughed.

"I don't know about that, but it'll be a happy day for us, the day he is ordained," Mrs. McCaffrey smiled, "but I think it's God we should be thanking. It was Him done us proud after all."

Later, Johny and Tom walked into town. In Kelly's pub, Jimmy shook hands with Tom and put up the first drink. All the other customers formally shook hands and muttered their welcome.

"Now, Tom, we'll get a wee bit of business out of the way before we go any further," Johny suggested, "I'm grazing your land since you left, as we agreed, but we agreed no price. I thought that forty-five a year would be a fair price, what do you think?"

"It sounds alright to me, Johny."

"There's another thing. I kept an eye on the house and lit the odd fire in it, so it's in fair good shape. But the thatch is getting shook. There'd need to be a job done on it fairly soon. But, of course, maybe you're going to stay at home now."

"No, I'm not. I'm going to England for a while. There's plenty of work over there, on the buildings and the like. Butsy Dwyer, a friend of mine in the army, went over about a month ago and he's going great."

"Whatever you say, Tom, but the thatching will have to be done."

"You'll be able to get someone, Johny."

"No problem with that, but it'll cost a few quid. Twenty should cover it."

"You can take it out of the letting money."

"I suppose I better pay you the rest some of these days."

"No, put it in the bank. It'll be a nest egg if I ever come home again."

Tom hired Jimmy Devine to drive him to his grandmother's house that night. His grandmother and grandfather were in bed when he arrived. His Aunt Bernadette answered the door in a long nightdress. It was a minute before she recognised him.

"Is it yourself that's in it? Will you come in out of that before I'm famished ?"

She opened the door wide. She went into the upper room and, when she came back, she was buttoning a coat and wearing unlaced men's shoes. She lit the lamp and, as she bustled around, reviving the fire and filling the black metal kettle, her long black hair fell about her face. A year younger than his mother, Tom had always been told that they were very much alike. Slightly olive- skinned and dark eyed, she was a good looking woman, who smiled a lot, showing white, even teeth.

"You have teeth like mine, Bernadette," Tom said.

"All the Burkes have good teeth," she laughed, "although when you look at my father with the one tusk in the bottom gum, you wonder where they came from."

"How are the old pair?"

"Great for their age. Himself is well over eighty and my mother was seventy last year."

"Johny McCaffrey told me you got married!"

"Aye, over two years now. I took on a big lump of a Monaghan man, but he's a good husband. Paul Comiskey. I'm Mrs. Comiskey now," she laughed and tossed her hair.

She took down the settle-bed and straightened the bedclothes in it.

"You'll stay the night?" she questioned.

"I might as well."

"It'll be the first time you slept here since you were a young lad."

His grandmother was bent over the fire when Tom awoke next morning. Standing up, she saw him watching her. She came over and stood over him.

"You're the last of the Burkes. Poor Rosie, God be good to her," she crossed herself.

"What about Bernadette?" Tom asked.

"Hasn't she her own man for over two years and not a stir out of her. Anyway, she's a Comiskey now. You're the last of the Burkes after himself beyant in the room, whatever way you look at it."

Later her husband hobbled up from the bedroom on two sticks.

"His hips are nearly gone. They've got shocking stiff on him this last lock of years," she said .

"But there's a bit of a kick in me yet," the old man cackled, "God, you're the boy that's looking well, Tom, all dressed up like the gentry. Come over till I shake your hand," he stood. swaying on his sticks.

He managed to grip Tom's hand, before being helped to his chair.

"It's a terror, a holy terror," he muttered.

Bernadette and Paul came in from foddering and looking after the stock. Paul was a big man with a cap on the side of his head. The bulk of him nearly filled the doorway.

On Christmas Eve, all, except the old man, went to Midnight Mass in a pony and trap.

"Where did this come from?" Tom asked, tapping his hand on the side of the trap.

"Your grandmother wouldn't let me in emptyhanded," Paul laughed, flicking the whip along the pony's flank.

"She's a hard woman, Paul," Tom laughed also.

"She's all that, but don't get me wrong." Paul flicked at the pony again. "It's the best thing ever happened me, marrying

Bernadette and I'm fond of herself there too, even though," glancing under his cap at his mother-in-law, "she might be a bit sharp in the tongue betimes."

"Get away out of that, Paul," Mrs. Burke slapped his knee, "sure, someone has to keep the Monaghan crowd in their place."

Tom enjoyed the good natured easy hospitality of his family for a few days. He was genuinely lonely leaving for Dublin, yet was happy to get away. Bernadette waved tentatively as the bus moved off, looking slightly forlorn beside her big, quiet husband.

Tom stayed in a hotel in Gardiner Street that night. Next morning he went down along the quays to Houlihan's shop. It was still closed. Tom looked at his watch. It was ten o'clock. He crossed over to the riverside and leaned across the wall. The tide was out and there was an old pram and a broken bicycle in a patch of mud underneath him. The water, sluggish on the turn, was dirty green on dirty brown. The sour, stale smell reminded Tom of the lake under Pakie's house when the rotten vegetation and the mud along the banks was disturbed and oozed up around one's ankles. There was plenty of pike in the lake. He hadn't fished since he joined the army. He hadn't milked a cow since either. Bernadette did the milking at his grandmother's. If his mother had lived, she would probably be milking cows too. Bernadette was like his mother. Everyone said that. Pakie used to say that they were "like two peas in a pod." She acted like his mother too. She even darned his socks and aired his shirts. Maybe, that was why she looked sad when she waved at the bus. She had been laughing and smiling during his stay. She had been delighted to have him in the house. His mother would have been delighted too, but she was gone. Bernadette could not take her place. Tunnygee was alright for a holiday, but he couldn't live there now. The army had shown him a whole new way of life. There was more to life than digging drains and milking cows in Tunnygee. Anyway, he would be in London tomorrow. He was looking forward to teaming up with Butsy again.

"Hey, Tom," Mike roared across the street.

Tom dodged over through the traffic to where Mike stood on the edge of the footpath.

"What time do you open this joint at?" Tom demanded.

Inside, Mike rubbed the bristles on his chin.

"Do I need a shave?" he asked.

"You need more than a shave by the cut of you. You must have slept in the suit."

"You're right there. I slept in a chair. I don't remember getting home."

"How are things at home, anyway?"

"Terrible. The old man's confined to bed and my mother's nursing him. You can imagine what it's like. When are you heading for London?"

"I'm on the boat tonight."

"I'll soon be out of this place myself. You won't believe this. I'm going to be a bankclerk."

"You're coddin'. Who'd let you near a bank?"

"They're letting me near one alright. My mother fixed it. Do you remember her going on about her friend, the bank director? Well, he came up trumps in the end. I did the interview before Christmas and I'm detailed to take up duty on Monday week."

"And what about this place?"

"It's a dead duck. Some weeks it hardly pays for itself, but wait for it, you didn't hear the best of it."

"What's your father and mother going to do?"

"That's taken care of. My father's going into the hospice next week and my mother has a few pounds put by. Everything's arranged to permit yours truly embark on a banking career. But I didn't tell you the best news yet."

"I'm all ears."

"I'm posted to Tunnygee."

"What?"

"You heard me. I'm to present myself to the bank manager of the Hibernian Bank in Tunnygee on Monday week."

"I don't believe it, Mike."

"You may and what would you say if I closed up here and we went off to celebrate the departure of Houlihan to Tunnygee and the departure of Burke to the land of the ancient enemy far beyond the sea."

"You're getting into your stride early in the day."

"You've seen nothing yet, Burke me boy. Wait till I get a few halfones in me."

In the pub Mike ordered a halfone and a cup of coffee. He poured the whiskey into the coffee and gulped it down.

"That's the breakfast, now for some serious drinking . I'll have a halfone and a pint," he called the barman, "and give my friend here another pint."

"No, I'll stick to a glass," Tom said, "I want to be on that boat."

"That's what's wrong with you, Tom, you're too serious-minded, too bloody cute. You never put a foot wrong, never let yourself go. Supposing you did miss the boat, what difference would it make? There'll be another one tomorrow."

"You're in right form this morning. The head must be bustin'."

"I'm sorry, Tom. I'm only shooting my mouth off. That hole of a shop and, then, the old man. I'm fond of him, you know."

"I know that, Mike but you're drinking too much. I know you're fond of your father, but you're not much help to him pissin' everything up again a wall."

"You have it all worked out, Tom."

"I've damn all worked out," Tom said, "but I'm my own man. I'm not full of self-pity, like you.

"Keep at it, Tom, you're going well."

"It's time someone put it straight to you."

"Keep going."

"Well, if you want the truth, here's it for you. What age are you? Twenty-three and your hurling days are over. You could have been a Dublin hero. You got out of the army to take over the bookshop. It was going well. You often said that yourself. A couple of years after you take over and that's a flop too. You want to know what's wrong with you, Mike. You got it too easy, everything came too handy for you."

"Ah, for Christ's sake, Tom."

"Never mind Christ's sake. It's for your sake."

"Come on, we'll go for a walk, unless you want to stay, mister.... no, sorry, Corporal Burke. Anyway, I'm off."

They walked the streets for an hour, ending up at Westland Row Railway Station.

"Never let it be said, Houlihan stopped you going to London," Mike stood on the footpath.

"Damn you, Houlihan, we're two hours too early."

In the hotel bar opposite the station, Mike ordered a coffee. He sipped it and spat the sip back into the cup.

"To hell with this. Bring us a whiskey, a large one, and another glass of stout," he shouted at the barman.

Three large ones later, Mike was talking about the wonders of television.

"In ten years time, there'll be a set in every house." he explained, "all you'll have to do is stick an aerial up on the roof and plug into the electricity."

"That wouldn't be much good in our place," Tom said, "unless an oil lamp would work the miracle."

"Is there no electricity in Tunnygee?"

"It's in the town itself alright, but not that long. I remember oil lamps in the shops, brass ones with big shades, hanging from the ceiling, like the ones you see in the Wild West films."

"It's a backward hole you come from."

"I never claimed otherwise, but the electricity reminds me of a story about a granduncle of mine, my mother's Uncle Martin. He went to America in the twenties sometime. That time, they stayed in Dublin overnight, before getting the train to Cork and Cobh the following morning. The hotel or the lodging house was somewhere around Gardiner Street. Anyway, Martin was in a room with two men from the West. When it got dark, someone suggested lighting the lamp, but the lamp was up near the ceiling, out of reach. Martin was the smallest of the three men. The other two lifted him up on their shoulders and there was Martin cracking matches and trying to puzzle out how to get the new-fangled Dublin lamp going. Suddenly, the door opened and a servant-girl came in and flicked the switch. The blaze of light frightened the men and they let Martin fall.

"That's a tall one," Mike said, "it never happened."

"It happened. What do you think three country fellas would know about electricity at that time?"

"And Humpty Dumpty came tumbling down," Mike laughed. "The poor oul' eegit. That deserves another drink," he lurched to his feet, knocking a glass to the floor.

He sat down again, looking at the broken glass.

"When a glass and the floor meet like that, something must give. How is it that it's always the bloody glass?" he asked.

"It's a mystery," he continued, still staring at the floor, "like a mystery of religion, past our....past our comprehension.....It's a mystery to me anyway.....But it's not a mystery to you, Tom. You have it all worked out. Do you hear me?" his voice pitching higher, "you have it all bloody well worked out, Mister Corporal Thomas Burke."

"Listen, Mike, I'm not going' to miss the train. Are you coming?"

"I'm staying here, Tom," Mike stood up. "I'll say farewell here. Then I'll have another drink and maybe puzzle out the mystery....the mystery of life. And then I'll be like you, Tom. I'll have it all worked out."

"You can drink your head off for all I care and work out any mysteries you like, but I'm off. I'll be seeing you."

"Are you not even going to shake my hand?"

They shook hands silently and Tom left. He looked back from the door. Mike was at the counter.

9

In Camden Town, at six in the morning, the gang to which Butsy belonged straggled along the footpath to stand in shop doorways or to hunker down along the wall. In donkey coats, cast-off army clothing or old suits, burst at the armpits and with ripped sleeves, they stood coughing, hacking and spitting. Some wore caps, one or two of the older men had hats, but the majority had berets sitting high on their heads. Most wore mud spattered wellingtons turned down at the top, with a few sporting equally mud spattered down-at-heel shoes. Each had an old biscuit tin or a tight brownpaper parcel gripped firmly under his arm.

Tom was an obvious newcomer in their midst, in his clean clothes and tight army haircut. Also, his wellingtons were new. A few glanced at him, but without comment. When the lorry came, they crowded in over the tailboard and sides and huddled down on the floor.

Fifteen miles out, the site was shrouded in mist, a halfmade motorway abruptly ending in a sea of mud. The biscuit tins and paper parcels were carefully put away in the hut and there was the clatter of picks, shovels and wheelbarrows. The mechanical diggers growled into life and the first loads of gravel arrived. The foreman came over to Tom and entered his name in a small notebook, that he took from his hip pocket.

"This is the best weapon to start with," the foreman handed him a shovel.

At lunchtime, the first blisters had burst on Tom's hands.

"That's the way the army softens you up," Butsy laughed.

"Hey, Jack," he called to the foreman, "you wouldn't have a bit of a bandage in that old box of yours?"

"What do you want it for?"

"Tom here has a few blisters."

"He can bloody work them off. You army fellas are too bloody soft."

In the hut, the parcels and tins were opened and billycans were crowded on the hut stove, stoked to red hot heat. Rough sandwiches were made and Butsy shared his billycan of hot, sweet tea with Tom. When they finally finished at half four that evening, the blisters were worn down and raw on Tom's dirt-grimed hands. An hour later, they were back in Camden.

On pay night, the gang went to Clancy's pub. Still in their working clothes, they drank pints of beer and stout, confidently assuring each other that they were not half as strong as the pints at home; that you could drink a barrel of the stuff without getting drunk. Yet the voices got louder and more boisterous and, invariably, someone was called on for a song. Quietly, at first, they sang songs of Ireland, but the sentimental soon gave way to the openly rebellious, and when *Kevin Barry* rang out, they shouted the chorus:*"Another martyr for old Ireland, another murder for the Crown, British laws may kill the Irish, but shall not break their spirit down".*

This was the high point of the evening, and, gradually, they drifted away, until a hard core of three or four were left. Clancy watched them from behind the counter, but he knew that the steam was gone out of them; that they might argue and talk vehemently for a while, but that they would soon depart.

Tom and Butsy stayed with the motorway gang until June. It was Tom arranged the first sub-contracting job.

"It's lumping," he told Butsy, "we get paid by the job, piece work, you know. They're paying thirty pounds a house to have the footins dug out by the railway."

"What the hell are footins?"

"The foundations, you bloody eejit. All you have to do is mark out the house and dig out the ground. It's money for jam. And we pay no tax, no nothing, that's the beauty of it."

"How would you get away with that?"

"Give a false name, if anyone asks you. Who the hell knows you in this country and isn't London a big place?"

"What'll we make?"

"Forty a week and more, if we work on weekends."

The first week, they earned thirty pounds each, but, as they became more experienced, they crossed forty most weeks. When the foundations were dug, they contracted for the internal plastering of the houses. The first few houses were a messy job, but they soon became experts at nailing plaster board and skimming it over. They went from that to another "lumpin" job, laying sewerage pipes on the same estate. Early in the new year, they laid the first stretch, connecting to the houses on the way down. That evening, on the instructions of the engineer, they filled the pipes with water, blocking the end one. Next morning, when the engineer opened the plug in the end pipe, it was soon clear that the water was not running properly. The pipes had to be relaid to permit the water to run freely. It took them two days extra work to remedy the matter.

In April, they laid the last stretch of pipes. They filled it with water as usual and went home. Next morning, about twenty yards of trench had caved in a third of the way down.

"That fucks it," Butsy said, "we'll have to lay every damn pipe again."

They walked down along the trench.

"If we get that clay out before the engineer comes, we could fix the damage," Butsy suggested.

"No leave it. Those pipes are well laid. There might be no damage done."

"Who do you think you're coddin', with that weight a stuff crashing in on them? We'll get dug into it."

"Leave it. We'll wait for the inspection and see what happens."

"I thought we were going back to Dublin tomorrow?"

"We are."

"And supposing, just supposing that we have to relay the pipes? Who's going to do it? It's Saturday. The engineer won't expect us to do anything before Monday."

The engineer arrived shortly after noon and declared the flow of water to be unsatisfactory.

"I'm sorry, boys. They'll have to be relaid. When shall I come back to inspect again?"

"It'll take two days at least," Tom rubbed his chin, "We should be ready on Wednesday morning.

"Right, I'll see you then," the engineer hopped into his car.

"Well, that fucks it. Our holidays bollocksed. There'll be no boat train the morrow. Now, what have you to say for yourself, mister know-all Burke?" Butsy threw a shovel clattering along the road.

"Fill in the trench", Tom said quietly, "we won't get paid until it's filled."

"I know that, but...."

"But what? Where will we be on Monday?"

"Laying bloody pipes."

"Use your head, Butsy. Fill in the trench and get paid. Our engineer friend can inspect as much as he likes on Wednesday. We'll be back in Ireland safe and sound."

"Oh, Jasus, where's that bloody shovel," Butsy dived after the shovel he had discarded a few minutes previously.

They finished at six that evening. The contractor was waiting for them, when, cleaned and dressed, they presented themselves at

Clancy's. He paid them and assured them that if they were ever back in London he would be only too glad to employ them.

That night they had no intention of going dancing. They just dropped in casually on the way home, to finish off the last night in London, as Butsy put it. They met Maisie, the row ensued, and Butsy was arrested in possession of the helmet.

Tom called to the police station next morning and asked to see Butsy.

"Not a chance, mate," a policeman told him, "you'll see him in court tomorrow morning"

Tom went around to Duncan's cafe. It was closed and there was no answer to his ringing.

He was walking away when he saw Maisie approaching.

"Hello, Tom," she said shyly.

"Howya, Maisie."

"I was at Mass."

"I was there earlier myself. I went down to the police station too, but they wouldn't let me talk to Butsy."

"What'll happen him?"

"He could get a couple of months handy enough. They have him on several charges, including assaulting a policeman and stealing the helmet and three or four others."

"Ah, poor Butsy. It was a foolish act, taking the helmet.

"The bloody clown. If he had dropped it when I told him, we were home and dried."

"And it was all because of me," Maisie smiled.

"Aye, it was over you I hit him. You seem to be happy enough about it too."

"I suppose I am. Well, to tell you the truth, I'm not sorry you hit him."

"Good girl, Maisie," Tom squeezed her arm.

When Butsy's case was called next morning, the magistrate had already dealt with two Irishmen, one for fighting, who got a month, and the other for begging, who also got a month. It seemed initially that the magistrate had no intention of sending the second man to jail. He asked the man how long he had been in London. When the prisoner replied that he had been there for a month, the

71

magistrate advised him that begging was an offence that could land one in prison in London.

"They don't give you a medal for it in Dublin either," the prisoner looked at him balefully. "The poor are as much the victims of the capitalist system in Dublin as in London."

"Are you a Communist?"

"No, I'm a Roman Catholic."

"I'm seriously considering sending you to prison," the magistrate warned.

"For being a Roman Catholic or a Communist?"

"A month's hard labour."

Whatever chance Butsy had of obtaining a sympathetic hearing was effectively eliminated. Despite the best efforts of the defending solicitor, assaulting a policeman and, then, compounding the crime by stealing a policeman's helmet, were offences that were not going to be tolerated, especially when another Irishman was involved.

"We seem to have a surfeit of Irish miscreants this morning and this court is not going to have the law brought into disrepute by the behaviour of such people. If a policeman cannot go about his duty without being upended by a wild Irishman, we are in an intolerable situation," the magistrate declared, before sentencing Butsy to six months with hard labour.

"I want to join the army, sir," Butsy snapped to attention in the dock.

"Are you a soldier?" the magistrate asked.

"Yes, sir, I was three years in the Irish army. I reached the rank of Corporal, sir."

"Sentence suspended, provided defendant enlists in Her Majesty's Forces."

Maisie and Tom went to a film that evening. He met her every evening that week and on Saturday he brought her out for a meal. They sat in plush seats in a corner of the restaurant. Tom ordered a steak and chips and a bottle of wine. Maisie had a salmon steak.

"Red or white, sir?" the waitress queried.

"Red."

"But for madame, sir? White is more usual with fish."

"Is that so? In the place I come from, we always have red wine with our fish."

72

"As you wish, sir."

"It's far from fish or wine, you were reared,"Maisie giggled.

"Ah, but we're not going to let them know that, especially now that I'm staying for another while."

"You're not going home, Tom? You've made up your mind ?"

"I think I'll stay around another while. Someone has to keep an eye on you, you know."

"Ah, Tom, you're not really staying, are you?"

"I am, and what's more, I'm starting work again on Monday. I went down to Clancy's today to meet the boss. I sub-contracted to do the footins for fifty houses."

"Did he say anything about the pipes?"

"He knew about it. The engineer had reported it. He was a bit surprised to hear it, he said, but what the hell, he laughed, there might never be another word about it.

"He's not so bad, Tom."

"He's no eejit. He knows that myself and Butsy are the two best lumpers he has. It'll be hard to get someone as good as Butsy."

"Poor Butsy."

"What's so poor about him?"

"He'll be two or three years in the British army now."

"Not at all. It's up to him. He can always skip back to Dublin the first week-end he gets."

"If he wasn't arrested, you wouldn't have stayed. It's funny the way things work out," Maisie said.

"If I hadn't met you I wouldn't have stayed," Tom told her, "I'd have been back in Tunnygee long ago."

10

Mike was no more happy banking in Tunnygee than he had been selling books in Dublin. The brass rails of the cashier's cage in the bank at Tunnygee had become as much his prison as the bookshop had ever been. Occasionally, he had the temerity to appear unshaven behind the brass rails.

"This will never do, never do at all. It may be the fifties, but banking is still an important profession and Tunnygee is an important market town," the manager told him.

"An important market town" became a phrase that stuck in Mike's gullet. All it meant to him was cowdung on the Monday and dirty, crumpled notes from satisfied, breezy shopkeepers on the Tuesday, while he counted the heads of passers-by for the rest of the week. He was in Kelly's pub most nights. One night, Tracker Duff was the only other customer there. A big, heavy-shouldered man with a round, outdoor face and a large moustache, Mike knew him by sight. As he sipped a halfone, he was aware that Tracker was studying him in the mirror behind the bar.

"The same again," Tracker called to Jimmy Kelly, who was reading the evening paper at the other end of the counter, "and when you're at it, give your man here his pleasure."

"No, not at all. I'll stay on my own," Mike said.

"Ara, never mind him, Jimmy. Shove them up there. Anyway, I want a word in your ear," Tracker placed a hand on Mike's shoulder.

"It's a shame, it's a shame," Tracker continued, "tell me, have you no wee bit of a lassie tucked away at all?"

"Is that any business of yours?" Mike asked sourly.

"You're right, son, dead right, its no business of mine, but I hate to see a man eating his guts out for no good reason at all."

"That's no business of yours either."

"No, I suppose it's not, but I'm not at the dog game this twenty years for nothing. When you're tricking around with them lads and some of their two-legged followers as long as I am, you get to know a few of the angles."

Tracker finished his drink and stood holding an empty glass.

"Well, are you going to buy back atself?" he demanded.

"Mr. Kelly, the same again please," Mike ordered.

"Come on, tell us what's eating you? You're standing there like a pup with distemper. What's biting into you?" Tracker asked.

"I'll tell you, Tracker. I'm fed up with this stinking hole of a town where nothing ever happens. A dead hole stuck away at the back of nowhere and . . . and I'm fed up to the back teeth. Now, are you satisfied?"

"Them's hard words, son, but do you know what's wrong with you?"

"What?"

"You want an interest, that's what you want."

"An interest in what?"

"I'm working round to that. Give me a minute."

"I'm all ears."

"You've no liking for the women, you say?"

"I didn't say anything of the sort."

"But you've no lassie?"

"No."

"No interest in women. A pity, but it'll pass. You'll grow into it yet."

"I'm twenty-five, you know."

"You'll be a divil yet. Drink and women, the two of them are the same. Them that takes to them late are blackguards out and out, but, of course, that's no good to you now. What you want is something to occupy you till you work your way round to them, the women, I mean."

"And what do you suggest, Mister Tracker?"

"A dog, get yourself a dog"

"A dog...a bloody dog ! Are you serious, Tracker?"

"I was never more serious in my life, son. There's nothing to beat a dog for taking your mind off things, nothing better or more interesting than rearing and training a racing dog, especially one of your very own."

Two nights later, Mike glanced warily up and down the street before leaving Tracker's gateway. There was no one about and he sidled off, dragging his new pup behind him. At Kelly's he had a hundred yards to go and still his luck held good. He quickened his pace and had his hand on the landlady's gate, when there was a shout from the direction of the pub. It was Willie McGinty, a small, little wisp of a man, with shoulders pointed in a coat too big for him. Eyes bright in a lined face, he eked out an existence driving cattle and walking dogs. He was known as a good judge of a dog. The pup lurked at Mike's heels as he approached.

"How much did you give for him?" he asked.

"Ten pounds," Mike reluctantly admitted.

"You paid ten quid for that fella. You've more money than sense. Ten quid for that bag of bones."

"He might be a bit thin, but that won't do him any harm. The breeding's good," Mike automatically quoted Tracker.

"The breeding would want to be shocking good. He'd want to be a cross between Mick the Millar and the English Rose to pay that for him. I hate to say it, but Tracker seen you coming."

"No one seen . . . saw me coming. I made a bargain and . . . and ten pounds is not a fortune in anyone's money nowadays."

"It might be no fortune, but I'd say Tracker's rubbing his hands this minute. A real back-tit merchant, that fella. Sure it was a Godsend for Tracker to get a tenner for the runt of the litter."

"We'll see, we'll see," Mike said, pushing open the gate and jerking the pup into the yard after him.

"No hard feelings," Willie called as the gate banged shut, "you know I only wish you the best of luck with him."

Next morning, when Mike had a good look at the pup, he could not altogether blame Willie. The pup looked much more dejected and lifeless than when Tracker had paraded him the night before. In the morning light, every bone showed through his rough, dry coat, while his anaemic - fawn, almost white -colouring did nothing for him either. Mike wondered if maybe Willie was right. Maybe Tracker had tricked him. Maybe that was why he waited until darkness before showing the pup. He probably knew that the lamplight would soften the hungry look.

"He's the makings of a top-class tracker," Tracker had emphasised, "he's made for speed with the light bone of him and . . . look at the width between the ears. Look at that, the width across there," he ran a stumpy finger from ear to ear, "that's what counts. That's where the brainbox is and that's what you want in a tracker . . . brains."

Weeks passed and the dog lost his hungry look. Tracker had become chief adviser on care and feeding and every other day he was in the yard to study the dog's progress. He brought Mike racing, claiming that it was a necessary part of an owner's education. Mike became a weekly visitor to the track and, on fair days, even the most taciturn of farmers made a point of alluding to his new interest.

"If you give me a winner for the night, I'll throw the lot on him," one of them was sure to mutter as he thumbed awkwardly through the notes Mike had handed out in change.

When the pup was six months old, Tracker and Willie came down the yard to see him one evening.

"Willie here would like to have a good look at him on his own ground," Tracker explained.

"Small yet of course, he'll never be a big dog," Willie said, "but he's coming on nicely and by the look of him he might have a turn of speed."

"Tell me," Tracker winked at Mike, "did I ever breed a bad one yet?"

"I wouldn't know about that," Willie said studiously, "but I know that your man here would want plenty of walking from this out."

Six months passed and the dog thrived in Willie's care. It pleased Mike to look at him through the wire and see the muscles ripple under the loose coat.

Mike went off on a fortnight's holidays in February, 1953. The night before he left, he gave Willie five pounds to purchase food and vitamin pills for the dog during his absence. On the first day, Willie bought the meat and pills as directed. That night he had several pints. The dog was not fed at all next day. On the following day, Willie bought two stale loaves. The pup lived on stale bread and an odd drop of milk for the rest of the holiday.

On the night of Mike's return, Willie was in Kelly's.

"He never went near the dog," he told Tracker gleefully, "he has a woman with him. A big horse of a one, she could ate hay off a loft. If she stays around for awhile, Mike won't be too worried about the dog."

Later, Mike and the woman entered the bar. She was tall, nearly as tall as Mike, a big, strong, thirtyish blonde. Mike introduced her as Olga Rasmussen.

"What'll you have, ma'am?" Tracker asked.

"I'll have whiskey," she said with a slight English accent.

"A fine drink for a fine woman and Jimmy here keeps only the best. A small one for the lady, Jimmy, and the same for Mike," Tracker ordered.

"Cheers everybody," Olga held up her glass.

"Some water, miss," Jimmy Kelly placed a jug of water on the counter.

"No, thank you, I like my whiskey straight. Water is only for the flowers."

"Well put, girl. That's what's wrong with half the country, drowning good whiskey with water," Tracker declared.

"I love the country. It's a tonic, the fresh air, the freedom and the peace and oh, the so relaxed people," Olga enthused.

"Is this your first time in the country?" Willie asked.

"Oh, I've lived here for the last five years. Maybe I'll go back to London some day, but now that I have met the handsome Mike with the soulful brown eyes, I may stay two years, three years more," she smiled at Mike.

"I think Willie meant were you ever down the country, away from the city like," Tracker grinned at a discomfited Mike.

"Yes, of course I was down the country, but I was never in Cavan. It is beautiful. It appeals to my artistic nature. I'm an artist you see. We were down by your lovely lake today. The quiet waters, so dark and so mysterious. Mike and I enjoyed our walk immensely didn't we, darling?" she tweaked Mike's cheek.

"Do you know that a fish is never caught in that lake, miss?" Tracker asked.

"No, Mister Tracker, but how interesting."

"It's interesting alright," Tracker left down his glass, "St. Patrick stopped here in his time on the way to light the fire at Slane. He said Mass, God be good to him, where the black church on the other side of the lake now stands. And there was this princess, the daughter of a king, you know, and she made a skit of the saint and all he stood for and . . . and what do you think happened? She was turned into a crow. Aye, a big black crow and when the Holy Saint was talking to the people after Mass, she flew around his head, cawing all the time. With all the cawing, the people couldn't hear a word the poor man was saying. In the end, he made a belt at her with . . . with, you know the lad a bishop carries . . .?"

"A crozier," Mike said.

"Aye, a crozier. Anyway, he just tipped the crow on the tail feathers with it and off it took up into the air with a fearful, wild scream. Up it went, straight as a die, until it was no more than a black speck in the sky. Then, you'll hardly credit this, down it came like a stone and plunged straight into the middle of the lake beyond. And . . . and that's why a fish was never caught in that lake since."

"Yes, Mister Tracker, I've heard stories like that before," Olga smiled.

"But this is a fact, ma'am. As true as God is my judge, a fish was never caught in that lake from that day to this."

"You must admit that it's a pretty tall story, Tracker," Mike said.

"Nothing tall about it. Haven't I often seen it meself. I've seen fellas, with more time than sense, sitting on the rocks below until they got calluses in their arses, excuse me, ma'am, and bad luck to the one of them ever even got a smell of a fish."

"So, you're from England, ma'am?" Willie questioned.

"I'm English. My father's from Norway."

"And you met Mike in Dublin, ma'am?"

"Yes, I met Mike on Saturday last in a ballroom. He was the most handsome man at the dance and I asked him to dance the ladies' choice. We became friends then."

"Are you happy now, Willie?" Mike asked, "Anything else you 'd like to know? The ballroom, for instance, was the Four Provinces in Harcourt St."

"I want to know nothing, Mike. I was only talking to Miss Olga."

"You know the lone bush in the field above the lake, did you see it the day?" Tracker asked.

"Yes, remember, Mike, I said it was like the fairy tree," Olga replied.

"You weren't up close to it, were you?"

"No, Mister Tracker, we were at a distance."

"Well, if you were up close you might have seen it. About two foot from the ground, there's a sort of a big knob on the trunk, like where a branch was broken off one time or another. If a woman can't have a child that bush is a certain cure. All you have to do is sit straddle ways on the knob with your arms around the trunk for a couple of minutes."

"I think that I do not want to sit on that tree, Mister Tracker," Olga laughed.

"You don't believe me?"

"Of course, I believe. I believe, like you say in Ireland, I believe every word you say, Tracker."

"You better give us another round, Jimmy," Mike laughed, "it'll give Tracker a chance to get his breath back."

"There's nothing wrong with my breath. Do you want to hear the story, or don't you?" Tracker demanded.

"Sorry, I thought you were finished," Mike grinned at him.

"Well, I wasn't, Mr. Houlihan."

"Don't get thick now, Tracker," Willie warned.

"Who's thick, McGinty? I'm not thick."

"I am very interested, Mister Tracker," Olga placed her hands on Tracker's arm, "I am all ears. I want to hear the end of the story of the fairy tree."

"There's not much more to it, ma'am. The woman must pull three strands a hair from her head, knot them together into a sort of string, sitting on the knob all the time, of course. That's all there's to it. They say it never fails."

"I'm afraid I 'd have a bad chance," Olga said.

"What do you mean?"

"This," she ran her hand through her close-cropped hair.

"You'd have to let it grow, ma'am, but if I'm a judge you want no fairy bush," Tracker told her.

"Thank you, Mister Tracker, you are much too kind. Mike, darling," she called to Mike, "it is past ten and your landlady said she would have supper ready at ten."

"Coming, Olga."

"Jasus, did you ever hear the bate of it? Coming, Olga and Mike, darling, I'd say she knows more than her prayers, that one," Willie declared when they left.

"She's a bit too smart for her own good," Tracker agreed, "Mister Tracker this and Mister Tracker that and you wouldn't know whether she was laughing at a fella or not."

"She was well able for you, Tracker. She wasn't swallowing any bullshit about fairy bushes, or black crows either."

"I wish Mike luck of her but she wouldn't be my dish, Willie, with an arse like wan of the Russian Tsars."

Olga left on the midday bus next day. That evening, Mike came bursting into Kelly's.

"What did you do to the dog?" he shouted at Willie.

"Nothing . . . not a thing. Why? What's wrong with him?"

"Did you feed him at all?"

"Of course I fed him. Isn't he jumping out of his skin?"

"He's not jumping out of his skin and all the condition is gone off him. What did you do with that fiver I gave you?"

"I spent it."

"Filling your gut with porter?"

"The dog got fed too. Anyway, he was getting too much red mate. Red mate killed many a good pup. It goes to their heads. It's the cause of half the fits in the country."

"You're very knowledgeable about dog diseases all of a sudden, Mr. McGinty."

"All I know is that too much red mate is bad for any dog," McGinty persisted.

Afterwards, the dog was known as *Red Mate*.

"I seen Willie with Red Mate the other day," Tracker told Mike, one evening in March, "bedad, he's a handsome looking baste this minute, but I wonder will he follow?"

"I'll tell you what," he suggested, "bring him down to the meadow next Sunday morning, when I'm blooding a couple of my own and we'll see what he's up to."

Mike and Willie were in the meadow on Sunday morning. Tracker let loose a rabbit with a broken back leg. Red Mate dived on it and, holding it with his paws, tore it apart.

"He'll follow alright. The speed is all he wants now," Willie told Mike.

A few days later, Mike, Tracker and Willie brought Red Mate and two of Tracker's dogs for trials. Tracker's two went first.

"The bitch has the legs of him, Tracker. What did I tell you?" Willie asked.

"Aye, she's fairly useful, I suppose," Tracker reluctantly admitted.

He owned the dog, a half-brother to Red Mate, but he was only training the bitch, which streaked home by four lengths.

"Come on, we'll try Red Mate," he said gruffly, "we'll put him in again the bitch."

"What's the betting, Tracker?" Willie asked, when the dogs were in the box.

"Never mind the betting," was the surly reply.

"So, that's the way of it. It's poor enough when a man won't stand by his own breeding. I'll give you two to one on her ladyship."

"Let's see the colour of your money and I'll cover it for you," Tracker growled.

"Sure it takes money to make money," Willie shrugged.

The traps sprung open and the dogs shot out. At the first bend they were neck and neck, but on the back stretch, Red Mate showed in front. Mike was thumping the rail and shouting at the top of his voice, when, at the finish, Red Mate was yards ahead. Tracker was delighted.

"With the well-fed moon face of him, you'd think he was after winning the big race at the White City," Willie said.

"Bedad, he can shift, that fella," Tracker fondled Red Mate's head.

"I'll give you two to one on her ladyship," he mimicked Willie, "what have you to say for yourself now, my boyo? Wouldn't anyone with half an eye in his head know by looking at him, that he has it in him? And you can't beat brains. See the way he took the inside corner on the far bend? He has the brains."

"Brains, who do you think you're coddin'?" Willie blurted. "If they had a glimmer of brains, do you think they'd bust themselves running after a hare that's not a hare at all? If it's brains they had, they'd be above in the stands watching me and you running, Tracker."

"You're too fuckin' smart, McGinty. You know everything and you know damn all . . . "

82

"Oh, Tracker, such atrocious language," the feminine voice took them by surprise.

"God, where did you spring from, Miss Macken?"

"Howya, Miss Macken," Willie touched his cap.

Blue-eyed, with high cheekbones and black hair pulled back under a red headscarf, Miss Macken's finely-boned, pale face contrasted with the chunky body in a suede jacket and straight skirt.

"So my poor Suzy met her match," she patted the bitch.

"Miss Macken owns her," Tracker told Mike.

"How do you do, Miss Macken?" Mike said.

"How do you do? He's a fast dog," she nodded towards Red Mate.

"Did you enter Suzy for the race, Miss?" Tracker asked.

"Yes, Tracker, I did."

"Well, she'll have a chance of getting her own back then. This fella's in for it too," Tracker jerked on Red Mate's lead.

Two weeks later, Red Mate and Suzy were in the first race. As far as Tracker and Willie were concerned, Red Mate was a 'dead cert'.

"Suzy is the best of the rest. They're only a bunch of duds. He'll skate home," Willie assured Mike.

They got their money on and the three of them took up position at the finishing line. At the first bend, Red Mate was well clear, but halfway up the straight, he checked and his head went up.

"Go on . . . go on, Red Mate," Mike roared.

When the first dog reached him, he pounced. The other four went past and the fighting, snarling pair were left to sort themselves out.

The stewards pulled Red Mate away and a cowed Suzy went slinking down the track. Mike and Tracker went back to the traps to collect their erstwhile hero. Miss Macken was already there, hunkering down beside Suzy.

"Oh, my poor Suzy . . . What did the beast do to you? Oh, my poor little pet."

"I'm sorry, Miss Macken, I'm sorry," Mike apologised.

"It wasn't your fault," she said.

11

Maisie was happy. She could not believe her good fortune . She had come out from Ireland a few weeks previously, half-believing she was pregnant, and now she had met Tom. He came to the cafe every day and often had his meals there. It became a habit for him to stay after closing-time and for Maisie and he to sit drinking cups of tea. On such occasions, they talked easily and happily, Tom about what happened on the site, and Maisie telling him about the cafe and what Jean or Mrs. Duncan had said. He told her about his Uncle Pakie and the arguments they had about politics, about Johny McCaffrey, and about his life in the army . She talked of home and about going to the hiring fair and how delighted she was to go to work for Peadar Kennedy in the town.

"You stayed with him less than six months?" Tom asked.

"He got the job for me here in the cafe."

"He was a bit of a lad for the women, according to Johny McCaffrey and a few more of them."

"I didn't care for him, Tom. I only want to forget about him."

"Did he do something on you?"

"I don't want to talk about it, Tom. I only want to forget all about it."

"Tell me. Tell me, what did he do? Did he go for you?"

"Don't ask me, Tom. It's all over now."

"I am asking you, Maisie. I have to know."

"He attacked me, Tom. He tried to........to rape me."

"The hoor's melt."

"But nothing happened, Tom. He was drunk."

"Tell me what happened, Maisie," Tom said quietly.

"I can't, Tom, I can't."

"You can and you will. You have to, it's important to me. You don't know how important," he gripped her shoulders tightly.

"You're hurting me, Tom."

"Tell me, tell me," he shook her.

"Don't look at me like that, Tom. You're frightening me," Maisie sobbed, happiness and confidence rapidly failing.

"Don't cry, Maisie, don't cry. Just tell me. I have to know," he still gripped her.

"Alright, Tom, alright, just let me sit down."

She told him the story. She finished and sat, blank-faced and dry-eyed, staring at the wall.

"McCaffrey was right. They should have debolicated the bastard thirty years ago," he stood up and walked down between the tables of the cafe.

He came back and stood over Maisie.

"I love you and I'm going to marry you," he took her head in his hands and pulled it against him.

"I love you too, Tom, I love you," she pressed against him, her arms around his waist.

Tom wanted to get married immediately, but Maisie said that she would like to have the wedding in Tunnygee.

Tom had a letter from Butsy at the end of July. You are not going to believe this, he wrote, but I am just back from Aden:

"When they found I was a Corporal in our own army, I was taken off recruit training and there I was, scarcely a month in the B.A., putting manners on the natives in Aden. It wasn't so bad, except for the heat. The beer was cheap and cigarettes were for next to nothing, but I couldn't stick it. I threw a glass through the canteen window one night and shouted that I would soldier no more, that no man with a drop of Irish blood in his veins would kick around people looking for their rights. Two or three of them jumped on me. They thought I was mad. I felt sort of mad myself.

"To tell you the truth I was well jarred, but it was a great act. You're all a pack of fuckin' Black and Tans, I roared, and I'm not going to be a Black and Tan for anyone. He's round the bend. someone shouted, he's frothing at the mouth. I wouldn't be a bit surprised. I had a bellyful that night.

"They threw me in a cell and left me there to cool off.

Next morning I stuck to my guns, ranting and raving about Black and Tans. They threatened me with the divil and all, but I was past listening to reason. I thought I was going to get my ticket for a while, but no such luck. They put me on a plane for home.

"I was in hospital for about ten days, but they threw me out and here I am now in a broken-down camp, about five miles from Newcastle, painting billets. A bit of a comedown for Corporal Dwyer of the 5th Foot. Somehow or other, I don't think I'll be too long here. Expect me when you see me."

During the last week of September, Butsy arrived in the cafe at breakfast time. He sat at a table and pretended to study a menu.

"Yes, sir," Maisie bustled up.

"How are things, Maisie?" Butsy grinned up at her.

"God, it's you, Butsy. I didn't know you for a minute. Are you out of the army?"

"Since yesterday, Maisie."

"I'm delighted to see you, Butsy. Tom'll be delighted too. Here, what am I thinking about, you'll have to have some breakfast."

"Aye, a few streaky rashers and a couple of eggs sunnyside up wouldn't go astray this minute."

Maisie sat with him as he ate.

"Many's the good laugh me and Tom had over your letter, the time they put you out of Aden."

"You never thought I was such a mad Republican?" Butsy laughed.

"That's what Tom said. He laughed his sides sore when he thought of you in the cell shouting and roaring about Black and Tans."

"Wait till he hears what I did this time and he'll have reason to laugh. Where's he working now anyway?"

"Just across from the underground at Piccadilly, straight across from the entrance. They're clearing a site for some sort of an office block. There's a big notice up in front of the place, you can't miss it."

"I think I'll go down that far. I want a bit of fresh air after twenty-one days in the glasshouse."

"The glasshouse?"

"An army prison."

"What happened, Butsy?"

"Well, if you have time to listen..!" Butsy looked around the cafe.

"God, Butsy, I'll have to go," she ran to serve a woman, puffing with vexed impatience on a cigarette.

"I'll see you tonight," he shouted after her.

Butsy walked to Piccadilly, the autumn sun warm on his back. It felt good to be out of the army, and better to be out of the glasshouse. The morning rush was over, but there were plenty of girls on the street, all shapes and sizes, old and young, short and long, fat and thin. He was free, all the field in front of him. Take your time. There is no hurry. Get down to Burke and get the pick in your hands. Swing the pick, the power flowing from the shoulders, down the arms, down into the wood of the handle. The metal biting into the ground. Give it the levering nudge. Up and swing again. Power, but not too much, or the jar will come back through the wood. Flex your arms. He felt the muscles cording from his ears down. The sun was warmer. Let him into a trench with his shirt off and he would dig for a week.

"The hero returns," Tom slapped him on the back, "where the hell did you spring from?"

"I'm out and that's all that matters. How much are they paying on this job?"

"Thirty a week, if you're up to it, and a bonus at the end."

"Let me at it," Butsy pulled off his jacket and shirt and grabbed a pick.

"You're glad to be out," Tom said.

"You can whistle that," Butsy drove the pick into the ground.

An hour later, he threw the pick from him. The sweat was running into his eyes and he rubbed it off with his shirt, as he pulled it back on over his head.

"I'm as soft as shit and that bloody sun is too hot," he scowled at the sky.

"You're giving up shockin' handy," Tom laughed.

"Ah, fuck you, Burke, I'm going for a drink. Are you coming?"

"No, someone has to work, but you go and drink your head off. Get it out of your system."

"I suppose you're looking for the soldier boy," Clancy greeted Tom and Maisie when they entered the pub that evening.

"Where is he?" Tom asked.

"Below in the bottling store. He's stretched out on the camp bed for the last four hours."

"I'll go down and give him a shout," Tom said.

"Was I in the cafe with you this morning, Maisie, or was it just a dream?" a bedraggled Butsy asked, having followed Tom into the bar.

"It was no dream, Butsy and you had a good feed of bacon and eggs."

"That's right, and I was going to tell you how I got out of the army."

"Go on, we're listening," Tom said.

"You're not going to believe this, but remember the time I wrote to you when I came back from Aden. Less than a fortnight after that I was transferred to the First Battalion of the Royal Sussex Light Infantry. A real gildy outfit they are too, at least in their own minds. There was only wan thing for it. Do what I done in Aden, go off me rocker. So, I started talking to myself, saying the first thing that came into my head. They put me on permanent kitchen fatigue. I suppose they thought I couldn't do much harm there.

"Anyhow, the Duchess of someplace-or-other is Colonel-in-Chief. Imagine that, Maisie, a woman head buckcat in an army."

"Never mind that, Butsy. Tell us what happened."

"What do you think I'm doing only telling you. On the day before your woman came on inspection....."

"What inspection?"

"You know, Maisie, the whole shooting gallery on parade on the square with chests stuck out and arses pulled in tight, and...and officers hopping around all over the place with medals jangling, all jittery and on edge. Then, when the old doll comes on the scene, they're all saluting and salaaming and....and all scratching around
88

after her like chickens after a clocking hen. Then she trots along, smiling at fellas and telling them they're great lads entirely to win all them lovely medals shooting all them savage foreigners."

"Don't overdo it, Butsy !" Tom said.

"Go on, Butsy, never mind him, it's great ," Maisie told him.

"Aye, where was I ?.... Aye, and the bands thumping away all the time, with the big drummer busting himself. You'd think he was trying to put the stick through the side of the drum. Then, when it's all over, the officers trot off to the mess and drink gins and tonics and tell themselves they're great fellas and that the Royal Sussex is the best bloody unit in the whole British army. All that sort of bullshit.

"The day before the inspection I was over in the medical hut and I lifted a bottle of cascara tablets."

"Ah, Butsy, you didn't," Maisie giggled.

"I did. I put them in the tea that evening and the lads were running all night. Only half of the battalion were on parade next morning, and, even then, two of them collapsed on the square. I kept mum at first and then it dawned on me that I was supposed to be half-mad anyway, so why not go the whole way? Pretend that I was stone-mad. So I spilled the beans."

"And what did they do, Butsy?"

"I'm coming to that, Maisie, I'm coming to it. They threw me in the guardroom and I got a fair old thumping from a couple of N.C.Os. Next morning, I was before the C.O. 'You're either a very vicious man, Dwyer, or a complete and utter fool,' he was stuttering with temper. I was getting a bit windy I don't mind telling you. 'Excuse me, sir,' says I, 'people might think I'm a bit of a fool, because I go round talking to myself but I'm no fool. With all due respects, I'm saner than you are, sir. I'm not a fool, sir.' 'What the hell are you, if you're not a fool?' he roared. 'I'm an Irish Republican, sir, and I was only doing my bit for the old sod.' You should have seen his face. He was ready to jump out of his skin. I thought he'd burst a blood vessel. I stood there looking at him, muttering away to myself. 'You're mad, Dwyer' he roared, 'completely and absolutely bonkers.' 'No, sir, I'm an Irish Republican and as long as British troops occupy........' I got no further. 'Enough, enough, get him out of here, get this lunatic out of here,' he roared. Left turn, quick march, right wheel, the Sergeant-Major roared louder. With all the commotion I think he forgot to sentence me, but I done me twenty-one days in the glasshouse all the same. I got out yesterday and I was discharged within the hour, services no longer required."

"You were lucky," Tom told him.

"Maybe I was. It was better than doing six months in jail, any way you look at it."

"Will you be down on the site tomorrow?"

"No, I'll head back to Dublin tomorrow. I'll be on the boat tomorrow night."

"Maisie and I are going back to Ireland."

"For good?"

"We are going to get married," Maisie said.

"Jasus, when's the big day?"

"It'll be after Christmas."

"Well, you're not rushing into anything"

"Don't look at me, Butsy," Tom laughed, "Maisie wants to do it in style, back home in Tunnygee."

"No better woman, Maisie. That's one day I'll be looking foward to."

"Are you sure you won't stay in London, Butsy?" Tom asked, "we could do with another man."

"No, thanks all the same, Tom."

12

I n November, Butsy met Tom and Maisie at Westland Row and bought them breakfast.

"You'll have to stay in Dublin for the weekend," he said, "Mossie Downey's giving one of his big parties tomorrow night and, what do you think, the bold Mike is coming up from Tunnygee."

"Nearly two years since he saw me off for England and neither sight nor sound of him since. I wonder how he's getting on in Tunnygee?" Tom asked.

"Flying. I was down there two weeks ago. We had a great weekend. Mike's as well known as a begging ass. Tracker, Willie McGinty and several others were asking for you and when I told them you were going to marry Maisie, they were all delighted."

"You shouldn't have told them, Butsy, you shouldn't have told them," Maisie exclaimed.

"Don't worry about it, Maisie. There's no harm done?" Tom told her.

"I suppose I should have kept my big mouth shut. I'm sorry, Maisie."

"Don't worry, Butsy, its not your fault. Its just...just that I was going to tell them in my own way," she assured him.

"Forget about it, Butsy. That big mouth will be the ruination of you one of these days," Tom laughed, "what about this weekend you've fixed up for us? We'll have to get somewhere to stay."

"Leave that to your uncle Butsy. Just follow me out of this eating establishment and we'll take the first taxi we see. Then we'll head southwards and I shall introduce to my good friend, Mrs. Murphy of Eaton Square."

"You got here in good time, Michael," Mrs. Murphy spoke to Butsy round the cigarette in her mouth, "and this is Maisie and Tom, I expect. You're both more than welcome. Any friend of Michael's is welcome."

Tom brought the bag upstairs. Mrs. Murphy accompanied Maisie into one room, while Tom followed Butsy into another.

"Any friend of Michael's! I was looking over my shoulder for Michael for a minute," Tom laughed.

"At least someone gives me proper respect. After all, I was christened too," Butsy grinned.

They were due to meet Mike in Guiney's at two o'clock. Maisie declined to accompany them largely on the prompting of Mrs. Murphy.

"Listen, girl, you're worn out and you're going to a party tomorrow night. Never mind the lads. What you want at the moment is rest to get the colour back in those cheeks. You go off, boys, and Maisie will be back to herself tomorrow."

Tom looked at Mike, then looked again. It was a different Mike, a well-dressed Mike, a man who epitomised small town success. A bright-coloured, single breasted crombie, over a double breasted, grey flannel suit, was set off by a pair of tan leather shoes. His black hair was sleek and shiny and not a strand out of place.

"You're the boy that's looking well, Mike. If you grew a wee bit a hair on the upper lip, Clark Gable wouldn't hold a candle to you," Tom greeted.

"Put it there, Tom. Its nearly two years since I left you at Westland Row that day. Time flies. I hear you're going to get married. My heartiest congratulations."

"Thanks, Mike, and how's life with you? How's Tunnygee?"

"Grand. Everything's fine. It was the best move I ever made, going to Tunnygee."

"Have you a woman for tomorrow night, Mike?" Butsy asked.

"Of course, I have, a six-foot half-Norwegian. Didn't the lads tell you about her in Tunnygee?"

"I heard more than that. What about this bit of stuff you have under wraps in Tunnygee, the Miss Macken, that Tracker was talking about? I thought you might bring her and give me a chance with the Norwegian."

"Sylvia Macken! Is she not a wee bit long in the tooth for you, Mike?" Tom asked.

"I wouldn't say that, Tom," Mike answered.

They went from Guiney's to a pub off O'Connell Street, ending up in McGovern's of Parnell Street. They left that some time after seven and made their way back up O'Connell Street. It was cold out on the street, with the first frost of winter. The breath of the hurrying people hung on the evening air and the speaker at Elvery's corner got scant attention. He stood on his box at the footpath's edge, a safety pin fastening a dirty mackintosh at his neck and long hair making a nest for his ears. A small, skinny, sharp-featured fellow, words flowed out of him.

"All politicians are rogues," he declared,

"Rogues, charlatans, knaves and fools. Small, little gombeen men, who by their chicanery, conniving and dishonesty plunge the world into misery and terror, generation after generation."

"He'd talk the hind leg of an ass, that fella," Butsy said.

"Who caused the last war? I ask you who caused the last war?" the speaker shrieked.

"Hitler," Tom shouted up at him.

"Hitler, Hitler, you say, sir, but you're wrong, very wrong. No one miserable, little dictator could have plunged the world into the horrors of war, if the politicians, our so called leaders, had wished to prevent it."

"Dev kept us out a the war and he was a politician and a leader," Tom shouted.

"Opportunists, each and every one. Politicians could have prevented the last war, but they hadn't the guts and, or, the principles. They still haven't. Name me one who has?" the speaker paused dramatically, finger pointing and eyes staring.

"A bloody frustrated public speaker if I ever saw one," Mike murmured.

"Did you say something? Did you mention a name, sir?" the speaker wiped droplets of sweat from his forehead.

"Go on, don't let me interrupt you. It's one way of keeping warm on a cold night," Mike belched.

"How long more are we going to stand here listening to this knucklehead? I'm perished," Butsy nudged him.

"Hold on a minute, Butsy, he's only getting into his stride," Mike said.

Leaning against Elvery's window, Tom heard the wailing music of the blind fiddler around the corner in O'Connell Street. He could see the man in his mind's eye, an old man with a long scrag of white hair floating free, standing dejectedly, jerking his shrieking bow, while he listened for the clink of the occasional dropping penny. His artistry long since gone, only his blind eyes appealed, as he stood on the fringe waiting for the tossed coins of pity to fall into the battered black hat. Tom walked round the corner and put a shilling in the hat.

"Come on, it's time we were moving," he called to the other two.

They caught a bus to South Richmond Street and went to Bessie's cafe. Bessie was leaning against the condiment shelf with its battery of sauce, pepper, salt and vinegar containers. She was reading a newspaper. Bessie folded the paper and placed it carefully behind the condiments. She pulled a wisp of hair back from her face and came towards them on flat feet, the expression on her round, placid face unchanging. Her apron was clean, but the blue dress was black damp at the armpits and as she leaned over the table on plump, dimpled arms, there was weariness in the flaccid droop of her body.

"Bessie, you look like a million dollars," Mike told her.

She did not answer and only her eyes moved as she gave him a glazed, noncommittal look.

"We're starved, Bessie," Butsy was practical,"what about three mixed grills, bacon, liver, eggs, the works?"

"Steak," she muttered.

"Yeah, and a pile of them grazy chips. I could ate a young lad this minute," Butsy told her.

She smiled, a bare tightening of the lips, and padded away.

"A good girl, Bessie," Butsy commented, "she knows what a man wants."

"I think you have a soft spot for her," Tom laughed.

"A soft spot is right. You'd be lost in the rowls of flesh."

The heaped plates arrived and Butsy attacked his steak.

"I could ate a bag of nails," he declared, shoving a lump of spongy, yellow fat into his mouth.

"She's not in the best a humour," Mike nodded back at Bessie, "Still, you better ask her, Butsy."

"Better ask her what?"

"Ask her will she go with you to the party tomorrow night."

"Ah, Jasus, Mike, give us a chance."

"Beggars can't be choosers. I often saw you with worse."

They mopped up gravy with pieces of bread and Bessie brought a pot of tea.

"What about the naggin you bought? A drop would go well in the tea," Butsy suggested.

Mike took the small flat bottle from his inside pocket and poured into each cup. He held up the bottle to Bessie. She took a cup from the counter and placed it on the table. Mike emptied the remains of the whiskey into it.

"What about a date, Bessie?" Butsy asked.

"I'm off at nine."

"Not tonight. It's tomorrow night, I mean."

"I'm off at nine then too."

On the following night, Butsy and Bessie arrived at Mossie Downey's flat in Ranelagh half-an-hour after the pubs closed. Butsy pushed open the basement door and stood in the flagged passageway with Bessie behind him.

"Who's there?" a tall figure, emerging from a door on the right, demanded, "and how the hell did you get in anyway?"

"We didn't come through the window," Butsy said.

"Ha," the tall man shoved past, banged the front door and shot a bolt home.

"You're still the same old bushy-headed skinamalink, you haven't changed a bit," Butsy said.

"Butsy, my old segotia, put it there," the tall man shook hands warmly.

"This is Bessie," Butsy said, "you know, Bessie from the chipper."

"You're welcome, Bessie. Come on, the two of you," Mossie Downey led them into the front room.

The only illumination came from a weak, red-shaded bulb over a radiogram in the corner. In the centre of the floor, a few couples swayed to the slow beat of the music.

"We'd want to get that stuff under cover," Mossie indicated the parcel under Butsy's arm.

In the back room, Mike sat on a bed with his arm around Olga, drinks in front of them on a small table.

"Put that stout in the wardrobe, Butsy," Mike ordered, "there's a terrible pack of scrubbers out there, with not a drop between them."

"You're Butsy," Olga stood up, "Mike has told me about you. And you are Bessie, Mike has told me about you too."

"They breed fine, big women in your part of the world," Butsy grinned up at her.

"In Norway, big men and big women, the ass is not too near the ground, like in Ireland. But I like Irishmen, even the short ones," Olga chortled.

"Where's Tom and Maisie?" Butsy asked Mike.

"In the front room there, mooching away with the rest of them."

"I'll sit down for a while, Tom. My head is going round. I shouldn't have drank that port," Maisie flopped into an armchair in the corner of the front room,"

"I wonder could I have a glass of water, Tom," she asked.

Immediately Tom left to get the water, a man sat on the arm of the chair.

"Hello, I didn't see you around before," he said.

"I only came over from London yesterday."

"What about a dance?"

"No, thank you, I'm resting for a moment."

Maisie felt a hand stroking her hair, and, then, it was on her neck, kneading gently. The other hand came down suddenly and grabbed the inside of her thigh.

"You're a fine looking bird to be left on your own," the man's face was a couple of inches from her face.

"A girl that's after coming from London is not afraid of a kiss," he attempted to kiss her.

"My boyfriend's in the other room," she turned her face away. She attempted to get up, but she was firmly pinned in the chair. Returning with a glass of water, Tom pulled back the neck of the man's coat and poured the water in.

"What the hell....!" the man jumped up, shaking himself.

He saw Tom's grinning face and he swung at it. Tom avoided the swing and rammed the palm of his hand hard up under the man's nose. Blood spouted, staining the front of the white shirt.

"I'll get you for this, you bastard," the man muttered, holding a hankerchief to his nose.

Tom took Maisie by the hand and they went into the back room.

Mike was pouring drinks.

"What about one for me?" a burly youth stood smiling in the doorway from the front room.

"No, nothing for you, nothing for any bloody chancer too mean to buy his own," Butsy moved towards him.

"Ah, come on, just one for myself and my partner," the youth cajoled.

"No, not even the smell of one and.....get to hell out of here as fast as you can, if you know what's good for you," Butsy threatened.

The youth moved to come towards him, but Butsy was faster. He slammed the door shut with a sudden kick, sending his would-be antagonist jerking wildly back.

"That'll larne him," Butsy laughed, "I'll take the square head of him the next time."

"Put the catch on the door," Tom advised.

"Aye, and we'll have a party on our own," Butsy slipped the catch.

Tom grabbed Maisie and swung her out to the centre of the floor. The music coming from the front room was fast, but Tom outpaced it, twisting, shivering, shaking, now down on one knee, now springing on his toes. Opposite him, a laughing Maisie attempted to keep pace, Bessie had her shoes off, gyrating slowly opposite a stifflegged Butsy. Mike took the top of another bottle and gulped at the spewing froth.

"It would be a shame to waste a drop of the precious stuff," he told Olga.

"Just like Norwegians, Irishmen are too fond of the beer and leave the woman sitting," Olga chided.

"But sure, the woman tastes all the sweeter after," Mike put his arm around a pouting Olga.

Someone was banging on the door.

"Who's there?" Butsy called.

"It's me, Mossie, the man who owns the bloody place. Open up."

"I'm sorry, Mossie. We don't want to let the scrubbers in," Tom opened the door.

"This fella says you invited him," Mossie nodded towards a man beside him.

"I'm bloody sure they did. The fancy gent and the big blonde. I'm the hackey that brought them here."

"Let him in," Mike shouted.

"I thought I was in the wrong shop for a while, the music whinging and a crowd of drips mooching around with not a sup between them. Like wan of them pits of hell." the driver announced, "this is more my notion of a hooley, a bit a life about it. Sure, I'll have a drink, maybe even two or three," he acknowledged Tom's offer.

"Jasus, will you look who's here," he shouted suddenly, catching sight of Bessie.

He rushed over and placed an arm in a playful wrestler's grip around her neck. A slow smile crept over her face, as an ignored Butsy's jaw muscles tightened and he shuffled uncertainly.

"How in hell's blazes did you get here anyway?" the driver demanded, holding her at arm's length.

"She came with me and she's staying with me," Butsy said.

"If you say so, pal, if you say so. No sweat as far as I'm concerned, but look after her well. She's a fine mott and that's from a fella who knows."

"As long as we know where we stand," Butsy muttered.

"I'll be seeing you, Bessie," the driver turned away.

"Come and dance," Bessie leant against Butsy, eyes soft in the bovine face.

A bored Olga yawned and lay back on the bed. Butsy, his arm around Bessie, came over and stood looking down at her.

"Can you not get a stir out of him at all, Olga?" Butsy asked.

"The whiskey and the stout, and he forgets about poor Olga," Olga nuzzled against Mike's back. A fly buzzed and landed on the table. Butsy banged down hard with the flat of his hand, killing the fly.

"That reminds me of the fly and the train," Mike looked up, bleary-eyed, "when two bodies meet head on like the table and Butsy's fist there, there's a collision and both must stop, both the hand and the table."

"My hand stopped alright, but wasn't the table stopped all the time?" Busty asked.

"One up for you, Butsy," Mike admitted, "but take a train, say the Enterprise, going at seventy or eighty an hour from Dublin to Belfast, a fly crashes into it and what happens?"

"One dead fuckin' fly, even deader than that one on the table," Butsy guffawed, as Bessie disengaged his arm from about her waist and sat on the edge of the bed.

"The fly may be dead, but did the train stop when the fly hit it?"

"I never heard of a fly stopping one yet, Mike," Butsy laughed.

"Fair enough, Butsy, but take the fly," Mike explained, "it stopped, didn't it? It had to stop before it could go back in pulp on the front of the train, and if the fly stopped, the train stopped. It's as simple as that."

"Who do you think you're coddin', Houlihan? Sure, there are thousands of flies on the track. If the train stopped for them all, the passengers would be dead of old age before they reached the Boyne."

"Do you not see it, Butsy? Do you not see the logic of it? If the fly stops, the train must stop."

"Shit, you're talking through your arsehole again, Houlihan."

"Oh, no, Mike is not so vulgar, he is always the gentleman, sipping the whiskey and the stout, but he does not dance with his poor Olga. Will you dance with me, Butsy?" Olga stood up.

"Where's Bessie?" Butsy asked.

"She is gone to the loo, maybe," Olga said.

"Maybe," Butsy put his arms around Olga and shuffled off looking up at her.

"I think we should get together again, Olga," he suggested, "I think we could make the sparks fly between us."

"Yes, Butsy, I think that we could."

"There's no sign of Bessie yet," he said, several minutes later.

"And there's no sign of that hoor of a driver either," he pulled suddenly away from Olga, jerked open the door to the front room and dashed through.

"The car's gone too. He sneaked her from under my nose," he was back quickly, "I knew he was up to no good, that fella. I should have clocked him on the spot," he punched the wall.

"My bloody hand," he sucked his bruised knuckles.

"Ah, your poor hand, let me look at it," Olga took his hand, "You need something on that. There is some antiseptic in the kitchen. Come with me."

Tom and Maisie sat on the bed, shoulders back against the wall, Maisie lying in the crook of Tom's arm. At the top of the bed, Mike sat, staring morosely into a bottle of stout.

"I'm tired and happy, Tom, I never enjoyed a night more," Maisie snuggled closer.

"You're a lucky man, Burke, but then you were always a lucky man. Everything always goes right for Mr. Burke," Mike muttered into his drink.

"Where's Olga?" Tom asked.

"You tell me. She's a long time fixing Butsy's hand," Tom said.

"Is Maisie asleep?" Mike asked, standing up.

"No, I'm only half asleep," Maisie smiled up at him, through half-closed eyes.

"You lucky bastard, Burke," Mike straightened himself and lurched towards the kitchen.

He pushed open the kitchen door, looked in and quickly closed the door again.

"I'll see you in Tunnygee sometime," he waved a hand to Tom from the door to the front room.

Tom eased his arm from under Maisie's head and went over to the kitchen door. He came back and woke Maisie.

"Hurry up, we're going home," he told her.

"What's the big hurry all of a sudden?" Maisie asked, out on the street.

"Olga and Butsy are at it hammer and tongs in the kitchen. God, it's a holy terror."

"What are you talking about?"

"You know well what I'm talking about."

"And where's Mike?"

"He's gone. He looked into the kitchen and saw them at it, I suppose. He went home."

"I don't believe you, Tom. Olga wouldn't do that. Olga's a lady."

"Have a titter of wit, girl. They're the worst kind."

"Ah, poor Mike!"

"Poor Mike, me arse, he skipped with his tail between his legs."

"What could he do, Tom?"

"Not much, I suppose."

"Anyway, I wouldn't do that, Tom."

"I know you wouldn't, Maisie. Are you still intent on going home tomorrow?"

"I hate going home without you,Tom."

"I know that, Maisie, but it was you decided that it might be as well if you didn't spring me on the family too soon."

"But I'll miss you all the same, Tom."

"I'll miss you too, Maisie. Maybe I should go home with you, after all."

"No, stay Tom, it will only be for a few weeks."

"Aye, you're probably right, Maisie. Anyway I promised Butsy I would take on the driving job until Christmas, and....and there's good money in it too."

"It's as well not to change the plans now, Tom. I can always come up to Dublin to see you."

13

On the last Saturday in November, Maisie arrived in Tunnygee on the evening bus and completed the journey home in Jimmy Devine's hackney. Her mother rubbed her hands on her apron before shaking hands with her smartly dressed daughter.

"You're welcome there, girl. You're doing yourself proud in London," Pat, her father, greeted her with pride in his eyes.

Maisie had presents for all the family, including a shirt for her father and a handbag for her mother. Both of them admired the fine texture of the imitation leather in the bag, and, when her mother realised that the small purse inside contained twenty pounds, her gratitude showed in the renewed warmth in her eyes and the new spring in her step as she fussed about the kitchen. The children opened their individual parcels and crowded close to Maisie clutching their gifts.

All the family walked to eight o'clock Mass next morning, up the hill to the church, and they were proud of Maisie, knowing that the neighbours were watching.

On the following Sunday, Maisie brought her parents to Mass in Tunnygee in Devine's car and they felt as good as any of the townspeople or big farmers in their own cars. After Mass, as they sat in the car, Maisie saw Mike Houlihan walking towards them.

"I know him," she told her mother.

"Who?"

"The tall man."

"He's the cashier in the Hibernian Bank," Jimmy Devine said over his shoulder.

Mike glanced at the car and Maisie thought he was passing by, but he glanced again and she saw his smile of recognition.

"Hello, Maisie, how are you?" he shook hands through the car window.

Maisie introduced her father and mother.

"No need to introduce this old scoundrel here," Mike clapped Devine on the back.

"True for you, Mr. Houlihan, true for you."

"Is Tom slogging away in Dublin, Maisie?" Mike asked.

"Yes."

"When's the wedding coming off?"

"We didn't talk about it yet," Maisie answered shortly.

"There's no doubt about it, Tom Burke's landing on his feet again. Still, no better man. I'll be seeing you, Maisie. Glad to meet you, Mr. and Mrs. Dempsey. All the best, Jimmy," he tapped Devine on the shoulder.

"And where did he meet Tom Burke, may I ask?" Mary Dempsey snapped.

"Himself and Tom were in the army together," Devine said, "a decent fella. Houlihan, myself and himself often have a jar in Kelly's"

"And where did you meet Mr...Mr. Burke, Maisie, might I ask?" Mary demanded.

"I met him in London, Mama."

"And there's talk of marriage, is there?"

"We're getting marrried in the New Year."

"I see," Mary Dempsey sat stern-faced.

"Still, yon Houlihan fella's alright and not a bit stuck up for a bankclerk," Devine broke the silence.

"I don't know what he sees in Burke then. You can judge a man by the company he keeps," Mary said.

"In truth and you're wronging Mike Houlihan, ma'am. Not a decenter man ever stood in shoe leather. There's no one knows it better than myself. I drive himself and Tracker to the dogs every week. And there's not much wrong with Tom Burke either," Devine declared.

It was a long, dull Sunday in Dempsey's. Mary went tight-lipped about her work, while Pat spent most of the day over the fire, smoking and spitting. Maisie brought the younger children for a walk in the afternoon, and little was said, until the rosary was over and Maisie and her parents sat at the fire.

"I'm surprised, Maisie, that you got yourself mixed up with that fella, Tom Burke, a man who doesn't know his own father," Mary started.

"Well, if he doesn't, we do," Pat took the pipe from his mouth and spat into the fire.

"Do you know who his father is?" Mary asked Maisie.

"No, he never told me."

"And you never thought of asking?"

"No, I never thought of it."

"Your father found out the last fairday. He was in Kelly's and there was loudmouth Willie McGinty telling the world and his mother that you were going to marry Burke, a bastard son of Peadar Kennedy."

"I don't believe it," Maisie found herself going cold.

"You can believe it," her father said, "Peadar was a whelp of a shopboy at the time when he got Rosie Burke in trouble."

"And why did you let me go and work for him then?" Maisie demanded.

"Sure, girl, what did we know about it? The Burkes are from the other side of the town," Mary told her. "All the townies knew about it right enough, but we haven't the same time as them to be poking our noses into other peoples' business. The first your father knew about it was when he heard McGinty mouthing at the fair. Do you think for a minute that I, or your father either, would let you next or near that house if we'd known the sort of man Peadar was."

"Maybe it's not true," Maisie said.

"It's true. I made my own enquiries since and it's well-known in the town. Of all the gassons around why did you have to pick up with the likes of Burke?" Mary asked.

"I'm fond of him."

"Well, you can't marry him now."

"I suppose I can't. I'm going to Dublin to see him tomorrow."

Despite the brave front, a knot was gathering in Maisie's stomach as she went out to stand in the frosty farmyard. Without realising it, she walked down through the little orchard, where the gnarled arms of the leafless old trees outlined against the starlit sky went unnoticed. She thought of Peadar Kenendy, the man who had tried to rape her, and who was now going to take Tom from her. She did not want to lose Tom, but could she marry him now?

She went back to the house, the void in her stomach settling to a dull ache. In her bed, she lay shivering and sobbing quietly for a long time before she fell asleep.

***

Next day in Dublin, Maisie walked across the half-empty car park and in under the arcade of the suburban shopping centre. It was only half past three and Tom would not arrive until four at the earliest. He and Butsy were transporting goods from the docks to the warehouse at the rere of the centre. She walked down along the line of shops and stood by the window of a dress shop, its goods splashed in arranged disarray.

"You'd look well in that," Butsy, coming up behind her, pointed to one of the outfits.

"Is Tom coming?"

"I was on the phone there and he won't be here for another while. He's delayed at the docks. What's wrong anyway, Maisie?"

"There's nothing wrong."

"Anyone would know by the face of you that there's something wrong."

"Ah, there is, Butsy, but there's nothing you can do about it."

"We'll have a cup of coffee. Maybe that'll help."

"Alright," she took his arm.

"There, that would suit you," he pointed at another outfit in the window.

"What would they say in Tunnygee if they saw me in that get up? My mother would have a fit."

"Aye, the bare belly would go down well. They'd think you were one of them belly dancers like they have in Aden."

"Belly dancers?"

"Sure, bare bellied and twisting themselves into knots. They used to have big lumps of glass stuck in their belly buttons. There was one of them, Selma she called herself, and she always had a lump of blue glass as big as an egg quivering on her belly. One of the lads asked her one night how she kept it in place. Chewing gum, she told him."

"Chewing gum, oh, the dirty divil."

"She was a bit yalla looking alright, but that didn't do her any harm. There wasn't a thing wrong with her, but she wouldn't hold a candle to you if you togged out in one of them outfits."

"Ah, Butsy, I'm sorry, but I'm not in the best of form."

"Come on, we'll have the coffee."

Across the corridor from the upstairs coffee-shop, Maisie could see a woman's head in the chair of the hairdressers opposite. Scraps of wet hair in crude, plastic curlers, intersected by delicate lines of white scalp, outlined the shape of the narrow, boney skull. A big, bucket drier was pulled across as Butsy returned with two coffees.

"I can't stay too long," he said, "I have to go out on another run. I have to be down at the docks before Tom pulls out."

"I'll wait here. Will you tell Tom?"

As Butsy left, the woman emerged from under the hair drier, her face hot and flushed, with her hair a halo round her head. She would go off to meet her man and neither of them would be aware of the fragile, brittle skull under the camouflage of shiny, lacquered hair. She would laugh up at him and squeeze his arm close to her side, her scalp still tingling. She would steal glances at the shop

105

windows and wonder if the crown of hair was really hers, before, reassured, holding her head high and assuming her own special mask of superficial sophistication. Maisie wore her mask also, but for her it was a real mask, covering the horrible emptiness of her tragedy. Tom was the off-shoot of a diseased and twisted tree, a healthy branch springing from rottenness and some of the rottenness was part of him. The rottenness of Peadar Kennedy, she was part of that rottenness also.

"I don't know what brought you to Dublin in such a hurry, but I'm delighted to see you," Tom sat down beside her.

"Oh, Tom, I thought you would never come."

"What's wrong? You're as white as a sheet."

"I'm not going to marry you, Tom."

"That's great. Who was talking to you?"

"My mother. She told me Peadar Kennedy is your father."

"She's right. Every dog and divil knows that."

"I didn't know it. My mother didn't know nor neither did my father, until McGinty told him the last fairday."

"Maybe I should have told you. Still, McGinty should have kept his mouth closed.,"

"You'd never have told me?"

"Of course, I would. I'd have to. Your parents might be a bit far out the country, but everyone on our side of town, and in the town itself, knows about it. There are very few around Tunnygee who don't."

"I couldn't marry you now, Tom."

"Couldn't, be damned. Peadar Kennedy's not going to come between us at this stage."

"It wouldn't be right, Tom, it wouldn't be right."

"What the hell are you talking about, it wouldn't be right?" Tom smacked the palm of his hand down on the table.

"They're looking at us, Tom," Maisie began to cry.

"God, Maisie, you're not going to cry here. Come on, we'll go."

He put his arm about Maisie's sagging shoulders and led her to the door.

"If that blonde one in there at the next table opens her mouth any wider she'll swallow herself," Tom said outside.

"She's not blonde."

"Are you mad? I'm not that damp in the peepers yet. My sight is not that bad"

"But," Maisie laughed through her tears, "she's not really blonde. She's as black as you are."

"What's the differ? She could be green white and yalla for all I care."

"But she's not really blonde," Maisie persisted, "she has black hair on her legs. I saw it, I saw it when she came in first."

"Are you alright? You don't know whether you're laughing or crying."

"But I know that she's black and that everyone, including you, thinks she's blonde."

"I know, I know, but I've got to go. I've another load to do yet. I'll be back about seven."

"Where?"

"Here, in the same place. Will you be alright until then?"

"I'll be alright."

"I'll see you at seven then."

"No, Tom, it's finished, finished, Tom."

"Cop yourself on, Maisie. I'll see you at seven here," he jabbed his finger down towards the ground in emphasis.

"What's the word, Maisie?" Tom asked when he came back.

"I can't, Tom, I can't."

"Forget about can't. There's no such word. If that one the day could change her hair from black to blonde, you can change your mind," he grinned at her.

"It's no joking matter, Tom. With Peadar attacking me and all, I'm a sort of like your own mother."

"Because an old drunken bastard like Kennedy attacked you. But nothing happened. You told me that yourself. He was too drunk."

"I know that, Tom."

"Well, forget about it then. He's my father, you know. Sometimes, I hate him. I could kick the hell out of him sometimes. But do you know something? He wanted to marry my mother, but Old Dancy wouldn't let him. Peadar often told my Uncle Pakie. Pakie said it soured him."

"And that excuses his attack on me."

"I didn't say that. I'm making no excuses for him, but they say he never got over my mother. And then he went off and married that old dried-up prune of a Suzanne one."

"He made his own bed. Suzanne may be a bit stuck up, but he married her. Suzanne's no excuse."

"I know that, but he would have married my mother only for old Dancy. They say he would have married her in the end, anyway, that is, if she'd.......she'd lived."

"Don't upset yourself, Tom," Maisie caught him by the arm.

"I'm not upset," he rubbed his eye with the knuckle of his thumb.

"My mother won't let me marry you."

"She can't stop us."

"Still, I wouldn't like to go behind her back."

"That means you'll marry me then," Tom caught her in his arms and danced her round on the footpath.

"I won't go behind my mother's back, Tom," Maisie half shouted at him.

14

Suzanne Kennedy died on March 3, 1954. She had entered a Dublin hospital in the previous December, where she had undergone two abdominal operations for cancer. She was sent home to die at the end of January. Miss Macken, who was a first cousin of Suzanne on her mother's side, moved into the house on the hill, from her home near Cavan, to look after Suzanne in her final illness. Tracker Duff maintained that her motives were not altogether altruistic.

"She's over to look after Suzanne right enough, but it gives her a good chance to keep an eye on Houlihan. I'd say she's taken a

New Year resolution that there will be no big blondes hanging round in 1954. Her second resolution is to have the banns read on poor old Mike before the end of the year," he declared.

"She could give Mike a good ten years," Willie McGinty remarked, "but I suppose when all's said and done she's a fine lump of a woman," McGinty scratched himself.

"And with a fair old lump in the stocking too," Tracker winked under his hat.

It was a big funeral. Tom and Maisie got a seat at the back of the church. The parish priest was reciting the prayers for the dead, the same man to whom Maisie had confessed nearly two years before. She glanced up towards the confessional, up on the right opposite the altar of the Blessed Virgin, remembering her terror on that morning.

"Will you look at who's on the altar, Eddie McCaffrey?" Tom nudged her.

"What?" she looked at him blankly.

"The young priest, that's Eddie McCaffrey, Johny's son," he whispered.

"Who?"

"What's wrong with you? On the altar, MacCaffrey's son, the young priest."

"He's a fine looking man," she said.

"The spit of the old fella, a quare old hero to have a son a priest."

"They'll hear you, Tom."

"Sure, they're all talking. You'll hardly pay any offerings."

"No. Only for you I wouldn't have come at all."

"I'll have to throw a few bob over her when I came this far."

The prayers ended and the two priests moved behind the table at the altar rails.There was an expectant quiet as the crowd concentrated on Peadar Kennedy. He left his front pew and, going to the altar, placed his offering on the table and joined the priests to supervise the ritual of collecting the money.

"He parted with a couple of fivers there at least," Tom whispered.

The other chief mourners, including Miss Macken, made their contributions and returned to their seats. This was the signal for a charge into the aisle by the main body of mourners. They formed up in a rough line and shuffled forward to bob a knee and place a half-crown, the tangible symbol of their respect, on the table under the watchful eye of Peadar and the priests.

The offerings were a survival from the old days, when the neighbours came to the burial house and put a coin on the discreetly placed plate, giving out of their poverty and misfortune towards the greater misfortune of the bereaved family. It became the custom to give the money to the priest and the custom became the tradition. It was one way of contributing to the support of one's pastor and what one paid over the dead was put to practical use. Few flowers or wreaths rotted on Catholic graves, but the priests had at least some of the wherewithal to meet their wordly needs. A good system, with a few shillings paid over a neighbour's coffin, to show respect for the dead and the family of the dead, serving a very practical purpose. But it was abused. It became an auction, taking from the dignity of the occasion. The family, by upping the contribution to impress the neighbours, or, simply, because it was an important or well established family, could so far outdistance others in moneys offered that comparisons became inevitable. Consequently, offerings became a symbol of standing in the community leading to the question as to what price Mary or Micky went. It was an abuse of an essentially sound system about which Peadar Kennedy did not have to worry. His wife would go a good price, befitting her and Peadar's standing in a community where material success was a very important criterion.

Tom could see Peadar start as he approached the offering table, but the ruddy, round face was bland and non-committal as Tom tossed the two half-crowns onto the growing pile of silver. Tom did not return to his seat, but went outside to smoke and chat until the coffin was carried out. Tracker and McGinty were already in position on the sheltered side of a yew tree.

"My sound man, Tom, how goes it?" Tracker asked.

"I didn't think I'd see you here?" McGinty was blunt.

"It's my stepmother's funeral, isn't it?"

"I suppose it is. A fair old turnout," Tracker commented.

"Big enough."

"Jasus, it's the biggest I've seen in a long time," McGinty said, "and did you see McCaffrey's young fella with the white collar on him?"

"There's Johny himself over by the door," Tom said.

"By God, aye, hey Johny, come over here and give us a bit of your chat," McGinty called.

"A nice collection of playboys," McCaffrey said, joining them. "Howya Tom, when are you giving us the big day ?"

"It might be a while yet, Johny."

"There'll be no talking to you now, Johny, that the son's ordained," McGinty nodded towards the church.

"Aye, isn't it a quare turn-up for the crawthumpers? They're all lifting their hats to me now."

"I don't wear a hat, Johny," Tom laughed.

"I suppose you'll be sporting one next. There's no doubt about it, but you've come a long way since you were cleaning the shucks for me with a patch on the arse of your trousers."

"I'd still have a patch if I'd stayed with you, Johny."

"You'd be lucky if you had trousers at all. Seriously though, Tom, when's Maisie and yourself going to tie the knot?"

"I told you, it might be a while yet."

"Why? Is the old lassie still putting a spoke in the wheel?"

"I wouldn't worry too much about that, Johny."

"It doesn't worry me, amhic."

"Good day to you, Gabriel," McCaffrey called to a big man, slouching past.

"That's the man who has come out of his shell a lot," McGinty commented.

"It's since he got the woman for himself," Tracker said.

"And, of course, he has a son now," McGinty laughed, "And there's a bit of a story about that too."

"I'd be careful there. After all he's another cousin of Suzanne's. But a fair bit of a lug in his own way," Tracker said.

"I know that, but he's not going to hear it," McGinty said, "Biddy was well past the forty when she married him. So you could say that the young lad was a bit of a miracle. But Gabriel O'Beirne wasn't satisfied with one. He got the notion that the missus was going to have twins. She's a big woman, you know, and she got shocking stout when she was carrying. The doctor told

Gabriel it was only one child, but Gabriel had his own know. Anyway, the night the child was coming, the doctor was a brave while upstairs. Gabriel was below in the kitchen, making tea and a sort of routing around. The next thing the doctor shouted down congratulating him on a fine son. Only one, doctor? Only one, Gabriel. But she was carrying two, doctor. I can only find one, Gabriel. Search her again, doctor, she's a shocking roomy woman."

"You'd think she was a bloody cow," McCaffrey said, "But he was always half a savage."

"Here she comes," McGinty whipped off his cap as the coffin was carried out the church door.

Peader stood, head bent, as the coffin was put in the hearse.

"Jasus, he's getting shockin' bald," Tracker said.

"And that runs in families. You'd want to watch it," McCaffrey nudged Tom.

The hearse moved slowly down the drive.

"Is that Houlihan up there with the chief mourners?" Tom asked.

"And with the bold Sylvia Macken hanging out of him," Tracker said.

"Come on, are you coming?" McCaffrey moved to join the cortege.

"I'll wait on Maisie," Tom said.

"My mother's inside, come on, before she comes out," Maisie hurried towards him.

"Running away is no help. Stand your ground everytime, is my policy."

"Come on, Tom, I don't want to meet her now anyway."

"Too late, Maisie, here she comes. You can't deny her. That's what you'll be like in a few years' time," Tom laughed.

Under a scarf, Mary Dempsey's once red hair was faded to near blonde with an occasional gold glint showing through. The light skin was soft-wrinkled around appraising blue eyes and she was apple cheeked from the weather. Compact in an old tweed coat, she marched towards them with the determined heel-toe tread of a soldier.

112

"Well, Maisie, I didn't expect to see you here," she spoke in a sharp, questioning tone.

"Hello, mama."

"And how is Mr. Burke this morning?" Mary was cynical.

"Very well, thank you, ma'am," Tom replied.

"I hope you are satisfied, taking my daughter from her good home to live in a room in the town."

"I didn't take her, ma'am. You threw her out. You told her she'd have to leave if she was going to marry me."

"She's still answerable to her parents. She's not twenty-one yet."

"She's old enough to get married and to make up her own mind about it."

"You're a smart boy, Tom, too smart for my poor old fool of a daughter. Neither myself nor my husband want you, you know that."

"And I know why too. Because my mother wasn't married, not respectable like the rest of you."

"Well?"

"Well, yourself!"

"Come on, Maisie, are you coming?" Mrs. Dempsey addressed Maisie.

"No, mama, I'm staying with Tom."

In the cemetery, Tom stood on the curb of an adjacent grave as the coffin was lowered and the prayers recited. The parish priest removed and kissed his stole and had a final word of sympathy for some of the mourners before leaving. The diggers sent the first shovelfuls of clay thumping hollowly in on top of the coffin, as Father Edward McCaffrey sympathised with Peadar, before moving to follow the parish priest. Tom went after him and caught him by the elbow as he skipped nimbly through the graves.

"Are you not talking to your old friends any more," Tom asked.

"Tom Burke! It's years since I saw you. How are you at all?" Edward shook hands warmly.

"I'm grand, Eddie. No need to ask how you are. You're the boy that's looking well."

"And I hear you are getting married to Maisie Dempsey."

"That's right. Come over and meet her."

"This is the man who will solve all our problems, Maisie," Tom introduced Edward.

"I'd say your problems are minor ones," Edward laughed.

"Well, Maisie's mother is not too keen on me," Tom said.

"I heard that."

"Maybe you'd have a word with her."

"Aye, I'll be around for another week. I'll do that, Tom. What do you say, Maisie?"

"I'd be delighted if you talked to her, Father."

"Fair enough, Maisie. I suppose you're both coming to the hotel."

"We weren't invited," Tom said.

"And you one of the chief mourners, the son of . . ." Edward stopped and looked at Maisie.

"The son of Peadar Kennedy. I don't mind, Father," Maisie said.

"You must come too, Maisie," the priest took her arm.

"No, Father, it would be too much meeting Peadar today, the day of Suzanne's funeral."

Peadar looked hard at Tom as they shook hands wearily in the hotel foyer. Sylvia Macken, as the other chief mourner, shook hands also and formally introduced a somewhat abashed Mike as her fiance.

"We're old friends, Mike and me," Tom grinned at Mike

"I am very pleased you came, Tom," Peadar said, "and now that we've made contact we must keep it up. You're my son and I'm happy to recognise that fact."

"It's a bit late in the day," Tom said shortly.

"There was not much I could do, when Suzanne was alive. I couldn't upset her."

"I suppose you couldn't."

"That's right, Tom, I couldn't," Peadar said quietly.

Later, Tracker stood at the bar, McGinty at his elbow.

"The Macken one has fairly got her hooks into Houlihan. She didn't let him out of her sight all day. Look at the two of them above in the corner holding hands, holding hands, I ask you?" he turned in disgust to McGinty.

114

"Jasus, she's kissing him now," McGinty said.

"Christ, and a big ould slobbery kiss too. Has Houlihan no shame? Fellas would do anything for money," Tracker declared.

"What money?"

"Are you stupid or something, McGinty? Isn't she Suzanne's nearest relation?"

"But what about Peadar? Won't he own the whole shooting gallery now."

"For his day, son, for his day. Do you think that Mick Dancy was that big an eegit? Kennedy only has it for his day and I hear that the bold Sylvia Macken is next in line after that."

A big hand grasped Tracker by the shoulder and spun him round.

"You're wrong, Duff, as wrong as blazes," Gabriel O'Beirne stood, eyes staring in a drink flushed face, the square block of him dwarfing the bulky Tracker. "You're a know-all townie, with not two halfpence to rub together, but that doesn't stop you shooting your mouth off. Well, let me tell you something, you're talking bullshit, pure unadulterated bullshit," Gabriel had Tracker by the shirtfront and grimaced down at him, showing strong white teeth.

"Stop that now, Gabriel, Tracker meant no harm," McGinty caught him by the arm.

With a backward swing of his arm, O'Beirne knocked McGinty into the corner, while with the other hand he shoved Tracker after him, also throwing him to the floor. With a further sweep of his hand he swept bottles and glasses from the bar.

"Silence," he roared, pounding the counter, "I want you all to hear me well. I'm Gabriel O'Beirne, first cousin to Suzanne Dancy on her father's side, the son of his eldest sister. As such I'm the late Suzanne's nearest surviving relative and there's no usurper going to step in and make claims in front of Gabriel O'Beirne. I'm talking to you," he pointed dramatically at Mike, "you, the stripe of a bankclerk, I just want to tell you that if you're thinking of marrying that Macken strap for her money you're making a big mistake."

Mike stood up, but Sylvia pulled him back.

"Ignore him, Mike. He's not all there. He was away in the big house several times," she whispered.

"Let him go, Sylvia. Is it a man or a mouse you're marrying? He won't always be able to hide behind your skirts," O'Beirne challenged, walking up the floor.

He stood in front of Sylvia and Mike, legs apart, jaw jutting forward.

"Stand up, you cowardly bastard," he roared at Mike.

As Mike stood up, Gabriel grabbed him by the throat with both hands. Mike attempted to pull free, but he was no match for an enraged Gabriel. He was forced to his knees, as Gabriel held on, babbling incoherently. Tom lifted a bar stool and, coming up behind Gabriel, hit him a hard blow with the seat of it on the back of the head. Gabriel sprawled unconscious across Mike.

"It's all I could do," Tom turned to the onlookers.

"Don't worry about that. You did the right thing," Peadar Kennedy assured him. "Will someone go for the guards?"

"What do you want the guards for?" Tom asked.

"If he wakes up and they are not here, you'd want to have another stool ready. Since they brought him away to the Big House the first day, and one of them had to clock him first with a baton, he treats them with respect."

"He might treat me with respect for clocking him too," Tom said.

"He just might. You never know how his mind works, but we'd be safer with a guard here all the same."

When Gabriel recovered consciousness, he nodded to the two guards standing over him, got to his feet and quietly left the bar.

A week later, Tom was alone in the Screelahan cottage, when Gabriel walked into the kitchen.

"O'Dea, the guard, and yourself were the only two men who ever downed me, the only two men who were not afraid of me. I admire that sort of courage in a man," Gabriel said and walked out again.

15

G od, these young clergymen are a terror, master, walking us into a thing like this. There's no doubt, we're a quare pair of matchmakers," Johny McCaffrey laughed as he drove his new car out towards Dempseys.

"Don't blame me. He's your son. He talked us into it," his front seat passenger, Sean Cosgrave, laughed.

"Aye, I suppose you're right, master. What do you think of this yoke?" Johny asked.

"She's going rightly. What breed is she anyway?"

"She's an Austin Devon, not even two years old yet. She should be going rightly."

"Remember the day you broke the fanlight over my head?" Cosgrave turned to Father Edward, who sat on the back seat beside Tom.

"I remember it well, Sean, and all the glass coming down around your head. I ran, if you remember."

"And how right you were. I'd have killed you if I'd got my hands on you that evening. Still, it was a great dropkick for a young lad," the teacher said.

"Remember the time Simon Deignan scored a point from a drop in Clones, master?" Johny asked.

"I remember it well. It must be six or seven years ago. It was in the final against Antrim. I thought the ball would never stop sailing."

"Aye, he kicked it from inside his own fifty yards," Johny said, "I can see it yet, a skyscraper of a kick. It kept coming and coming and a sort of steadied over the posts before dropping like a stone on the top of the net."

"I don't think there was anyone more surprised than Simon himself when the ball went over the bar, Johny."

"I'd say you're right, master, but it was a great dropkick."

"No better than Edward's, the day he broke the fanlight. Your

117

son was bit of a blackguard in his youth," the teacher winked at the priest.

"He wouldn't be like his father if he wasn't," Johny chortled, hunching over the wheel.

"Who's going to do the talking to Mrs. Dempsey?" Tom asked suddenly.

"You better keep well in the background anyway, Tom," Johny still chortled, "I'd let the Master and Father Edward do the talking if I were you."

"Have you any idea how to approach this, Edward?" Cosgrave asked.

"We'll just play it by ear, Sean," the priest said.

"Ear be damned. I told Edward what to do, Sean, but he won't listen to me,"exasperation was in Johny's voice, "I know the crowd Mrs. Dempsey comes from, the seed, breed and generation of them. All as thick as double ditches and high and mighty at the same time, in their own minds anyway. Don't beat about the bush with her. If you want my advice, get the boot in straight away."

"How do you suggest we do that, Johny?" Cosgrave asked.

"Just remember that her own sister, Josephine, went to Canada in a bit of a hurry herself the time of the Eucharistic Congress."

Mrs. Dempsey came to the door at the sound of the car. Obviously impressed by the high powered delegation, she approached, smiling.

"You're welcome, Master, hello, Johny, and how are you, Father Edward," she ignored Tom.

"Will you sit in there beside Father Edward, Mrs. Dempsey?" Cosgrave requested.

Tom and Johny got out and went across the yard to stand in an outhouse door. About twenty minutes later, Cosgrave beckoned them over.

"Shake hands and seal the bargain," he instructed Tom.

"You're free to marry my daughter," Mrs. Dempsey said formally, holding out her hand, adding, "she's made her own bed and she can lie on it."

"Did you hear the old hairpin?" Tom asked, when they were back on the main road.

"It's the grudging nature of the baste. She'll come round in her own time," Johny said.

"What brought her this far?" Tom asked

"Who else, but the old scandal monger himself," Cosgrave clapped Johny's shoulder, "we couldn't get a stir out of her at first. All about Peadar being a decent man and that he was going to marry your mother and the rest of it was all a waste of time. Father Edward here gave you a great write-up, Tom, but it was in vain. Evenually, I asked which of us can throw the first stone. There were no bastards on our family, she said."

"That's the bitch," Tom cut across him.

"Anyway," Cosgrave continued, "wasn't it the year of the Congress that your sister, Josephine, went to Canada, I quietly threw it across her bows. She collapsed after that. It took all the steam out of her."

"It didn't take half enough out of her," Tom said, "did you hear her about Maisie making her own bed and lying on it?"

"She agreed and that's what counts. You can name the day now," Cosgrave said.

"I'll have to wait until Lent is over, I suppose, unless His Reverence here gets me an exemption," Tom said.

"My authority doesn't extend that far yet, but I'll marry you the third week after Easter. Monday, Tuesday or Wednesday of that week, take your choice. I'll be back home that week," Edward said.

"Shake on that,Eddie," Tom held out his hand.

Tom and Maisie went to Kelly's to celebrate that night. Tracker and McGinty were there. It was McGinty who suggested going to Fairyhouse on Easter Monday.

"Tracker and myself go every year and it'll be your last chance of an outing before you tie yourselves down," he said.

Tom and Maisie spent the Easter weekend in Dublin. On Monday, Tom waited for her on O'Connell Bridge. The east wind that came across Europe from the steppes of Russia still had a bite to it. Tom looked at his watch. No sign of Maisie! Leaning across the parapet of the bridge, he flicked a match from him and watched its wavering flight downwards. He lost sight of it before it reached the swirling waters. With the tide in, the river was backed up all the way down past Guinness's wharf to Kingsbridge Station, muddy, brown and sombre. The sun was shining, but the wind made it a cold Easter Monday.

Already, the 'racing specials' were pulling out. Tom waved to Maisie who was crossing from Westmoreland Street.

"Hurry up and we'll get the next bus," he shouted when she came within range.

***

Fairyhouse racecourse is to the north of the city, lost in the long grass and high hedgerows of the lush Meath countryside. A pilgrimage for Dubliners on Easter Monday, out to see the lithe horses match paces. British soldiers were there in 1916, when the Revolution was sprung upon them. The horses were charging up the finishing straight at the end of the second race, when Tom and Maisie finally found Mike, McGinty and Tracker in the long bar.

"Where's Sylvia?" Tom asked.

"She changed her mind. She decided not to come," Mike said.

"Ah, she didn't want to be seen with two old yobs like myself and Tracker," McGinty said.

"Hasn't she been trotting off to the dog track with both of you for years?" Mike reacted, slight irritation in his voice.

"But the racecourse is a wee bit different. You'd have more nobs at the racetrack than at the dogs. You know well she's a wee bit of a snob, Mike."

"She's not a snob. She just didn't want to come."

"God bless your wit, gasson. You're a city man born and reared, you don't know the country at all. Three ha'pence looking down on a penny, the farmer with two cows looking down on the cotter and the like of Sylvia looking down on the whole lot of us because she had a gombeenman of a father who had the wit to grab all he could. All that crowd are snobs," McGinty declared.

"I didn't think you were such a vicious little bastard, Willie," Mike said.

"No offence meant, son. I'm only wising you up," McGinty declared.

"I don't want to be wised up by you or anyone else. I'd advise you to forget about it," Mike warned.

"Fair enough, if that's the way you want to take it."

"That's the way I want it."

"You were always a troublesome little bollocks, Willie," Tracker said, "always letting your mouth run away with you."

"Shut up, Tracker. Are you having another drink there? And what about the rest of you? The same again, is it?" McGinty asked.

"I'll get it, Willie," Tom said.

"I see you're still sporting your Easter Lily, Willie," Tom remarked, when he came back with the drinks.

"Amn't I entitled to?"

"You were fairly young then, Willie?"

"Not that young. I'm fifty this year."

"Sixteen in nineteen twenty, you were young enough."

"Well, let me tell you something, mister Tom. Sixteen was old enough to carry a rifle that time. Tracker there, he was only a year older, he carried one too. We did our bit, me and Tracker."

"Aye, them were the days," Tracker squared his shoulders. "Remember the ambush, Willie? We were all set, lining the ditch, with the tree down around the bend and the whine of the Crossley tender in the distance, remember, Willie?"

"Will I ever forget? I was pissing in my trousers and my forehead was awash in the sweat of fear, Tracker."

"And then the Tan and the lassie walked down the road. You won't believe this, lads and ...Maisie, where do you think they picked to do their courting? They went in through a gap in the ditch across the road from us. Johny McCaffrey was in charge and he came creeping along telling us to hold our fire. He tapped me on the shoulder and the shot went off. You see, the rifle had a hair trigger on it and the least touch..."

"Sure, sure, we heard it all before, Tracker," McGinty cut in, "you needn't make a meal of it."

"Never mind him, Tracker, finish the story," Tom said.

"What's biting you, anyway, Willie?" Tracker asked. "You're as ill-mannered as an old sow the day."

"Go on. Finish it, but make it quick. We want to get a few bob on before the next race," McGinty said.

"Fair enough. The trigger. As Willie there knows well the sear was filed to a whisper. I was working on it for days. Anyway, the shot went off and the Tan went scooting like a rabbit along the back of the ditch. Myself and McCaffrey fired off a shot apiece after him, but he got to the bend and warned the boys in the Crossley. It was save our own necks then. There were only five of us and twelve or more of them. As it was, only they were a bit slow organising themselves, we would never have got away. Isn't that right, Willie?"

"That's right, Tracker. We got away up by the rectory and down by the sandhole to the chapel. We spent that night in the old cornmill..."

"What about the race?" Mike interrupted. "Are we going to get our money on?"

"That's on my hands, son," McGinty assured him, cupping his whiskey in the palm of his hand, "when I get this wee drop to the right temperature, I'll swallow it and the job will be as good as done. The rest of you get out there and study the field. You better go with them too, Tracker. The sight of you with the stirabout face on you, and the sweeping brush across the middle of it, would frighten any bookie."

In the saddling enclosure, seven horses were being led around. Five walked quietly, with long strides, heads down and forward. The other two were skittish, pulling against their handlers, prancing and jerking. The big black horse neighed and reared up on its hind legs.

"That's our lad, that's The Dancer," Tracker said.

"Feeling his oats by the look of him," Tom commented.

"See that wee mare over there," Tracker pointed out a brown animal, "she's our biggest danger."

In the centre of the ring, men and women were horsey in sheepskin coats and outsize binoculars, the men topped in snappy hats, the women shod in cossack boots. Beside them, the jockeys, elfin-faced under the deformity of their safety helmets, looked frail, edgy and incongruously cocky. Suddenly, they were mounting. "The Dancer" sidestepped away, but a final heave and the jockey was astride. The half gallop down past the stands to the starting post as the bookmakers shouted the odds, two to one bar one, and the wee, brown mare was favourite.

"We'll get a good view from up here," Tracker led the way to the back of the stand.

The crowd was milling around the bookmakers, banknotes held up to catch the eye. The bookmakers grabbed the money and stuffed it into open, leather satchels, tossing the odds and docket numbers out of the side of their mouths back to the scribbling clerks. McGinty, hunched into his black coat, hovered on the outskirts, before moving in a fast, outflanking walk. He was lost to view momentarily, but soon his cap appeared at a clerk's shoulder and there was his fist, with the money in it, up against the red waistcoat of a florid bookmaker. The bet was laid and he was coming back.

"Hey, Willie, up here," Tracker called, waving his programme.

"What did you get?" he demanded when McGinty was still yards away.

"Five to two."

"God, you're a genius, Willie, he was no better than two to one anywhere."

"They're off," Tom shouted, but it was a false start.

They lined up again. To the murmur of the crowd they were off this time.

Tracker took a small pair of glasses from his overcoat pocket.

"The mare's in front. Our lad is last," he announced,

"He got off to a bad start...

"He's coming now, though, but he's still tossing the head..."

"The seven of them in a lump together with the mare still holding her own in front..."

"Hold it, The Dancer flew over that jump. He's second now. There's six lengths in it....."

Two jumps from home, he was eight lengths behind. Over the last jump, the mare was still holding on well.

"Come on, you big lug, get a move on," McGinty roared.

"So much for your dead cert, McGinty," Mike shouted in his ear.

"Hold your water, son, the race is not over yet," McGinty told him.

McGinty was right. The mare was tiring rapidly and The Dancer was full of running. The mare's jockey had his whip out and was lashing rhythmically. The Dancer came alongside and was over a length clear at the winning post.

"Now, who was right!" McGinty reached up and thumped Mike's shoulder.

"Thirty five pounds, not a bad return for a tenner, I suppose," Mike smiled down at him.

Tom grabbed Maisie and swung her round. Tracker stood at his expansive best, hat shoved back on his head.

"Did you see The Dancer?" McGinty exulted, "he came like a swallow rising from a lake on a Summer's evening."

"In troth and a poet couldn't put it better, Willie. What would you say to a drink now?" Tracker asked.

"Not for me, Tracker. I'll stick around till they pay out. Business first and play after is my motto," McGinty laughed, narrow shoulders shaking in his coat.   •

"It's lately it happened you," Tracker told him.

That night, back home in Kelly's, Tracker bought a round for the house and Mike bought two. Tom bought another, before leaving Maisie at her flat. It was almost closing time when he headed back to the pub. At the door he met Sylvia.

"Would you please send Mike out. Tell him I'm waiting," she requested.

"Would you please send Mike out. Tell him I'm waiting," a half drunk Tom announced in a high-pitched voice, when he entered the bar. "You better get out fast, Houlihan," he continued, "her ladyship is waiting and she is not too happy."

"Bring her in, bring her in, Tom, my boy," Mike shouted, "she'll show McGinty that she's no bloody snob. She'll come in and tell it to him right up to his face. Call her in," he waved a disjointed hand in the air,

"He wants you to come in," Tom put his head out the door."She won't come in," he called over his shoulder.

"Tell her McGinty's right that she's only a bloody snob and that Houlihan doesn't like snobs," Mike shouted.

"I heard that," Sylvia told Tom, walking away.

"She's gone," Tom announced from the open door.

"Come in and close the door then. McGinty's ordering aother round," Mike told him.

16

Butsy arrived in Tunnygee on the Friday before Tom's wedding driving a Volkswagen Beetle. His first call was on Mike at the bank.

"I'm told they're a great little car," Mike stood on the footpath, admiring the Volkswagen.

"Would you like a drive?" Butsy asked.

"Sure."

Butsy was enthusiastic about the merits of the Volkswagen, explaining how the rear-mounted engine gave greater stability with consequent faster cornering.

"Also, it's air-cooled," Butsy explained."You have no worry about water freezing in the wintertime. It has only one disadvantage as far as I'm concerned, the lights could be better."

"I understand they're putting twelve volt batteries in the newer models," Mike said.

"Then, Bob's your uncle, you couldn't have a better car. Are you thinking of buying one?"

"I'm considering it."

"Well, while you're considering that, here's something else for you to consider."

"What?"

"Did you ever hear of Saor Uladh?"

"That's the I.R.A., isn't it."

"No, it's not."

"Don't split hairs with me, Butsy. They're the one sow's pigs."

"In the sense that they both want to get the British out of Ireland, you're right."

"What gave you the notion that I would have any interest in

the I.R.A. or Saor Uladh, or any other group of half-witted, so-called patriots?"

"I had no notion about anything. I only asked you a simple question, did you ever hear of Saor Uladh?"

"You were leading somewhere."

"Do you think I'm a police informer or something?"

"I don't know and I don't care."

"Well, let's say we were only making conversation and leave it like that."

"That's okay with me, Butsy," Mike agreed.

"Do you see much of Maisie?" Butsy asked.

"I see her nearly every day. She has a flat in the town. I'm best man on Monday, you know."

At her small flat, over Clarke's hardware shop, Maisie threw her arms around Butsy.

"It'll be eight or nine before Tom comes to town," she told him. "He'll have to do the milking first. He bought two cows, you know."

"I'll drive out and surprise him," Butsy said."Do you want to come?"

"I'd love to, Butsy."

They found Tom whitewashing the outside of the house.

"Give me ten minutes more and I'll have it finished," he said.

Proudly, Maisie showed Butsy around the three-roomed cottage, two bedrooms freshly wallpapered and the newly whitewashed kitchen. She brought him up to the loft tucked in under the thatch and, hunkering to the little window in the gable, she pointed out the view over the lake. She was making tea when Tom came in.

"A typical man," she scolded him,"not a thing in the house, only loaf bread and a heel of butter. Things are going to change around here after Monday, I tell you."

Tom brought Butsy for a walk round the fields.

"And we call this the Crockaun*," he stood on the narrow strip of sloping ground bordering the lake."

"It would make a great miniature range, Tom," Butsy said.

* Small hill

"I often thought that myself, Butsy. Come on, what's on your mind? You're like the proverbial hen with an egg."

"Jasus, I got a bit of a suck-in the day already. I thought Houlihan might be a bit of a Republican."

"Who? Are you serious? Houlihan a Republican? He's the original West Brit. As far as he's concerned we should never have left the Commonwealth. As far as that goes, I don't remember you as much of a Republican yourself, Butsy."

"Maybe I was and maybe I wasn't. Tell me something. Did you ever hear of a fella called Liam Kelly?"

"The Tyroneman, the boy from Pomeroy. He got nine months last year for sedition."

"Do you know anything about Saor Uladh?"

"Another I.R.A."

"That's what Houlihan said. There's a difference you know."

"I know that, Butsy," Tom said. "There are a couple of Saor Uladh men around this area and, between the two of us, I told them I might give them a hand."

"God, you're a deep one, and Houlihan knows nothing about it?"

"Not one bloody thing."

"Do you think would he give a fella away?"

"I don't think so. He just doesn't want to know, doesn't want to be bothered. All he wants is an easy life. He's back in with Sylvia Macken too."

"I didn't know he was ever out with her."

"They had a bit of a tiff on Easter Monday. Anyway, she's coming to the wedding with him on Monday. Sure, it's thanks to you, Butsy, they're together at all. He was straying with the big Norwegian for awhile until you put a halt to his gallop."

"Shut up, Tom. It just happened. It wasn't my fault."

"It's a wonder Houlihan talks to you at all after wiping his eye that night. And then you charge down to Tunnygee and ask him to join the I.R.A."

"I didn't ask him to join any I.R.A."

"Some emissary for an underground force! Listen, I'm getting married on Monday, as you know. I'm not getting involved in anything for a while anyway."

"Still, it would be a great training area and this would be a great range," Butsy persisted.

"I agree with you, I agree with you, Butsy," Tom thumped him on the shoulder,"but leave it for the moment."

The wedding took place on the Monday at the Mountainy Chapel, Maisie's parish church. In high heels, Maisie was nearly as tall as Tom,and her *New Look* tweed suit, with calf length skirt and small fitted jacket, complemented her undoubted good looks. Tom's double-breasted worsted brown suit sat well on his lithe figure, leading Tracker to declare that they were "as fine a pair as came out of the Mountainy Chapel this forty years".

Mike was best man, with Betty, Maisie's sister, as bridesmaid, and Father Edward was the officiating priest. Peadar Kennedy sat at the back of the church during the ceremony. Outside, afterwards, Tom, acting on the spur of the moment, invited him to the reception in Shaffrey's, Tunnygee's only hotel.

"Who invited that fella to the breakfast?" Mrs. Dempsey demanded of Maisie on arrival at the hotel.

"I don't know, mama."

"I did," Tom said.

"You had no right to. It's the Dempseys are paying for the breakfast."

"I'll pay for Peadar if you like."

"And I suppose you'll have him speaking at it too as father of the groom."

"I never thought of that," Tom said,"but now that you mention it, I might."

"That will be the day," Mary Dempsey declared.

Father Edward was lavish in his praise of Tom and Maisie in his after breakfast address.

"They are two of the finest individuals it has been my pleasure to know," he said, but when he went on to praise both families, Willie McGinty found it difficult to control himself.

Eventually he turned to Johny McCaffrey.

"Will you get the young lad to shut up before he makes a liar of himself altogether?" he asked in disgust.

"Whist, McGinty."

"Whist, my arse. Isn't Mary Dempsey one of the Sullivans of

the mountain and wouldn't every one of them skin you for a ha'penny?"

"You don't point out the faults at a wedding. Anyway, they're not two bastes at a fair and . . . and what the hell's wrong with the Sullivans of the mountain for that matter?" McCaffrey demanded.

"Hypocrisy, I hate hypocrites. If the young lad keeps going the way he's going now he'll soon be as bad as the rest of them, a master of the soft word. Why doesn't he tell us about Peadar Kennedy? The Burkes may be all he says they are, but it's only half of Tom's breeding."

"You're drunk, McGinty."

"I have a few, but I'm not drunk, mister McCaffrey."

"Well, if you're not drunk, you're a bigger bloody eegit than I ever gave you credit for, McGinty."

"Don't get up on my back and piss down on my belly, McCaffrey. I'm no eegit. Willie McGinty's no bloody eegit," McGinty shouted. He was drunk.

"Is that Willie's voice I hear?" Edward asked, stopping in his speech. " By the sound of things there'll be no need for any water to be turned into wine at this wedding."

"Tell us about Peadar Kennedy," McGinty shouted through the general laughter.

There was a shocked silence, interrupted by the scrape of a chair, as Peadar Kennedy got to his feet at the end of the room.

"There's nothing to tell about Peadar Kennedy, that my friend , McGinty, and the rest of you, do not know already," he said evenly into the silence. "Now that I'm on my feet, however, I've a few words to say. I'm very happy to be here today and more than happy to be invited by my son, Tom Burke. There's some may say it's late in the day for me to claim him as my son and there's some truth in that. There's just one thing I'd like to say about it. I should have married his mother. I had reasons for not doing so at the time. At least, I thought I had, but they were not valid reasons. I know that now, twenty five years on, as I have known it for most of those twenty-five years. It is impossible, at this stage, to remedy that mistake, but, today, the day of Tom's marriage, I wish to make a gesture in that direction by publicly recognising Tom as my son, secondly, by wishing to himself and his young bride,

Maisie, every blessing and every happiness and, thirdly, by presenting them with this small token of my regard," Peadar finished.

He walked up the floor, shook hands formally with Tom and Maisie and handed an envelope to Tom. He shook hands with Pat Dempsey and then turned to Mary. It seemed for a moment as if she was going to ignore him, but she finally held out her hand.

"I don't blame you," he said quietly, holding her hand.

There was a spontaneous clap as Peadar returned to his chair. When word was passed around that the envelope contained a cheque for £500, the news was put in perspective by Tracker Duff.

"Jasus, it would buy a good sized farm,"he said.

The honeymoon was spent in Glengariff. At about four o'clock in the afternoon, the newly married couple set off in Johny McCaffrey's car for the journey south. Three hours later, on the straight on the Cork side of Cahir, Tom's head was nodding over the wheel.

"I just can't stay awake," he told Maisie."We'll have to pull in somewhere."

About a mile further on, they stopped at Kilcoran Lodge Hotel. The hallway was empty. Tom rang the handbell on the desk. A blonde woman in her thirties, apparently the manageress, eventually appeared, seemingly rubbing sleep from her eyes. Having pondered the question, she agreed that the dining room was open, but that she was on her own and that the best she could do was two mixed grills. She brought them into a little bar at the back, where having poked up the smouldering fire, she served Tom with a pint of stout and Maisie with an orange drink.

When the meal was served, they sat in the bay window of the dining area as the rays of the setting sun slanted in from the west. The meal wakened Tom up and he suggested continuing the journey, but Maisie was doubtful.

"How far is it to Glengariff?" she asked the woman.

"The best part of a hundred miles," was the careless reply.

"It's not a hundred miles," Tom said.

"As near as makes no difference," the woman said.

"Could we have a room for the night so?" Tom asked.

"Do you want the bridal suite?"

Tom blushed and Maisie tittered.

"How do you know?" Tom stammered.

"It's as plain as the nose on your face," the woman laughed, "I'll be in the bar when you finish your meal. Just give me a shout."

It was getting dark when they left the dining room. In the foyer they stood in the gathering darkness. They could hear someone laughing in the bar.

"Are you coming in?" Tom asked Maisie.

"No, Tom, I'll wait here. You go in and get the key."

The talk and laughter died suddenly when Tom opened the bar door. Three grinning men stood looking at him, while the woman smiled behind the counter.

"Are you alright?" she asked and one of the men stifled a laugh.

"The room, what about the room?"

"Come on, I'll show you," she came out from behind the counter.

As Tom followed her into the hallway, the men were laughing again.

"Your friends are in great humour," Tom said to the woman.

"They're locals," she said, "the season didn't start yet. You're the only visitors."

With a flourish, the woman threw open a door at the top of the stairs.

"There you are," she said, flicking on the light, "the first occupants of the bridal suite for nineteen fifty four."

"God, Tom, it's magnificent and look at the size of the bed. I never saw anything like it, "Maisie stood in amazement in the middle of the floor, when the woman left.

"And you better take a look in here too," Tom opened the door to the private bathroom.

Tom was in bed first. Maisie was a long time in the bathroom.

"Put out the light," she called from the door of the bathroom, before running across and getting into bed.

"God, you're frozen," Tom said, as she lay stiffly beside him.

He put his arms about her and she turned to him.

"I love you, Tom. I'm glad we're married," she whispered into his shoulder.

Casey's Temperance Hotel in Glengariff had a reputation for food, with fresh salmon and fresh cream figuring prominently on the menu. For three days, Tom and Maisie did little but eat and sleep. On the fourth day, they rowed to Garninish Island, where they marvelled at the formal symmetry of the Italian garden. On the following day, they drove to Killarney. Up at Kate Kearney's cottage, a small, black-haired Kerryman talked them into hiring two scraggy ponies. It was the first time Maisie sat astride a pony and she found it difficult to keep her seat. She gripped the spikey mane tightly as she bobbed up and down in the saddle.

"I'm getting sick, Tom," she shouted.

"Seasick on a runt of a Kerry pony," he laughed.

"I'll have to go back, Tom. I can't go any further."

The small Kerryman was delighted to get his ponies back so quickly. He had two other customers waiting.

"Can I drive through the gap?" Tom asked him.

"Sure, but it's fairly tight in places."

"We're in Killarney and we're not going home without seeing the Gap of Dungloe," Tom declared.

"Take it handy and you'll be okay," the Kerryman assured him.

Round the first bend after leaving the cottage, and the loneliness and solitude of the place began to impress itself on Maisie. The little mountain lakes, with the MacGillyguddy Reeks towering on the right, and with the Tomies and Purple Mountains on the left, awed her. She felt small and insignificant in the enclosed wilderness above the lakes, with the odd white cloud high and stationery in the blue sky.

"It would make you think of God," she told Tom.

"Aye, I suppose it would," he said absentmindedly, as he manoeuvred the car round a projecting rock at the side of the track.

As they went further into the ravine, the track became narrower and narrower.

"Maybe we should go back," Maisie suggested.

"It's a bit late now to do that. There's nothing for it only to keep going forward," he told her.

At the top of the Gap they stopped and stood, looking down at the Upper Lake and the Long Range stretching away below it.

"It's beautiful up here, all the brightness and light after the gloom and the sort of closed in feeling on the way up. It's like being on top of the world," Maisie enthused.

"This is where we are," Tom pointed to the map he had got at Kate Kearney's Cottage,"and that's the Upper Lake down there, the grandest sight that Sir Walter Scott ever saw."

"How do you know that?"

"Isn't it written down here," he laughed, putting his arm around her.

"Oh, Tom," she said,"I was never so happy."

They sat down on the sunny side of a large rock, at ease in the warmth and with the world to themselves. Maisie lay on her back and pulled Tom down on top of her.

"I love you, Tom, I love you," she whispered.

They were drowsy and half asleep, when the sound of the car horn impinged on their consciousness. Maisie heard it first.

"What's that noise?" she asked.

"I don't know," Tom said, half awake.

"It's a car," she pushed him to one side and stood up, ducking down again quickly.

"There's a big car below and it can't get past," Maisie straightened her clothes and rubbed at her hair.

Tom got up, pushing his shirt into his pants.

"Jasus, it's a big Yankee car and the head's busting on your man ," he sat down and laced his shoes.

"Come on," he told Maisie, pulling on his coat and walking sheepishly towards the cars.

"I always heard the Irish were romantic. Now I know it's true," the American called, as his wife sat grinning beside him.

A mile or so on, Tom turned to the right down towards the Glen of Owenreagh. The Americans, who had stuck on their tail all the way from the Gap, tooted on the horn, and grinning and waving, turned to the left.

Next day, Sunday, Tom and Maisie returned to Tunnygee.

17

Tom was a good hardworking small farmer in the traditional manner, following the three year cycle of potatoes, grain and hay before letting a field out to grass. A year after his marriage he had five cows and sent the milk to the creamery. The two creamery cans of milk were placed on a sled, a wheelless wooden box on iron shod runners, known as a *slipe*, in Tunnygee. Pulled by his Uncle Pakie's pony, it was brought out the lane to the road, where it was picked up by Red James Smith's creamery cart. It was thanks to Johny McCaffrey that the pony was still around. When Tom left to join the army, Johny took care of it and returned it to him the week he returned from his honeymoon.

Over twenty years old, the pony had been bringing milk to the road for Pakie for years. She was so well trained that, when one unloaded the milk, she automatically turned and went back in the lane. In fact, on occasions, Tom let the pony go to the road on its own with the creamery cans, while he followed casually later. On one occasion, the creamery cart had come before Tom had even left the house to follow the pony. Red James, finding the pony waiting at the end of the lane, unloaded the milk and the pony turned for home. About ten minutes later, Tom, who was finishing a final cup of tea in the kitchen, heard the hoofbeats in the yard. Afterwards, he often let the pony deliver the milk on her own.

Maisie was happy, but somewhat disappointed, when a year after marriage, there was still no sign of a baby.

"There's plenty of time yet," Tom told her when she voiced her concern.

"But it's over a year now, Tom. I think I should go to the doctor."

"Whatever you like. You could go in to the wee specialist on Saturday."

On Saturday evening, Maisie came flying into the yard on her bicycle, skidded to a halt and dumped the bicycle on the ground.

Breathless, she rushed into the house and threw her arms around a startled Tom.

"There's nothing to stop me, nothing wrong with me. I could have twenty yet, Doctor Carroll told me."

"That's great news," Tom laughed, pulling her tight.

She pulled away from him, wiping tears of happiness from her eyes.

"Maybe it's my fault," Tom said.

"No, it's not your fault, you old fool," she laughed. "I asked him that and he told me to have sense. I'm over-anxious, he said."

"Over sexed, if you asked me," Tom told her.

"Are you coming to bed?" she asked later that night.

"Don't be over-anxious now," he jibed.

"I'm not over-anxious," she threw the sock she had darned at him.

"If you're not over-anxious, I am," Tom jumped up.

"I bet you I'll be in bed before you," he ran towards the bedroom.

Several hours later Maisie nudged him.

"There's a car in the yard," she said.

"I hear it. It sounds like the clatter of a Volkswagen. It's hardly Butsy, is it?"

It was Butsy.

"I thought it was you. The Volkswagen gave the game away," Tom told him, turning the bellows to blow the fire to life. "Anyway what has you rambling at this hour of the morning?"

"It's not that early. It's nearly six o'clock, time any self respecting farmer was up and about," Butsy laughed.

"It's you, Butsy," Maisie came from the bedroom.

"You're looking great, Maisie, isn't Tom one lucky man?" Butsy kissed her.

"Well, what's the news, Butsy?" Tom asked.

"I want to set up a training camp, Tom."

"Where?"

"Here. Just for a week, four fellas and myself."

"I.R.A.?"

"No, Saor Uladh, Kelly's organisation."

"I thought that was confined to Ulster."

"Isn't this Ulster? Isn't Cavan part of Ulster?"

"You know well what I mean. I thought it was confined to the Six Counties."

"It's organised solely in the Six Counties and it recognises that Oireachtas Eireann is the sole legitimate authority in Ireland."

"You're well briefed."

"That's my army training, boy. I don't go into things with my eyes closed. What do you say to the training?"

"When?"

"Starting on Friday and finishing the following Friday."

"I don't mind. What about you, Maisie?"

"It's your decision, Tom?"

"Okay, Butsy, that's fair enough. I suppose we can put them in the top room, Maisie."

"There's not much there except the bare boards," Maisie said.

"Don't worry about that, Maisie. They'll have sleeping bags and all," Butsy answered her.

"Sit over to the table," Maisie told him.

"Bacon and eggs cooked on the open fire. I don't know how you manage it at all," Butsy said.

"I'm used to it all my life, Butsy. It's the best fire of all. I don't like the ranges everyone is putting in nowadays. You couldn't even warm your shins at them."

"I didn't think you were such an old fashioned girl," Butsy said. "By the way, talking about old fashioned lassies, did Mike marry Miss Macken yet?"

"Aye, they tied the knot during the summer. Sneaked off to Rome to some cousin of Sylvia's who's a priest in one of the colleges there," Tom answered, "that way Mike didn't have to invite the wrong people."

"That's not fair, Tom," Maisie said.

"Of course, it's fair. Do you think Miss Macken would have McGinty or Tracker at her wedding? She'd even look askance at me and you too, Maisie."

"And what did Mike say to all this?" Butsy asked.

"Wasn't it the handy way out for him too, although there's nothing wrong with Mike. He still drinks with the boys in Kelly's. Anyway, he was moved. He's working in Navan now, driving up and down every day. They moved in with Peadar Kennedy in the house on the hill after the wedding. We don't see that much of them," Tom told him.

There was a knock on the door and Gabriel O'Beirne entered.

"I came to borrow the pony," he announced.

"She's all yours, Gabriel."

"Thanks," Gabriel turned on his heel and walked out.

"I wouldn't like to cross that fella, he's a brute of a man," Butsy said, "and he doesn't believe in wasting words either."

"No," Tom chortled, "he's the man nearly throttled Mike, you know. Did you hear about that?"

"It was at a funeral. Tracker told me about it at your wedding. So that's your man."

"That's your man right enough. He bought a bit of land the far side of the lake during the Summer and he's living there now. The wife and son left him. They went to live with a sister of hers in California."

"And you downed him with a stool!"

"That's why we're friends. He admired my courage, he told me."

"He's not right in the head."

"I know he's not, but I'm not going to fall out with him, especially now that he's a close neighbour, whatever he wants the pony on a Sunday for."

Butsy brought Tom and Maisie to first Mass in Tunnygee and brought them back to the end of the lane afterwards.

"I'll see you on Friday," he called, driving away.

Butsy and three men arrived on Friday as scheduled.

"I thought there were four coming," Maisie said.

"One of them got cold feet at the last moment," Butsy told her, ushering the three men into the top room.

Instruction began that evening on the care and maintenance of weapons. The group had a Bren gun and three rifles and Maisie could hear the drone of Butsy's voice, and the clatter, as the weapons were assembled and reassembled.

Tom was helping out at Johny McCaffrey's that day and it was nearly nine o'clock when he returned. He had a quick cup of tea and joined the men in the room. Soon, Maisie could hear his voice, louder and sharper than Butsy's, issuing instructions. She went to bed.

Next day was spent in the fields. Butsy and his men returned, wet and tired, as darkness fell.

"I'll cook you something while you're changing your clothes," Maisie said.

"No, Maisie, thanks all the same. As I explained last night, we want to be self-contained. That's why we have our own stove and grub. We're training for active service, you know."

"Go way out of that, Butsy, you like playing at soldiers."

"It's serious this time," he told her.

The pattern was the same throughout the week, all day in the field and back to the house as darkness fell. After a meal prepared by themselves and a short rest, Butsy lectured the men on fieldcraft, camouflage and musketry, while on two or three nights Tom supervised weapon training.

They left on Thursday night shortly after dark.

Next morning, between five and six o'clock, a mine went off at Roslea R.U.C. barracks in County Fermanagh. The attackers charged in through the breech, but Sergeant Morrow, who was living in the barracks with his wife and family, opened fire from the stairway. In the battle, a Constable Knowles was severely wounded, but the determined Sergeant forced the withdrawal of the raiding party. Maisie heard the report of the raid on the eight o'clock radio news.

"There was a raid on an R.U.C. barracks this morning," she shouted to Tom, who was still in bed.

He ran up to the kitchen in his bare feet, his trousers in his hand.

"What did he say?" he asked.

"Not much. Just that a policeman was injured and that the raiders withdrew after about fifteen minutes."

"None of the raiders were injured?"

"No. Why? Butsy and the boys weren't mixed up in it?

"I don't know, but they were heading somewhere last night."

"Did Butsy not tell you?"

"He didn't and I didn't ask him."

In the early hours of Sunday morning, Butsy and one of his men arrived in the Volkswagen.

"What happened the other two?" Tom asked.

"It's alright, they're safe and sound in Dublin. They went back on the bus yesterday," Butsy assured him.

"Were you on the raid?"

"A sort of. We were on outpost duty, to cut off reinforcements. We hadn't to fire a shot."

"They were beaten off?"

"That's right."

"There was a policeman badly wounded?"

"There was, but one of ours was badly wounded too."

"There was nothing about that on the news, or in the newspapers either."

"When the lads went in after the mine exploded, the Sergeant had them covered from the stairs and one of them was badly wounded. We got him away across the border, but he died yesterday morning. The doctor could do nothing for him, only send for the priest."

"Lord have mercy on him," Maisie crossed herself.

"Amen to that, Maisie," Butsy said.

"Can we leave the weapons here?" he asked Tom.

"I'm not too sure about that, Butsy. What about the guards?"

"I wouldn't worry too much about that, Tom. Sure wasn't Liam Kelly on to the Government about the man that was killed. He wanted to have him buried without an inquest. The Minister for Justice said there would have to be an inquest, but that it could be held in secret. The inquest was held last night at a farmhouse in Monaghan."

"How do you know all this?" Maisie asked.

"I was there. I was one of the jurors. Myself and five others acted as jurors. The Coroner was there and so were the superintendent of the guards and a detective. The farmer gave evidence about the man being brought to his house and the doctor gave evidence about a bullet wound in his left side. The Coroner's verdict was death due to shock and haemorrhage. They're burying him this morning at Carrickroe, to the north of Monaghan town."

"God, that's a terror," Tom said.

"And do you know who guarded the farmhouse during the inquest?

"Uniformed guards and detectives. And when the inquest was over, I came out to the car and there was a guard talking to Tony here," Butsy nodded at his companion.

"That's right," Tony said,"and before that, one of them sat in beside me to have a smoke."

"And where do you think the guns were, Tom?" Butsy asked.

"I don't know."

"On the back seat, with nothing only a groundsheet over them and the muzzle of the bren jutting up through it."

"I suppose you better bring in the weapons," Tom said.

"Are you staying the night?" Maisie asked.

"That's if you have no objection, Maisie."

"None at all, Butsy."

"Right, Tony, bring in the guns and two sleeping bags and put them in the room above," Butsy ordered.

18

In the following May, Tom met Butsy in Cavan's Farmham Hotel. He had got a letter from Butsy in the previous week requesting the meeting.

"This is Charlie Daniels, the man I mentioned in the letter," Butsy introduced a tall, slim, grey-haired man.

"He's interested in Thomson-O'Cleirigh, the British General. He doesn't live too far from you."

"No, he's about ten miles down the road, but he's only five from here."

"We know that. We're on our way to meet him. We thought we should have a local with us and Butsy suggested you," Daniels said.

"Fair enough."

"You don't mind?"

"No. I suppose you know all about him? He stood for election, for example."

"Of course. He didn't do too well. He was a bit too much for the people of Cavan, but his heart's in the right place," Daniels said.

"More Irish than the Irish themselves," Butsy laughed.

"That's not fair, Butsy, he's an Irishman." Tom objected, "his grandfather came from County Down. He made his fortune on the docks in Liverpool and came home and bought Blackhorse Forest and the big house."

"Tom's right," Daniels cut in, "he's as good an Irishman as the rest and better than most."

"They say he's a military genius," Tom remarked.

"Do you hear the Cavan man? There's no doubt about it, but they always stand up for each other," Butsy laughed.

"But Churchill sacked him!" Daniels said.

"I know that," Tom replied, "Churchill sacked him, but he sacked him wrongly. He was looking for scapegoats in 1942. Churchill was bad news politically himself at the time, and he charged out to the desert, and it was a good ploy to dump Auckinleck, O'Cleirigh and the rest of them. It gave the impression he was doing something."

"You're well informed on the General," Daniels commented.

"Aye, Johny McCaffrey knows him well. Johny and I often talked about him."

"Who's Johny McCaffrey?" Daniels asked.

"He's a farmer from home. I used to work for him. He buys and sells cattle for the General. O'Cleirigh told him the whole Churchill story, how Montgomery took over and the rest of it."

"How did Montgomery take over?" Daniels asked.

"Thompson O'Cleirigh had the plans made to defeat Rommel and Montgomery just put them into effect. The only thing about it is that Montgomery was slower about going into action than O'Cleirigh planned. The plans worked and Montgomery took all the credit. O'Cleirigh got no credit for the part he played as planner-in-chief. And once Churchill dumped him his army career was finished."

"That's his story," Daniels said.

"What do you mean?"

"There are two sides to every story."

"You don't believe Thompson O'Cleirigh's story then?"

"I never said that, just that there are two sides to every story."

"Jasus, Charlie, will you give over. You'd aggravate a saint sometimes," Butsy said."What the hell does it matter how your man was sacked? Or why he was sacked? Anyway, that old bastard, Churchill, would sack his own grandmother if he saw any advantage in it."

"Sorry, Tom," Daniels tapped Tom on the shoulder. "I'm inclined to split hairs sometimes. It's a weakness of mine."

"Don't worry about it, Charlie, we all have our faults," Tom replied.

"We better get on the road," Butsy stood up."We're supposed to be at your man's at four."

Butsy turned in through the heavy iron gates and swept up the driveway.

"It would remind you of one of those films about Germany, with the trees growing down close to the avenue," Tom said.

"Christ, it would be a great place for training. With the woods all around you could hide an army on the place," Daniels enthused.

The General received them in his basement study. Dandified in appearance, he was tall and thin, with a white shirt and blue cravat. He sat opposite a large mirror in which he studied his appearance, as he rubbed a hand over his well groomed red hair. Butsy looked at Tom and frowned.

"Gentlemen," the General turned round from the mirror, "I suggest we get down to business straightaway. Perhaps you would care to introduce yourselves."

"Charles Daniels, Director of Organisation, Irish Republican Army, General," Daniels clicked his heels.

"And this is Michael Dwyer, a provincial organiser," he introduced Butsy, "and Tom Burke here is a local man from Tunnygee."

"We haven't met, have we, Mr. Burke?" the General asked.

"No, General, but you know Johny McCaffrey, a friend of mine."

"McCaffrey, yes, another old soldier. We were on different sides in 1919 and 1920."

"Did you serve in the first world war, General?" Daniels asked.

"Yes, I was a young officer then."

"Did you see any action in Ireland?"

"No, but I was often home on leave. I remember on one occasion when I was on leave, the Black and Tans were searching houses in the local town, and let me say straight away, as a professional soldier, that the Black and Tans were a disgrace to the profession of arms. Anyhow, they were carrying out a search. The housekeeper's husband was the local I.R.A. leader. The family were fully aware of this, I might add. She was very agitated that morning. Eventually she approached me and told me that there were five grenades in her house. I strolled down to town in uniform, went into her house, and had her sons bury the grenades in the potato garden at the back. The Tans arrived a few moments later, and, of course, as a British regular officer I assured them they were in a completely loyal house."

"And there was no conflict?" Daniels enquired.

"None," the General looked at him sharply. "I already indicated to you that I considered the Black and Tans beneath contempt. Gentlemen, I am very sorry, please sit down," he took a seat at the mahogany table in the centre of the room, angling the chair so that he could glimpse himself in the big mirror.

"Mr. Daniels, you queried the possibility of conflict in relation to my little vignette concerning the Black and Tans, and quite rightly too, I may add. Consequently, I would like to make very clear my motivation in relation to current events and, in particular, in relation to your presence here. You're here," he patted his hair in the mirror in what seemed to be a strangely conscious gesture, "you're here because I'm an Irishman first and I believe that my native country should be free and independent," he looked at each of them in turn, smiling broadly.

"We accept that, General," Tom said.

The General turned back to the table and opened a book.

"I'm going to read to you part of a letter which I wrote to Basil Liddell Hart," he said. "It was published as the foreword to this book, *The Indirect Approach*, by Basil, published in 1946. Basil Hart, as you may know, was one of the foremost military thinkers between the wars," he grinned at his listeners.

"Yes, I read the book," Daniels said.

Butsy looked at Tom and shrugged.

"I gather Mr. Dwyer is not over familiar with Captain Hart. What about you, Mr. Burke?" the General asked.

"Not over familiar, but I heard of him," Tom said.

"What I would like to do, if I may," the General patted his hair, "is to read you a couple of snippets from this letter here. I believe it conveys my thinking on warfare. Shall I begin?"

"Yes, of course, General," Daniels answered.

"Critical readers," the General began to read, enunciating carefully and obviously placing value on each word,

"I quote from the letter, critical readers of your book will find in it no ritual formulae for success - instead they will discover a key to a method of approach to the solution of the problem of war on all planes of action, and that key is obliquity. It is a purely mental instrument, and only for the use of the critical and unorthodox - those open-minded soldiers who can say with Brian Boru before the Battle of Clontarf, what sort of a war will it be today?" - he looked up and his glance moved along each man seeking approbation.

"The object of obliquity," he continued reading, "is to find the chink in the armour, the mental armour at that. One's object is the psychological disruption of the opposing command, and the yardstick of success is the degree of freedom of action one enjoys at the end of the process. To this end one seeks all possible means of keeping the enemy guessing, hence the value of alternative objectives.

"There is little doubt that the true mental qualities for success on all the planes of military action are common sense, reason and obliquity: and the last quality becomes the more necessary as one ascends the scale to the plane of independent command," he closed the book and turned to the three men.

"You all look a small bit stunned," he said, smiling broadly again, "And I can't say that I altogether blame you."

"No," Tom said, "we're with you. As I understood it you are talking about surprise, using imagination, doing the unexpected, catching the other fellow off guard."

"Precisely," the General held Tom's eyes."You're Burke, aren't you, McCaffrey's friend?"

"Yes, Burke, Tom Burke, Johny McCaffrey's friend."

"I see, Burke," the General ignored the emphasis on christian names. "You seem to have a good grasp of the meaning of obliquity. It is important in conventional war, but it is much more important in an unconventional situation, in a guerrilla situation such as you men envisage. Firstly, I referred to independent command in that letter. Every guerrilla leader is an independent commander. He is on his own, operating in enemy territory. If he has not the quality of obliquity he is lost. In the Irish situation, Collins and Barry had it. Like Brian Boru, they were open-minded soldiers, capable of being critical and unorthodox. Lawrence of Arabia had this quality of obliquity, but in the Irish context, it was probably Collins who epitomised it."

"All I.R.A. men are students of the Irish War of Independence," Daniels said.

"I appreciate that, Mr. Daniels, but the problem is its application in current circumstances. To take one simple and straightforward operation, the silent removal or elimination of say two sentries at a military base. Knives come first to mind, but not all men are willing to use a knife. Think of it, would any of you three men walk up to a man and knife him in cold blood? Put it another way, would you prefer to shoot a man?"

"Yes," he continued, "you all nod. You would all prefer to shoot. Shoot with what? A gun, what else, but supposing a crossbow was used to eliminate the two sentries, what would be the effect? The relieving sentries would stumble across the body of their comrade with an arrow jutting out of their backs. Think of the shock, of the consternation the sight of two dead bodies killed by arrows would cause. The soldiers would think they were back somewhere in the Middle Ages. Supposing the same happened at three or four other military bases. Suppose the I.R.A. was to open a guerrilla campaign in this manner. Can you imagine the psychological disruption of the enemy security forces? They would be wrong footed from the start."

"And we wouldn't have to smuggle guns and ammunition across half the world," Daniels said with a grin.

"Seriously, though, "Daniels continued, "it's interesting what you say about knives in light of what happened on one of the raids in '54. The raiders, sixteen of them, got over the back wall. Three of them had knives with the job of silencing the sentry, but instead of using the knives, they tried to knock out the sentry with revolver butts. The result was that the sentry was permitted to shout a warning, alerting the guard, which immediately opened fire. The sixteen raiders got back over the back wall, while the twenty waiting at the main gate got away as best they could, but the alert was out and eight of them were arrested. The raid was a failure for the very reason that you suggest, General. The men hesitated to use their knives."

"That is indeed interesting. It is a perfect illustration of my knife theory, confirming my belief that not all men will use a knife," O'Cleirigh said.

"Maybe it is an Irish characteristic," Daniels suggested.

"I doubt that. Although upon reflection, I would feel squeamish about using a knife," the General admitted.

"Yes," he said as he stood up and went over to a map on the wall. "Before you go, I would like to give you another example of obliquity. In the desert in December 1940, the Italians were a formidable force. They were a major threat to Egypt. O'Connor was the British commander charged with eliminating that threat. The Italians were in position with their left flank at Sidi Barrani on the Mediterranean, occupying a series of camps or boxes running south to the escarpment," he pointed out the positions on the map. "In November a full-scale rehearsal of an attack on one of these desert camps was held. I was there as an observer on behalf of Wavell, Commander-in-Chief, Middle East.

"The rehearsal was carried out according to the book. As an exercise in military orthodoxy it was perfect. The artillery registered for two hours and then after the barrage, the infantry and tanks went in. I was among those who criticised the two hours' waiting time during which the entire striking force would be exposed to attack by the much larger Italian air force. Also, aerial photographs showed a minefield in the path of the proposed advance. In the face of Italian superiority on the ground and in the air, I did not see the attack succeeding if pursued in the orthodox manner. Orthodoxy did not make use of the speed and surprise that mechanised warfare made possible. How to do so was the problem.

"Further examination of the air photographs gave the answer. This showed that all vehicle tracks led into the north-west corner of the Italian camp, suggesting an absence of mines. The final plan was now evolved, a daring and imaginative manoeuvre that ran counter to every concept of military orthodoxy.

"The attack went in from the Italian rear at the unmined north-west corner. There were many problems and very definite risks involved in moving thousands of men over sixty miles of desert, but O'Connor succeeded. The infantry followed the tanks in trucks and on the morning of December 9, 1940, the attack force was in position to the west and in the rear of the Italian position. When the artillery bombardment, put in from the east, the Italian front, lifted, the British force went in.

"The Italians were taken completely by surprise. Nevertheless, they fought well, attacking heavily armoured tanks with grenades and machineguns, but the position was hopeless. Two thousand men and thirty-five medium tanks were captured for the loss of fifty six British officers and men.

"Other Italian camps quickly fell and two days later Sidi Barrani itself fell. In three days' fighting O'Connor had ended the Italian threat to Egypt and nearly forty thousand Italian prisoners had been taken at the cost to the British of something over six hundred casualties, killed, wounded and missing. It was one of the great victories of the war and the key to it, gentlemen, was obliquity.

"By using the intelligence at our disposal, specifically, the information gleaned from the aerial photographs, we found the chink in the enemy armour and, by that, I mean the mental chink, or the failure by the Italians to conceive of an attack so completely at variance with military orthodoxy. In the words of my friend, Burke, here, the Italians did not conceive of using imagination, doing the unexpected, catching the other fellow off guard," he finished and stood patting his hair in the mirror.

"General," Daniels stood up,"thank you very much for giving us so much of your time. We are sincerely appreciative."

"Not at all, Mr. Daniels, any time I can be of help."

He accompanied them outside and, standing on the steps, shook hands with each in turn. Tom was last.

"I think you have a very good military mind, Burke," he said, "I hope we meet again."

"I hope so too, General, but my friends usually call me Tom."

"Well, I would be happy to be numbered among your friends, Tom," the General said good-humouredly.

As they drove down the avenue he stood, chin up, standing to his full height, patting the red hair into place.

"Jasus, he's a fucking quare," Butsy said. "Did you see him looking in the mirror and rubbing the dyed hair?"

"I don't think he's queer," Daniels said, "in my opinion he's a very shy man."

"I think you're right, Charlie. He might be a bit vain, but there's nothing quare about him," Tom said.

"He's a bloody quare," Butsy persisted, swinging the car on to the main road.

"Where are you going?" Tom enquired.

"Back to Cavan."

"How do you think I'm going to get home. The bus is gone long ago."

"Hold your water. I'll drive you home."

"It's six or seven miles longer through Cavan."

"Don't let that worry you, Tom. What's six or seven miles to old Bessie here? She'd do them without drawing a breath."

"You got very uptight about the use of your surname, Tom," Daniels said.

"Maybe I did, but I noticed he was mistering you, one general to another, I suppose."

"By God, you handled him well, Tom, put him in his place nicely," Butsy said. "My friends usually call me Tom, says you. You were bloody well right."

"I don't know, but it annoys me, a fellow like that who doesn't even know you, using your surname. It's different if a fellow knows you well."

"It doesn't matter one whit what he called you," Daniels

declared, "what's important is that he's willing to help us. He's a man of ideas, who could be very valuable."

"I grant you that, Charlie, but where do I fit into this picture of yours?" Tom asked, "I'm not a member of the I.R.A."

"I'm fully alive to that fact, Tom, but I understand that you accommodated some Saor Uladh men last year."

"So what?"

I thought you might give us a hand in training some men. I understand you were a first-class instructor in the army?"

"I don't want to get entangled with the Twenty-Six Counties authorities. Saor Uladh confines itself to the Six Counties."

"The policy of the I.R.A. is to drive the British Forces of Occupation out of Ireland and under section eight of army orders, all I.R.A. volunteers are forbidden to take any militant action against Twenty- Six County forces under any circumstances whatsoever. If necessary, arms are to be abandoned rather than take military action."

"What do you say to all this, Butsy?"

"I've thrown my lot in with Charlie, Tom. As I see it, it makes no difference. We are all after the same thing. We all have the same aim, get the British out of Ireland."

"We would like if you would run a small training camp for us, Tom, say a half dozen men at a time," Daniels suggested.

"And there's no question of getting involved with the authorities here?"

"I didn't say that, but there's no question of using arms against Twenty Six County forces."

"I suppose that's fair enough," Tom said.

19

T he first I.R.A. group arrived in October. On this occasion, Tom was well organised. On his land, further in along the lane than his home, was an old building called *The Farhouse*. Built of loose stone and roughly thatched, it had been the family home two generations back. The dividing wall in the two-roomed cottage was partially broken down, but the old hearth and chimney breast survived. The pony was housed in one end of the cottage, while the other end was a calfhouse. In preparation for the advent of the I.R.A. group, the calves were moved to a shed near the home house and the broken down centre wall was made high enough to stop the pony putting her head across it from her own loose box in what was the former kitchen. Tom put a rough board floor about two feet above the ground in what was the former bedroom. He half-filled this room with hay.

Butsy appeared on the Sunday before the arrival of the group.

"You're still driving the same old heap of scrap," Tom kicked the wheel of the Volkswagen.

"Who owns that yoke?" Butsy pointed to the Austin Devon.

"It's mine. I bought it of Johny McCaffrey."

"You might as well drive a tank and you'd want a private oilwell to keep it in juice."

"Little you know about it," Tom put his arm around Butsy's shoulders. "Come in. Maisie has the tea ready."

Afterwards, they inspected *The Farhouse*. Butsy pronounced it ideal.

"You can light a fire here too," Tom pointed out the fireplace.

"What about herself?" Butsy nodded at the pony.

"You need only bring her in at night. Anyway," Tom patted the pony on the forehead, "she's so old and quiet she won't disturb anyone."

"Hey," Butsy opened the door into the other room, "we can always sleep here."

"That's the general idea and there's false floor here also," Tom said, "it covers about two-thirds of the floor space."

"Could men hide in it?"

"Aye, it would take six or seven, or maybe more, lying flat."

"How do you get into it, that's the next question?"

"Bend down and you'll see it."

Butsy got down on one knee and pushed his hand under the hay.

"You wouldn't have to search too far to find that," he said.

"That's true, but once in, all you have to do is to take the props from under the first plank. The hay will fall down and there'll be no opening."

"Maybe no fresh air either," Butsy said.

"I've thought of that too," Tom looked at him. "There's plenty of fresh air."

"Are you staying tonight?" Tom asked on the way back from *The Farhouse*.

"Yes, I'm staying in town."

"Why stay in town? The settle bed is still there. Maisie will be delighted to have you."

"Thanks all the same, Tom, but . . ."

"But what . . ? What the hell's wrong with you? Are you hiding something?"

"Olga's with me."

"God, no, I thought she had gone back to England, or back to her father in Norway, or someplace?"

"Well, she's back. She's in Shaffrey's and the two of us are staying the night. Yourself and Maisie should come into town and we'll have a few drinks."

"I'll have to take you up on that," Tom said.

"Who?" Maisie demanded, when Tom told her of Butsy's invitation.

"Olga, the big Norwegian from London. Butsy and herself are staying in Shaffrey's tonight," Tom said.

"I don't believe it. I'd love to see Mike's face when he hears she's in town."

"What about Sylvia's face?" Tom laughed.

"I'd love to be a fly on the wall when she hears the news," Maisie smiled.

"Don't be vicious now," Tom said.

"It would be worth a million pounds to see her, Tom. Who does she think she is, anyhow, with the stuck up head of her. I met her in town last week and she could hardly bid me the time of day. Hello, said she in that thin polite voice of hers. Poor Mike."

"I don't think I'd worry too much about Mike. He seems to be happy enough, the real gentleman. I hear the two of them are now golfing every weekend."

"Still, I have a soft spot for Mike," Maisie said.

Olga burst into Kelly's, pulling Butsy by the hand after her. With blonde hair piled high on her head, she held out her hand to Jimmy Kelly.

"Oh, Jimmy, it is my great pleasure to be back again in Tunnygee."

"You're more than welcome, ma'am," Jimmy shook hands warmly.

"And Tracker," she turned to that broadly smiling individual and kissed him straight on the moustache.

"I love kissing men with face hair. It adds the necessary spice," she stood back.

"God, I haven't a chance so," McGinty said at her elbow.

"Oh, Willie, of course you have. I love small men too," she lifted him up and kissed him as Tracker and the others cheered.

"She's a gas character," Tom said.

"I don't know what you're grinning about," Maisie retorted. "She's just a big vulgar woman. You men are all the same."

"You're jealous, Maisie," Tom laughed.

"And her behind is bigger than ever too," Maisie said.

"I'm delighted to see you again, darling," Olga kissed Maisie on the cheek, as Butsy winked over her shoulder at Tom.

She kissed Tom on the cheek also, before sitting down opposite Maisie.

"You have no baby yet, Maisie. I must talk to Tom," she smiled.

"I don't think Tom needs anyone to talk to him," Maisie said.

"I'm sorry, Maisie. I don't mean to be rude. I was just making a little joke. I hope you are alright?"

"I am alright."

"Then you have no need of the lone bush by the lake."

"What lone bush?"

"You should ask Tom about it, darling. You do know the story, Tom, don't you?" Olga turned to Tom.

"It's all nonsense, another Tracker yarn."

"It's no Tracker yarn," Tracker declared, "I heard my own father telling the story and he got it from his own father."

"All bloody superstition," Tom said.

"But the Irish are superstitious, Tom, and religious too," Olga said.

"All foreigners think that," Tracker said."It reminds me of the story of the fellow who toured the country before the war. He was from the Middle East somewhere, but he went back and wrote that the Irish were very religious, especially those living in rural areas. He reached this conclusion on the basis of what he saw with his own two eyes. At every crossroads in the country on a Sunday afternoon, he wrote, the local men gathered. One of them tossed two coins into the sky, while the others, muttering prayers, looked up towards the sky. Then, when the coins fell on the ground, they all bowed down, heads close to the ground and said, oh my God. They did this for hours, the man wrote, and never in his experience had he come across a more religious people," Tracker stood, fingering his moustache.

"They play pitch and toss in England too," Olga said. "Nevertheless, the Irish are religious and, I think, superstitious too."

"Maybe we are, but we don't believe in *pishrogues** about lone bushes," Tom said.

"I am sorry. I started all this because I talk too much. I am sorry, Maisie. Tonight is not a night for serious talk. We should all be happy, laughing and singing."

"It's a pity Mike Houlihan is not here," Maisie said quietly, "I'm sure he'd love to see you again, Olga."

"Maybe on another occasion, darling, but not on this visit. I am happy to spend this little holiday with Butsy."

*   myths

"We're only staying for the night," Butsy said. "I have to be back in Dublin before eleven tomorrow morning."

"That means early to bed tonight for Butsy and me," Olga fixed a loose strand of hair into place on the top of her head.

"Did you ever see the bate of it?" Tracker demanded, when Butsy and she left shortly afterwards. "Her with the trousers on her and dragging Butsy after her like a calf after a cow. Some fellas have no respect for themselves at all."

"By God, she's a quare cow," McGinty said, "and Butsy's no harmless calf. There's more the touch of the young bull about him. I don't think she has too much dragging to do on him."

"What was all that about the lone bush?" Maisie asked on the way home.

"Just an old *pishrogue* of Tracker's that a woman is sure to have a baby if she visits the lone bush over the town lake."

"And that's what she was hinting at?"

"Never mind her. There's not a word of truth in it. You know that and I know that."

"I don't like her, Tom, and I don't trust her either. She's far too smart. You wouldn't know what that old fool, Butsy, tells her."

"Butsy's no fool. He wouldn't tell her much."

"You know I'd never let you down, Tom, even though I mightn't agree with the shooting and guns. But I wouldn't trust that Olga one."

20

Tom brought the General to his home on Friday, the last day of the October course. On the Monday, he had gone down to Blackhorse House and suggested to O'Cleirigh that he might give a lecture on "Obliquity" to the personnel on the training course. The General had readily agreed.

Tom and Butsy had fixed up the upper room of the house with a table and some forms. As the General entered, Butsy called the students to attention. Tom introduced the visitor, giving a short rundown on his career. The lecture proper lasted an hour, and an hour later the General was still answering questions. At that stage, Maisie brought in tea and sandwiches, but the question and answer session continued for another hour.

"That was the most satisfying afternoon I've had in years," the General told Tom on the journey home."All the questions were pertinent and showed a keen appreciation and understanding of the subject matter of my lecture."

"They are all potential leaders, but, for all that, still only a bunch of enthusiastic amateurs," Tom replied.

"You may have something there, Tom. In fact, I think you have put your finger on it. That describes it precisely, a bunch of enthusiastic amateurs, and that is what came across, the interest and spontaneity of the amateur as opposed to the more cynical approach of the professional. I tell you that it is a joy to an old warhorse like myself to find it at this stage of my career.

"And something else, Tom, that added to my joy in the afternoon was my pleasure in meeting your charming wife. A beautiful young woman of a particular Irish type, titian-haired and fair-complexioned, she is also capable and intelligent, altogether, a very impressive person."

"Thank you, General."

"You mentioned earlier, future lectures," the General went on. "After today, what can I say but that I shall be delighted to assist you on any future occasion, if at all possible."

The next course took place in March and the third and final course was held in May. The General attended the March course and was in the middle of his May course lecture, when warning of an impending raid was given.

Mike Houlihan had not gone to work that morning. He had a heavy cold and lay in bed until lunchtime. After lunch, he went down to buy cigarettes and noticed the army lorry outside the garda barracks. There was something familiar about the Sergeant standing at the tailgate. It was Pat Layde, the man who had replaced Corporal Duggan in the Training Depot.

"Hey, Pat," Mike shouted at him.

"God, if it's not the bold Mike Houlihan," Layde shook hands, "I'm delighted to see you."

"I'm delighted to see you too, Pat. I see you're a Sergeant now."

"That's right, Mike, do you touch a hurl now at all?"

"No, Pat, I gave all that up. How about yourself?"

"I still keep my hand in. I'm on the Battalion team and I'm a sub on the Command."

"What about a drink?" Tom suggested.

"I'd love to go with you and have a good old chat, but I can't move. We're just waiting on the word to move out."

"What's up?"

"Some tip-off about an I.R.A. training camp out the road somewhere," Layde lowered his voice, "probably another wild goose chase."

"I never heard of any training camps around here. Will you be in town tonight, Pat?" Mike asked.

"I don't think so. We'll head straight back to Dublin as soon as this is over."

"Hey, Pat," a guard called from the barrack door, "you're wanted inside."

"Right, Mike, I'll have to go," Layde held out his hand.

"Good luck, Pat, I hope it's not as long the next time," Mike shook the proffered hand.

"All the best, Mike," Layde hurried into the barracks.

With studied casualness, Mike walked back towards the main street. Having turned the corner, his pace quickened and he hurried home. He jumped into the car which was parked in the driveway and drove out towards Tom's place. At the sound of the car, Tom came out into the yard.

"Have you an I.R.A. course on here?" Mike shouted through the car window.

"What are you talking about?"

"Cut the shit, Tom. There's a raiding party at the barracks in Tunnygee, ready to move out. It could be on its way here now," Mike began to turn the car.

"What are you doing?" Tom shouted over the noise of the engine.

"Getting out of here before I'm trapped in the lane," Mike shouted back.

156

"Hold on a minute. Don't go until I come out again," Tom ran into the house.

A minute later he reappeared, ushering a bemused General towards the car. He pulled open the door of the car and shoved the General in beside Mike on the front seat.

"Away with you," he ordered. "The General here will tell you where to go."

"Who the hell are you anyway?" Mike demanded, changing gears.

"I'm General Thompson O'Cleirigh."

"Of Blackhorse House?"

"That's right."

"What's a British General like you doing at an I.R.A. training camp?"

"I'm an Irish General who served in the British army. There's a distinction, you know."

"I'm quite aware of that."

"And who are you?"

"I'm Mike Houlihan from Tunnygee. I'm a friend of Tom. I served with him in the army. That does not mean that I agree with his politics. I don't. I have absolutely no time for the I.R.A."

"You are a forthright person, Mr. Houlihan, but you better turn left here if you intend delivering me to Blackhorse," the General said at the end of the lane.

Back at the farmhouse, Tom instructed one of the men to burn the blackboard on which the General had been illustrating his lecture.

"Just break it up and throw it on the kitchen fire," he ordered.

"And you there," he told another man, "get the floor swept and remove any cigarette butts."

Butsy dashed to the farmhouse with three men and brought back all the weapons.

"Why did you bring those here?" Tom demanded.

"You said yourself that the lake was the safest place, safer than the hide," Butsy explained.

"Alright, get them wrapped up and get them down to the boat. Row out about thirty yards, veering a bit to the right. There's a good deep hole there."

Gabriel O'Beirne came running into the yard. Tousle-headed and unshaven, braces over a collarless shirt, boots unlaced, he had come over the fields.

"They're the far side of the hill," he panted, "a whole lorry load of them. They're spreading out along the road, twenty soldiers at least."

"They'll be coming in from the main road too," Tom said. "I'd say we have about fifteen minutes before they reach the brow of the hill at your place, Gabriel."

"That won't give us much time to dump the arms," Butsy said.

"It gives you no time, but Gabriel here will do it. Bring them down to the boat, Gabriel,   and dump them in yon deep hole about thirty yards out," Tom instructed.

"They're a bit heavy," Butsy said, as he and another man lifted the bag of weapons.

"Show them to me here," Gabriel put his powerful arms around the bag.

"I'll manage alright," he said, breaking into a half run in the direction of the lake.

"I know you don't trust the hide, but there's not much we can do now. There's no way the lads would get through the cordon. There's nothing for it, only *The Farhouse*," Tom told Butsy.

At *The Farhouse*,the men scrambled in under the hay. Butsy went to follow them.

"Where in the name of God do you think you're going, Dwyer?" Tom half-shouted in exasperation. "Your car's in the yard. How do you think I'm going to explain it away?"

"Christ, I forgot all about it."

""A cool head is needed now," Tom said."You're just an ordinary visitor. Put the collar and winkers on the pony there and bring her over to the house. The milk has to go to the road. Let everything be as normal as possible. Just pretend you're giving Maisie a hand. If anyone asks you, say you came down on Wednesday. You come down regularly."

"Fair enough, Tom, I never thought of the bloody car."

"Go on, get the pony ready."

"Right, lads," Tom shouted in under the hay, "there are two props under the plank nearest to me. Pull them and the plank will fall down. Then the hay will come down in front here."

When the hay settled, Tom jumped up on it and, carefully, moved a few forkful towards the front. He stuck the fork back in the thatch and jumped down. He walked back towards the house, following Butsy and the pony.

Back at the house, Tom had a last look round the upper room. Butsy's revolver was on the mantelpiece. Tom grabbed it and rushed out to the yard, where Butsy was loading the two creamery cans on the sled.

"You're a right bloody eegit, Dwyer. You left that bloody revolver of yours in the room. Do you want to get us all caught?"

"I'm sorry, Tom."

"Sorry's not much good, what are we going to do with this thing?"

"Give it to me," Maisie said quietly.

"What?"

"I said, give it to me," she held out her hand.

She took the revolver, lifted the lid of one of the creamery cans and dropped the gun in. She put the lid back on and tapped the pony on the rump.

"Giddy up, Polly," she said, as the pony moved off.

Two gardai led the soldiers into the yard. Tom recognised Layde through the kitchen window.

"How are you, Pat?" he called, going out the front door.

"Hello . . . you were on the Curragh with Mike Houlihan, Burke, Tom Burke. You were a corporal in Dublin after, I heard," the Sergeant said.

"That's right. What's up?" Tom asked.

"Who is this man?" a young officer asked, walking briskly into the yard.

"He was a corporal in the army, sir. I knew him as a recruit in the Curragh, sir."

"Yes, he was a corporal in the army," one of the guards confirmed.

"I'm sorry, Tom, but we have to inspect the place on foot of a report that there is an I.R.A. training camp on your land," the guard told Tom.

"Fire away," Tom said.

"Who's in the house?" the guard asked.

"The missus and a friend of mine, another former corporal. You know him well, Butsy Dwyer. Sure, he comes to see us regularly."

"That's right, sir," the guard told the officer,"Butsy's a regular visitor. Now that I think of it, that's his car," he pointed to the Volkswagen.

"You better inspect the house, guard," the officer said.

"You don't mind, Tom, do you?" the guard looked at Tom.

"No one there, sir, only Mrs. Burke and Butsy Dwyer, just like Tom said," the guard announced a few minutes later.

"Why doesn't this Dwyer man show himself?" the officer asked.

"Any reason why he should? Isn't it enough that the guard identified him, or do you not trust Guard Maguire?" Tom asked.

"It is not a question of trust, mister. . mister . ."

"Burke, Tom Burke. Do you want to speak to Mr. Dwyer?"

"No, it's not necessary," the officer said shortly.

"Have a couple of the men search the out-offices," he turned to Layde, "And let the rest of them spread out and search the fields in the immediate vicinity."

About half-an-hour later all the soldiers and four or five guards were congregated in the yard.

"There's a house further over in the fields," one young soldier reported."There's hay in it in one part and the other part is obvious-ly used as a stable."

"No signs of occupation?" the officer snapped.

"No, sir."

"If you gentlemen are satisfied, there seems to be nothing to hold us here," the officer addressed the guards.

"We're satisfied," one of the guards said.

"Another tip-off from the know-alls in Dublin that was wide of the mark," another of them growled.

"I was talking to Mike Houlihan in town," Sergeant Layde told Tom as the others strolled off down the lane."He tells me that he never takes a hurl in his hand now at all."

"That's true, Pat, but this is not a great area for hurling."

"It's a crying shame," Layde said, "he could have been up there among the stars, if he'd kept at it. He was the equal of any of them."

"He was all that, Pat," Tom agreed.

"A shocking waste of talent," Layde shook his head as he walked off.

"Are they gone?" Butsy asked, when Tom entered the kitchen.

"I hope so."

"What about the lads?"

"Leave them for awhile. Hold it . . Is that someone outside?"

"It's only Gabriel," Maisie said from the window.

"Did you meet the soldiers?" Tom asked when he came in.

"Aye, when I dumped the stuff, I went up and sat in at the butt of the hedge at the top of the Crockaun. One of them nearly fell across me. I have one of them, he shouted, and him pointing his gun at me. He was only a skitter of a gasson. He was shaking. I just sat on my hunkers, a sort of half-laughing up at him. Then this other young fella, a long skinamalink, came over, with two or three shiny belts on him. What's your name, says he. It's none of your business, says I. It is, said he, and if you don't give me your name, I'll have to arrest you. You and how many more, says I, standing up and looking down upon him from the higher ground by the ditch. Where do you live, sir, he asked, a sort of calmer like. See that house over yonder on the hill, says I, that's where I live. And what are you doing here, he asked. I'm looking for a calf, says I. Would you mind giving me your name, sir, says he. My name is Gabriel O'Beirne, says I. I could see him looking at me. I was a sort of half laughing. You know the way I go on. . ."

"We know that alright, Gabriel," Tom said.

"Anyway, I think he thought I was a sort of half mad. He looked at me fairly tight before he walked away. They all came up here to the yard. I waited a while before I came after them."

"You did right, Gabriel," Tom told him.

"I better go over to the lads," Butsy said.

"Forget about the lads for a while. The revolver is more important. It would never do if it turned up at the creamery. I'd say Red James hasn't collected the cans yet," Tom said.

"I'll get the bicycle and go for it," Maisie suggested.

"The soldiers might still be around," Tom said.

"I can always say I'm going to the shop."

"Off you go so. Gabriel, go up to the hill behind your house and check if the soldiers are gone. You'd want to give us some sort of signal. Wave your shirt or something if they are gone," Tom suggested.

"That's what I'll do. I'll take off my shirt and wave it if they're gone," Gabriel laughed in his slightly manic way.

"You scoot up the hill behind us here and come back and let us know the situation," Tom told Butsy.

Butsy was first back, with nothing to report. Maisie returned, driving the pony before her, as she wobbled on her bicycle behind.

"I just bet Red James to it. I could hear the cart in the hollow below," she said, "I had to spill out half the milk before I got the revolver out. Here it is," she took it from the bicycle carrier.

"There's the all clear," Tom said as Gabriel frantically waved his shirt in the distance.

Butsy released his men from under the hay.

"I thought we would never get out," one of them said.

"What are you cribbing about? You were only in there for a hour altogether."

"It was too long, with about ten generations of mice crawling around," the man said.

That night, Butsy made two trips to Dublin, safely delivering the six men to their homes.

"I'm telling you, Tom, that if this is ever traced back you'll find it is her that gave the game away," Maisie told Tom.

"I don't know, Maisie. I think you're a bit hard on poor old Olga."

"You men are all the same. She can twist you all round her little finger."

"That's not fair," Tom protested.

"Fair or not, if the truth ever comes out, you'll find I'm right."

21

Butsy was back on the Monday after the raid, accompanied by Charlie Daniels. He had come to hold a court of inquiry into the cause of the raid, Charlie told Maisie.

"Where's Tom?" he asked.

"In the bog."

"Where's that?"

"Down by the lake," Maisie replied..

"Come on, I'll show you," Butsy led the way out of the yard.

At the lake shore, a barefooted Tom stood practically knee-deep in mud.

"What the hell are you at?" Butsy asked.

"This is the way we make turf in this part of the country," Tom replied.

"It looks like heavy work," Daniels said.

"It is, but you two fellas hardly came to talk about making mud turf."

"No, but I'm interested. I've heard of mud turf, but that's about all," Daniels said.

"I'll give you a quick rundown if you like," Tom offered.

"We're on business, Tom, and Charlie here ...," Butsy said.

"We can always spare a few minutes," Daniels cut in, "I'd like to know something about it."

"Right, come on up along the edge, on the left there," Tom directed, "unless you want to go to your knees in mud . That's it, come over this way to the boghole."

"That's where the mud comes from," Tom pointed down into the hole. "All you have to do is shovel it up on the bank here and then you add water and mix it until all the lumps are out of it. You have to turn it about twice or three times. You then spread it on the bank the way I've done her to a depth of about eighteen inches. All you have to do is mark it after that. That's what I'm doing now. Watch and I'll show you," Tom made his way back into the spread mud.

"You hold your hands this way," he clasped one thumb on the

other and pointed his fingers downwards, giving a dome-shaped effect. "You move backwards through the mud then, marking out the shapes of sods of turf with your domed hands, " he demonstrated. "About every eighteen inches you mark off each individual sod," he demonstrated with the side of his hand. "After that you leave it there to dry".

"How long does that take?" Daniels asked.

"That depends on the weather," Tom smiled. "Anything from a week in good drying weather to three weeks in bad weather. If the weather was real bad you might lose it altogether, but it's seldom that happens. When it's dry enough to handle, that means when it won't fall apart, you lift it."

"Lift it?" Daniels looked at him.

"That's right, and dirty, backbreaking work it is. Starting at one end, you use your hands to ease a sod free from the rest and up on its end. You do that with every sod until they're all standing on end. About ten days later when the drying stage has gone a bit further, you foot the turf. That means, you build one sod across two others, turning each of the two bottom sods in the process, to ensure that the bottom end gets a chance to dry."

"I think I'm with you," Daniels said.

"I'm nearly lost myself, Charlie, at this stage, but we're nearly finished. All that remains to be done is clamp the turf. There's the end of last year's clamp over there."

They walked over to the old clamp, and Tom lifted a sod of turf.

"Feel that, how hard it is," he handed it to Daniels."That's the finished product and it's as good as coal."

"What about the raid?" Daniels said suddenly.

"What?" Tom said.

"You heard me. What about the raid?"

"I thought you were interested in turf."

Tom turned and walked towards where his boots and socks were placed under his folded coat. He pulled on his boots, and stood up, leaving them unlaced. He put the socks in the pocket of his coat, which he threw over his shoulder, before walking off towards the house. Butsy and Daniels followed at a slower pace.

Gabriel O'Beirne was in the kitchen, sitting on the table, swinging his legs, when Tom entered the house.

"I wasn't expecting you for awhile yet," Maisie said. "Did you not meet Butsy and the other man?"

"I did. Do you know what that fella Daniels is about, inquiring about the raid?"

"He told me that."

"Who is he, anyway?" O'Beirne asked in his manic fashion. "I'll handle him, Tom, if you like."

"May we come in?" Daniels knocked on the door.

"Of course, come in," Maisie said.

I don't think I've had the pleasure of meeting you," Daniels addressed Gabriel.

"You're dead right, you had not, but we'll soon remedy that," Gabriel sprung from the table, landing out in the centre of the floor. "I'm Gabriel O'Beirne and I came over to give my friend, Tom Burke, a hand with the turf."

"It's not turf he's interested in," Tom said, "he has other things on his mind."

"Butsy told me that I might be able to use your room above, Mrs. Burke," Daniels said.

"I didn't hear your name and I told you mine," O'Beirne said to Daniels.

"Daniels," Daniels threw the answer over his shoulder.

"Were you not christened, man?"

"I'm not used to been spoken to like that," Daniels turned to Gabriel.

"Were you christened?" Gabriel repeated with his little broken laugh.

"I was."

"What were you christened then?"

"I don't think that's any business of yours."

Gabriel grabbed Daniels by the lapels of his coat and stood leering at him.

"Let him go, Gabriel. He's not worth bothering with," Tom said.

"What's his name then?" Gabriel asked

"He's Charlie Daniels," Tom told him.

"An uppity wee whipper snapper," Gabriel let Daniels go.

"What about the room?" Butsy asked.

"Fire away," Tom said.

Butsy opened the door and let Daniels go before him.

Close the door," Daniels instructed, as Butsy followed him into the room.

A few minutes later, Butsy swung open the door again.

"Tom Burke, first witness," he called.

"Listen, Butsy, will you tell that self-styled general to cop himself on. Tell him that he's holding no court of inquiry in this house, but that if he's willing to come down and sit by the fire and act like a human being, we might be willing to talk to him".

"There was a tip-off about the raid and I must find out where it came from," Daniels stood behind Butsy.

"Come down to the kitchen and we'll talk about it," Tom said.

"I think I'll head down to the bog," Gabriel said, "that's if you don't want me round here."

"No, we don't need you," Tom said.

Gabriel stared at Daniels for a moment, before going off, laughing to himself.

"How much does he know?" Daniels asked.

"Do you mind if I tell you something, Charlie?" Tom asked, "You've been here about an hour and you've got under everyone's skin. You're a Dublin jackeen, I think,"

"I'm a Dublin man, if that's what you mean."

"I mean that, but I mean more " Tom said. "I knew a lot of Dublin men in the army. All and all, they were a grand crowd of fellas, but there was always one or two of them who never understood us country lads. They seemed to look down their noses at us. I can't help but think, Charlie, that you might be one of that type of Dublin man, a self-important little bastard."

"I don't have to take that sort of abuse, Burke."

"There you go again. As Gabriel would put it, I was christened. The plain, fact Charlie, is that we are all just culchies to you, stupid culchies. That's why you come down here with a file under your arm and announce that you're holding a court of inquiry. I'm not a member of your organisation, neither is Maisie, neither is Gabriel. Who might I ask are you going to question?"

"This is where the raid took place".

"Did you go to Blackhorse House yet?"

"No."

"Do you intend going there?"

"No."

"Why not?"

"I don't believe he gave away information."

"But we did."

"I didn't say that."

"You don't have to. You trust a British army general, but you don't trust us."

"That's not true."

"If it's not true, it means you're afraid to go to the General. You know well he'd throw you out on your neck, and he'd be bloody well right too."

"Is that what you are going to do?"

"No, but we're answering no questions, no court of inquiry, but we're willing to talk about it. I told you that already."

"Alright," Daniels sat down at the table and wearily wiped his hand through his hair, "where do we begin?"

"By eliminating a few people. Gabriel O'Beirne, you don't seem to trust him. I'd depend my life on him. Maisie told no one anything and neither did I. I'm sure the same goes for Butsy and I'd say the General kept his mouth shut."

"That's grand, Tom, but as I understand it, it was a Mike Houlihan who gave you the tip-off. How did he know about the course? If he knew about it, how many others knew about it ? He's a friend of yours, Tom, and he's a friend of Butsy's too. That's why I decided to start my inquiry here."

"I suppose you have a point there, Charlie," Tom conceded.

"I think I have, even though I am a Dublin jackeen."

"Fair enough, you have us there. What do you say?" Tom turned to Butsy.

"Aye, you're right, you're right there," Butsy jerked out.

"What's wrong with you, Butsy?" Daniels asked.

"Nothing, nothing at all."

Daniels looked at him closely.

"Hold it everyone, before we go off at half-cock again. The

man we have to see is Mike. We'll call into him this evening", Tom said.

That evening, Tom drove Daniels and Butsy into Tunnygee. He pulled up at the foot of the stone steps. Sylvia answered the door.

"Oh, Tom, you are a stranger. I didn't see you in months," she greeted

"Maisie just said the same the other day, Sylvia. Mike and yourself should come out to see us sometime. Is he in, by the way?"

"He is. Guess who's here, Mike?" she shouted back into the hall. "An old friend of yours, Tom Burke."

"Bring him in," Mike's muffled voice sounded from one of the rooms.

"No, no, I've a few friends with me. I won't go in, thanks all the same, Sylvia."

"Alright, Tom, I'll tell him." Sylvia went back down the hall.

Mike sat on the back seat of the car, beside Butsy.

"This is Charlie Daniels. He's an I.R.A. man from Dublin," Tom introduced Daniels.

"You know what I think of the I.R.A., Tom ?"

"I know, but Charlie wants to ask a few questions."

"About what?"

"How did you know there was a training course in progress at the Burke farm last week?"Daniels asked.

"I didn't know."

"That's strange. How could you warn them if you didn't know?"

"I guessed."

"What do you mean?"

"Exactly what I said. I guessed that Tom would be fool enough to be involved and I knew that he was a friend of Butsy's here."

"How did Butsy come into it?" Daniels asked sharply.

"Hold it, Mr. Daniels, don't jump to any conclusions," Mike said. "I know that Butsy comes down to see Tom regularly. I know both of them well and I knew it was something that both of them might be involved in."

"And you went out to Burke's on the off-chance?"

"Of course, wasn't it lucky I did, or the two of them would be in jail now?"

"All I know is that there's a leak somewhere and that it's here in Tunnygee," Daniels said.

"I wouldn't be too sure about that, Charlie," Tom said.

"I'm sure about it," Mike declared. "The leak didn't come from here. It came from Dublin and that's straight from the horse's mouth."

"How's that?" Daniels asked.

"I was playing golf with the Garda Superintendent yesterday up in Kells and he happened to let drop that the tip-off came from Dublin."

"I just don't believe it. It couldn't have happened. Only a handful of us knew about it. The lads themselves did not know their destination until they got here."

"There were two other courses," Tom said.

"We thought of that, but none of them would know the date of this course. Anyway, we checked them all out. They're all in the clear," Daniels said.

"How can you be sure?" Tom asked.

"That's the problem, you can never be sure," Daniels admitted.

"I'll leave you, lads," Mike said. "Sylvia and I are going to a concert in Carrick tonight."

Back at his own house, Tom stopped the car at the front door.

"Listen, Charlie, will you sit there for a minute?" Butsy requested Daniels, "I want to have a private word with Tom and Maisie."

Fifteen minutes later, Tom tapped the window of the car and signalled Daniels to come into the house.

"Sit at the end of the table here," Maisie told him. "We're just going to have a cup of tea."

"Butsy wants a word with you, Charlie," Tom said.

"I think I might be the cause of the leak," Butsy scuffed the floor with his shoe.

"Go on," Daniels looked at him.

Butsy told how he had come down to Tunnygee the previous October, accompanied by Olga.

"I didn't tell her anything," he said, "but she sort of guessed there was something up."

"You must have said something to her, Butsy," Daniels said.

"As true as God is my judge, I didn't, Charlie, but she got suspicious, because I left her in the hotel and went off to see Tom on my own. She knew we were near the border too. She said to me that night that she believed I was in the I.R.A., and that so was Tom, that we were planning something. I laughed it off, but I don't think she believed me. We broke up after Christmas, I heard last week that she was doing a line with a guard."

"And you think she told him?" Daniels asked.

"It would be like what she'd do. She'd bladder away about knowing an I.R.A. man. She'd like to boast about it sort of thing," Butsy explained.

"That could explain it. I hope it does," Daniels said.

"What's going to happen now?" Butsy asked.

"We'll go back to Dublin and take it from there," Daniels told him.

***

That evening Olga answered the phone in her Ranelagh flat.

"It's me," Butsy said. "I want to talk to you."

"Oh Butsy, I'm delighted to hear from you. What do you want to talk about?"

"I'll call up to the flat."

"No, not this evening, Michael is coming. He should be here any moment."

"Is that the guard?"

"He got promotion, he is now the Sergeant."

"That's the bastard."

"No, he's not a bastard. He's a very nice man."

"That's worse."

"Are you in bad humour, darling? You sound unhappy."

"Never mind that. Listen, Olga, I want to talk to you."

"I'm all ears, darling."

"Not on the phone. Can I meet you someplace?"

"Yes, maybe. I'm not working tomorrow morning."

"I'll meet you in Searson's then about eleven o'clock."

"Searson's?"

"Yes, Searson's pub at Portobello Bridge. You know it, with the clock outside?"

Next morning, Olga, blonde hair piled carelessly on her head, came striding into Searson's and plonked a kiss on Butsy's cheek.

"I love a mystery," she said, "and I had no breakfast, Butsy. I would love one of those Irish coffees."

"You always had expensive tastes," Butsy signalled to the barman.

"What is so serious that you could not talk about it on the phone?" Olga asked.

"Some people think that you're an informer, Olga."

"What do you mean?"

"Answer me straight, did you tell that policeman friend of yours that I was in the I.R.A.?"

"How could I? I didn't know."

"But you guessed?"

"Maybe I did."

"Aye, and what you didn't know you made up."

"That's not fair, Butsy."

"But you blabbed. I know you too well, Olga. You told him something."

"I didn't mention your name."

"What did you mention then?"

"I just told him that I thought an old boyfriend of mine was a member of the I.R.A."

"Yes?"

"And . . . and I talked about Tunnygee. I told him that a friend of ours, Tom Burke, lived there."

"How stupid can you get?" Butsy asked in disgust.

"But we were just chatting, Butsy. It was not a serious conversation. Michael was not even very interested. he did not ask any questions, not even one."

"He didn't have to, with you babbling away at his elbow."

"Oh, Butsy, I'm very sorry. Did something happen?"

"You might say that. Tom's place was raided just because you couldn't keep your mouth shut."

"I really am very sorry," she reached forward and gripped Butsy's hand.

"And so you should be," he half-grinned.

"You're not angry with me, darling," she smiled at him.

"I'm bloody sure I'm angry with you," he said.

Daniels waited for Butsy in the back garden of a house in Templeogue that afternoon. Seated on a garden bench close to the high laurel hedge, he was stiffly erect, white shirt spotless in the May sunshine. The jacket of his suit was neatly folded on the bench beside him.

"It was her," Butsy said, standing in front of him

"Informers, the scum of the earth, I hate them," Daniels spat out.

"Be fair now, Charlie. Olga's no informer."

"What is she then?"

"It was an accident, Charlie. She was just talking, boasting that she knew an I.R.A. man, a sort of. She meant no harm. She didn't get paid or anything," Butsy attempted to explain.

"Forget the explanations. Just have her here at nine this evening," Daniels ordered.

"I told you, Charlie, she meant no harm."

"Listen, Butsy, I'm not concerned with what she meant. Her state of mind doesn't matter one whit to me. Not only did she compromise the Tunnygee set up, but good men could have been captured or even killed. It wasn't her fault that didn't happen. And we can never use the Burke place again. Let yourself and herself be here at nine this evening. Both of you have questions to answer".

"Supposing we don't turn up?" Butsy asked.

"That's up to you", Daniels said curtly.

"We could take the boat, Charlie."

"If I was in your shoes I might just do that, Butsy."

That evening, Daniels sat in a public house on the Dublin quays, from where he could observe the Liverpool boat. He watched as the taxi dropped Butsy and Olga and sat until the boat moved down the river. He then went to the telephone and dialled a number.

"Is that you, Chief? Daniels speaking, " he said curtly.

"I've tied up that leak business," he continued after a pause. "The birds have flown. I'll have a full report tomorrow."

On the following Sunday, Tom and Maisie returned from

Mass to find Daniels leaning across the field gate, scratching behind the pony's ear.

"It's only me," he said, walking towards them.

"Where did you spring from? Is Butsy with you?" he asked.

"No. I'd say that Butsy's in London at this stage."

"What are you talking about?"

"He went to England on Tuesday last, himself and his blonde friend, Olga."

"Why?"

"She was the guilty party. She spilled the beans."

"And you let her go to England?"

"Shall I say that I created the circumstances where both of them could go to England. Butsy was in trouble too, you know, and he was a member of the organisation. They had a few hours to get out and they took it. A nod was as good as a wink to Butsy."

"Would they have been court-martialled?"

"Butsy would have, anyhow. As I said, he was a member of the organisation and he was responsible for jeopardising a very successful operation. It could have gone hard enough on him. That's why I gave them the chance to get out."

"And you came down to tell us?" Tom queried.

"I did."

"You have a heart in there," Tom tapped his forefinger on Daniel's chest, "even though you are a Dublin jackeen. Butsy's a good friend of mine and...and.....and I appreciate what you did, Charlie."

"Go on, finish it. You were going to say that you have a soft spot for Olga too," Maisie nudged Tom,"But what did I tell you, if the truth ever came out you'd find that it was the bold Olga who gave the game away?"

"I don't think she was an informer, not a real one anyway," Daniels said.

"I suppose to be fair, she just gets it hard to keep her mouth shut," Maisie agreed.

22

A month later, Butsy wrote to Tom and Maisie that Olga and he had got married in a London registry office.

"I wanted to have a proper marriage," Butsy wrote, "the works, white veil and all in the chapel, but Olga wouldn't hear of it. She'll get married properly, she says, when they let her back to Ireland. Then we'll do what Jack Doyle and Movita did, she says, we'll get married in Westland Row."

A son was born in the following March.

"What else could we do but call him Patrick," Butsy wrote, "But he's no Paddy. He's a real Norwegian, the spitting image of Olga, with a fuzz of white hair on the top of his head."

Two years later, at the end of April, Butsy announced the arrival of a daughter, Marie.

"And here are we married for six years, and us with neither chick nor child," Maisie declared the morning the letter arrived.

"Plenty of chickens out in the yard," Tom was jocose.

"That's not one bit funny. You're just as insensitive as the rest of them."

"I was only joking, Maisie. I was only joking."

"It's no joke to me and it should be no joke to you either. I went to the doctor and you didn't. It could be your fault."

"What are you talking about?"

"I know what I'm talking about. It's unfair that yon big cow of an Olga should have two children and us with none."

"And you want me to go to the doctor?"

"I don't want you to go anywhere."

"You think there's something wrong with me?"

"I don't."

"You do."

"Are you afraid to go to the doctor?"

"No, I'm not."

"Why don't you go then?" she stood up, knocking a cup from the table.

"Now, look what you've done" he demanded.

174

"It's only a bloody cup," she kicked at a broken piece with her toeless shoe.

Blood spurted from her big toe.

"That's all your fault," she shouted.

"Don't be ridiculous," he retorted.

She ran at him where he sat in the chair and beat a tattoo on the top of his head with both hands, as the tears streamed down her face. Suddenly, she stopped and ran to the bedroom, bolting the door after her. Tom heard the creak of the bed as she threw herself on it. He listened to her sobbing for awhile before knocking on the door.

"Is that foot still bleeding?" he called.

"A lot you care," she mumbled.

"What did you say?" he asked.

"A lot you care," she shouted.

"I don't want you to destroy the bed. I've to sleep in it too, you know."

"For all the good you are."

"What did you say?"

"For all the good you are," she half chuckled.

"Come on, open the door," he called.

She opened the door and stood in front of him, wiping tears from her eyes.

"I'm sorry," she said, with a trace of a smile.

"Come on," he took her by the arm, "that toe is still bleeding. We'll have to get a bandage on it."

Tom went into town that evening. He had a half intention of going to the doctor, but he had not the courage to face the cynical "wee specialist". Instead, he went to Kelly's. McGinty and Tracker were there and Mike arrived, having come in on the Dublin bus. Mike had the evening paper with him, which he spread out on the counter to read.

"See where they finally sent poor old Caryl Chessman to the gas chamber," he said. "What time is it now? A quarter to nine. It was all over nearly three hours ago. He was scheduled to die at six o'clock Irish time in San Quentin Prison, California. It was the ninth date set for his execution."

"He made a quare fight for it," Jimmy Kelly said. "It's a terror to keep a man in Death Row for twelve years. There's nothing right about that."

"How many did he kill?" McGinty asked.

"That's the funny thing about it, he killed no one," Kelly said.

"What was he sentenced for, then?"

"He was sentenced for kidnapping and rape. There were seventeen charges against him. He was sentenced to death for the kidnapping," Kelly explained.

"The Red Light Bandit, he claims he was innocent, but whether he was or not, twelve years was too long to keep him on Death Row," Tom said.

"You seem to be fairly well up on him," Kelly commented.

"Like yourself, I read the papers an odd time," Tom told him.

"I don't think he's innocent," Mike cut in. "I got a book in the library a couple of weeks ago and it tells the whole story. He was as guilty as hell, I would say, He was a right blackguard."

"Maybe he was, but twelve years on Death Row, that was twelve years of torture." Tom persisted.

"He's played the law. That's what the judge that tried the case said. I was only reading it the other night. As the judge saw it, if the death penalty was going to be rescinded, just because Chessman could write and get a book published, we might as well forget about the law," Mike explained.

"Come off it, Mike. Being in the bank doesn't mean that you have to support the death penalty."

"You know bloody well, Tom. I'm not supporting any death penalty. I'm only telling you what I read."

"Will you stop prodding him, Tom, and let him talk. What did your man do anyway?" McGinty asked.

"Well, one of the lassies, that your man is supposed to have raped, is in a mental hospital ever since. She was only seventeen at the time."

"Jasus, any fella that done that deserves to swing. If it was me I'd castrate the bastard first," the hitherto silent Tracker declared.

"Whether he was guilty or not, he was a quare bucko. He deserved to swing," McGinty drained his glass.

"Good man, Johny," Jimmy Kelly laughed. "No better man to put the tin hat on it."

176

"Aye, you're right, Jimmy, but will you put up two more bottles and Tracker'll pay you. You'd think he was handcuffed, sitting looking at two empty glasses."

"It's your turn, McGinty," Tracker said.

"Fair enough, Tracker," McGinty banged out three pennies on the counter. "Give us tuppence worth of porter, Jimmy, and let Tracker keep the change."

"Give us two more bottles, Jimmy," Tracker said with resignation.

"As a matter of interest," Kelly put the two bottles on the counter, "Chessman didn't get the rope, he went to the gas chamber."

"Did you ever see a man hung?" McGinty asked.

"No, did you?" Kelly asked.

"I did. Do you remember round the end of the war, the lad that hung himself in the cottage below at the end of the town."

"Aye, I remember him well, a dacent wee divil he was," Kelly said.

"Well, I saw him before they took him down. There he was hanging from the rafters and his neck was two foot long."

"Get away out of that, Willie, how could it be two foot long?"

"Well, Jimmy, if it wasn't, it was a good foot anyway."

"Good man, Willie, no better man," Mike laughed.

"The death penalty, it's a terrible sentence. It should be abolished," Tom said.

"You'll be glad to know that no less a person than Governor Brown of California agrees with you. He's quoted right here in the paper: *I regret equally every execution in California, past and future, including the one today. My personal opposition to capital punishment remains as profound as ever.* There you are, no less a person than the Governor and yourself think the same way, Tom," Mike said.

"Well, I'll tell you one thing," McGinty asserted, "Dev should never have hung the Republicans."

"What could he do? He had to keep order," Mike said.

"I agree with Willie," Tom said, "if he'd put them in jail and let them out after the war, he might have saved himself a lot of trouble."

"What do you mean?" Mike asked.

"He mightn't have been thrown out of power in '48?"

"How's that?"

"Wasn't it Republicans, most of them Fianna Fail men, who supported McBride and his party," Tom replied.

"What about the teachers? It was the teachers that made the Clann and you know that," Mike said.

"Yes, they were the front men, but the grassroots support came from the Republican Fianna Failers, the men and women who objected to internment and the executions. They put McBride's ten Clann na Poblachta men in in 1948 and they put them out again in 1951, just because McBride entered into a coalition with Fine Gael."

"I don't think it was as simple as that, Tom," Mike said.

"Fair enough, Mike, but I've heard no other explanation for the sudden rise of McBride in 1948, winning ten seats and, then, the sudden drop to two in 1951."

"I think Tom's right," Jimmy Kelly said. "Sure, I voted for Tully myself in 1948 and most of the others round here, who did the same, were Fianna Fail men too. But it stuck in our craw when McBride went in with Fine Gael. A good few of us stuck with Tully in this part of the country - he's a dacent man and good Republican - but the heart had gone out of us as far as McBride was concerned."

"God, you're the right traitor, Jimmy. I'm proud to say that I never changed my colours. Since I joined Fianna Fail at the first meeting in this town in 1926 I've soldiered under the same flag. McBride didn't cod Duff," Tracker declared, "Fianna Fail never struck the Republican colours. We never joined with the Fine Gael Blueshirts."

"Good man, Tracker, you were never a *souper**. You never sold out for the *Indian male* *and *hairy bacon**," Willie emptied his glass and put it back on the counter with deliberate ostentation.

"You think the soft soap will get you another drink," Tracker said.

* Refers to people who allegedly changed religion for food in the 19th century

178

"Aye, another one wouldn't go astray. Anyway, I'll have money tomorrow. I've a few bob to collect from old McClelland."

"Are you still tricking with him, the bloody Orangeman?"

"Damn the hate wrong with him. It's a great house for a feed. More than can be said for some of the Catholic places. I had a feed in it last Friday that would do your heart good."

"What did they give you, Willie?" Mike asked.

"A plate of cabbage and nearly a pound of boiling bacon. My mouth tightens up yet when I think of it."

"But Friday's a fast day. You didn't eat meat on a Friday?" Jimmy Kelly queried.

"What are you talking about?" Willie demanded.

"You can't eat meat on Friday. It's a sin, against the law of the Church."

"It's alright for you, Jimmy, with meat on your plate every day of the week. It's different for fellas like me, with every day a fast day except the day you get a dinner on a plate."

"But it's a sin," Jimmy persisted.

"It's no sin for me. I'd be lucky if I got meat twice in the week."

"You fast five days a week against Jimmy's one. I think we'll absolve you," Mike assured him, "but do you know that they are allowed to eat barnacle geese on fast days in the diocese of Kerry?"

"Not a word of truth in it," Tracker declared. "You couldn't have a differ between one part of the country and the next. The church is universal, didn't you learn that from the penny cathecism?"

"They still eat barnacle geese on a fast day in Kerry. Did you ever hear that, Tom?" Mike asked.

"I did. I knew a couple of Kerry fellas in the army and they swore it was true."

"I don't believe it," Tracker said.

"Do you believe this?" McGinty held up his empty glass.

"What?"

"The glass, it's empty for the last half hour," Willie said.

"Go to blazes, McGinty, I'm going home," Tracker moved away from the counter.

"Just a minute, Tracker, before you go off in a huff," Willie said.

"I'm in no huff."

"Well, hold on a minute so. Do you want to know why they eat geese in Kerry on fast days?"

"A lot you know about it, McGinty."

"Alright, so you don't want to hear it, or maybe you think you might have to buy again."

"Go on, Jimmy, give us two more. It might shut his mouth," Tracker ordered.

"I knew you had it in you, but you're puzzled about the geese too," Johny carefully poured his bottle.

"Tell us, then."

"Don't you know that them Kerry geese eat fish and you're allowed to eat fish on a fast day. Eating them geese is the same as eating fish."

"Bullshit," Tracker declared.

"But, it's true, Tracker," Mike laughed, "that's the reason as far as I know."

"And you all thought Willie McGinty had no head on him. Now you know, he knows more than you think," Willie grinned over his stout.

Maisie was in bed when Tom got home. She grunted in her sleep and turned towards him, when he got in beside her.

"Did you go to the doctor?" she muttered.

"No, why should I?"

"I'm glad you didn't. Tom. I'm sorry for what I said."

"How's the toe?" he asked.

"As sore as bedamned, but it's stopped bleeding."

"I suppose I should see the doctor?" Tom said.

"Ah, not at all, Tom, we'll wait for another while."

23

In the June of the following year, Tom went to Cavan to buy a new cow. The man he hired to bring the animal home was not available until late in the evening and, when the cow was eventually tied in the byre, it was close to nine o'clock. When he entered the house, Maisie sat engrossed in front of a television set.

"It arrived today," she said, "And Josie Tynan put up the aerial on the old tree at the back. Isn't it a grand picture?"

A short religious programme followed the news. When it ended, syncopated sales music burst through and an advertisement flashed on the screen. Clean, painless removal of hair guaranteed with Ditzo. The model's head was hirsute enough, if sleek and well groomed, but the rest of her was suitably hairless, from the artistic shot of a shoulder blade with the hint of a breast underneath the arm, down to the coyly placed, shapely leg. The towel, draped over the thigh, would cover little if she were to turn round, but the niceties were observed and the viewers were left guessing. A quick fade-out and the lady was gone with her story half told, but the message was clear: use Ditzo if you want a hairless body. A new picture fluttered into focus and *Weekly Round-Up* was under way. The American girl was first. Yes, she was half Irish, entitled to an Irish passport, she giggled. She would love an Irish passport, but she wanted to keep her American one also.

"Have her bread and eat it," Tom muttered.

"Shush," Maisie said.

"Grandmother was a Murphy from Kildare and grandfather was a Kane from Cavan. She was enjoying her visit to Ireland immensely. The people were just as hospitable as she had been led to believe. Dublin was a wonderful city. The singing pubs were marvellous. The singers were so brashly uninhibited. Wonderful, just wonderful.....That's right, she guessed that she was a singer.

She was especially interested in traditional singing. No, she had not appeared on television as a singer, but she would certainly welcome the opportunity. Yes, thank you very much, she hoped some producer would have similiar ideas.

"Thank you, Miss Hanson, I hope you enjoy the remainder of your stay equally well."

"I sure will. I just love this little, old, green isle of yours."

"All we want now are the fairies," Tom said.

"That's not fair, Tom. The poor girl was only doing her best," Maisie laughed, pouring boiling water into the teapot.

The showband was good and the lead singer was jerkily confident, soaring towards the top of the hit parade once again. The latest hit, sure, here goes. He still loved her, but more and more, and forever, and ever their lives would interwine. No, the band had not toured the States yet, but it expected to do so in the Autumn. Yes, of course, coast to coast, all the way from the Statue of Liberty to the Golden Gates. Yes, they hopped over to England every second week. In fact, they were booked into the Hippodrome in Birmingham on Sunday next. The singer drove a Mercedes now. He traded in the Jag last week.

Mrs. Cusack made lampshades. It started as a hobby. Now, it was big business. Her husband had given up his job and the garage was a fullscale workshop. They would have to expand soon. A factory on the outskirts of the city was a distinct possibility.

The soapsuds obliterated Mrs. Cusack's smiling face. It was detergent time again. Ours washes whiter, so white that even a dead man would sit up and take notice. Whiteness to dazzle, but legs are important too. They look lovelier in salmon pink, treble-stretch. No depilatory necessary with salmon-pink. Ditzo be damned. Let salmon pink give your legs, hair and all, that healthy, rosy glow, so natural and so chic. A quick flicker and a new advertisement is on. Our filtertips are dipped in genuine fifteen-year-old. Guaranteed to remove all impurities. Careful not to light the wrong end though. They might explode. The man took his first satisfied pull.

"Sit over," Maisie poured the tea.

Tom sat at the table, eating automatically, eyes on the television screen, until Maisie walked over and switched it off.

"What did you do that for?" Tom demanded.

182

"I want to talk to you," she flounced back to her chair and sat smiling at him.

"What's got into you,? You're like the cat that's swallowed the cream."

"I'm going to have a baby," she announced.

"I don't believe you," he jumped up , took her in his arms and waltzed her around the floor.

Suddenly, he threw his arms up in the air and, with fists clenched, he let out a wild cheer.

"I knew you could do it, Maisie, I knew you could do it," he exulted.

"And I knew you could do it too," Maisie put her arms around his waist and buried her head in his shoulder.

"I'm delighted, I couldn't be more delighted," he told her.

"You're squeezing the life out of me," she laughed.

"But are you sure? How do you know it's true?" he asked.

"I went in to see Carroll today."

"What did the wee specialist say?"

"What the hell do you think it is, woman? It could be nothing else only a baby," she attempted to imitate the doctor's gruff tones, before breaking down in laughter.

"And I gave him a kiss on the cheek," she blurted between bursts of laughter.

"I'd love to have seen his face," Tom laughed.

"He took it well, with a sort of half grin on him and then... then, says he, there's murder where they are and there's murder where they're not. What, I said, looking at him openmouthed. There was a woman in here the other day, he said slowly, fifteen years married, and she has eleven children. Here's you, after seven or eight years, only with one on the way. That's what I meant, I suppose. Nature's strange. There's either a feast or a famine. There's no in-between"

"What was he talking about?" Tom asked.

"Where there's children......."

"I know, I know, but one will satisfy me......for the time being anyway," he grinned down at her, "but I might start kicking up trouble if you stop there though."

Maisie was accustomed to riding the pony bare backed around

the farm, the animal invariably contenting himself with a sedate walk. On one occasion in the previous summer, the pony had run away and reached the main road before the terrified Maisie succeeded in bringing her under control. It was never fully explained why the pony ran away. She was never known to have done it before and she did not do it afterwards, even though Maisie continued to ride her regularly. On the day after she announced her pregnancy, she rode the pony out to the field where Tom was working.

"I don't think you should be riding that fella" Tom said.

"It's like sitting in an armchair, the way she danders along. It's safe enough," she said.

"She ran away before. She could run away again."

"Don't be such an old fuddy-duddy," Maisie laughed.

"You can't be too careful, the way.... the way you are now," he said.

"Don't worry. Do you hear that, Polly, he doesn't trust you," she patted the pony's neck.

In September, she went out one morning to catch the pony to bring the milk to the road. She mounted her on the way back to the yard and they were just a few yards from the gate, when a hen flew out from the hedge, pursued by the rooster, practically under the pony's front feet. The pony reared up and Maisie, sitting carelessly and unprepared, was thrown. In the yard, Tom heard the commotion and, then, the riderless pony appeared at the gate. When Tom opened the gate, he saw the sprawled figure of Maisie., She was semi-conscious and groaning. He picked her up and brought her into the house, laying her on the bed. She was deathly pale, but her lips were moving.

"Get the doctor, get the doctor," she whispered, when he bent down towards her, "I have a terrible pain. I think I'm going to lose the baby."

Within the hour, the doctor arrived, but there was nothing he could do. Maisie had already lost the baby.

For a month afterwards, she went about pale and lifeless, and, when alone with Tom, burst into tears on the slightest provocation. When he tried to touch her, she pulled away and, at night, she rolled up in a ball in the bed, cold and unyielding. One day Tom met the doctor in town and suggested that he might call out to see her. He did so on on the following day and advised Maisie to have another baby.

"It took me years to have the last one," she muttered.

"But you've got the knack of it now. You'll have the next one in no time,"he told her.

"I hope you're right," she gave him a hesitant, forlorn smile.

Within a month, she was pregnant again and a son was born in the following July. Father Edward McCaffrey was home on holidays from his English parish and, on the Sunday, he officiated at a special afternoon baptism. Among the guests were Tom's grandparents, the old man, then over ninety, still hobbling on his sticks, but lively enough and cackling away over his one stump of a tooth. His wife did not stand it half as well. She was like a little bird, wispy, white hair half covering a pale, delicate skull, with her once tart tongue silenced. Their daughter, Tom's Aunt Bernadette, looked well, her face rounder, but still beautiful, in its dark-complexioned way. Her big stolid husband, Paul, was as quietly good-humoured as ever. Bernadette congratulated Maisie and asked if she could hold the baby in her arms.

"Wouldn't you love to have a wee baby like that?" she looked up at Paul.

"I would," he said simply.

"I think it's too late for us now, Paul."

"I think it is," he agreed.

Maisie's father, Pat, was more bent than ever, but he had a new pipe with a crooked stem, which he smoked incessantly. Mary Dempsey had changed little since the wedding. She was still apple-cheeked, although the blonde hair was fading quickly to grey. She was immensely proud of her latest grandchild, fussing over it during the ceremony.

"Isn't he the grand wee man, with the chubby cheeks on him?" she poked at him, adding as she looked across at her daughter, "he's the death spit of your father, Maisie".

Maisie glanced quickly at her father and turned to smile at Tom. Peadar Kennedy caught her eye and smiled too. Johny and Alice McCaffrey grinned also. Jimmy Kelly and his wife, Joan, were talking to Tracker, who stood twisting his hat in his hands , the high, bald crown of of his head white over the red face.

McGinty stood beside them, his cap shoved into his overcoat pocket. Butsy and Olga arrived late, home from England for the first time since the raid.

Mike and Sylvia were Godparents and the baby was christened Thomas Patrick, after his father and my father, Maisie said; after me and my Uncle Pakie, Tom insisted, smiling at Maisie, having gone through the charade of ensuring that Pat or Mary Dempsey were not in earshot.

"No Burke was ever that good looking," Maisie whispered.

After the ceremony, the party adjourned to Kelly's, where Jimmy had closed the bar for the day. Upstairs, in the dining room, his wife had several plates of sandwiches, each covered with a damp teacloth, ready. Jimmy opened a well-stocked sideboard. McGinty took off his cap and blessed himself when he saw it. He then put his cap back on again and rubbed his hands in anticipation, winking at Tracker at least three times. Mary Dempsey bustled around between the dining room and the kitchen next door, helping Mrs. Kelly to make tea. Jimmy Kelly started the men off with a glass of whiskey and served port to the women. Olga handed her glass of port back, saying she wanted whiskey instead.

"I'm sorry, Olga," Jimmy said, "I should have known that you drank whiskey."

Shortly after the tea and sandwiches were served, the Burke and Dempsey families went home.

"How long are you staying for?" Tom asked Butsy.

"We're going back on Saturday".

"What about the I.R.A.? There's no danger, is there?"

"I took no chances there, Tom. When the Movement announced the end of the campaign in February, I wrote to Charlie Daniels. To give him his due, he replied straight away. The war was over, he said, there was no longer any reason why we should not return home. He's a decent enough fella," Butsy said.

"Not a bad fella at all," Tom agreed.

Peadar Kennedy stood on the fringe of a group that included Tracker, McGinty and Olga, the three of them in high good humour. Peadar caught Tom's eye and beckoned him one side.

"I'd like to have a private word with you," he told Tom.

They went downstairs to the deserted bar, where Peadar came

quickly to the point.

"Do you know that Jimmy's thinking of selling this place?" he asked.

"I heard that rumour. He's not getting any younger, I suppose."

"How would you like to take it over?"

"Me.....It never even struck me."

"It's a good business."

"I know it is, but where would I get the money to buy a place like this?"

"Your son and my grandson was baptised the day. As far as I'm concerned, that's a big occasion, and I'm not short of a few bob, you know. To put it in a nutshell, I'd like to buy this place for you and your son."

"God, Peadar, I don't know what to say. It's too much, it's too much altogether."

"I'm your father."

"I know."

"Well, shake on it so," Peadar held out his hand.

"Hold on a minute. I better have a word with Maisie first."

"She's at home in bed," Peadar objected.

"I know, but I'd like to talk to her.

"No better time than now. I've the car outside the door," Peadar suggested

"What about the crowd upstairs?" Tom asked.

"We'll be out and back before they know it. Come on," Peadar pulled open the shop door.

Maisie was sitting by the fire when Tom and Peadar arrived.

"You are supposed to be in bed," Tom said.

"Don't worry, I'm fine," she assured him.

"You're a bit of a stranger here" she greeted Kennedy.

"Peadar wants to talk to you," Tom said.

"Where's the baby?" Maisie asked."He's due a feed, you know."

"Mike and Sylvia will bring him home."

"You should have brought him with you."

"I know, I'll go in for him if you like, but, before I do, I've news for you. Peadar wants to buy Kelly's pub for us."

"What?"

"That's right, Maisie," Peadar said,

"To celebrate the birth of my grandson, I would like to purchase Kelly's pub for Tom and you."

"I don't believe it," Maisie said.

"It's true. You just say the word and I'll arrange an immediate purchase."

"All I want is the baby. He's nearly an hour overdue and the milk is running out of me."

"What about the pub?" Tom asked.

"I want my baby. Where's my baby? Something happened him. Why did you come home without him? Something happened."

"Nothing happened. We only came to ask about the pub," Tom attempted to assure her.

"It's an excuse. There's something wrong. I want my baby. Get my baby."

"We'll get your baby. We'll be back in about ten minutes. Come on," Peadar took Tom by the arm.

"I'm going with you," Maisie said.

In Tunnygee, Sylvia brought the baby out to Maisie in the back seat of Peadar's car.

"Oh, Sylvia, I thought there was something worng, when Tom came home without him. I'm sorry, I really am sorry," she turned to Tom on the seat beside her, with tears in her eyes.

Peadar drove them home and when Maisie had the baby fed and settled, she made tea.

"I'm sorry we frightened you this evening," Peadar said as they finished the meal.

"It was my fault, Peadar. I was a bit hysterical, I think, but I really did think that something had happened."

"And we thought we were the bearers of good news," Peadar laughed.

"But you were. Of course, you were. I can't believe that you want to buy the pub for us, Peadar."

"I'm buying it for my grandson," he told her.

24

The following May, the Burkes moved into Tunnygee and took over Kelly's bar. The sale, at £3,500, had gone through quickly enough, but Mrs. Kelly wanted a house in the Wicklow seaside resort of Bray, and it was months before she found the bungalow she desired on Bray's Meath Road. In the meantime, Butsy, Olga and the two children had returned from England. It was arranged that they would occupy the Burke farmhouse, but when they arrived in April, the Kelly pub was not yet vacated. Consequently, the Burke household was overcrowded for a few weeks, but it emerged, during this period that Butsy and Olga were very much at home on the land. Originally, the Burkes intended to sell the stock and let the land, but when the Dywers showed such an aptitude for farming, arrangements were made to have them run the farm as it stood.

The pub reopened under Burke management on the first Friday in June. Butsy was there, but Olga did not attend. One of the cows was due to calve that night and she stayed at home. Butsy left the bar after midnight and his car crossed the hedge a mile outside the town. A following car stopped, but when Butsy was taken from the practically undamaged crashed vehicle, he was dead. He had a broken neck.

The full shock of Butsy's death did not hit Olga until some days after the burial, but, when it did, it affected her grievously. Within a short space of time, the outspoken effervescence that characterised her was replaced by the dour sullenness of depression. Either Tom or Maisie, and sometimes both, went out to see her practically everyday, but before their eyes, she faded and the big body sagged more and more. The facial muscles drooped around the blue Scandinavian eyes, the despair in which reflected the depth of her grief. Her only consolation was to talk of Butsy. Both Maisie and Tom noticed that when conversation turned to him she brightened up considerably.

"He was a good Irishman," Maisie commented casually one evening, as Olga reminisced about Butsy's I.R.A. days.

"No, Maisie, he was a great Irishman," Olga corrected her, "I will tell that to my children and teach them to be proud of their father, a fighter for Irish freedom."

"Another Dan Breen," Maisie said, somewhat facetiously.

"Sorry, Maisie, what did you say?" Olga asked with something of her old sharpness.

"Oh, nothing, Olga, nothing really, only....just that what you said about Butsy reminded me of Dan Breen."

"Who was he?"

"An Irish hero, a great fighter during the War of Independence. He wrote a book about it, *My Fight For Irish Freedom.*"

"I'd like to read that," Olga said.

Next evening, Tom brought the book out to Olga. Two days later, she was in the pub for the first time since the death, the Breen book in her hand.

"It was great. I only finished it an hour ago. I wonder could I keep it for another while. I'd like to read it to Patrick," she said, emotion in her voice.

"He might be a bit young yet," Tom looked at her, "but I'll tell you what, I 'll give you a present of it."

Tom gave her the loan of his copy of *Guerilla Days in Ireland* by Tom Barry that evening also, and all during the summer she avidly read books on revolutionary Ireland. It gave her a new purpose in life and the desolation and grief that had engulfed her in the aftermath of the death was so effectively ameliorated that she even resumed swimming. From her arrival at the farmhouse, Olga had gone swimming in the lake every morning. She had ceased doing so when Butsy died. It was September when she started again and there was already an autumnal nip in the air, but Olga continued swimming until the first week in November.

Over the Christmas period, Olga and the children moved in to stay with Tom and Maisie in the pub, Tom going out every day to look after the stock. Going back to the farm in the New Year, Olga was practically her old self. She was happy that spring, although she was vaguely disturbed and uncomfortable, when, on the odd occasion, her neighbour from the other side of the lake, Gabriel O'

Beirne, called and sat for an hour or two, not saying much, but grinning at her across the hearth.

She went for her first early morning swim in May and because of the remoteness of the lake and the early hour at which she swam she went unnoticed until mid-August. One morning, shortly after dawn, Gabriel O'Beirne went pike fishing. He was on his third cast when he heard the splash of Olga diving into the water. He took cover in a clump of willows as she came stroking strongly up the lake. Most mornings after that, he was at the lake and watched as she threw her old terry-cloth dressing gown over a bush, stretched both arms above her head and dived naked into the water. Towards the end of September, the early morning swims ceased. Gabriel waited a fortnight before walking over to Olga's one night.

Olga was brushing her hair at the fire when, after a peremptory tap, Gabriel lifted the latch on the door and walked into the kitchen.

"It's only me," he said.

"You frightened me. You shouldn't have walked in like that," she said, half rising from her chair.

"I wouldn't say you frighten that easy," he stood, grinning inanely at her.

"What do you want, Gabriel?"

"I just want to have a wee chat with you," he took the chair on the other side of the hearth.

"I am waiting to hear what you want, Gabriel."

"I seen you swimming in the lake."

"So......!"

"I seen you with the arms stretched above your head like a big white statue before you dived and I said to myself, so I did, there's a woman for you, Gabriel, a fine big lump of a woman as strong as yourself."

"I'm surprised to learn you are a peeping Tom, Gabriel."

"I'm no peeping Tom, Olga," he grinned, "I only watched you swimming and I said to myself that's the woman I'm going to marry. Will you marry me?"

"I....I don't know," Olga stammered, for once at a loss,"Butsy is not long dead."

"Aye, but I'd wait.Maybe you're still in mourning."

"It's not that, Gabriel, but I don't think I want to marry anyone again."

"That would be a waste, a fine woman like yourself. And you could do worse than marrying Gabriel, girl. I'm a finer man than Butsy, you know, and....I've money in the bank and there's over thirty acres in that bit of land across the lake yonder."

"But I loved Butsy, Gabriel."

"And he wasn't half the man I am," Gabriel did not even hear her. "I'm fifteen stone weight, you know, and not an extra pound on me," he stood up, expanding his chest and flexing his biceps.

"But I don't want to marry anyone. It's too soon to even think about it."

"It's too soon to do it, but not too soon to think about it," Gabriel chortled, still standing with his arms muscles flexed.

"See that," he bent down suddenly and touched his toes; "I'm as fit as a fiddle. Fifteen stone of muscle and bone and no man in the country better equipped."

"You are a......fine man, Gabriel."

"You'll marry me so?"

"I'll have to have more time to think."

"That's what I said, think about it. That's all I'm asking. I only want to have me spake in early. There'll be plenty more smelling around." Gabriel stood looking down at her.

"Oh, God, I hope not. I think you should go home now, Gabriel."

"Aye, I'll go, Olga, but I'll be back."

On the following Friday, Olga attended a function in Tunnygee Community Hall, organised by the G.A.A. to honour the Tunnygee hurling team which had won the county title earlier in the year. Mike, of course, was one of the heroes and at the presentation of medals that night, he was lauded not only as a star of the team, but also as an inspiration to the youth of the town and district.

"Mike Houlihan may be a veteran," the club chairman enthused, "but his dedicated skill still permits him to show a trick or two to young lads twenty years his junior. Mike may be a Dublin Jackeen by accident of birth, but, after his exploits on the field of play, Tunnygee has taken him to its heart. We now declare him one of our own. I am proud to stand up here tonight and honour a true sportsman, a gentleman both on and off the field....."

"Bejasus, Mike, you'll be going for election yet, "Tracker declared in Tom's pub that night.

"And what's more, he'll get in too," Johny McCaffrey asserted, "that's if he joins the right party."

"If he stands for the Soldiers of Destiny, he'll head the poll and when you do, Mike, there'll be no man prouder than me to carry you shoulder-high through the town," Tracker squeezed his moustache dry between thumb and forefinger.

"Don't let Tracker lead you astray, Mike," McCaffrey advised good-humouredly. "Never mind that old died-in-the-wool Fianna Failer. Fine Gael's the party for you, Mike, me boy."

"Fine Gael, me arse, all blueshirts, every one of them. Not one of them wouldn't sell his mother," Tracker glared round him, his face purply-red under the hat."As true as God is my judge, Houlihan," he continued in a strident voice, his eyes bulging from a suffused face. "If you join that crowd, I'll never talk to you again."

"Quit that, Tracker," Willie McGinty caught him by the arm and pulled him to the seat.

"Where are they?" McGinty plunged his fingers into Tracker's waistcoat pocket and pulled out a small box of tablets.

"Give us a glass of water," he called to Tom behind the bar, pushing a tablet into Tracker's mouth.

Some minutes later, Tracker was back at the counter.

"Give us another drop of water, Tom, and...and a bottle a stout for Willie," he said quietly.

"You can take off that long face now, Johny," he told McCaffrey, "I'm not on the way out yet. I'll be around for another while to keep the blueshirts in order."

"Are you alright?" Olga came up and put her hand on Tracker's shoulder.

"It's only the old blood pressure. I forget to take the tablets sometime," he assured her.

"Maybe you should let Willie take you home, Tracker," Tom leaned across the counter, "that was a fair old attack."

"Will you quit, Tom, there's not a bother on me once I got the tablet into me. Did you hear that Olga's getting married again?" Tracker winked at Tom.

"There's absolutely no truth in that. I have no intention of getting married again," Olga said with vehemence.

"That's not the way I heard it," Tracker said.

"What did you hear?" she asked.

"That you're marrying Gabriel."

"You're not serious, Tracker. The man's not all there, he's bats ...he's nuts...he's off his head....he's batty."

"He was not too batty to ask you to marry him and, according to Gabriel, you didn't refuse."

"And you wouldn't refuse either, Tracker, if you were sitting at the fire in your nightdress and Gabriel standing over you," Olga said, "but I didn't say yes, either. I said I'd think about it."

"Maybe, that's what you told Gabriel, but he reads it different-ly. Do you know he was married before?" Tom asked.

"No."

"He was. The wife's still alive. She had a son by him. The two of them left about a couple of years ago. She had to get out. There's definitely a screw or two loose."

"And he asked me to marry him. He must think I'm mad too."

"He'll pester you from this on. It's awkward enough with him living across the lake from you."

"I am not leaving. It is my house. That is my home. I stay there."

"He'll make it awkward for you, I'm afraid," Tom said.

In the months before Christmas, Gabriel only called on Olga twice. On each occasion, he came in, squared his shoulders and shaped around the kitchen, grinning vacantly. On the night of the second visit, Olga took Butsy's old single-barrelled shotgun from the chest in which she stored it in the loft. She cleaned and loaded it and, having warned the children not to touch it, placed it in the cupboard in the corner beside the fire. On Christmas Eve, Gabriel called again. He placed a square, cardboard box on the table.

"There's a cake in that. I came to wish you all a happy Christmas," he said, as the children stood watching him, Marie sucking her thumb, and Patrick standing warily, a slight frown on his face.

"Where's your mother?" Gabriel asked.

"Did you hear me?" he demanded, when there was no reply, "Where's your mother?"

When there was still no reply, he took a step forward and gripped Patrick's shoulder.

"I want an answer," he said, tightening his grip and squeezing tears from Patrick's eyes.

"She's foddering," Patrick said.

Gabriel found Olga at the hayrick, cutting out a block of hay with a hay - knife.

"I came to wish you a happy Christmas," he said, as she shook out the hay and picked up an armful.

"Thanks," she said, over the top of the prickly hay.

"Is that all you have to say?" he demanded, the grin set in place.

"I am grateful," she said, "but I have to finish feeding."

"First, the wee brat of a Patrick wouldn't talk to me and now you're gone high and mighty on me," he reached out to pull the hay from her arms.

Resisting, she clasped the hay to her and fell to her knees. He knocked her on her back and threw himself across her, the wad of hay still a barrier between them. With one arm across her throat, pinning her down, he jerked the hay away with the other. Over his shoulder, Olga got a glimpse of Patrick with the shotgun in his hands.

"Stop," she screamed, as the blast reverberated and Gabriel jerked half to his feet, before falling limply across her.

He was dead, when she dragged herself out from underneath him, a hole in his back, gristly white and oozing blood. A white-faced Patrick lay on the ground, the side of his chest bleeding. He had fired the gun with the butt under his arm and, in the kickback, the hammer had torn him.

"My hand is sore," he held up his right hand to show two fingers skinned by the trigger-guard.

"Oh, my poor Patrick," she picked him up and ran with him into the house.

Marie, still sucking her thumb, stared wide-eyed, when they came into the kitchen. When Patrick's clothes were removed, his chest wound proved to be a jagged tear, which did not run very deep and, once bathed and bandaged, ceased to bleed. The skinned fingers were much sorer and Patrick whimpered as his mother dressed them. She then gave him a sedative and put him to bed. Marie crept into bed behind him and, within minutes, both of them were asleep. Having watched for awhile, Olga pulled on a coat and walked wearily to the end of the lane, where she told the first passerby to get the guards.

Sergeant Murphy and two guards arrived first, closely followed by the curate from Tunnygee, who whispered an Act of Contrition in Gabriel's ear, before giving him the Last Rites. Gently, the Sergeant questioned Olga and was soon in possession of the facts. He went down to the bedroom and stood looking at the sleeping figures of the two children for a moment.

"The poor little fella," he said.

Tom, who arrived shortly after the curate, insisted that Olga and the children should again spend Christmas with Maisie and himself in the pub. Initially, Olga demurred, but when the undertaker came and removed the body, and the police and everyone else had gone, she changed her mind. The sleeping children were carried out and placed on the back seat of Tom's car and the four of them arrived in Tunnygee as the people returned from Midnight Mass. There was a light spattering of snow as Maisie greeted them at the entrance to the private quarters of the pub.

"Hey, is that Olga and the children?" it was Willie McGinty's voice from the far side of the road.

"Hold on there, Maisie, don't close the door. Me and Tracker would like to have a word with her," he shouted, crossing the road, a slower moving Tracker behind him.

"I'm shocking sorry, Olga," McGinty took off his cap as he came into the hall."

"I'm sorry too, ma'am," Tracker, puffing stertorously, held out his hand.

"Are you alright, Tracker?" Maisie asked.

"A bit winded, ma'am, that's all."

"In truth, he's more than a bit winded, Maisie," McGinty said, "he's blowin' worse than yon old broken-down horse McCaffrey used to have."

"Maybe a drink will do him good," Tom said, returning, having left the two children upstairs.

"I've a fierce pain in the chest," Tracker grabbed Maisie's arm.

"And you're as white as a sheet too," Tom said.

"Here," he grabbed McGinty by the shoulder and pushed him towards the door, "get the doc as fast as you can. He's in a bad way."

They helped Tracker into the bar and stretched him out on a seat. Tom opened his collar and tie, took off his boots and he lay, mouth open, snoring loudly.

"I'm going for the priest," Maisie said, leaving.

Tom filled a large measure of brandy and handed it to Olga.

"Get that into you. It might do you some good," he told her.

"It's all too much, Tom. I can't take any more," she sobbed, "and now poor Tracker. He is going to die too."

As Maisie cried, Tom noticed that Tracker's loud snoring had ceased.

"How are you feeling now, Tracker?" Tom asked.

"Not too bad," Tracker said, his eyes still closed. "You can tell Olga there that I won't be kicking the bucket for awhile yet."

"Oh, Tracker," Olga fell to her knees beside him and, resting her head on his chest, wept, her shoulders shaking spasmodically.

"What in the name of God is going on here," the doctor bustled in. "She'll kill him, lying across his chest."

Olga stood up and looked down at the neat, dapper figure of the doctor with disdainful, tear-filled eyes.

"I'm, sorry, Mrs Dwyer, I didn't know you," he said, before turning abruptly to the prone figure of Tracker.

Quickly and efficiently, he examined the patient.

"You'll live," he said, "but not for too long, if you don't take your bloody tablets."

"How do you know, doc?"

"Do you think I'm a quack? Your blood pressure's gone through the roof. Have you any tablets?"

"I ran out of them, doc. I thought I'd get through the Christmas without them."

"Here," the doctor riffled through his bag and produced a small bottle of tablets, "take these and you'll live for another while."

"He's all yours, Father," he turned to the priest, as Tracker popped a tablet in his mouth.

"It seems you're going to live, Tracker," the priest said quietly.

"Aye, it looks that way, Father."

"Well, you've no need for me so."

"I suppose not, Father."

Ten minutes later, Tracker sat nursing a brandy. McGinty put coal on the fire and poured more brandy for Olga and himself, both Tom and Maisie refusing.

"It was a terror about Gabriel," McGinty said.

"A holy divine terror. May the Lord have mercy on him," Tracker crossed himself.

"A pair of hypocrites," Maisie stood up, "Where's your sympathy for Olga and her son, Patrick? They are the people who need your sympathy, not a madman who brought his troubles on himself. I'm going to bed. Are you coming, Olga?"

"Yes, Maisie."

"I think I'll go to bed too," Tom said.

"Pull the door after you when you leave," he told Tracker and McGinty.

25

Old Burke, Tom's grandfather died in his sleep in January. His funeral took place at the Mountainy Chapel.

Peadar Kennedy, a year short of his sixtieth birthday, was there. Only slightly more rotund than he had been fifteeen years earlier, he was bald with closely cropped grey hair fringing the pink dome of his head, but still soft-skinned and fresh-complexioned. At the funeral, he was in the pew behind Olga. She left the church ahead of him, her head above that of many of the men, and he stood beside her at the graveside.

"How are you enjoying life in town?" he asked, when the ceremony was over.

"It's good, but I enjoy the farm more. We 're going back there again next week."

"You like the farming?"

"I like the country life, the peace and quiet of living surrounded by fields. My father's people were small farmers in Norway, you know, small farmers and fishermen. It might seem a strange life for me, the farming, but I have it in my blood," Olga smiled.

"I suppose you came with Tom," Peadar said.

"I did."

"I'll give you a lift home, if you like, Olga," he suggested.

"I'd be delighted, but...oh, there's Tom. Yo ho, Tom," she waved her hand, "I'm getting a lift home with Peadar."

Gabriel O'Beirne's place was auctioned at the end of the month. It was bought by Kilbride, the solicitor, in trust for an unnamed client. Speculation was intense as to the identity of the purchaser and when Patsy Carolan, the builder, moved in and demolished the old house in preparation for the erection of a bungalow, many approaches, both direct and indirect were made to him to find out the name of the mysterious person, but to no avail. As Patsy said: "I am no wiser than anyone else. I take my instructions from Mr. Kilbride."

At the end of April, a Dublin firm of landscape gardeners arrived on the site and concentrated on opening up a vista to the lake, while laying out a half-acre garden planted with many well-matured shrubs. The bungalow was finished in July and the following Sunday, Peadar Kennedy called on Olga as had become his weekly custom since the Burke funeral.

"We're going on a special trip this evening," he announced.

"Where, Mr Kennedy?" Patrick asked.

"You'll know when you get there," he lifted Marie on to his knee.

"Would you like sweets?" he asked, smiling down at her.

"Yes, Mr. Kennedy," she lisped.

"No, not that pocket," he told Patrick, "try the other one."

It was a well tried game, and Peadar smiled up at Olga, as Patrick found the packet of sweets and Marie slipped from his knee.

"Are we all set?" he stood up, brushing his knees.

"Lead on, sir," Olga laughed, ushering the children before her.

He turned left on the main road, and a half mile further on, he turned into the new bungalow. Olga looked at him sharply.

"I thought we might have a look at this house that's causing all the talk," his mouth tightened in a suppressed smile.

"It's yours, it's yours, Peadar, the house is yours, Peadar," she shrieked, "and you never told...you never told me."

"Didn't I keep the secret well?" he laughed, pulling up at the front door.

"We'll go down to the lake first," he suggested.

He had enclosed an old laneway, lining it with trees on one side and using the original whitethorn hedge on the other. At the water's edge, he pointed out a small concrete pier.

"I'm thinking of getting a boat," he said.

"And, anyway," he added slyly, "I hear you're a great swimmer, Olga, that you'd go up and down the lake four or five times."

"I stopped swimming," she said shortly.

"No matter," he said, his equanimity undisturbed. "We'll go up and see the house.,."

"Would you like to live in that house?" he asked Patrick on the way back in the car.

"I would."

"Would you like to live there?" he asked the girl.

"I would, Mr Kennedy," she replied.

"It's up to your mother now. I wonder would she like to live there?"

"I would like it very much, Peadar, but the price might be too high," she said lightly.

"Do you think your mother will marry me?" he asked the children.

There was no response.

"They seem to know that it's my decision, Peadar," Olga said.

"Maybe, you think I'm too old for you," Peadar said quietly.

"Better an old man's darling than a young man's slave," Olga laughed.

"I'm not that old, Olga."

"I know that, Peadar," she squeezed his arm.

Later that evening, Tom Burke was suprised when Peadar entered the bar.

"It's not often we see you here, Peadar. You're more than welcome, however," Tom greeted.

"I've news for you, Tom, I'm going to marry Olga Dwyer," Peadar announced.

"That's not news, Peadar. Everyone in Tunnygee knows you're courting hard for the last six months."

"What are you talking about? Just because I go out to see a woman and her children on a Sunday and bring them for an odd drive, everyone thinks the one thing."

"Aye, you're probably right, but it's good news all the same. I'm delighted. Olga's a grand lassie. I wish the two of you the best of luck."

"Thanks, Tom, but there's something else I want to talk to you about. That place of yours, would you sell it by any chance?"

"You're not going to move in there with Olga?"

"Why? Are you going to object?

"No. The place is all yours anytime you want it. I'll sign it over to you anytime you like."

"No, I want to buy it. I'll give you the full market value. I can well afford it."

"You bought me this place. I feel I owe you something."

"Aren't you my own flesh and blood? Anyway, I'm retiring from business. I did a deal with Mike. He's leaving the bank at the end of the month."

"I always knew the bold Mike would land on his feet."

"He's paying well for the privilege, I don't mind telling you. I'll give you fifteen hundred for the place."

"Give me a thousand and I'll be happy enough."

"I'll give you the fifteen hundred. It'll be the last chance you'll get, now that I'm taking on a woman and a readymade family."

"Fair enough, Peadar. I can only wish you the best of luck so and many years of happiness in the old place."

"I'm not going to live there. I'm only extending my interests in the area around the lake, you might say."

"It was you bought Gabriel's place. The bungalow belongs to you, you old reprobate."

"That was one bit of information I kept to myself. All the old newsbags round the town got it wrong, bad cess to the lot of them. Anyway, myself and Olga are getting married the week after next."

"That soon.......?"

"Aye, we'll do the job quietly above in Dublin. Then, what will the newsbags have to say for themselves?"

"God, Peadar, that's a fret."

"Two terrors and a fret," Peadar laughed."Your old father's not bet yet, you know."

26

O lga and Peadar were in Burke's one night in the October after their marriage. With other customers, they watched an hour hour long television programme which dealt with evolving events in Northern Ireland. Dr. Ian Paisley was to the forefront, with a rundown on his career from 1964, when he originated what became known as "The Tricolour Riots". The riots occurred, when under pressure from Paisley, the Home Affairs Minister in Northern Ireland, had sent in a detachment of R.U.C. to remove an Irish Tricolour, which flew from Sinn Fein headquarters in Belfast 's Divis Street.

The police succeeded in seizing the Tricolour, but two days later, another Tricolour was hoisted as several hundred people cheered and sang "A Soldier's Song", the National Anthem.

The result was a riot that night in which over thirty people, including eighteen policemen, were injured.

"Another Paisley target has been the ecumenical movement and the World Council of Churches," the reporter announced. "In June of last year he led his followers in a march on the General Assembly of the Presbyterian Church in protest against what he claimed was its Romeward trend. The result was the Cromac Square riot. Several people were injured in a short and sharp confrontation and material damage was extensive, with shop windows smashed and cars wrecked. At the Assembly Hall, the Paisleyites hurled verbal abuse at the Governor, Lord Erskine, who shortly afterwards resigned the governorship and returned to his native Scotland."

"Good on you, Paisley," a young farmer at the bar said. "You should have shot the bastard."

"You're right, Timmy," his father, who was drinking with him, agreed, "the bloody Queen's representative , over here living on the fat of the land, drinking brandy and smoking big cigars. Pity is we haven't a man like Paisley on our side."

"He's a bad man. He's the cause of all the trouble. It is wrong to praise him," Olga said with some feeling.

"And look who's talking," the man chided. "Weren't you a Protestant yourself before you married the Dwyer fella?"

"What do you mean, married the Dwyer fella? You're not very polite, little man. And it's no business of yours what my religion is. That's what's wrong with this country, too much religion and no...no christanity. That's what's wrong with Paisley. He may be a Protestant, but he's not a christian."

"That's a quare bit of a spake, ma'am, but it changes nothing. You have your know, but I still have mine," the man said.

"I don't support Mr. Paisley, anyhow," Olga rejoined.

"And now if we could see the rest of the programme," Tom suggested from behind the bar.

"You get some great programmes from the B.B.C. on the North," Tom said, when the programme ended.

"Yes, Tom, I agree it was a good programme," Olga said, "but I do not think that civil rights alone will solve the problem. There is also the question of national identity."

"God bless us and save us, woman," the older farmer intervened, "but, aren't you shocking knowledgeable for a foreigner? What the hell do you know about the situation?"

"I have told you already that you are not a very polite little man. I think I am very right."

"I think you're coming the heavy a wee bit on the old fella," the son intervened."He only asked you a simple question and you didn't answer it. What does a foreigner like you know about the situation anyway?"

"I'm no foreigner. My mother was English and I married an Irishman and now I'm married to another Irishman."

"And what do you know about this country? That's a simple question." the son asked again.

"I'll answer your simple question, Timmy," Tom said, irritation edging his voice, "there's no one in this town better informed than Mrs. Kennedy on the Irish situation. I'd say she's read every book published on it since her first husband was killed. Isn't that right, Olga?"

"That's right, Tom. It kept me sane in the months after his death."

"Now, are you satisfied?" Tom asked the older man.

"Maybe I am and maybe I'm not, but I still say Paisley's right. He's only standing up for his own."

"Have it your own way" Tom said.

"Aye, sure you're all a nest of Republicans in this pub anyway. I don't know what they're all shouting about in the North. Look at the roads they have and the dole money and everything. I'd say most of them are happy enough the way they are," the older man declared.

"But they are not free," Olga protested.

"Free! Who're you coddin'?" the son demanded. "It's the money in your pocket that sets you free, not the flag above your head. What's wrong with England anyway? It gave a good living to many an Irishman. If you ask me, we should all join up together."

"The slave mentality," Peadar whispered in Olga's ear.

"That's right.....that's right," Olga laughed.

"Whatever you have to say, Kennedy. Spit it out and not be coggering in her ear," the older man was loudly aggressive.

"I'd say a man's entitled to have a private word in his own wife's ear," Peadar said.

"We'll get out of this joint," Timmy put his hand on his father's arm. "There only a bunch a gammon Republicans, wrap-the-green-flag-round-me merchants."

At a meeting in Tunnygee's Community Hall, called by Johny McCaffrey in support of "The beleagured Nationalists in the North", Olga was one of the speakers.

"Last week, you had the Glorious Twelfth on your televisions screens," she began. "They talk about religion, Mr. Paisley and Mr. Clark, but they try to fool you. Religion is not in question. I was born a Protestant and I know that. The question is about nationality. One is either Irish or British. I am Irish, because I married an Irishman. I have read all the Irish history. The question is one of nationality and as Irish people it is our duty to suppport the people in the Six Counties. I suggest that we form a support group to assist our fellow Nationalists in the North."

"Hear, hear," Johny McCaffrey, as Chairman, led the applause of the eight people present.

"I second what Olga said," Tracker got heavily to his feet.

"Aye, Aye," McGinty nodded his head in agreement beside him.

Tom sat beside Olga's eleven year old son, Patrick, tall and broad-shouldered for his age. The other two men present were former Irish soldiers. Nicky Coffey was small, thin-faced and alert, his hair jet-black and curly. He was a former Corporal. His cousin, Ned Coffey, was more strongly built, but with the same sharp features and black curly hair. He was a former Sergeant. It was Ned who suggested that they should get some training in firearms.

"The way things are going at the moment," he said, "those unfortunate people could be under attack at any minute and they'll be shouting for help then. If we weren't ready to help them, we wouldn't be much good. To do that, we might have to fire a shot or two."

"Aye, I think Ned's right," McCaffrey agreed, "I'll tell you what we'll do. We'll all meet out at Peadar's place next Sunday morning after second Mass, that's unless Olga here objects."

"No, I've no objection. I just look forward to seeing you all on Sunday morning."

"What about some more recruits?" Nickey Coffey enquired.

"No, Nickey, we'll keep it to ourselves. After all, this is a public meeting, and anyone that was interested could have come. We'll leave it the way it is for the minute. Less chance of informers that way too."McCaffrey said.

"Whatever weapons you have, bring them with you next Sunday," Olga ordered.

The weapons were limited - two World War 1 Lee Enfield rifles, which Johny McCaffrey produced, and about one hundred rounds of .303 ammunition of the same vintage. Two shotguns and three .22 rifles, plus Butsy's old revolver, completed the armoury.

"Aye, the two guns and the ammo have been safe and snug in the old loft at home, since I led the two of you into battle fifty years ago," McCaffrey told a surprised Tracker and McGinty.

"This is Butsy's .45," Tom presented the revolver to Olga. "It survived the raid on the farmhouse in the bottom of a creamery can. I suppose you could say it is an historic weapon."

"Oh, Tom," Olga grabbed the revolver and kissed him on the cheek, "I am delighted to get back my late husband's gun after so many years. He was an Irishman, who longed to see his country freed from British rule and, Patrick," she called her son, "this is your father's gun, the one he used in the last I.R.A. campaign against the British. I present it to you now with pride. I want you to have it in remembrance of your father and to treasure it in honour of a good Irishman who loved his country."

"Aye, I suppose he might as well have it," the practical McCaffrey declared. "There's no ammunition for it anyway."

Because of the scarcity of ammunition, the two Coffeys were appointed as riflemen and were allotted ten rounds each of the precious .303 to test the Lee Enfields. The test firing took place on the Crockaun, the Coffeys showing, with the ten rounds at their disposal, that they were skilled riflemen. The others fired the .22s and the shotguns.

"What did you think of Olga the day?" McGinty asked in Burke's that night."All that rubbish about Butsy's gun. It would give you a pain in the arse."

"Aye, she's a changed woman this last while," Tracker agreed, "a sort of harder like. Butsy's death took more out of her than you think."

"I'll tell you one thing," McGinty shrugged, "she frightens the wits out of me. Before you know where you are, she'll have us firing at the B Specials and us three old age pensioners."

"Aye," McCaffrey laughed, "we might be better at home preparing to meet our Maker. Anyway, it could all blow over. The British government might cancel this Apprentice Boys' parade in Derry yet".

The parade was not cancelled and on August 12, the barricades in Derry's Bogside were strengthened as the music of the Orange bands wafted down from the walled city above, and that evening the battle was joined. On the previous day, when it was obvious that the parade was going to go ahead, Olga had organised her troops. The Coffey brothers were agreeable enough to travel to Letterkenny with her, but Tom was appparently evasive.

"I can't go with you," he told her, "I have made arrangements to meet a man. He won't be here until midnight."

"I just don't believe you, Tom," Olga finally declared, "and Johny McCaffrey and those two fools, Tracker and Willie McGinty, won't go, if you don't go."

"Is McCaffrey at home?" Tom asked.

"He is."

"I'll go out and have a word with him," Tom said.

Peadar Kennedy was looking out the picture window of his bungalow, when McCaffrey, accompanied by Tracker and McGinty, drove into the forecourt.

"Your army has arrived, Olga," Peadar shouted to his wife in the kitchen.

"Did Corporal Burke grant you permission, Johny?" Olga was cynical.

"Surely to God, you're not bringing Tracker with you?" Peadar called Johny one side.

"You try and stop him, Peadar."

At seven the next morning, the two car convoy left Kennedy's and headed west towards Glan Gap, arriving in Bundoran shortly after ten o'clock. At lunchtime, they were in Letterkenny, where they pulled up at the Northern Lights restaurant. It was packed, soft Donegal accents intermingling with the harsher tones of Derry and the rasp of Belfast. They had to wait over two hours for a meal, after which Tracker fell asleep in an armchair, while the other five held a council-of-war. It was Johny McCaffrey who suggested that they should go to confession before "going into action". He also suggested that they should not move round town in a group.

"We would only draw attention to ourselves that way," he said."We should walk about two by two."

Johny and Tracker went off together to the Parochial House, where both went to confession. Olga and McGinty walked up the street.

"I don't want confession," McGinty said, "a nice creamy pint would be more in my line."

They went into the nearest pub. The Coffeys were already there.

"I thought you two were going to confession," Ned greeted.

"What's going to happen now?" Nickey asked, "they're killing each other in Derry."

"We'll have to wait and see ." Olga said.

"Turn up that TV," someone shouted to the barman.

"It's war, it's a full-scale battle here in Derry's Bogside," the reporter shouted into his microphone, "stones and bricks and petrol bombs are the currency of this war and there are rumours of shots being fired. Ambulances are racing through the streets. Another police charge, youths scattering in every direction. We must get out of here," the reporter's voice rose to a scream as the camera cut out.

Petrol bombs and stones, police advancing and retreating with a mob howling in support was the pattern of the day. Night came and the blaze from the burning buildings reached towards the sky, while from the roof of the new high-rise flats youths hurled petrol bombs at the police below. Tortuously, canisters of CS gas curved upwards to land on the flat roof and, momentarily, the youths disappeared to come back hurling further petrol bombs.

Olga and her friends stayed in Letterkenny that night, the restaurant proprietor advising against any attempt to go into Derry. Next morning, at breakfast, the proprietor approached and told them that Tom Burke had called from the City Hotel in Derry.

"How did he get there?" Olga asked.

"I don't know, Mrs. Kennedy, but he'll be here later in the day."

Tom and Charlie Daniels arrived in late afternoon, tired and worn-out.

"We arrived in Derry at three o'clock yesterday morning and we haven't closed an eye since," Tom explained."It's rough over there, I don't mind telling you."

"Can we do anything ?" Olga asked.

"No, I don't think so. It seems the British army is on its way in. I hear Toler is going to make a statement this evening."

That night, Jack Toler, the Taoiseach,* made his "not stand

*Taoiseach - Prime Minister

by" speech from Dublin. Looking pale and drawn, Mr. Toler's accent, with intonations of his native Cork, was unmistakenly southern in the context of a Donegal pub.

"It is with deep sadness that you, Irish men and women of goodwill, and I, have learned of the events which have been taking place in Derry and elsewhere in the North in recent days," he began with the hesitancy of emotion lending dignity to his words,

"The Government have been very patient and have acted with great restraint over several months past.... but it is clear now that the present situation cannot be allowed to continue. It is evident that the Stormont Government is no longer in control of the situation......the Irish Government can no longer stand by and see innocent people injured and perhaps worse......R.U.C. is no longer accepted.....request United Nations for urgent despatch of a peace-keeping force.....Recognising that the reunification of Ireland provides the only permanent solution.......End soon by granting all in the Six County area full equality of citizenship and by the eventual restoration of the historic unity of our country."

The pub was engulfed in a deep primeval roar. It was minutes before the crowd settled down to a high buzz of excited conversation.

"I never thought I'd find myself cheering a Free State Taoiseach," Daniels said, "I wonder does he mean it?"

"Don't be a begrudger, Charlie," Tom nudged him, "we're all on the same road now."

"I hope you're right, Tom." Daniels said.

"Of course, he's right. Ireland long a province be, a nation once again," Olga asserted.

"Do you know this man, Olga ?" Tom asked.

"No."

"Did you ever hear of Charlie Daniels?"

Olga looked at Tom, questioning with her eyes.

"Yes, it is the same Charlie Daniels," Tom said.

"Oh, I am very glad to meet you, Mr. Daniels," Olga said, formality covering her momentary confusion.

Olga's squad left for home next morning. They had a midday meal in Donegal town and stopped for drinks in Cavan town arriving at the Kennedy bungalow in late afternoon.

"You know bloody well I was the best shot in the country when I was a young lad," Tracker declared, following McGinty into the Kennedy kitchen.

"I can vouch for that," Peadar said, closing the kitchen door after them. "When I came to Tunnygee first, and that wasn't the day or yesterday, it was always said that Tracker was the best man to handle a rifle in the country."

"Give a man a name for getting up early and he can stay in bed till dinner-time. Who do you think won the biggest shoot ever held in this part of the county?" McGinty asked.

"You won once and you're talking about it ever since. Only big Jim Williamson's gun jammed on the five rounds rapid, you'd never have smelt it. You were only a flash in the pan, McGinty," Tracker said.

"A quare flash and me only a runt of a gasson. I was barely fourteen at the time. It was in 1919 and all the soldiers home from the big war. I bet them all. Admit it, Tracker, I was the best man that day."

"I'm not denying it, but you won nothing after. It was between meself and Big Jim after that and I won two out of three."

"There's an easy way out of this," Ned Coffey said. "We'll go down to the Crockaun. We've eighty rounds and two rifles and we won't be long finding out who's the best shot."

"I want to be in on this too," Peadar said. "I wasn't a bad shot in my L.D.F. days."

"What about you, Olga?" Johny McCaffrey asked.

"Count me in," she said.

"What about Nickey and Ned here?" McGinty demanded. "The two of them were army marksmen, you know."

"Alright, Willie, me and Nickey will supervise," Ned said.

"Have you a bag of spuds around the place?" he asked Peadar.

"Aye, in the garage."

"Right, I'll get the spuds, You get the rifles and ammo," he told Nickey.

Down at the Crockaun, Ned speared ten potatoes on sticks which he stuck in the ground. He paced back to a rise down towards the lake.

"It's about forty yards," he said.

"They couldn't miss at that range," Nickey laughed.

Olga, Peadar and Johny McCaffrey fired fifteen rounds each without a hit.

"Three whitewashes," McGinty said, "now, it's myself and yourself, Tracker. Who's going first?"

"We'll toss for it," Tracker said.

Tracker won the toss.

"Off you go, McGinty," he ordered.

Willie knocked off three potatoes and broke the skin on another. He was credited with four hits.

"That's putting it up to you, Tracker," he laughed.

Tracker knocked four potatoes with his first ten shots and then rested the rifle, butt on ground. The sweat was running down his face, as he took two or three breaths. McGinty looked at Ned Coffey.

"Are you alright?" Coffey asked.

"Give me a minute to get my breath," Tracker grunted.

Slowly, he lowered the muzzle of the rifle and, steadying himself, butt into his shoulder, fired.

"I shouldn't have missed that," he muttered.

Deliberately, he fired three more shots, but with no luck. He rested the rifle on the ground again, before easing it into position for the final shot. There was a spontaneous shout from the six onlookers, as a potato burst open. Tracker got slowly to his feet, wiping a handkerchief over his face.

"What have you to say for yourself now, McGinty?" he growled.

"Fair play to you, Tracker," McGinty eyed him closely, "You're still the daddy of us all, when it comes to the shooting."

27

T racker positively luxuriated in his victory at the Crockaun, accepting the congratulations of the town as if they were his right. It was as good as a new lease of life to him, Willie Mc Ginty said, but, when Tracker was not at Dockery's corner at eleven one sunny morning a month later, Willie was worried. He went over to Tracker's house to find the front door locked. He was trying to open a window when Sergeant McGladdery appeared.

"What's wrong?" the Sergeant asked.

"I'm looking for Tracker."

"And when you find him," the Sergeant laughed, "tell him that I'll have to pull him in if he doesn't stop talking about the couple of spuds he blew to pieces in Kennedy's Crockaun."

"I'm serious, Sergeant. He's always out and about before this. We'll have to get in, his old ticker's not the best."

"I know that, Willie," the Sergeant grabbed the doorknob and shook the door vigourously, before stepping back and bursting the door open with the sole of his boot.

Tracker lay on his back on the bed, his face doughey-white under the criss-cross of broken veins. The Sergeant had to bend down to hear his shallow breathing.

"At least, he's still alive," the Sergeant was not too hopeful.

"The poor old Tracker's done for, I'm afraid," McGinty was even less hopeful.

McGinty accompanied Tracker in the ambulance to hospital, where, to McGinty's surprise, Tracker lived for a week.

"With the shaking we got on that humpy road to Cavan, with potholes where you could drown a cat's kittens, Tracker must be an iron man to live as far as the hospital," he declared.

It surprised many people to learn that Tracker was not a native of Tunnygee. He came from the neighbouring parish of Bunmore, where he was buried in the mixed graveyard at the back of the Church of Ireland parish church. As a former I.R.A. man, Tracker was entitled to be buried with military honours. The rifles and blank ammunition were supplied by the local battalion of the F.C.A. ,while a regular army bugler travelled from Dublin. As the two surviving I.R.A. men in Tunnygee, McCaffrey and McGinty were on the firing party, with the addition of another survivor from Bunmore. Three volleys were fired and the bugler played Reveille and The Last Post. Tom and Olga folded the Tricolour before the coffin was lowered into the grave, and Fr. Edward McCaffrey said the final funeral prayers.

In Burke's later, Maisie made sandwiches and her son, Tom Pat, helped to distribute them.

"What age is Tom Pat now?" Sylvia Houlihan asked, patting the boy's head.

"Seven, Sylvia, he was seven last July. He's about a year younger than your Canice."

"That's right. Canice was eight in June."

"Mike's taking Tracker's death very badly," Maisie said.

"He has a soft spot for poor Tracker. As he says it was Tracker who introduced him to dog racing and that it was through dog racing he met me."

"And that was his lucky day," Maisie said sweetly.

"Yes, I expect it was," Sylvia was her serene self.

"I'd love to take that Sylvia down a peg or two. She's too smug by half," Maisie whispered with feeling to Tom, shortly afterwards.

"You'll get that knife of yours into her good and proper one of these days," Tom laughed.

"And when I do, it'll stay stuck," she said grimly, moving away with her plate of sandwiches.

"Maisie," Tom called her back, "I'll be leaving in an hour or two with Charlie. He wants me to go to Belfast with him."

"Did you tell him you had a business to run?"

"I did, and do you know what he said?"

"Go on."

"He said it was you had the business head."

"You're a chancer, Tom Burke," she turned and offered a sandwich to McGinty, who was nearest her.

In a house in Belfast's Whiterock area at nine that evening,

Tom and Charlie were offered bottles of stout by the man of the house. Tom took one, but Charlie refused, accepting a cup of coffee. A tall man came in and told them about police raids, bus burnings and petrol bombings in a rapid Belfast accent.

"I'd say things are quieting down a bit now," Tom said.

"You're mad, man. It'll never quieten down again until the Brits get to hell out of the Wee Six here."

"We might as well go down to Leeson Street, down to the Long Bar, and see what's stirring ," the man of the house suggested.

There was a hum of excitement in Leeson Street, with people moving up and down, over and across, in the twilight of a soft September evening. Security was tight, however, and a Citizens' Defence Committee member was called to identify the Whiterock man, who vouched for Tom and Charlie. Only then were the three of them allowed through the Falls Road barrier. The Long Bar was packed and the two visitors were introduced to several people by their host. In all cases , conversation followed the same pattern. Talk of attacks, shootings and burnings in the previous month, with the hope, forlorn in some cases, that the "Twenty-Six Counties" would come to the rescue. A man, with curly red hair came from the back of the premises. Someone said that he helped to operate the radio station further along the road. He went over to talk to two men at the counter.

"One of those is an Irish Army Intelligence Officer," the host said, "I think the other fella's a newspaper man from Dublin."

Soon, the redhaired man and the newspaper man were deep in conversation, which quickly became heated. The Intelligence Officer stood watching, a half smile on his face. The red-haired man stood back and said something to the newspaper man with a dismissive wave of his hand. The latter turned round to him.

"You socialists are all the same," he said. "All suffering from chronic indigestion, caused by an overdose of half-baked ideas, culled from Marx and Engels and the rest of them. And I bet the half of you haven't even read the Communist Manifesto."

"Maybe we haven't."

"There y'are. You bloody well haven't. Well, let me tell you, I have," the newspaper man turned back to the counter.

The Intelligence Officer put his hand on the arm of the red-haired man, who was turning away in disgust and spoke to him for a minute or two in an obvious attempt to mollify him. The man, however, pulled away and went towards a door at the end of the bar.

"Did you see them?" the Whiterock man asked."The two of them at each others throats like a pair of fighting cocks and the officer laughing at them."

"I saw that officer someplace before," Charlie said.

"Aye, and do you know where it was? It's coming back to me now. It was in Derry. It was on the Wednesday," Tom recalled, "remember the three police tenders zig-zagging up the road, breaking through until the young lad ran out and lobbed the petrol bomb into the right-hand tender. And then the policeman on the ground, rolling around in agony, trying to quench the blazing clothes. Remember we were at the corner of the Bogside Inn and the woman came up to this fella standing beside us and asked him what he was doing skulking around when all the men were needed up front. He walked away towards the highrise flats and I said, we better follow him, or we'll be in trouble too."

"You're right, Tom, you're right. That's the very man."

At a public meeting in a small hall across the street, later in the evening, the officer was also present.

"He must be following us around," Tom said to the Whiterock man.

"You'd never know what the bastard's up to," was the reply.

The Chairman of the meeting was terse and to the point. He wanted suggestions on how best to defend the area against another invasion similiar to that of August. How are we going to stop the armoured cars, he put a specific question.

An intense young man jumped to his feet immediately.

"There's only one way to block them,"" he said. "Put the women and children out in front. Sit them in rows across the road."

"And supposing the armoured cars drive across them like the Russian tanks in Prague?" an older man demanded.

"That would be the end of Stormont," another man declared. "The whole country would rise up and tear the R.U.C. limb from limb".

"And you're willing to sacrifice the women and children?" the older man was outraged.

"I'm willing to sacrifice nothing. I'm only telling you what would happen if they crossed the women and children. Anyway, you can't....you can't make an omelette without breaking eggs. You can't make a revolution without losing a few lives."

"Who are you? Where did you come from? You're not from the area?" the older man accused.

"No, I'm not from this area, but I'm as good a Belfastman as yourself. But, as I see it, this is the pre-revolutionary phase and it's only something like a few deaths that will shake the people out of their lassitude. We have to stir the proletariat into action to permit them to take their place in the new socialist Ireland."

"A bloody commie, the end justifying the means, throw him out," someone shouted.

Several other people took up the cry and two or three men elbowed towards the alleged Communist.

"Stop it," a hard, guttural voice, with about it an air of command, erupted from the end of the hall, and a tall, pale-faced man got to his feet.

"We don't want a split before we start," he said, "but we don't want to hide behind women and children either. There's only one way to protect ourselves and that's to get the means of protection. That means guns and the men to use them," he stopped to a muted, if general, murmur of approval.

"And where are you going to get these guns from? I hope you're not depending on the green capitalist government in Dublin. Even if you got them, that wouldn't be much help to the workers in Belfast, or the workers anywhere, for that matter. Connolly had it right, we don't want to exchange flags and still remain slaves. No, thanks, Mr. McBrien," a crew-cut blonde youth stared defiance at the tall man.

"Watty Cox has his men well placed the night. Isn't that right Watty?" McBrien addressed the alleged Communist, whom he'd defended earlier.

"But Watty's not interested in protecting the people of the Falls," he continued. "He has bigger things on his mind. He doesn't want to protect anyone. He only sees this as the pre-

216

revolutionary stage on the road to a Socialist Republic and if women and children die on that road, what matter? Ten children, twenty children, a hundred children sent to an early grave doesn't matter to Watty and his young friends. As someone said earlier on, the end justifies the means. Watty wouldn't take arms from Dublin. He'd prefer to have them from Russia, but after the women and children are dead. Mr. Chairman, I don't think we should waste any more time with this ideological nonsense. I propose that we seek aid, including arms for defence, on behalf of the Nationalist people of the Six Counties and that we send a delegation to the Dublin Government for that purpose."

"You propose that a delegation go from this meeting? " the Chairman clarified.

"That's right. That it goes to Dublin tomorrow."

"I put that proposal to the floor," the Chairman said.

Agreement was practically unanimous, with only Cox and five or six of his supporters not holding up their hands. McBrien was proposed as leader of the four-man delegation.

"McBrien, Norbert McBrien, he was in the internment camp in the Curragh with me during the war," Daniels said, as he and Tom left the hall.

"Himself and the officer are having a bit of a pow-pow inside now," Tom said.

"I saw that, Tom. We'll wait for them on the street," Daniels suggested.

McBrien and the officer came out together.

"How ya, Norbert, It's been a long time. " Daniels greeted.

"Come over to the light," McBrien walked back to the door, followed by Daniels.

"God, It's you, Charlie Daniels, the Curragh, nearly thirty years ago. God, time flies. I'm glad to see you, Charlie."

"I'm glad to see you too, Norbert, but who's your friend?"

"He's a Captain in Irish Army Intelligence from Dublin.

"Hey, Ned," Daniels called, "come over till I introduce you to some friends of mine."

"Captain Ned Roche, Army Headquarters, Dublin," McBrien introduced the officer.

"Tom Burke, a friend of mine. He was in the Irish army for awhile too," Daniels said.

They chatted for a few moments on the side of the street. It was Roche suggested that they keep in touch

"I'll probably set up a further meeting," he said.

A week later, Tom had a phone call from Daniels.

"Remember that meeting Roche was talking about. It's on next Saturday."

"Good. Where?"

"You'd never guess. McBrien left the meeting place up to me and I suggested the hotel in Tunnygee."

"I don't believe you."

"It's true enough. Roche was on to me a minute ago and he booked it for the weekend."

"Are you coming?"

"Of course. I arranged with McBrien to represent Donegal and I arranged further, that your good self should represent Cavan. There'll be a couple of people from the Civil Defence Committees representing each of the Six Counties."

"What time on Saturday?"

"Three o'clock."

Captain Roche chaired the meeting and immediately came under strong pressure from some of the delegates to explain why the training of Derry citizens in the use of firearms by the Irish Army at Donegal's Fort Dunree had been aborted.

"I've told you already, but I'll tell you again," Roche said slowly. "Nine or ten people underwent a week's training, but the news leaked out. One of the Sunday papers threatened to publish it. This came to the notice of the Director of Intelligence on Friday. He tried to contact the Minister for Defence or the Chief-of-Staff. Neither was available. Rightly or wrongly, he cancelled the training on his own initiative."

"That's what I don't understand," a Tyrone delegate persisted. "Why the hell did he have to cancel at all? It's not as simple as you put it, as I see it."

"Do you not trust me?"

"No, to put it bluntly, we had promises from Free State Army Intelligence men before and they didn't amount to much."

"Have it your own way. What I've given you are the facts."

"When's the training going to start again?" another delegate asked.

"How the hell do I know?" Roche was obviously annoyed. "The Minister authorised the training originally. I told you that already and he'll have to re-authorise it. To date, he hasn't done so."

"You're some help. Do you know what I think? I think you're bluffing us," the Tyrone delegate said.

"Maybe, we should call off this meeting, Mr. McBrien," Roche suggested.

"Hold on, Captain," McBrien said. "Listen, Mick, you're going a bit too far," he told the delegate. "Anyway, leave it for now. There are more important issues on the agenda."

"Thanks," Roche said. "You're looking for arms and training. What are you going to use the arms for?"

"What do you mean?" one man asked.

"Are you going to use them for revolution or what?" Roche asked.

"No, not at all, we've enough on our plate without planning revolution," an Armagh man said. "Defence is our only concern at the moment. There are isolated pockets of Nationalists all over the Six Counties. They are completely defenceless. Any of them could be wiped out in one night, like Bombay Street in Belfast. We have to have arms to defend those communities. It's a matter of self-protection. Anyone who'd talk about revolution in the current situation is mad, a nutcase. Defence is all we are concerned with."

"Fair enough," Roche said. "That seems to answer my question, unless some of you disagree. What about yourself?" he addressed Mick, the Tyrone delegate.

"I'm half satisfied," Mick grunted.

"Okay. Now, the next item on the agenda is gas masks, the provision of same," Roche continued, "I don't see any problem there. The stores are full of them."

"The thing is to convince the politicans," Mick was still disgruntled.

"Well, our politicians in the north are fully convinced," McBrien said, "and most of them are running to Dublin looking

219

for arms since last August. I'd say the lads in Dublin are fully convinced at the moment also."

"Never trust the Free State, I always heard. And I don't give a hate, I can't bring myself to trust the bastards yet," Mick declared.

"That's as maybe," Captain Roche said, "but the fact remains that this meeting delegates me on behalf of the Citizens' Defence Committees in the Six Counties to put the following requests to the Minister for Defence. One, to have arms made available for defensive purposes, two, to have training in the use of arms resumed, and, third, to have gas masks made available. I can assure you that these three requests will be brought to the attention of the Minister."

"Maybe that's fair enough," Mick muttered.

"Once you're satisfied," Roche said.

When the meeting broke up and the Northerners had departed, Tom invited Daniels and Roche down to his bar.

"I'd be delighted," Roche said, "I think we deserve a drink after all that."

After closing time, Tom invited both men to stay and Maisie made tea.

"Tom was in the army too," she said.

"He told me that, but, when he was soldiering with the Fifth Battalion, I was doing hard labour as a Cadet."

"You were one of the privileged," Tom said.

"I probably was, but we didn't think that at the time, with Johny McEoin as Cadetmaster and Slim Donoghue in overall charge. The first year was tough but, curiously enough, looking back on it, we enjoyed it. I suppose, it gave one some sense of achievement to survive in an authoritarian situation where the superior officer had the last word."

"That's the type of discipline that's missing today," Daniels said. "Youngsters nowadays get it too soft. You can't tell them anything. They know it all."

"I'm not too sure about that, Charlie," Maisie said, "I don't believe in the heavy hand. I think you have to talk to people, persuade them."

"I'm inclined to agree with you, Mrs. Burke. Personally, I feel that if you want to get the best out of someone, persuasion is the best approach," Roche said.

"Do you think it would work on the Orangemen in the North?" Daniels asked.

"No, I don't think so. As long as Britain guarantees their position, they're not subject to change, regardless of whether the approach be authoritarian or persuasive. That's why I was so delighted when today's meeting was so adamant about concentrating on defense."

"What do you mean?" Tom asked.

"As long as Britain guarantees the present postion, Orangemen or Unionists are practically immune to change. They can neither be forced nor persuaded, but if Britain were to remove the guarantee, the possibility of consent to change increases immeasurably. That's why the defence option is so important. If adhered to, it practically removes the possibility of the situation degenerating to civil war, a battle between Orange and Green, the classic colonial result of divide and conquer. To avoid that is the trick. We can then concentrate on persuading Britain to go. Afterwards, we can then use Mrs. Burke's approach on the Unionists."

"And we'll still have to fight the Orangemen," Daniels said.

"I'm not so sure, Charlie. In the changed circumstances where Britain declares that British citizenship will not be indefinitely granted to any group of Irishmen, they might, at least, be more amenable to persuasion."

"That sounds reasonable," Tom said.

"Thanks," Captain Roche stood up, "it's getting late. I'll have to go. I enjoyed the evening very much. It's now up to the Minister."

"What do you think of the bold Captain?" Daniels asked when he left.

"He's a nice enough fella," Maisie said. "And he seems to talk a lot of sense."

28

About two weeks after the Tunnygee conference, Tom had a call from Roche requesting a meeting.

"Just the two of us, face to face," Roche said. " Where would you suggest?"

"I don't know, what about Kells? Say, the Headford Arms Hotel."

"Fine. Would six o'clock suit you?"

"Okay. I'll see you then."

"I'm sorry for dragging you up here like this, Tom," Roche apologised when they met, " but I might need your help. You heard what went on at the Tunnygee meeting and I might want you to give me a hand at some stage. What do you say ?"

"I don't know. If I help, Captain, I won't cut across the lads from the north."

"Don't worry about that. I've no intention of doing so either."

"Well, I suppose that's okay then."

"There's something maybe you should know. We ran a check on you," Roche told him.

"I'd be surprised if you didn't," Tom laughed.

"Well, you'll be glad to hear you had a good army record. P.M. Quinlan, your old army commander, described you as one of the best NCOs he ever had, and I met another army friend of yours too, Sean Sheridan - he gave you a great write up . Do you know him?"

"Of course I do. Isn't he another Cavan man, an old IRA man and a great Fianna Fail man, to quote my uncle Pakie."

"Who?"

"My uncle Pakie. He reared me."

"Screelahan ?" Roche gave him a quizzical glance.

"That's right. How do you know? You got it from the army I suppose."

"Yes, but I had other sources also. You were never an I.R.A. man?"

"No."

"But you helped them? Butsy Dwyer, another former Corporal, was a good friend of yours."

"He was."

"Well?"

"You know bloody well that men were trained at Screelahan during the fifties."

"And that's when you met Charlie Daniels first?"

"You did a good job. You vetted me well," Tom said.

"No hard feelings, Tom, but I like to know the fellas I work with. What do you say we shake on it ?"

"Okay," Tom hesitated momentarily before holding out his hand.

"Come on up to the bar and I'll buy you a drink," Roche invited. "Did you ever meet General O'Clerigh?" he asked Tom, when the drink was served.

"You're not still checking, are you?" Tom looked at him.

"No, no," Roche assured him. "But, I admit, it might look that way. No, there was a story current at the time that O'Clerigh did train the IRA, in the fifties that is. I was just wondering if you ever came across him."

"I did. He gave lectures to some of the courses that Butsy and myself ran."

"That's a good one. There was a rumour, but you're the first person who ever confirmed it to me. The British, you know, believed that he was Chief-of-Staff of the I.R.A. in the fifties."

"You're having me on, Captain. If he was, I never heard it."

"Well, someone must have convinced the British. I heard about it when I attended a seminar on revolutionary war at a British university in '67 or '68. The man who told me had his ear to the ground and he was obviously quoting British Intelligence sources."

"He was still wrong. The General only lectured a few groups in his own area, as far as I know."

"Yes. I made some enquiries myself, Tom, and I'm inclined to agree with you. He certainly was never Chief-of-Staff."

"Any results from the Tunnygee meeting yet?" Tom asked.

"No, but the report's gone in to the top-man, request for arms and all, and he hasn't shot it down."

A week later, Charlie Daniels arrived at Tunnygee and asked Tom to accompany him on a trip to England.

"Now that the Dublin Goverment has come up with the money," he explained, "the Defence Committees are looking for arms."

"Why the Defence Committees?"

"They'll be untraceable that way and the Dublin crowd won't be embarrassed."

"Embarrassed?"

"That's right. Dublin has plenty of old rifles. It was going to sell them. The Minister has cancelled the sale and he's holding the guns. The only snag is that they can be traced back to Dublin very easily."

"And they won't be distributed so?"

"To use the official phraseology, they'll be held in reserve in case it should become necessary to distribute them to a defenceless minority in Northern Ireland. It's felt that if Dublin arms were found in the North prior to a fresh outbreak of violence that it would preempt the situation."

"What you mean is that they won't be sent in until the trouble actually starts?"

"Precisely. Dublin doesn't want to be seen jumping the gun," Daniels said drily.

"Not a joke, I hope," Tom said, "but what about the isolated communities there was so much talk about at the hotel above?"

"What do you think we're going to England for?"

"That raises another question. Why the hell should an Irishman go to England for arms. Didn't two Irishmen get jail over there not that long ago, trying to buy guns?"

"That's the problem. But the contact's good. Still, I suppose it could be a set up."

"Who's the contact."

"It came through Big Jack O'Mahony."

"Who's he?" Tom asked. "The contractor?"

"That's right, the one and only Big Jack."

Both men flew into Heathrow early in the following week.

224

From the airport, Daniels rang the London number he had been given. He was told by the man who answered the phone that they would be met at the entrance to the Underground in Oxford Street.

"Just turn to the left when you leave the station," the man told him.

"How will I know you?" Daniels asked.

"Don't worry, we'll know you," the man said.

"I'm telling you there's something wrong," Tom said as the train rattled towards Oxford Street.

"Give it a rest, Tom. Big Jack could have given our descriptions."

"Strange he didn't mention it. I'd say we're under observation since we landed. Yon two at the airport were Special Branch lads. And how the blazes could the fella on the phone know us?"

"I told you, Tom, give it a rest. We'll find out soon enough. Here's Oxford Street coming up."

Leaving the station, Tom bent, ostensibly, to tie his shoelace.

"You keep going, " he told Daniels.

On the footpath, Daniels went left. A second or two later, Tom angled out to the right. He was certain that the man at the bus stop, one of the suspected Special Branch men from the airport, did not spot him. He turned and came back down towards the bus stop. The man had his back to him, stretching, half on his toes, watching Daniels, while talking into a small walkie-talkie in his hand. Tom edged closer to him.

"Negative. I confirm non-arrival of second man at Oxford Street," he said into the radio, a hint of irritation in his half-whispered voice.

Instinctively, Tom ducked back, and moving round the end of the queue, crossed the street. He walked quickly down the footpath on the far side and saw two men approach Daniels. As the trio stood talking, Tom noticed a middle-aged, blonde woman, about twenty yards to his right, apparently using a walkie-talkie. He moved towards her, as she bent down at the rear of a large station-wagon. One hand was hidden in a holdall held across her stomach. She crouched, peering through the rear window of the station wagon. Suddenly, she jerked a walkie-talkie from the bag. All

Tom heard of the message was "...down Greek Street", as she ended on a high-pitched note.

Glancing across the street, Tom saw the three men turning down a sidestreet. Moving quickly he got to the corner of what was Greek Street to see the three entering a cafe. When Tom entered the cafe a few minutes later, Daniels introduced his companions, one, a small, lightboned, swarthy man with a neat black beard, who claimed to be an Arab. He said he had served in the British army and had reached the rank of Captain. He was called Markham-Randall.

"That's an unusual name for an Arab," Tom commented.

"You are quite correct, Mr....err"

"Burke."

"Mr. Burke, you are quite correct. As an observant man, you may note I look like an Arab. But what is not so obvious is that I also feel like an Arab, think like an Arab. My father may have been an Englishman, but I am one of my mother's people. I served in the British army. So did many Irishmen. That does not make them any less Irishmen, as it does not make me any less an Arab. I trust you understand me, Mr. Burke. There are many Irishmen and many Arabs who do not like the English."

The second man was in his thirties, about six feet tall, with round strong shoulders. Fresh-complexioned with a scrub of blonde hair, his features seemed to have an unfinished look. He did not say so, but from the few words he uttered, it was evident that he was Cockney.

"Call me 'Enery," he told Tom.

The conversation centred on the mechanics of obtaining arms. Markham-Randall made it all sound very simple. He spoke of a warehouse full of arms and ammunition down in Essex which included grenades and anti-tank weapons.

"In fact, we can supply whatever you require," he said.

He suggested that Tom and Daniels should visit the warehouse.

"Whenever it suits you," Daniels said.

"That's very satisfactory. Henry and I will meet you here again tomorrow morning. Say tennish. We might be able to arrange something then," Markham-Randall said.

"Where are you staying?" he asked casually as they parted.

"At the Irish Centre," Daniels answered.

"The more I see of it, the less I like it," Tom said when they were shown their bedroom at the Centre.

"We'll see it through when we're here," Daniels declared.

"You better listen to me first, Charlie," Tom launched into a description of the Oxford Street observation team.

"God, you made great work, Tom," Daniels said ten minutes later.

"I was just lucky that I spotted your man as I was coming up the station steps," Tom was deprecatory.

"It's a set up. There's no other explanation," Daniels said.

"Aye, you're probably right, but they've nothing on us yet."

"Except that we're looking for arms. That in itself would be enough to put us away for a while."

"I'd say we're safe enough yet. We should at least meet them in the morning."

"I'm not sure. I propose we call a taxi and head for the airport."

"Steady on, Charlie, we'll wait till morning."

"It's against my better judgement, Tom."

"Phone call for Mr. Daniels," Charlie was paged later in the evening.

"That was the bold Captain Randy," Daniels said, when he returned to the dining room. "He wants money. He suggested that we bring one thousand with us tomorrow as a sign of good faith, as he put it."

"What did you say?"

"I hedged as best I could. Muttered we'd have to get authority from Dublin. He got very uppity all of a sudden. Thought we were the principals and all that sort of rubbish. Anyhow, the meeting in the morning still stands."

Markham-Randall's approach on the following morning was aggressively business like.

"I am very disappointed," he said, when Daniels told him that the money would not be available for a day or two. "Listen, I've South American clients to take all the weaponry off my hands. I can't afford to fool around. Either you have authorisation to purchase tomorrow morning, with a thousand up front, or the deal is off."

"I didn't know we had a deal," Tom said quietly, "You ask for a thousand pounds. How do we know we're not buying a pig in a poke?"

"I beg your pardon?"

"How do we know there is a warehouse in Essex?"

"You'll have to take my word for it."

"And pay a thousand for the privilege. You must think we're a right pair of Paddies. You're talking about calling the deal off. There's no deal until we see the goods. Bring us out to this famous warehouse of yours and then we'll talk business."

Markham-Randall sat fingering his beard for a moment, looking from Tom to Daniels.

"Yes, I grant that you have a point. Excuse me, until I make a phone call," he stood up and left the cafe, ignoring the public phone on the wall.

"Where's he gone?" Daniels asked Henry.

"To make a phone call," Henry answered between smoke rings.

"Will he be long?" Daniels persisted.

"I dunno," Henry blew another smoke ring.

"I've made arrangements for both of you to visit the warehouse tomorrow afternoon. I'll pick you up here at two o'clock, if that suits," Markham-Randall announced upon his return.

"Fair enough," Daniels said.

"Suits me," Tom nodded consent.

"Right, Henry," Markham-Randall said, heading for the door.

"Right, Sir," Henry jumped up, topped his cigarette and put the butt in his pocket, as he followed him.

"A soldier if I ever saw one," Tom said. "This whole sheebang gets more suspicious by the minute."

"And the money. Once we handed over the money, we'd be in the manure business good and proper. The defendants paid over one thousand pounds as a deposit on the weapons. Can't you see Captain Randy standing up in court?" Daniels asked.

"Listen, Charlie, money or no money, I'd say we're for the high jump. They'll get us down there and they'll produce a few weapons and, then, they might string us along for another day or two. But, as sure as eggs are eggs, they're trying to walk us into something."

"What'll we do, Tom?"

"Get the first flight out of here, Charlie."

***

Back in Tunnygee that night, they discussed the various aspects of the trip. It was Maisie, who, finally came up with a solution. She suggested ringing Markham-Randall and inviting him over to Ireland to continue discussions. Daniels, who had driven Tom home, rejected the sugggestion.

"As far as I'm concerned, I want nothing more to do with it," he said, as he left to drive back to Dublin.

"Here," Tom called him back, "give us that London number. I might chance ringing it."

When Tom rang next morning, there was a considerable delay before Markham-Randall came to the phone. Meanwhile, Tom heard typewriters working and the ringing of at least two phones in the background. As he listened, he got the impression of a large general office, which was confirmed when the noise was cut off and the phone switched to what was obviously a more quiet, private office.

"Burke here,"Tom said, "Charlie and I were recalled to Ireland by our superiors."

"You're in Ireland?" Markham-Randall was obviously surprised.

"That's right. We want to continue negotiations here in Ireland."

"Hold on a minute," Tom heard the phone left down and a door opening.

"Where can I meet you in Dublin?" Markham-Randall was back in a few minutes.

"The Gresham," Tom said, naming the first hotel that came to mind.

"Alright, let me see. There's a six o'clock flight to Dublin. I'll take that and meet you in the Gresham, eightish, say."

Maisie travelled to Dublin with Tom, Olga, taking charge of the bar in their absence. Daniels was in bed when they arrived at his flat.

"You're not serious," he said, when Tom told him about Markham - Randall's expected arrival.

"I am. He's on his way, and you better get out to the airport to meet him. We won't let him out of our sights for a minute," Tom told him.

Markham-Randall did not pass through Dublin airport. Yet, when Daniels arrived back to the Gresham Hotel, the "Captain" was there before him.

"He came in a car about an hour ago, came straight in, checked in, left his bags and walked straight out again," Tom explained. "I ran out after him, but he was gone. I couldn't believe it. He must have been picked up by a car immediately. Anyway, he's back now. He's in Room 321."

"He must have come through Belfast, flown into Aldergrove and come down by car. He didn't come through Dublin. He's Military Intelligence," Daniels said.

"He's a bloody spy of some sort, that's for certain," Tom said. "Still, we better have a word with him. Come on, Charlie, the two of us will go up."

"I won't go near the bastard. Plugged, he should be," Daniels said.

"I'll go up. I want to see what makes him tick."

When Tom came down an hour later, Maisie was having coffee with Captain Roche in the foyer.

"Where did you spring from, Ned?"

"You're not going to believe this, Tom. I walked in off the street and who did I bump into but your beloved wife here. Sure, the least I could do was offer her a drink and when she wouldn't have that, I did the next best thing, I bought coffee."

"And you knew nothing?"

"Actually, Charlie Daniels gave me a ring" Roche grinned up at him. "He told me you were meeting a British spy. He thinks he should be arrested. Maisie was briefing me when you interrupted."

"Oh!" Tom glanced at her.

"Oh, yourself," Maisie laughed, "I told him what happened and that you had your man hidden away upstairs."

"God, I'd love a drop of coffee," Tom said.

Roche signalled a waiter and ordered another pot of coffee.

"And bring a cup for my friend," he called after him.

"Where's Charlie?" Tom asked.

"He went home in disgust," Maisie said. "The thought of even talking to a British spy was too much for him."

"Poor Charlie, but tell me something, Ned," Tom addressed Roche, "What do you think of a thousand rifles, a couple of hundred grenades and several thousand rounds of ammunition for thirty thousand pounds?"

"It sounds a lot of money, but, God knows, I haven't a clue, Tom. I suppose I could find out. I'll make a few enquiries tomorrow."

"Don't bother because, before I left him, the bold Markham-Randall offered me the same amount of stuff for three thousand."

"You couldn't go wrong there, Tom," Roche said. "But what does he want in return?"

"Information, Ned. For example, he wanted to know what is Minister McAtavey's attitude to the Six County situation. He was also interested in your boss. He wanted to know if he'd send in arms to protect the Nationalists."

"And what did you say?"

"I played dumb, but we arranged to meet tomorrow evening again, at nine. That gives him the whole day tomorrow. We have to go home, but he should be kept under observation."

"Leave that to me," Roche said.

Tom arrived at the hotel about eight on the following night. Roche was already there.

"Did you leave Maisie at home this time?" he asked.

"Aye, I asked her, but she didn't want to travel. She says one member of the family has to stay and keep the home fires burning," Tom sat down beside him.

"Well, how's our friend?" Tom asked.

"He didn't stir out of the hotel all day. He made one call to England. It was only about arrangements to meet him at the airport in London. The lads at the desk tell me that he spent most of the day in bed. He's a lazy bloody fecker as well as everything else."

"Here's trouble now," Tom said, as Charlie and three other men entered the foyer.

"Who are they?" Roche asked.

"Jackie Bell from Belfast is one of them," Tom stood up and went over to greet them.

"These are two friends of Jackie's," Daniels said.

"Is your man still around?" Bell asked.

"Aye."

"He won't be around for too long," one of the men said.

"I sent for them," Daniels said. "They think the same as I do. As far as they're concerned he should be eliminated."

"You'll have to hold on for another while, lads," Tom turned to the Bell. "Myself and himself are going to have another chat. I want to get all the information I can out of him. Anyway, we're not certain he's a spy."

"I'm certain" Daniels said. "Didn't you say yourself last night that he was a bloody spy?"

"Leave it till I come back down," Tom advised, "and then we'll see."

"Fair enough," Bell said, "we can have a feed in the meantime. Although I don't think we could afford this joint."

"I saw a chipper on the way in," one of his friends said.

"Aye, that'll do us."

"We'll see you later, Charlie," Bell said.

Daniels went over and sat beside Roche.

"We can't let them kill him," Roche said.

"Why?"

"It would spoil everything."

"Spoil what?"

"I'm sure you could guess, Charlie, The Government here is willing to give all the help it can. You know that. You've been with delegations that met government ministers."

"I still agree with Jackie. We can't let a spy go. Anyway, I don't know how you're going to talk them out of it."

"We'll see," Roche said.

"He's a wrong one, he's as wrong as be damned," Tom said when he came back downstairs. "All he wants is information, about the Dublin Government, about the I.R.A., about everything. The arms were only a bluff. There are no arms."

"The bastard," Daniels said.

232

"Hold it Charlie, you haven't heard the half of it yet. He was testing me out, trying to bribe me. The final thing was that he had been a training officer in the British army; that he was an expert in small arms and guerrilla warfare; that he had a lot to offer a force like the I.R.A. As an Arab, he said, it would be a pleasure for him to train an anti-British force like the I.R.A. Bring me to one of your training camps, he said, and I will demonstrate my expertise."

"That's it," Jackie Bell, who had returned to the hotel, said. "Go back.....Go back and tell him that you would be delighted to bring him to a training camp. Then hand him over to us and we'll find his own very special boghole for him in Leitrim, or Sligo, or someplace."

"No, Jackie, you can't do that," Roche said.

"Who are you?" Bell asked.

"I'm Ned Roche, a Captain in Irish Army Intelligence."

"And I'm Ian Paisley," Bell said.

"He's an Irish Intelligence officer alright," Daniels said, "I suppose you better listen to him."

"I'll make it short, Jackie, "Roche said. "The Government here wants to help. By shooting this Markham-Randall fella, you could queer the pitch. Also, you'll be putting Charlie and Tom here in danger. Their movements are well logged by British Intelligence. If Markham-Randall dies, where do you think the finger will point, straight at Tom and Charlie."

"God, I never thought of that," Bell said.

"Neither did I, for that matter," Daniels said, half to himself.

"I'll go up and tell him that the I.R.A. has condemned him to death as a spy. That might frighten him," Tom said.

"I hope it puts the shit crossways in the bastard," Bell said.

"He's no joke, that fella," Tom said, when he came back. "Do you know those little cases that spies are supposed to carry, you know, you see them in the James Bond films. He has one of those, that he keeps on the table in front of him. You're sentenced to death by the I.R.A., says I. No sooner were the words out of my mouth, then he snapped the case open and shoved his hand in, but I was too quick for him. I jammed his hand with the top of the case. If anything happens to me, I said, there are two or three fellas downstairs who'll look after you. Now, I said take out your hand slowly. He did that, as gingerly as you like. Now, I said, I'll give you one piece of advice. Get out and get out fast."

A few minutes later, Markham-Randall came down the stairs and checked out. Jackie Bell followed him to the front door and squeezed into the taxi after him. The taxi swung across the road and did a U-turn into the down carriageway. It screeched to a halt at the Parnell monument after what seemed to be the muffled sound of a shot. Before it moved off again, Jackie Bell jumped out.

"Did you kill him?" Daniels asked running up,

"No, I only frightened the fucker. I fired into the seat, but I destroyed me effin' coat trying to smother the shot," he held up the burnt side of his tweed jacket.

29

Olga Kennedy attended the Sinn Fein Ard Fheis in Dublin's Intercontinental Hotel in January, 1970. At an I.R.A. convention in the previous month, a resolution was accepted advocating a change of policy, from abstentionism in relation to the two Irish parliaments and the Westminster parliament, to one of the participation in all three. When this resolution was put to the Sinn Fein gathering, about one-third of the 257 delegates walked out and held their own Ard-Fheis. Provisional Sinn Fein was born. Apart from the abstention issue, some of the reasons later given for the break were the failure to provide adequate protection for Nationalist areas in Northern Ireland in August and the adoption by the parent body of an extreme socialist policy, which was seen as leading to totalitarianism.

As one of the delegates who had walked out, Olga returned to Tunnygee a convinced Provo.

"The I.R.A. was a laugh in Belfast in August," she told the crowd in Burke's. "*I.R.A., I ran away,* the kids were shouting in the street. My late husband, Butsy, would have turned in his grave if he had known what took place. It brought disgrace on a once proud organisation."

"Poor Olga, she's a bit hard to take this minute," Johny McCaffrey declared when she left. "Converts, they're all the same.

There she is, not an Irish woman at all, and her going to free the country."

"Pearse had an English father too," Maisie said.

"True for you, Maisie, true for you, Olga's in good company, there's no doubt about it. Anyway, wasn't the lad himself, above in the park, half Spanish?" McGinty added his pennyworth.

"If you farted, you'd bring Dev in to excuse yourself, McGinty," McCaffrey said in disgust. "Who brought the country to its knees in the thirties? Dev, him and his old economic war."

"But he got us the ports," McGinty objected.

"The ports be damned. He destroyed half the farmers of the country. Davitt got the land back for us and, fifty years after, Dev tried to throw us out again."

"But he got the ports and kept us out of the war. Was that not a good day's work?" McGinty asked.

"Aye, maybe it was, but Dev was wrong all the same. He should have supported Mick Collins, the best soldier Ireland ever had."

"Fighting the civil war again, I thought the two of you had more sense," Tom came in behind the counter. "Between you, you left the job half done, as the bold Olga won't be long in telling you."

"For a bloody foreigner she has a lot to say for herself," McCaffrey said sourly.

"She's going ahead with the meeting next Friday to form a branch of Provisional Sinn Fein," Tom said.

"Well, here's one bucko she won't see," McCaffrey declared.

McCaffrey's absence from the meeting did not surprise Olga, but she was very disappointed when Tom did not appear.

"Where is he?" she asked McGinty.

"He's below behind the bar. He told me he wasn't coming. I asked him."

Otherwise, the meeting was very successful, about twenty, mostly younger people, attending. As the only veteran of the War of Independence present, Willie McGinty was appointed President, with Olga unanimously acclaimed as Chairman.

Afterwards, Olga made clear to Tom her displeasure at his failure to attend.

"Listen, Olga, I'll be very frank with you," he told her. "While I fully accept, as you do, that there will never be permanent peace in Ireland until the Brits get out, I , unlike Provisional Sinn Fein, accept the Dublin Parliament as an Irish parliament representative of the bulk of the Irish people. I'm opposed to abstentionism. As far as I'm concerned it's a complete waste of time."

"One thing certain, Butsy would not agree with you, if he was alive. And....And Charlie Daniels is on the National Executive. He's a good friend of yours, isn't he?"

"That's right, Olga, he is," Tom said.

"Is that all you have to say for yourself?" Olga asked.

"That's all, Olga."

In the first week in March, it was well after midnight when two cars pulled up at the Burke pub. Tom, Maisie and Tom Pat were in bed, but the persistent knocking eventually forced Tom to open the door. One car was from Derry and the other, driven by Jackie Bell, was from Belfast.

"Sorry for disturbing you at this hour of the night, but Jackie insisted," one of the Belfastmen explained. "We were above in the Dail."

"You're Billy Jackson, you were at the meeting in the hotel above," Tom said.

When Maisie heard who the callers were, she got up and made tea and sandwiches. Three of the visitors were from Derry and three from Belfast, and they had come from a meeting with government ministers in Leinster House. The visitors were highly elated, all in high good humour at the outcome of their Dublin visit. Billy Jackson, in particular, could scarcely contain himself. He paced up and down the floor, talking rapidly, machine-gunning his words.

"Even the Taoiseach," he explained, "couldn't have been more forthcoming. He's with us all the way."

"The Taoiseach! You didn't say the Taoiseach?" Maisie practically dropped the cup of tea she was pouring.

"Aye, I did. We were talking to the man himself, myself and two of the Derry lads there. He talked about what Dublin could do as a sovereign government working in conjunction with Westminster. In the end he asked us if we'd be satisfied with the abolition of Stormont..."

"We couldn't believe our ears," one of the Derrymen interrupted. "The abolition of Stormont, what more could we ask for?"

"And the Minister for Defence, he was away with it altogether," Billy enthused. "I put it to him that if we were attacked again the same as in August we would need a means of defence, that guns would need to be readily available. He was aware of the situation, he said, and he talked about forming a fictitious company to purchase arms. He talked about street fighting and about how to counteract armoured cars in the city streets and ....and told us how he would love to see the Tricolour flying over Belfast City Hall."

"Sit down, Billy Jackson, you'll wear out the carpet," Jackie Bell said."But," he turned to Tom and Maisie, "every word he says is true. Billy, as usual, did most of the talking, but I was listening. I listened to every word the Minister said and all I can say about him is that he is so Republican he makes me suspicious."

"Aye," one of the Derryman left down his cup, "I was a bit suspicious for a while too, but, then, I thought, he couldn't be that good an actor. In the end, I was convinced that he would do all in his power to assist us. You weren't so sure, Sean," he turned to one of his fellow Derrymen.

"Aye, I think Sean went a bit far, calling him back to the table and challenging what he said," Billy Jackson said.

"But you must remember, Billy," Sean Devlin spoke in his soft Derry accent, "I am the oldest man here and I heard Free State promises before. That's why I called him back and asked him if he meant all he said, if it wasn't so much water under the bridge."

"And he came back , pulling on the black overcoat. He was mad," Jackie Bell laughed at the memory. "He thumped his fingers on the table and if looks could kill, Sean was dead. He stared straight at him and said he was not that sort of man, that his word was his bond and that he stood over every word he said. I suppose it was a bit of an insult to him right enough, Sean."

"Maybe he was insulted," Sean said quietly, "but it's a serious matter for us. Promises are easily made after all. That's why I had to be sure."

"Are you sure now?" Tom asked.

"That's still the big question," Sean said.

As the party left an hour or so later, Billy called Tom to one side and asked him if he could have a lorry available on the weekend of the 17th March.

"And I want a good reliable driver, one who will keep his mouth shut," he added.

"I'm not too sure where I'd get a lorry," Tom said.

"Listen, Tom, I'll leave it with you. I'll give you a call at the end of the week."

"What's it for?" Tom asked.

"You could make a guess and it could be right," Billy grinned, "but I'm only a messenger. Captain Roche told me to tell you".

"Are you in contact with him?"

"He was at the meeting with the Minister. He told me you'd be able to get your hands on a lorry."

"Right, Billy, I'll see what I can do."

Roche arrived in the following week.

"I was in Dundalk for the last few days. I met Billy in The Imperial last night. He told me you got the truck," he said.

"That's right."

"Who's the driver?"

"I was thinking of driving it myself."

"Grand. You'd want to be at the North Wall on the morning of the 17th, St. Patricks Day."

"What's it all in aid of?"

"We're expecting a consignment of arms and we want the truck to remove them down the country."

"I thought as much. Where?"

"Where what?"

"Where are you going to store the stuff?"

"Did you ever hear of a place called the Black House?"

"Sure, It's only down the road a bit. It's deserted for years. Down in the middle of the wood, how did you find out about it?"

"I have my contacts." Roche laughed.

On St. Patrick's Eve, Roche rang to inform Tom that the arms were not coming on the following day.

"The ship, *City of Dublin*, that they are scheduled to arrive on won't be in Dublin until the 25th. Can you cancel the truck?" he asked.

"No great problem."

238

"What about the 25th? Will it be okay?"

"Okay, no problem."

On the 25th, Tom was at the dockside, his lorry parked not twenty yards from the *City of Dublin*. In his rearview mirror he saw a car pull up with a jerk behind him. Jackie Bell hopped out of the driver's seat. He came running forward as Tom watched in the mirror.

"Billy said it was you, I didn't recognise you against the sun," Jackie said.

"Who else is with you?" Tom asked.

"Just the three of us, Sean Devlin, Billy and myself."

The March sun was warm in the lee of the goods piled up along the riverside. The four men stood around smoking and watched the *City of Dublin*, on which sailors moved around in a desultory fashion. A crane moved alongside and dockers seemed to appear from nowhere, moving with the confidence of familiarity to the ship.

"What's going to happen now?" Tom asked.

"Captain Roche is supposed to be here," Billy said.

At that moment, two soldiers, Gustafs at the ready, came running around the piled-up goods, one of them brushing against Jackie Bell as he rushed past.

"They're going to seize the stuff," Jackie said. "Where's that bloody bastard, Roche?"

The two soldiers took up position at the bow of the ship, while two others appeared at the stern. Another stood at the gangplank.

"And there's five other of the bastards in a truck behind," Devlin said, looking round the end of a stack of timber.

"There's something wrong, lads. I feel it in my water," Jackie said.

"Never mind your water. Just play it cool," Billy told him. "There may be a reasonable explanation," he added after a pause. "Wait till we hear what Captain Roche has to say."

"You won't have long to wait," Devlin said from his post at the timber. "Here he comes and company with him."

Roche, flanked by a tall civilian and an army Sergeant, walked purposely to the gangplank, where he seemed to dismiss the Sergeant, who stood back and saluted as Roche followed the civilian aboard.

"See that," Billy said, "Roche and the Sergeant are friendly enough, it seems."

"Too bloody friendly for my liking," Jackie rejoined.

"Let us get out of here as fast as we can. I don't like the way that Sergeant is staring at us," Devlin came over to Billy.

"Stand your ground. He's coming over," Billy watched over Devlin's shoulder.

"Excuse me, gentlemen," the Sergeant said, "have you any business here?"

"Aren't we entitled to be here?" Bell demanded.

"We're waiting on Captain Roche," Billy cut in.

"Do you know the Captain?" the Sergeant looked at him sharply.

"Aye, we know him," Billy said.

The Sergeant looked at them for minute, and, still, obviously suspicious, walked slowly back to the gangplank. A few minutes later, he gave Roche a perfunctory salute as he stepped off the gangplank and had a quick word with him. Roche turned and waved at Tom and his friends, before giving the Sergeant a reassuring pat on the shoulder. He then went over to the tall civilian who was waiting a few yards away. After a moment or two, he shook hands and walked across to Tom and the others.

"I don't know what your story is, Captain, but it better be a good one," Bell said, "I nearly had a stroke when the two soldiers sprung on us from nowhere."

"I'll tell you one thing," Roche said, "I didn't expect to find half the army on the quayside either."

"Will you, for God's sake, Captain, tell us what in the name of God is going on and put us out of our agony?" Devlin demanded.

"Did you ever hear of Murphy's law?" Roche asked, "I think it's in operation on this quayside this morning."

"Forget about Murphy's law. Tell us about the army," Devlin insisted.

"A pure coincidence, just a pure coincidence. There are army munitions and stores on the boat and, in such a case, it is simple army routine to send down a guard to escort the cargo back to the barracks. That's where Murphy's law comes in. The absurdity of it.

On the one day in years that undercover arms are scheduled to come in, a routine consignment of arms arrives, not only on the same day, but on the same bloody ship. If that's not Murphy's law in action, I don't know what is."

"But....but," he looked at the three watching faces, "you haven't heard the worst of it yet. Our stuff didn't arrive at all."

"I don't believe it," Billy said, "you must be having us on, Captain."

"Unfortunately not, Billy," Roche said. "That tall man I was talking to. He's from Customs and Excise and he sent a telex to Belgium. The stuff was not put on the ship for some reason or other."

"Because the arms dealer is a crook. From what I hear he's one slippery customer," Devlin declared.

"How do you know him?" Roche asked.

"I don't know him, but I've a friend who does. I think I'll give him a ring."

"It mightn't be a bad idea," Billy agreed.

They were in the North Star Hotel an hour later when Devlin's friend arrived. A square man in a double-breasted suit, he was of average size, with big feet and hands, giving an impression of bulk and strength.

"This is Mick Spillane. I filled him in on the situation," Sean said.

"I suppose I can talk openly here," Spillane rubbed his hand through a mop of springy, brown hair.

"Talk away," Roche said shortly.

"Fair enough, Captain," Spillane grinned at him, "I heard about you."

"You have the advantage of me," Roche was on the defensive.

"Don't worry about it," Spillane assured him. "It's the boyo in Hamburg we should be worrying about. I've a few friends there and, to put it mildly, they have their doubts. They think he might hold on to the arms and the money."

"We all have doubts at this stage. What do you suggest.... What do you think we should do?"

"If you give the say so, Captain, the lads in Hamburg wouldn't be long putting the tighteners on him."

"What are you talking about?"

"Come off it, Captain. You and I know there was a business deal done, but in this sort of deal it's cash, spons, up front. As I see it, you should get the spons back if the goods don't arrive."

"And you're in a position to arrange that?"

"Let's say I know a few lads who'll give it a helluva good try."

"Perhaps, you'd tell us your exact interest in this, Mr. Spillane."

"Mick, my friends call me Mick, Captain. My interest, a fair enough question. Let me put it this way, me and Sean here go back a long way. Now, the question arises, can we trust you? Me and Sean here, are Republicans from way back, but you're a Free State officer."

"Listen, Mr. Spillane, I'm doing a job and I make no apologies for doing it. I'm cooperating with Sean and the rest of them on that job. How much Sean has told you about the operation I don't know."

"I trust Mick," Sean said simply. "But I trust you too, Ned. Otherwise, I wouldn't be here at all. It's the man in Hamburg we're not too sure about, isn't that it? I know Mick here can put the clampers on him. Should we let him go ahead?"

"No, under no circumstances. As you know Sean, the Minister for Defence, you met him yourself, is backing this. I still don't know how much our friend knows...." Roche nodded at Spillane.

"As Mick himself put it, we go a long way back," Sean said. "You can take it he's in the picture."

"I wonder who the hell else is in the picture? As I see it, the dogs in the street will be barking it next."

"I'm no dog, I don't bark, you needn't worry about me," Spillane said curtly.

"Alright, alright, we're getting off the track a bit. To get back to the issue, I don't think we should take any strongarm action in relation to the dealer. As yet he has given no indication that he's welching on the deal. There may be some good explanation for what has happened," Roche looked at Spillane.

"I'm all ears," Spillane said.

"What do you suggest then, Ned?" Sean asked.

"That someone should go over and talk to him. We've waited

this long, another week, or even two, is not going to make any difference."

"It's up to you, Captain, if you want to give him another chance," Spillane said. "But it might be no harm to warn him."

"What do you mean?"

"Don't worry, when I say warn I mean warn, nothing more. For example, a phone call from the right man telling him to either shit or get off the pot."

"That would do no harm, I suppose," Roche agreed.

30

L isten, Ned, it has to be said, there are a lot of people very un-happy about this arms business," Tom told Captain Roche, having gone to Dublin to meet him. "Billy Jackson was in Tunnygee last night and he says that there are Defence Committee people all over the North very doubtful about the whole operation."

"What do you mean?"

"I'm just telling you what Billy said."

"Why doesn't he come down and talk to me himself?"

"He can't leave Belfast. You know what happened in Bally-murphy last weekend. The whole thing nearly blew up. He wants to be on the ground there this weekend."

"He's right, I suppose, but what does he expect me to do?"

"I told you. As far as the Defence Committees are concerned, you'd want to get shifting and try and pin down the arms."

"And what the hell do you think I'm doing ? I was in Germany last week, and as far as I can make out, the stuff is in Vienna. I'm flying out this weekend to check. Schleuter says he'll meet me there."

"Who's Schleuter , is he the arms dealer?"

"That's right."

"Is he on the level at all, that fella?"

"I honestly don't know. That's why I'm going to Vienna. Up

to this, he's always had some excuse or other, why the stuff was not where it was supposed to be. He says I'll see it with my own two eyes in Vienna."

"I might go with you."

"Why?"

"The Defence Committees want someone to look after their interest and I volunteered for the job."

"You're not checking on me, by any chance, Tom?"

"No more than you checked on me, Ned."

***

In Vienna, Schleuter brought Tom and Roche to a customs compound in the airport complex, where an official opened up a grilled cage and indicated several wooden crates.

"Now, Herr Captain," Schleuter said in his guttural, broken English, "you don't fully trust Otto, maybe, but I would not be around all those years as an arms dealer, if I was not trusted. In this business, one keeps bargains. Crates! You select one, Captain".

"I beg your pardon?" Roche said.

"The crate you want to see, you want a crate opened, no?"

"Oh, yes, I'm sorry," Roche laughed, " I didn't understand you for a moment. Open that one," he pointed.

"Open it, please," Schleuter instructed the customs official.

Using a pinch bar and hammer, the official prised loose a board from the top of the crate and Schleuter waved Tom and Roche forward. Roche took out one of the guns; he passed it on and they all, including the customs official, examined it minutely.

"Are you satisfied, Herr Captain?"

"I'm not satisfied," Tom cut across Roche. "There could be anything in the other crates. Open that one there," Tom pointed to one in a corner, "and take a board from the side this time, the one second from the bottom," he said as he went over and tapped the board with his foot.

"You are satisfied, Herr Burke?" Schleuter asked, when the official prised the board off and pulled out a gun.

244

"At least, Tom, you can now assure Billy and the rest of them that the stuff actually exists," Roche said.

***

Back at the hotel, Roche rang Dublin.

"I was talking to the boss of Aer Turas*, the carriers. They'll have a plane out here on Tuesday morning," he told Tom afterwards.

"That's great. What'll we do, hang around until Tuesday?"

"There's not much else we can do, but if you want to get home...."

"No, I'll see it through when I came this far. I'll give Maisie a ring and tell her."

"Hello, Maisie, everything is hunky dory out here," he enthused on the phone. "They should have sent me to sort it out long ago. The stuff is okay and a plane is coming out to collect it on Tuesday. You won't see me until then, I'm afraid."

"I'm sorry, Tom, but there is nothing hunky dory at this end. The whole thing is going up in smoke. No one seems to know what is going on, but, apparently, the Special Branch have got the wrong end of the stick. They are waiting to seize the goods and to arrest you and Ned. Billy Jackson was here this morning on his way through to Dublin. He rang from Dublin a few minutes ago and he's flying out to Vienna. He'll be there sometime tomorrow. He'll put you in the picture."

Next day, Billy had not much to add to what Maisie had told Tom on the phone:

"All I can tell you is that the Special Branch are on full-scale alert, with orders to seize the plane and everyone and everything on it. As far as I can see, the Secretary of the Department of Justice is gone off at half cock and he thinks he's running the country. He's ordered every airport and every half-airport and every big field, according to some reports, to be covered. He's quoted as claiming to have a ring of steel around Dublin and Cork airports. You'd

---

*   Air Freight Division of Aer Lingus, the Irish National Airline.

think he was expecting a platoon of commandos on the plane instead of a harmless pair, like the two of you," Billy grinned.

"The bloody fool," Roche said, "he's being fed stuff and nonsense by the two boyos who've been planted on the Special Branch, and it's being regurgitated to him, all that junk and crap about coups and takeovers, as if it was genuine intelligence, to which it bears as much relationship as the blue shark to the baboon."

"That's not much good to us now, Ned," Tom said.

"I know bloody well it's not, but a fella has to let off steam an odd time."

"But what are we going to do?" Tom persisted.

"There's nothing you can do," Jackson told him. "First off, no plane is going to come from Dublin. All we can do is leave the stuff here and pick it up when the scare blows over. I'll tell you one thing, there'll be a few Ministers in the Government who'll have some explaining to do, especially the brave Mr. McAdoo, with his flag flying over Belfast City Hall.

"It seems Sean Devlin was right to challenge him, after all," Tom said. "Maybe, like Sean said, all the promises are so much water under the bridge."

"Whether they were or not, it seems everything is scuttled for the time being and we are stuck in this place until Monday at least," Roche was tight-lipped with annoyance.

"Why?" Billy asked.

"I'll tell you why, Billy. I had to take over the stuff officially from Schleuter. Otherwise, I would not have been permitted to put it on the plane. But now that the whole thing has blown up in our faces, I have no authority to keep it under my control in Austria. But Schleuter has a license to cover it. So I've to formally hand it back to Schleuter's agent and I can't do that until Monday," Roche explained patiently.

"Why hand it back at all?" Tom demanded.

"Come off it, Tom. The way things are going in Dublin, we mightn't be able to do much about it for a while. At least, by handing it back to Schleuter, we're keeping our options open."

"You could be right, but do you know something, and I don't

mean anything by this, Ned, you could be keeping Schleuter's options open too," Tom said.

"And what do you suggest?"

"I suppose you're right, Ned, to hand it back. When you think about it, it gives more freedom of action."

"I'm glad you agree," Roche said curtly.

"That means we'll be kicking our heels around here for another day," Tom went on.

"For God's sake, Tom, will you cheer up?" Roche clapped him on the shoulder. "You're in Vienna, you know, that famed and historic city on the banks of the blue Danube."

"From the glimpse I got of it, the same Danube is not too blue," Tom said sourly.

"Someone better ring home and tell them we won't be home until Tuesday morning at the earliest," Billy suggested.

"I'll do it," Tom moved off towards the phones.

"A word with Maisie might put you into better humour," Roche called after him.

Tom stuck up his two fingers and grinned back.

***

At Dublin Airport, on Tuesday morning, there was no overt sign of the Department of Justice's "ring of steel", but it was obvious that some new arrangements had been made to receive the travellers from Vienna. They were directed into a special area away from the other passengers and their passports were checked with great care. They were the only people to be given such special attention.

"Did you see the face of your man behind the desk?" Billy asked when they got to outside. "He was as tense as a rattlesnake. He must have thought we were going to pull a gun on him or something. I wonder was he a policeman?"

"Whoever he was, he was well psyched up. And did you see the fella to the left? He was like a coiled spring, with the new suit on him and the bulge of the gun under it. He was a policeman, anyway," Tom said.

"I'll have a few words with the Minister for Defence about

247

this," Roche declared angrily. "You'd think the Government knew nothing about the operation with McAdoo briefed to the last and all. I don't know who organised this reception, but if O'Brien did it, he has a lot to answer for."

"O'Brien, who's O'Brien?" Tom looked at him.

"Who else but Timothy O'Brien, the Secretary of the Department of Justice."

"Ah, that fella."

"They don't normally check passports, when you come through London like we did? " Billy enquired.

"You're right," Roche agreed. "It was all a set up this morning."

"I suppose we're lucky we weren't arrested."

"You could be right, Billy," Roche smiled wryly.

***

In the following week, a meeting was held in the office of Mick Slaney, the Minister for Agriculture. McAdoo, the Minister for Defence, Colonel Boylan, who had retired as Director of Intelligence a few days previously, and Roche attended. Both Ministers seemed puzzled as to why the Special Branch should have mounted the weekend operation to seize the arms. After some general conversation, which seemed to be getting nowhere in particular, McAdoo suggested to Roche that he was in trouble, intimating, that he, McAdoo, was not going to accept any responsibility for the arms importation.

"You're in the hot seat," he told Roche.

Roche reacted with some passion to this remark, stating that if anyone was in the hot seat, it was the person who had authorised this operation, McAdoo himself.

***

Roche , and his wife, had arranged to meet Tom and Maisie in the Russell Arms Hotel in Navan, later that evening.

"Where's Stella?" Maisie asked when Roche arrived alone, "I was looking forward to meeting her."

"She's at home. She was too upset to come, after what happened today."

We're waiting. What happened?" Tom asked.

"I got some shock today, I tell you. See that?" Roche held up his hand with a cigarette in it, "see the shake in that hand? I never had that before. But do you know what caused it? I met McAdoo who told me I was in the hot heat. When I took him up on it and put it to him that if anyone was in the hot seat it was he, he put on an air of injured innocence and referred to me as a brazen bastard."

"You mean he's going to deny he knew about the arms" Maisie asked.

"That's the way I read it, Maisie."

"I don't believe it. He just can't do that. I heard the lads in my own house. Bill and Sean and the others, the day they met him in Leinster House. He can't go back on all that. I just don't believe it, Ned," Maisie was shocked.

"I wish I had your faith in human nature," Roche half smiled at her.

"No, he can't go back on you now, Ned. We all know he's part and parcel of it. I wouldn't take too seriously what he said today, if I were you," Tom advised.

"Funnily enough, Colonel Boylan said exactly the same thing, but he thinks everyone is like himself, basically honest."

"What did Slaney say?" Tom asked.

"I didn't see him afterwards. He went off with McAdoo, the two of you are going to appreciate the irony of this, the pair of them with McAdoo, after condemning me to the hot seat, rushed off to attend the handing over to the nation of St. Enda's, Padraig Pearse's school out at Rathfarnham. Wasn't there someone who said that patriotism was the last refuge of the scoundrel?"

"You're not putting Slaney in that category?" Maisie queried.

"No, of course not. I'd say McAdoo's duplicity shook him too," Roche told her.

31

I s it not a bit pointless going to Dublin tomorrow?" Tom asked Maisie.

"Why?"

"It's Friday."

"That's right, Friday, May 1st. What difference does that make?"

"Not much, I suppose, but Friday's often busy enough here. Anyway, you've no business in Dublin."

"I could have business that you know nothing about, Mr. Burke," Maisie smiled at the mirror over the bar fireplace.

"I suppose you could," Tom said, absentmindedly stacking bottles.

"Well, if I have no business, your stepmother has plenty. She's going to buy a suit, shoes, a hat, a complete new outfit. And she wants to give the new car a run."

"What new car?"

"The new Cortina. Gibson delivered it on Wednesday."

"A Cortina, no less. I knew they were talking about a new car, but I was thinking of something smaller."

"So was Peadar, I'd say, but Olga's the boss there now. She can wrap him round her little finger."

"Poor Peadar must be gone soft in the head."

"Divil the soft, " Maisie said.

"Talking about soft. You and Olga are all one this last while. There was a time when you didn't trust her too far."

"She's alright, but I still wouldn't trust her too far with a man around."

"You'd trust me?" Tom grinned up at her.

"I might trust you, Tom, but I don't trust her."

"That means that you wouldn't trust me with her around," Tom said.

"How right you are," she cuffed him playfully on the back of the head.

"It might be a good idea to ring Roche when you get to Dublin," he suggested.

"That's exactly what I'll do. There hasn't been a word from him since the night we met him in Navan."

When the two women left next morning, Tom strolled up to Kangley's for the morning paper. He came back and prepared breakfast before calling Tom Pat. When his son left for school, Tom made a second pot of tea and sat back with the paper. He had left the halldoor on the latch to permit the barman to enter. Consequently, he paid no attention when the halldoor was pushed open, scraping on the tiled floor.

"Anyone at home?" the strange voice from the hall startled him.

"Up here," Tom called down to the two men in the hall.

"Are you Thomas Burke?" one of them asked.

"Yes."

"We have a warrant for your arrest under the Offences Against the State Act," the man said, coming up the stairs, the other man remaining in the hall.

"Where did you come from?" Tom asked.

"Dublin. We've instructions to bring you to the Bridewell."

The two detectives agreed to wait until Sean, the barman, came in.

"I have to go to Dublin with these men," Tom told him, "Maisie's gone already, gone to Dublin, and Tom Pat's at school. Get word out to Peadar Kennedy and I'll be home as soon as I can."

The unmarked police car made good time on the journey to Dublin and, within less than an hour, it was speeding through the Phoenix Park. It cut in past the front of Collins Barracks and across Blackhall Place to the Bridewell, swinging through the iron gates into the yard. In the back door through a dingy hallway and Tom was in an enclosed square in the heart of the station, a heavy iron-barred gate and cold stone steps running up from it. He was ushered into a rectangular room, two barred windows, a table and a few chairs. A man came in as the arresting officers left. Tom and he were to sit talking in a desultory fashion for an hour or more, killing time. A uniformed jailer brought in hammered down fish and potatoes on a plate. Tom pushed the plate one side.

"I'm not too hungry," he told his guard.

A mug of tea and a small packet of bread and butter was brought in next. He ate the bread and drank the tea.

The door opened. The big chief, a tall man, the head of the Special Branch entered, accompanied by an Inspector, also in plain clothes. The guard nodded and left. The newcomers did not even sit down. They went into the attack from a standing position.

"You're in a spot, a statement."

"No statement."

"We know all about it. You're up to your neck in it."

"Where were you last October, the beginning of November?" the Superintendent asked quietly.

"I don't know."

"Come now, you were in London. What were you doing there?"

"Just a visit."

"To purchase arms?"

"Who briefed you? British Intelligence?"

"So the Super's right," the Inspector said, "it was to purchase arms."

"I didn't say that. I just mentioned British Intelligence."

"Don't try to be smart with us, Burke," the Superintendent warned.

"Alright, I'll shut up. I want a solicitor here before I say any - more."

They continued questioning, one cutting in on the other, but Tom ignored them, concentrating on a spot on the ceiling. Eventually, they left. The guard returned and they sat looking at each other for several more hours. Tom was brought upstairs to a cell in the late evening. The only furnishing were a chug-chug toilet bowl in the corner and an iron bed with filthy bedclothes. There was nothing for it but to get into bed. Pick a clean place on the floor to put his clothes and squeeze in between the sheets. The opening cell door awakened him. The Superintendent wished to see him downstairs.

He got dressed and went out into the passageway. A quick dash of cold water in the grimy sink at the corner of the passage, a run of wet fingers through his hair, and he was escorted down to the interrogation room. It was well past midnight.

"We brought in Captain Roche," the Superintendent said, "He made a comprehensive statement."

"I'm making no statement. I told you that earlier."

"What's the point? Roche made a full statement. I'd advise you to get your statement on record."

"You're wasting your time, Superintendent."

He was released next morning. He rang Roche's from the pub at the corner.

"Is Ned under arrest?" he asked Stella, Roche's wife.

"Yes, they took him away yesterday. Where are you ringing from?"

"A pub beside the Bridewell. I was held overnight too. I'm just out."

"Are you coming out?"

"Yes, I'll take the bus."

When Tom reached the Roche home, he rang Maisie.

"We knew you were arrested, when Sean told us about the two men. Stella told us earlier in the day that Ned had been pulled in. We were home about eleven and I rang the barracks. They knew nothing, of course, but I insisted, and about two this morning, one of them came down and said you were in the Bridewell; that you'd probably be released today."

"I'm out here at Roche's. There's no need to come up. I'll get the evening bus," he assured her.

Roche arrived home about an hour later. No, it wasn't so bad, he told them, the Special Branch were kind enough. No, he wasn't allowed to make any phone calls; it seemed one had no rights under the Offences Against the State act. It was a bad Act. Under it innocent until proven guilty was a misconception. The assumption of guilt was axiomatic. After the initial excitement of the home-coming, Tom and Roche sat in the front room. Roche brought Tom up date on events:

"On the Monday after I met yourself and Maisie in Navan, I had another meeting with McAdoo in his office in Leinster

House. At this meeting, and this is going to surprise you Tom, after the 'brazen bastard' incident," Roche leaned forward in his chair, "the Minister indicated that the arms could still be imported, provided secrecy was maintained. He then told me that, in the interests of security, he was having me transferred from Army Intelligence to an undemanding position in Dublin from where I could carry on my work and report directly to himself. Now what do you think of that?" Roche asked.

"A bit of a switch from the week before. He must be playing some game of his own. What do you think yourself, Ned?"

"He's too much of a chameleon for my liking, but to finish the story. The next morning I was brought to Army Headquarters by two of my colleagues, obviously under some sort of restraint, and marched into the new Director of Intelligence's office. It was pure farce in the Director's office with your man, a grim-faced automaton, and a staff officer, another equally grim-faced automaton, standing by with pencil and paper poised. It was hard to believe. It was like something you'd read about in a Russian novel. It reminded me of Kafka, standing there, watching the two of them.

"I'll tell you one thing, it was a sobering experience to see my comrades converted into machines without a trace of humanity at the whim of a political master. Anyhow, Fitzgibbon, the new Director had a document in his hand and he read from it to the effect that I was to discontinue my present duties, break all contacts established in the course of those duties, concentrate on legal soldierly duties in future, and finally, that I was to be transferred to the Command Training Depot in Cathal Brugha Barracks. That was, obviously, McAdoo's 'undemanding position' in Dublin, so I wasn't too worried at that stage. If that was McAdoo's way of doing things, well, fair enough, even if it did not show my army friends up in the best light," Roche stopped to take a sip of water from a glass on the table. "Anyhow, I made an appointment to see McAdoo again that night, who, as soon as I arrived in his office, announced that the Director of Intelligence had overreacted.

"I asked him why the leave I'd applied for that day had been blocked. Without blinking an eye he told me that it was probably his fault, that he had told the army that I was not to get leave. I couldn't believe my ears. In the circumstances, I said, I could understand the army overreacting. They could only assume that I was *persona non grata*. McAdoo still insisted that the Director of Intelligence, through ignorance of the situation, had overreacted, stating that the sending of two officers to my home to collect me was a disgrace.

"His protestations rang false to me and my gut reaction was that he was going to deny authorisation of the arms importation. I asked him how he could reconcile the Director's very specific order to break all contacts with his instruction of the previous night that I should keep up my Northern Ireland contacts. He insisted that I should still maintain the contacts. When I queried how I should resolve the contradictory orders, McAdoo gave no direct answer, assuring me that as far as I was concerned everything would be alright. I left him convinced that somehow or other he was going to attempt to make me a scapegoat. I was certain that he was changing his stated policy vis-a-vis the northern situation; that he was placing me in a compromising situation with the army authorities, in a position where I could be court-martialled for disobeying a lawful order."

Roche sighed and continued: "As an army officer I was in a virtually impossible position. As the leave incident indicated, I was already under partial restraint on McAdoo's orders and I knew that it would be easy to hold me completely incommunicado, debarred by military law and the Official Secrets Act from giving my interpretation of events.

"It seemed that I would have to leave the army As I saw it, I had to get out. I had no choice. The decision was inevitable. I applied to retire two days later, on May 1st. McAdoo did not want to sign the application, indicating that I would be looked after. I insisted he sign".

Roche was finding it hard but he continued: " I was arrested on May 1st under the Offences Against the State Act and like you, Tom, brought to the Bridewell. I demanded that McAdoo be brought down to talk to me. After some argument I was brought to Dublin Castle, to the Special Branch Headquarters, to meet the

Minister. In the end, I refused to make a statement. That evening I was brought to talk to the Taoiseach in Government Buildings."

Roche sipped some more water and went on: " The Taoiseach accepted that there would be no formal statement, but he still wanted information. I told him that the matter should be sorted out at cabinet level, that I was only at the operational end, putting policy into effect, and that, anyhow, I was not going to be a stool-pigeon for him or anyone else. I was taken back to my cell in the Bridewell soon after that and was finally released today."

32

Tom was awakened in the early hours of May 6 to the insistent ringing of the telephone in the hall downstairs. It was 3.15 a.m. and he was still half-asleep when he lifted the phone, but the caller soon shook him wide awake.

"Did you hear the news?" Billy Jackson asked, "Toler has sacked Slaney and McAtavey, and O'Donnell has resigned."

"You're not serious."

"I'm dead serious. Here, there was a statement by the Taoiseach, it came out a few minutes ago."

"In the middle of the night?"

"No better time to do the foul act, when half the country's asleep. Then everyone wakes up in the morning and the deed is done and they all shake their heads and say there's no smoke without fire."

"The shit will hit the fan now," Tom said.

"You don't know the half of it. Wait till the muck spreaders shift into high gear. We'll be plastered with the stuff," Billy laughed.

"Where are you ringing from?"

"From Dublin. Where the action is. The word is that the whole thing will break today. You should get yourself up here."

That afternoon, Tom and Maisie arrived at Buswell's Hotel in

Dublin's Molesworth Street, directly opposite Leinster House, the seat of parliament. It was packed.

"There's nothing happening across the road, I'm telling you," a man, flushed with excitement and drink, said loudly."The first thing Toler did this morning when the Dail met was to call for an adjournment till ten tonight. It'll give him a chance to get his story right."

"Hey," Billy called from a corner of the lounge, "we've a table over here."

"I love the air of excitement around this place," Maisie pushed her way through.

"Maisie, I love excitment too," Jackie Bell grinned from behind a tall vase of flowers in the centre of the marble table.

"Hello, Jackie, I'm glad to see you," Maisie said.

"Is there no one glad to see me?" the third man at the table asked.

"This is a Monaghan man, Padraig Sweeney," Billy introduced a lightly-built, intense, young man. "He was just telling us that another Minister has resigned."

"Aye, Andy O'Byrne, he's a parliamentary secretary, he's resigning too. And do you know, it's nearly killing him. I met him on the way in here and he told me that Fianna Fail was like a second religion to him."

"That's four gone now,"Billy said.

"Five, four Ministers and a Parliamentary Secretary. You're forgetting Doran, the justice man, Toler got rid of him the night before last. At this rate, all the Government will be gone before the end of the week," Sweeney declared.

"They say Toler will hold on as Taoiseach all the same." Tom said.

"I wouldn't put it past him, but do you know where he is this afternoon? Do you know were they all are?" Sweeney asked rhetorically. "Up pounding around Arbour Hill, honouring the patriot dead. The 1916 Commemoration at Arbour Hill is on today and there they are above dancing on the graves. There's something wrong there."

"There certainly is," Maisie agreed.

"Is there any way we could get into the Dail tonight?" Tom asked.

"I doubt it," Billy said.

"God, I'd love to be in there," Maisie declared. "You've no pull, Mr. Sweeney, have you?" she asked.

"You're right there, I've no pull," Sweeney told her, "but I might know someone who has. No time like the present. They should be back from Arbour Hill by this. I'll go over and have a word with Slaney. He knows me."

When the Dail met that night, the Taoiseach, Mr. Toler, proposed the nomination of Darragh O'Looney as Minister for Justice to take the place of Mick Doran.

"A jumped up jack, stepping into Doran's shoes," Maisie said and Sweeney cackled in laughter.

"Silence," an usher glared down at them. "Any more of that and you'll have to leave," he warned.

Meanwhile, Toler droned on, explaining that he had requested the resignations as members of Government of Deputies McAtavey and Slaney "on the basis that I was convinced that not even the slightest suspicion should attach to any member of the Government....I may say that on the question of suspicion Deputy McWilliams came to me yesterday evening to say that he had some information from an anonymous source connecting the two Ministers concerned with this alleged attempt at unlawful importation."

The leader of the Opposition, Oscar McWilliams, spoke after Toler:

"Last night at approximately 8 p.m. I considered it my duty in the national interest to inform the Taoiseach of information I had received and which indicates a situation of such gravity for the nation that it is without parallel in the country since the foundation of the State.....Yesterday when I received a copy of a document on official Garda notepaper which supported the information already at my disposal and which also included some additional names, I decided to put the facts in my possession before the Taoiseach. This particular document says : a plot to bring in arms from the continent worth £80,000 under the guise of the Department of Defence has been discovered. Those involved are a

Captain Roche, the former Minister for Agriculture and two associates of the Ministers."

McWilliams went on to state, in his rasping voice, that not only was the security of the State involved, but that those drawing public money to serve the nation were attempting to undermine it. He stated that "the lives of the people not only in the greatest part of Ireland for which freedom was won at such great price have been put in peril, but even worse than that, the people, particularly the minority about whom we are so concerned in the Six Counties, have their lives and their welfare put in jeopardy."

"What do you know about the minority, you old bollocks?" Billy was on his feet, his Belfast accent ringing out loud and clear. "Lives and welfare put in jeopardy, did you ever hear of last August? Did you ever hear of Patrick Rooney, nine years old, and his father, down on his knees, scraping up his son's spattered brains? Did you ever hear of Hugh McCabe in the same Divis Tower flats, shot down by the same so-called forces of law and order? And you talk about lives in danger. Lives have been lost long ago, do you not realise that, Mr. McWilliams? It is not more hypocritical cant we want at this stage, but protection."

"You'll have to leave, you'll have to leave, sir," an usher had a hand on his shoulder, pulling at him.

"I'm going, I'm going. Get out of my way," Billy brushed past the usher and walked rapidly down the aisle.

Some people looked at him with disdain, muttering under their breaths, but some were clapping. When he reached the exit from the public gallery, more than half were clapping, some were standing. Ushers were rushing hither and thither, attempting to restore order, and the Superintendent of the house nearly knocked Billy down as he came charging up the stairs. Tom, Maisie and the two others caught up with him in the downstairs corridor.

"Did you ever hear the like of the piosity of that bastard, McWilliams?" Billy asked.

"Are you another northern troublemaker?" a man, who had overheard, demanded aggressively.

Billy hit out with his fist and blood spouted from the man's nose. In the general melee some of the heavy paintings on the wall were knocked out of position, but Billy kept pushing towards

259

the door, where an usher caught up with him.

"You'll have to leave," the usher said.

"That's exactly what I'm doing," Billy told him.

Out in Kildare St., a crowd was milling around, some of them the worse for drink after the long day, while many were huddled around transistor radios.

"One could start a riot here very handy," Billy glanced around, "that's if one wanted to ," he grinned at a worried looking Maisie.

"I thought you were serious there for a minute," she said.

"I think we should go out to see Captain Roche," Tom suggested,

"Aye, not a bad idea," Billy agreed.

Bell and Sweeney remained in the city centre, while Billy accompanied the Burkes to Roche's Terenure home.

"I'm not long home myself. I left Dail Eireann not much more than an hour ago," Roche told them.

"What do you think now?" Tom asked.

"I'm disgusted, absolutely disgusted at the duplicity of both Toler and McWilliams. I've a copy of the note McWilliams quoted from," Roche produced a photostat from the inside pocket of his coat. "There are three Ministers named on it, McAtavey, Slaney and the Minister for Defence, Willie McAdoo. Why was McAdoo's name left out by McWilliams? The only explanation is that McWilliams entered into an agreement with Toler not to mention McAdoo's name."

"Why?" Tom asked.

"Quite simply because under the law of the land, McAdoo, as the Minister for Defence, is entitled to authorise the importation of arms. As far as I'm concerned it's all a set up."

"But why? It still does not explain why," Tom said.

"Never mind the why," Billy interjected, "the fact is that I was at the meeting back there at the beginning of March. McAdoo knew all the about the arms. Sure, when you went to the phone, Captain, he even made a joke about Ho Chi Minh. There goes Ho Chi Minh, he said, when you left the table."

"The Ho Chi Minh trail. It could mean only one thing, arms," Tom said,"but it still does not explain why the Taoiseach and the leader of the Opposition should collude and, in effect, mislead the Dail by concealing McAdoo's name."

"For Christ's sake, Tom, you're like a dog with a bone," Billy accused. "It's between the three of them. The fact is that McAdoo was in on the arms importation. If he pulls out now we are all going to be dropped in the shit. I say we should jump the gun on him and the other two conspirators, Toler and McWilliams, by going to the papers. Blow the whole lot to hell."

"We could do that, Billy. We might even succeed too, but what about your fellow Nationalists in the Six Counties?" Roche asked.

"I agree with Ned," Tom said."McWilliams was right in one thing if wrong in everything else: lives could be involved if this is mishandled."

"I couldn't agree more, Tom," Roche said. "Look at it this way, Billy. Many Six County people have placed their trust in the Toler Government. They felt that Dublin would come to their rescue if there should be another pogrom like August in Belfast...."

"I know, Ned, I know", Billy interrupted. " No one knows better. Wasn't I on two delegations to Toler? Now, we're thrown to the wolves. It's either back to Croppies lie down, or fight our own corner. Either way, we're now on our own. That emerged clearly from that talking shop you call a parliament this evening. But if the Croppies don't lie down this time, what's going to happen. What's going to happen?" he finished with a shout pounding his fist so hard on the coffee table that he cracked the glass top.

"Take it easy, Billy, take it easy," Tom advised. "It mightn't be as bad as you think. Maybe McWilliams walked Toler into it. He got the note from the guards and used it to put the screws on Toler, that might have happened."

"Yes, Tom, you could be right," Maisie concurred.

"Maisie, you are a great girl, but you're an innocent abroad," Billy declared. "You don't know the Tolers of this world. A bloody Holy Mary milk and water, neither fish nor flesh, everyone's friend. Ditherers, they don't know their own minds, with you one minute and sticking the knife in your back the next. Toler, mark you, will find a good excuse for selling us down the river, to avoid greater violence, for example. Is there no way of getting through to him that if he deserts us now he's setting the stage for violence?" Billy's voice was charged with emotion.

"You're probably right, Billy, especially after Ned's arrest and the sacking of the Ministers," Maisie agreed.

"We may forget about Toler," Roche said. "The only hope now is McAdoo. He's fully briefed on the probability of major violence in the Six Counties if the Dublin Government turns tail. In fact he firmly believes that large scale violence is inevitable if the Dublin Government does not exert its full authority as a sovereign government on behalf of Six County Nationalism, firstly, to give protection and, secondly, to have Stormont abolished as outlined by Toler to Billy and the other boys on the delegations."

"What are you getting at, Ned?" Billy asked testily.

"Maybe, it's wishful thinking, Billy, but maybe, just maybe, there is a possibility that McAdoo won't back down: that he'll stand by his word, as he told Sean Devlin at the meeting in Leinster House. No one knows better than him the lines of trust that have been established between Six County Nationalists and the Government here since August last and no one knows better than him that violence will be the result if he breaks those lines."

"Would you not say they're broken already?" Billy asked.

"Maybe, but I find it hard to believe that McAdoo, knowing all he knows about the Six County situation, will callously throw the Nationalists to the wolves, despite my suspicions of him over the past few weeks."

"According to some of them in Buswell's today, it's a foregone conclusion that McAdoo will replace Slaney as Minister for Agriculture. That would be a fair jump up for him," Tom said.

"But he hasn't sold out yet, not as far as we know anyway," Roche persisted. "All I'm asking is that we wait till he does, before we go off at half cock. Wait till he publicly commits himself. It would be time enough for us to talk about going public then."

"But didn't Toler blow the gaff below in Leinster House today?" Billy asked.

"But if McAdoo doesn't back him he's out on a limb, do you not see that, Billy?"

"I don't know whether I do or not, but the way I see it, Toler must be fairly sure he has him in his pocket at this stage."

"Granted, granted, but we have to wait for McAdoo to make his move. It would be wrong for us to preempt the situation."

"I see that, Ned, but with a sort of blurred vision, like a mirage in the desert, now you see it, now you don't. You're a bit too optimistic for me, I'm afraid, Ned."

"I don't think it's anything got to do with optimism, Billy," Maisie said, "it's more a question of hope, hope that McAdoo will yet back away from betrayal, from betraying the Nationalists in the Six Counties. If there's any possibility that he might do that, it would be wrong of us to speak out."

33

When the Dail met at half past ten on the morning of Friday 8 May 1970, the Ceann Comhairle announced:

"Before the order of business I would inform the Dail that there was a defect in the bells, and at the last division at 2.30 a.m. on Thursday I extended the period of their ringing beyond the usual time on receiving complaints from the Chief Whips..."

This low-key, mundane introduction was the prelude to a historic debate in the Irish Parliament. The opposition decided to filibuster and the debate went on for thirty-six hours. Much of the verbiage evoked was uninformed and speculative but some of it was deliberately and positively misleading. The debate, with its mixture of hyberbole and falsehood, did not end until eleven o'clock on the night of the following day, Saturday. In the circumstances it was probably fitting that the proceedings should have opened on the farcical note of the bells that would not ring.

That morning, Captain Roche and Tom were out on Tunnygee Lake fishing for pike. About twelve, they pulled into the promontory in the centre of the lake for tea and sandwiches.

"I never saw it worse," Tom said. "Not a rise and we're out nearly three hours."

"I don't care if I never caught a fish, Tom," Roche leaned back on the grass, his shoulders against a root, "it's just a relief to be here, away from that mob of cowboys in Dublin."

"Forget about them, Ned. That's why Stella and yourself came down with us yesterday, to relax and enjoy the fishing."

They arrived back in the pub shortly after five. Sean, the barman, stood staring at them when they entered, while the two customers at the end of the counter sat silent, looking down at their drinks.

"Anything wrong?" Tom asked the youth.

"No, Tom, no, nothing wrong."

"Where's everyone then?"

"Herself is upstairs, herself and the Captain's wife and daughter."

In the kitchen upstairs, the two women and the twelve year old girl sat huddled around a radio on the table. It was obvious that they were not listening to the music coming from it. Tom stood in the door, the Captain behind him. The girl, who was crying, jumped up, pushed past Tom and put her arms around her father's waist.

"He told lies about you, Daddy. Mr. McAdoo told lies about you on the radio," she eventually blurted out between sobs.

"He said you were under suspicion. He said terrible things about you, Ned," Roche's wife, Stella, rubbed away her tears.

"Don't cry, Stella," Maisie stood up and patted her on the shoulder, "please God, it will work itself out yet."

"What exactly did McAdoo say?" Roche looked at the women.

"That you were untrustworty, that you weren't fit for your job, that you were under surveillance. He ruined you, Ned, he ruined you. The Minister for Defence ruined you," Stella spoke through her tears.

Roche took his daughter by the hand and sat down at the end of the table, where she sat on his knees and held him tight.

"I'm going to find out what was really said," Tom threw his coat over a chair and went pounding down the stairs.

"Bring me out money for the phone and some pencil and paper," he roared from the hall to the barman.

Soon, those upstairs could hear him speaking loudly into the phone.

"Yes, it is a pay phone," he shouted at someone at the other end of the line. "Alright, alright," he lowered his voice slightly,"I'll put it down, but make sure you ring me back.."

"Yes," he grabbed the instrument from the cradle on the very first tinkle, "Burke here again. Fire away, but not too fast. I want to get it down."

Several minutes elapsed before Tom came running up the stairs and burst into the kitchen.

"McAdoo got the pay off," he shouted. "Toler appointed him Minister for Agriculture and he betrayed everyone. He denied any knowledge or consent on his part in relation to what he'd described as an attempt to smuggle arms. Here, I wrote this bit of it down:

> I was aware through the Director of Intelligence that attempts to smuggle arms were a constant danger, and these attempts were kept under surveillance at all times. I wish to say I discharged my duty to the full extent of my knowledge of the situation. I want to say also that in recent times I formed the opinion that Captain Roche was becoming unsuitable for the type of work that he was employed in. I want to say that certain suspicions were forming in my mind. I was kept informed by the Director of Intelligence but nothing concrete emerged.

That's the guts of it."

"Who were you talking to?" Roche asked.

"I rang your friend in *The Irish Times,* Mick Cash. He said you'd probably want to make a statement. I said I would drive you back to Dublin. I told him we'd be at your house in two hours."

Mick Cash was standing on the Roche doorstep, when Tom and Roche arrived. Sitting at his dining-room table, Roche dictated a statement to Cash in which he referred to McAdoo's reference to him in Dail Eireann as a tissue of lies, stating that "the man is an unmitigated scoundrel and I say that not under privilege of Dail Eireann." It concluded: "What Mr. McAdoo has done is nothing better than character assassination obviously intended to preserve his position at any cost to his honour and integrity."

"Were you surprised, Captain, that Tommy Moloney, the Belfast M.P. defended you at his press conference?" Cash asked.

"What press conference?"

"He gave a press conference in the Gresham Hotel at eleven this morning."

"The first I heard of it," Roche said.

"You're not serious. McAdoo referred to it in Dail Eireann," Cash said in surprise.

"We were out fishing today," Tom explained. "Ned only knows what you told me on the phone."

"I'm sorry, Captain. I assumed you heard the six o'clock news," Cash said. "That means that you didn't hear about the second press conference in the Gresham today either."

"No, I'm afraid I'm a bit out of touch," Roche rubbed his hand through his hair. "That's what comes from running down to Tunnygee to fish," he smiled ruefully at Tom.

"And we're heading back there as soon as we straighten out Mr. McAdoo," Tom told him.

"Yes, there were two press conferences in the Gresham, today," Cash said, "the Moloney one was at eleven, as I said. I have a note here of what he said," he flicked back through his notebook. "Here it is. I would be surprised - assuming that there is any truth in the allegations - if any action he, that's you, Captain, took was not known to his superior officers and even to the Minister for Defence."

"Good man, Tommy, at least someone is willing to come out in the open and tell the truth," Roche said.

"He went further," Cash flicked over a page, he said:

As far as I know, Captain Roche was not asked to resign. He tendered his resignation, so that it would be possible for him to tell whatever he had to tell, rather than remaining muzzled within the army.

Cash continued, "As I see it, McAdoo could have interpreted this as a threat issued on your behalf, Captain, by a friend of yours. Moloney is a good friend of yours?"he asked Roche.

"Yes, a very good friend."

"That's it, then. It was the threat that triggered the McAdoo reaction. On the face of it, it was a stupid move on McAdoo's part attacking you the way he did, but if he had seen Tommy Moloney issuing a threat on your behalf, it would explain why he felt it incumbent on himself to get in the first word, a form of self protection."

"Well, whatever the reason," Roche smiled wryly at Cash, "there's no longer any doubt about McAdoo. He's sold out."

"Sure, you expected nothing else since that day in Slaney's office," Tom said.

"Still , it's hard to accept. It's a strange feeling to be finally let down by a man whom I looked upon as a friend once. There's something particularly rotten about it. It lowers everyone. That's it, I suppose, it lowers everyone. It lowers humanity."

His two listeners sat looking at him.

"There was another press conference?" he questioned quietly, breaking the silence.

"Yes, yes, there was. A group of people from various parts of the Six Counties denounced the Government for betraying the Defence Committees. Yes, here it is," Cash found the page. "They claimed there was only despair for the northern minority as they listened to politicians in the Twenty Six Counties try to make cheap political capital out of the situation. As far as they were concerned, Toler threw them to the wolves, to quote one of them."

"How right they are," Roche said.

It was late the following evening when the two of them got back to Tunnygee. Two or three people stopped and looked after the car as it went down the street. Two youths at Dockery's corner shouted something, while, McGinty, who was standing beside them, waved his cap. As they entered the bar, the nine o'clock TV news started. The first item showed Roche and Tom standing on the doorstep of Roche's home. The announcer stated that both had been questioned by gardai in relation to the alleged arms importation.

"They should have kept you, when they had the pair of you," McCaffrey shouted across the heads of the crowd in the bar.

Olga ran forward and kissed both of them on each cheek to the amusement of a group at the lower end of the counter. McGinty came in behind them, panting, having rushed down from the corner.

"Give the two of them their pleasure," McCaffrey called to Maisie.

"What about me, Johny?" McGinty asked between pants.

"Give him one or I'll never hear the end of it," McCaffrey said resignedly.

"He's some boy, that McAdoo fella," McCaffrey declared, holding out his hand to Roche, "but he met his match last night. You gave him his answer, Captain Roche. You were great on the television. Even though I never had the pleasure of meeting you before, I was proud of you last night and it's proud I am to shake your hand now."

"He's some tulip, that McAdoo fella, right enought," McGinty said, holding out his hand for the pint of stout that Tom passed to him.

"There's nothing wrong with McAdoo," an overweight, white-haired man of about forty said, "he was only doing his job, blocking McAtavey from walking the country into civil war."

"Who are you?" Roche asked.

"It doesn't matter to you who I am, Captain Roche," the man said, "but I'll say one thing, the truth will come out yet and when it does, McAdoo will be shown to be right,"

"I'm telling lies so?" Roche questioned.

"I didn't say that."

"What the hell did you say then?" Roche demanded.

A tall, thin man, gaunt under a cap, caught Roche's eye and tapped his temple with his index finger.

"I only said the truth will come out yet," the overweight man said. "Give us another drink there, ma'am" he called to Maisie.

"No more drink, " Maisie removed his glass from the counter top. "Out you go and don't come back. Your type is not welcome here."

"Now, Mrs. Burke, that's strong talk for a wee woman like you," the man said.

"There's the door," Tom pointed towards the door, "I'd advise you to start walking towards it."

"You're a big man, Burke, with all your friends around, but that won't always be the case," the man blustered as he left.

"He's not just like another," the tall, gaunt man said as he followed him out. "And he's not too bright either. He's a neighbour of mine and maybe I shouldn't say it, but he's so thick that he couldn't write his name with a burnt stick on a whitewashed wall."

"He's a bollocks, that's what he is," McGinty was more forthright.

The party lasted until the early hours of the morning, and Tom and Maisie were in bed at noon next day, when the barman knocked on the bedroom door.

"Come in," a half-awake Tom grunted.

"There's four men downstairs to see you," the barman said.

"Who are they?"

"I don't know, but they've Belfast voices, I think."

"Alright, I'll be down in a minute."

"I guessed it was you, Jackie. What's up?" Tom greeted Jackie Bell, who was accompanied by three others.

"Not much, but me and the lads here, thought we should do a wee job on McAdoo."

"I must admit that the thought crossed my mind yesterday too," Tom went behind the counter and pulled a small bottle of lemonade.

"Sorry, would you care for something? " Tom asked, pouring the lemonade and gulping it down.

"Too early," one of the men, with a small blue cardboard case in his hand, said shortly.

"We're serious about this, Tom," Bell said.

"What are you going to do?" Tom asked.

"Shoot him."

"Go up and call Captain Roche," Tom told the barman.

"Howya, Captain," Bell greeted cheerily when Roche appeared.

"Hello, Jackie," Roche said and nodded at the other three.

"They're going to shoot McAdoo," Tom said.

"What?"

"A lot of good men are going to die because of him," Bell said.

"We should discuss this in a more private place," Roche glanced up along the counter at the barman busily polishing glasses.

269

"What exactly do you intend doing," Roche asked, when Tom had ushered them upstairs.

"Go down to his hometown and shoot him."

"You can't do that, Jackie," Roche said.

"He's a traitor as far as we're concerned. I know what I'm talking about too. I was on a delegation to Dublin, remember?"

"You called him an unmitigated scoundrel yourself," one of the other men said.

"I did and that's what he is, but shooting him is not going to get you anywhere. You'll make a martyr of him and you'll be classified as murderers, bloodthirsty gunmen. Have sense, Jackie," Roche begged.

"But how many are going to die in Belfast, Derry, Dungannon and other areas because of the actions of McAdoo and the rest of them?"

"I know, Jackie, I know and you know, Jackie, and McAdoo knows too, that violence is inevitable now that the Dublin Government has not kept faith with the Nationalists. God knows I've spelt it out in enough reports to the same McAdoo, but what do the general public know? How could they? They have not been briefed on the inevitabiltity of violence, but I'll tell you one thing, if you shoot McAdoo you will simply undermine the Nationalist case."

"I don't see it that way," Jackie persisted.

"Quite simply, you will hand Toler and the rest of them several trumps. The security of the State will be trotted out as under attack. The right of an elected representative to freedom of speech in parliament will be portrayed as under attack. The integrity of parliament itself as an institution of state will be said to be under attack. I could go on, the list is endless. Against that, the possibility or even the probability of violence will be of little account. That argument will be dismissed out of hand. Listen, what you suggest is complete madness."

"It's a shame to let the bastard away with it." Bell said.

"The worst thing you could possibly do is make a martyr of him at this stage," Roche declared.

"Okay, Captain, you win," Jackie conceded, after some argument.

"Now that that's decided, will you take charge of this for awhile," the man with the case stood up and handed it to Tom.

"What's in it?" Tom asked.

"A couple of short arms and here's the ammo," the man handed two battered Players 20 packets to Tom. "You better stick these in along with the weapons."

Tom felt the shape of the bullets in the heavy packets, as he opened the case.

"This is a bit ancient looking," he said taking out a snub-nosed revolver, "and the other two don't look much better."

"They work, all the same," Billy said.

"What do you want me to do with this cargo?" Tom asked the man who had given it to him.

"Stow it away somewhere safe for an hour or two. It's a bit heavy to be lugging around. And I could do with a bit of grub and maybe a drink or two, now that the operation's off," the man grinned.

"Fair enough, I'll put away the weapons," Tom closed the case, "and then we'll all have breakfast."

"That's the best news I heard in a long time," a blonde sharp-faced youth, who had sat on a chair, pulling hard on his cigarette, spoke for the first time. "I came off without my breakfast this morning and my stomach thinks my throat is cut."

34

Wednesday morning, May 27, was bright and sunny. Billy Jackson had come down from Belfast to Captain Roche's on the previous evening and had stayed overnight. The Roche children had gone to school, when Billy left the house for a morning newspaper to be arrested by Special Branch Officers waiting outside. He was whisked to the Bridewell to appear in the Dublin District Court later in the day, where he was charged with conspiring with people unknown to import arms and ammunition into the state in contravention of the Firearms Act between March 1 and April 24. He was remanded in custody until the following Wednesday.

As Billy was on his way to Mountjoy, there were two other visitors to the Roche home. Both of them, one from Limerick and the other from Derry, were in their penultimate year at Maynooth College, where they were studying for the priesthood. The Limerick man was going north with his Derry friend to spend a short holiday at the latter's home. They had stopped for a meal at the County Club on the Navan Road. The restaurant was full, but eventually they were allotted a table, where two other men were finishing a meal. When the latter addressed them as Father, the Derryman expained that they were not yet ordained, despite the round collars.

"We've still a year to go," he said.

"What do you think of this arms business?" he asked after a few minutes.

"There never was such a threat to the institutions of State, since the State itself was founded," one of the men said portentously. "It's a communist plot with the arms coming in from behind the Iron Curtain."

"You don't expect me to believe that," the Derryman objected.

"There is a lot of truth in what he says," the second man said.

"Are you policemen?" the Derryman asked.

"We are, how did you guess?" the first man grinned.

"Have the arms not something to do with the Six Counties?" the Derryman asked,

"That's only an excuse. It's an attempted left wing coup."

"Surely, you don't mean to say that McAtavey and Slaney are left-wingers?" the Limerick man asked.

"No, but they're being used."

"By whom?"

"By Captain Roche, or whoever's behind him."

"You're not serious?"

"I am. Wait till you see. It'll all come out in the wash."

Shortly afterwards, the policemen excused themselves, saying that they had to be on duty in Dublin Castle within fifteen minutes.

"What did you think of that?" the Derryman asked.

"It's nonsense, of course, absolute nonsense. Nevertheless, it's dangerous nonsense," his Limerick friend replied.

"It's worse than that, it's Alice in Wonderland stuff, and it's being fed to them. That's the sinister part of it. Did you hear that first policeman, he's semi-illiterate? Someone had to brief him. The second boy supported him all the way. It's obvious he was briefed too."

"We should tell someone about it," the Limerickman suggested.

"We'll go back and tell Captain Roche. He lives in Terenure," the Derryman agreed.

The students were in Roche's home relating the story, when Roche was arrested by a quiet voiced and polite Sergeant. He was brought to the Bridewell where he was held overnight. In the next cell, was Albert Horan, from Flanders, who had come to Ireland at the end of the war and was a naturalised Irish citizen. Because of his linguistic capability, he was brought to the Continent to act as interpreter for Captain Roche in dealings with the German arms dealer. Both men were charged with the same offence as Billy Jackson, Horan contenting himself with a plea of "not guilty" and Roche stating:

"I plead not guilty as charged and I wish to state further that anything I did while a serving officer I did with the knowledge and approval of the then Minister for Defence, William McAdoo."

Next morning, having spent the night in the cells, both were in court. The former Ministers, Slaney and McAtavey, the latter with his arm in a sling, were also there. Roche was the first to be arraigned on the charge of conspiring to import arms. The head of the Special Branch automatically opposed bail on the basis of the seriousness of the charge and of the likelihood that the defendant would interfere with witnesses. When pressed for evidence, the Superintendent claimed privilege, but the District Justice was having none of it. All four were released on bail.

"You were lucky," a prison warder whispered to Roche as he left the court precincts. "There were four cells scrubbed out above in the 'Joy. We all thought you'd be joining Billy Jackson."

Meanwhile,Tom, who had left the court when bail was granted, was on his way to the home of Kevin O'Donnell in the foothills of the Dublin Mountains. O'Donnell had resigned from the Government as Minister for Local Government, in protest at the manner in which the Taoiseach had acted and had called a press conference that afternoon. When Tom reached O'Donnell's home, the narrow approach road was blocked by cars, with media men and women all over the place. It was not possible to get into the house, but Tom secured a vantage point at an open window. Resting his elbow on the dining room mantelpiece, Kevin O'Donnell, calmly and unequivocally, put the blame for all that had taken place squarely on the shoulders of the Taoiseach, Mr Toler, calling for his removal from office.

O'Donnell was particularly incensed by the arrest of Jackson, whom he described as a man who had stood between the defenceless Nationalist people in Belfast and slaughter in the previous August. Since then, he declared, he was permitted to go freely about his business in Belfast, yet, when he came to Dublin, he was arrested by the Irish Government. He went on to say that he considered it to be felon-setting by the leader of the Irish Government and that it appeared to him to be deliberate a effort to deliver the Nationalist population of Belfast into the hands of their enemies.

"As far as I am concerned," he said, "it constitutes the ultimate treachery of which an Irishman could be guilty."

When asked if Mr. Toler should give more background information in relation to the case, he replied: "I would not be interested in whether he does or not. Whatever evidence he has does not interest me in the least. It comes from a source of a man of no honour. It's tainted evidence."

"That's fairly sewing it into him," Tom said to an older man in working clothes, who stood behind him.

"He couldn't sew it half hard enough," the man said between puffs on his pipe, "and I'll tell you something for nothing, young lad, you can believe every word Kevin O'Donnell says. I know him all my life. He got out, you know, as a matter of principle. He wasn't pushed or asked to go."

"So did Captain Roche," Tom said. "In fact, they wanted to keep him, but he wouldn't let down the people in the north. He got out on principle too."

Billy Jackson remained in prison until June 10. On that day, Terry Tone, the business man with the black patch over one eye, who had already gone bail for Captain Roche, was in court again.

"Will they let Billy out today?" Tom, who had met him in Roche's house, asked.

"If they stick to this nonsense about his home being outside the jurisdiction, they may not."

"Those fellas mightn't be too happy," Tom indicated some of the thirty or so Belfastmen, who had travelled down for that day's hearing. "There's a rumour that they're going to attempt a rescue, if Billy doesn't get bail."

When the case was called, the Belfastmen crowded into the court, mostly youngish men, shirt-sleeved and bare armed.

"It looks a bit like intimidation to me," Tone said out of the side of his mouth.

"Those Special Branch men round the dock might agree with you," Tom whispered.

"I notice that," Tone said, but isn't it a mockery of Irish justice that Billy, a representative of the minority in Northern Ireland, whose only crime was in coming south to seek assistance, should have been incarcerated?"

The case was called and the State prosecutor suggested a figure of £10,000 bail. It was the highest bail figure ever demanded by the State to that date, but Tone was equal to the occasion.

"I would be proud to go £10,000 bail for a man like Billy Jackson," he calmly announced.

The Justice showed some sense of proportion when he said that £10,000 was an exaggerated figure, but he still placed a high price on Billy's freedom when he fixed bail at one personal surety of £1,000 and an independent surety of £5,000, accepting Tone as bailsman.

With a shout, the Belfastmen seized Billy and chaired him from the court.

Some of them attempted to grab Tone, and carry him shoulder high also, but he declined. The group burst out through the heavy iron gates of the Bridewell, joyous and elated that one of their townsmen had secured a modicum of freedom, that he was at least as free as his co-accused from the South.

"You bastards must think Belfast is a different country. He was the only one held. One law for down here and another for us," one Belfastman shouted at a policeman.

"I'm just as glad as you are he's free," the policeman shouted back.

On July 2, Billy was before the court again, this time in company with McAtavey, Slaney, Roche and Horan. Informations were refused against Slaney on the ground that the prosecution had failed to make a *prima facie* case, his counsel pointing out that the evidence against his client was at best mere hearsay, much of it based on alleged phone-calls at that. The other four were remanded on continuing bail.

"It's absolutely scandalous that you were returned for trial," Roche told Horan, "when all you were was a bloody interpreter."

"Don't worry, Ned. I have been in worse spots before," Horan laughed, lighting a small cigar.

The trial proper opened in the Central Criminal Court on September 22. The main prosecution witness was McAdoo. He denied any knowledge of the Tunnygee meeting with the Defence Committees in the previous October. He also denied authorising the arms importation, but he was forced to admit, under cross-examination, that he had been briefed on aspects of the operation by Captain Roche.

Colonel Boylan, the former Director of Intelligence, was another prosecution witness. He contradicted McAdoo in relation to the Tunnygee meeting, stating that the Minister had been briefed about it shortly after it took place. Probably the most significant piece of evidence given by the Colonel was that McAdoo had issued a Directive to the Chief-of-Staff of the Defence Forces on February 6 instructing the army to prepare for incursions into Northern Ireland, to set aside surplus arms for that purpose, and to provide gas masks. He stated that at all times McAdoo had been fully aware of Roche's activities.

"That should establish to everyone's satisfaction that I acted with due authority at all times and that McAdoo is giving false evidence when he indicates otherwise," Roche said to Tom in the foyer of the Four Courts during a break in the trial.

"The judge might throw it out," Tom suggested.

"That won't happen," Roche said. "They'll pull some stroke or other in an effort to confuse the issue."

On the sixth day of the trial, the Secretary of the Department of Justice appeared in the witness box. He began to read out a letter about Albert Horan to which Horan's counsel took exception on the grounds that it contained personal matters and was of no relevance to the trial.

"Why Mr. Horan's affairs should be bandied around the court, I don't know. I don't know what they are, but I strongly suspect that your Lordship thinks they might hurt Mr. Horan in some way." Horan's counsel paused and glared at the bench before continuing. "It is only illustrative of the rather unfair tone in which your Lordship sometimes has conducted this trial."

The judge called a recess and then aborted the trial. Apart from the challenge posed to him as impartial arbiter and his right to take the action that he did, the effect of the judge's decision was to put the defendants at hazard in another trial where the prosecution would have an opportunity to mend its fences and strengthen a case which, it seemed , might have been thrown out at the end of the prosecution evidence first time round.

The ground rules for the second trial, which started on Tuesday, October 7, were quickly evident. To the consternation of the defence, Colonel Boylan was dropped as a prosecution witness on four grounds, two of which were false and two irrelevant. Secondly, the judge ruled that there could be no reference to the aborted trial, a decision which worked very much to the disadvantage of the defence, because the stated grounds for excluding Colonel Boylan arose from the first trial and, because it also gave an opportunity to prosecution witnesses, already heard, to amend and change evidence without fear of referral back to the first trial. There were rumours of even more sinister developments as the second trial opened. There was a story going the rounds in the precincts of the court that morning which seemed scarcely credible. It was claimed that a meeting had taken place in a hotel in the Wexford area where the recently appointed Minister for Justice, Darragh O'Looney, the slightly more recently appointed Minister for Agriculture, McAdoo, and the Attorney-General, Reg Donlon, had discussed prosecution strategy for the second trial, which resulted in the expedient of dropping Colonel Boylan as a prosecution witness and, secondly, a decision to change the record in relation to McAdoo's Directive of February 6.

In the first trial, leading counsel for the prosecution had stated that they did not know where to get the terms of the Directive, claiming: "Quite a detailed search has been made already and no such record can be discovered so far."

Yet, a retired officer, Colonel Boylan, by making a simple phone call to Army Headquarters, obtained the terms of the Directive, as had emerged at the first trial. Was it possible that the prosecution, with all the resources of the state behind it, could not find a record available in such an official place as Army Headquarters? It was possible but clearly not credible. It was obvious that it would be a factor in the second trial. Both the prosecution and defence realised this.

On the day before the second trial, a man visited Tom's bar. It was a few minutes before Tom identified him as a spectator at the abortive trial on practically every day. A tall, middle-aged man, erect and square shouldered, Tom assumed he was a policeman. He did not identify himself, stating that it did not matter who he was; he was merely concerned with having a message conveyed to Captain Roche.

"I know you're a good friend of the Captain's," he said. "I've seen you together in the Four Courts several times. That's why I'm using you to convey my information. I do not want to be seen talking to the Captain directly. First, Colonel Boylan is going to be dropped as prosecution witness when the trial opens tomorrow."

"Why?" Tom asked.

"Basically, because he told the truth and undermined the concocted prosecution case. Part of his evidence was about McAdoo's Directive to the Chief-of-Staff. I haven't the full details, but I've enough information to know that it's the intention to produce a different version of the Directive than that given by Boylan in the first trial..."

"Who's going to produce it?" Tom interrupted.

"The prosecution and . . . and that's why they're dropping Boylan as a witness. They don't want him telling the truth about it and upsetting the applecart."

"That's a terror," Tom said. "It's hard to believe."

"Well, that's it and the Captain should know about it. Can you drive up to see him today?" the man asked.

"I suppose I could."

"I'd suggest you do. I'm glad to meet you," the man held out his hand, shook hands and moved to the door.

"I'll see you in the court tomorrow," Tom called.

"No, you won't," the man said cryptically, pulling the door after him.

Next morning, in the Four Courts, it seemed that the Wexford meeting, and what transpired there, was common knowledge.

"The place is buzzing with it," Billy Jackson told Roche and Tom, as they stood in the foyer of the Court, waiting on the trial to start.

"There's no doubt that the meeting took place," Roche said. "Tom's caller yesterday seems to have been well informed. Did you tell your counsel about him Billy?"

"Aye, he's briefed alright, and do you know, he didn't seem a bit surprised. That's obviously what they were planning in Wexford, was all he said."

"What did your counsel say?" Tom asked Roche.

"I went out to his house last night. It seemed to take him by surprise, he didn't say much. He pondered for a while and said, they'll have to call the Chief-of-Staff to substantiate any purported change in the Directive, and if they don't call him, we'll call him. Also, even if the prosecution drop Colonel Boylan, we can always call him, he said."

A few mornings later, Kevin O'Donnell approached Tom and handed him a letter.

"I can't see Captain Roche around." he said. "I would like if that letter was delivered to his counsel."

The letter contained information which had been conveyed to O'Donnell concerning the rewriting of the record of the February Directive. In the wake of Colonel Boylan's evidence in relation to the terms of the Directive which existed in written form at Army Headquarters, evidence which went a long way towards demolishing the prosecution case in the first trial, it had been decided as arranged at the Wexford meeting, to change the official record. Accordingly, a meeting was called in the office of the Minister for Defence, attended by various departmental officials and army officers, and chaired by the Defence Minister. In his letter, Mr O'Donnell named the officer who had recorded the substitute version and it was interesting to note that, belted and uniformed, the man was daily present in court, obviously detailed to stand by as a witness.

"That explains why the bastard's hanging around," Roche said.

"Precisely," his counsel replied, adding drily. "And it seems that the good Mr. Toler was also consulted."

"You mean the Taoiseach?" Roche asked.

"Yes, it says in the letter that the Minister for Defence phoned the Taoiseach twice to give his *imprimatur* to portions of the revised text."

"They're trying to hang us on forged evidence, it's as simple as that," Roche said.

"Yes, but that won't happen. I heard that the Chief-of-Staff won't be available to give evidence," the counsel told Roche.

"Where did that information come from?" Roche asked.

"I am not at liberty to disclose a confidential source, let us say," the counsel smiled, "but the Chief-of-Staff has gone or is going to Cyprus to inspect the troops."

"He could be recalled," Roche said.

"I don't think that will happen. If he was willing to give evidence he would not have decided to go in the first place. Without him, the...the amended version of the Directive won't be put in evidence. It just would not stand up and, anyhow, we have another trump card," counsel held up the letter, "we can call Mr. O'Donnell if neccessary."

Counsel was right and the reconstructed record of the Directive was not introduced by the prosecution. The unadulterated record of the Directive as given by Colonel Boylan to the court was unchallenged and a major effort to subvert the course of justice had been thwarted. In relation to the evidence of McAdoo, counsel for the defence stated:

"Forget that he is a Minister of State. He is now down in a court of Justice, one man against others. Remember, gentlemen, what were to me at any rate and I am sure to some of you, some of

280

the things, shocking things he said...Don't let's mince words, he's a liar...This is the man on whose evidence you must act and whose evidence you must accept as the truth beyond all reasonable doubt, when he swears he did not authorise the importation of arms. This is the man, you will remember, this is the man who told Dail Eireann and the populace of this country that although he had certain suspicions in his mind, no concrete evidence had emerged.....He had been told time and again by Colonel Boylan and by Captain Roche just what Captain Roche was doing. He made his own classical remark that comes from his own mouth, that when the army turned up to collect the official consignment of arms that he supposed Captain Roche melted into the shadows. This man, to use his own adjective, had the brazen effrontery to tell Dail Eireann that no concrete evidence of importation had emerged....What is this trial about? I think it is an asinine pantomime, sheer waste of your time and everybody else's time, except the lawyers like me who are paid for it ....Mr. McAdoo reminds me of a character in Pilgrim's Progress, Mr. Fancey Motface, who was notable for facing both ways...In the witness box, he was evasive, prevaricating, confronted with his own false statement in parliament...For God's sake, gentlemen, throw out this smelly, shameful, disgraceful prosecution."

The four defendants were found not guilty. Immediately the court erupted into a wild scene of cheering and shaking hands. People jumped for joy and Roche, escorted by Tom and Mike Houlihan, who had travelled up with Tom for the final day of the trial, pushed through the crowd. The three arrived on the street, battered and in disarray. Billy Jackson was carried out shoulder-high and the crowd burst into wild, uninhibited song.

The Taoiseach, Mr. Toler, was in New York when the trial ended. Immediately upon his return to Dublin, he called a press conference and announced that there would be an investigation into the source of the money that was paid for the arms.

The first sitting of the Inquiry was held in Leinster House on January 7, 1971. Two witnesses at the Inquiry, Superintendent Carlton of the Special Branch, and the former Secretary of the Department of Justice, Timothy O'Brien, sought direction from the

Minister for Justice, Darragh O'Looney, in relation to attendance at the Inquiry and the evidence they should give.

The Superintendent was told to be frank, even though he had little or no direct evidence to give. As it emerged, the vast bulk of what he told the Inquiry was purely hearsay and, on his own admission, would not be permitted in a court of law. Worse, the bulk of this so-called evidence was false, based on information supplied by two informants who had infiltrated the Special Branch to forward the aims of their own organisation which pursued a policy involving the retention of the Stormont Government in the Six Counties and, related to this, the blocking of any interference by the Dublin Government in the area.

Secretary O'Brien, during his years in the Department of Justice, had become a major cog in the security network of the State, but he depended completely for his information on the Special Branch and, as we have seen, that evidence was tainted. An example of this was the report of the Tunnygee meeting which had been passed on by the Superintendent to O'Brien. It was slanted in such a way as to indicate that Captain Roche was attempting to foment revolution, was throwing money around, buying drink, and generally behaving in a very irresponsible manner. The reality was, as reported by Captain Roche on the day after the meeting, a sober discussion to find out the Defence Committee's needs and intentions. O'Brien gave his particular version of the meeting to Toler in October, 1969, but in January 1971, Messrs Toler and O'Looney did not want this fact brought to public notice. As far as they were concerned, O'Brien had one weakness, he spoke the truth as he saw it, and they knew that if he was allowed to appear at the inquiry, he would tell it about the Tunnygee meeting. Conse-quently, O'Brien was instructed by O'Looney's private secretary to the effect that anything which O'Brien might usefully say would be contrary to the Official Secrets Act and that the Minister would not agree to release him from his obligations under the Act.

O'Brien then enquired of the Minister if he should reveal that he had informed Toler of the Tunnygee meeting, when Toler came to visit him in Dublin's Mount Carmel Hospital shortly after the meeting had taken place. In reply, he was told that the Taoiseach had no recollection of what was discussed and that the Taoiseach deprecated any reference to this visit. In the event, O'Brien told the Inquiry about Captain Roche's activities and the Tunnygee meeting in October 1969, supporting Roche's contention that the Taoiseach was aware of the proposed arms importation from the beginning.

McAdoo, however, denied knowledge of the Tunnygee meeting to the Inquiry, stating: "This meeting ws mentioned at the Arms Trial. As I recall it, I said I had no recollection of any de-scription of having been told about that meeting. I have thought a great deal about that since; I racked my brains for any detail about it, the purpose of it, the people who attended it, what was decided, and I am absolutely certain that I was never informed of the Tunnygee meeting and that the reference to it in the Four Courts is the first reference I can recall."

Yet both Mr. Toler and Colonel Boylan had discussed the meeting with McAdoo shortly after it took place, as did Captain Roche later, as evidence before the Inquiry indicated.

Another peculiar aspect of McAdoo's evidence was his admission to the Inquiry that he had been informed by Captain Roche of where the money had come from to purchase the arms. It was put to him that in May, the Taoiseach had told Dail Eireann that he had "made specific inquiries as to whether any monies could have been devoted or could have been paid out of Exchequer funds or out of any public funds in respect of a consignment of arms of the size we have been dealing with and I am assured that there was not nor could not have been."

Asked why he had not informed the Taoiseach as to his knowledge concerning the source of the money, Minister McAdoo blandly told the Inquiry that: "The Taoiseach had not asked me that question, as far as I can recall," refusing to give any logical explanation as to why he chose to remain silent, and, as a Minister of Government, permit the Taoiseach to mislead the Dail and the people of Ireland.

The Inquiry dragged on for nearly a year, coming to basically the same conclusion in relation to the source of the arms money as that given to Minister McAdoo by Captain Roche in April 1970; that it came through agents of the Defence Committees in the north, who had obtained monies from various sources, including the Dublin Government.

"There's someone codding someone some place," Johny McCaffrey said, "McAdoo knew where the money came from all along, and I'd say Toler knew bloody well too. I wonder how much did the whole exercise cost the country," he continued, "and did you see where they brought over a whole fleet of stenographers from England? Could they not get Irish lassies to do the job?"

"They wouldn't trust the Irish lassies not to leak the private sessions," Mike said.

"Do you mean to say they could trust the Brits?" Tom asked.

"Not at all. Knowing the way the Brits operate I'd say there were a few Intelligence agents planted," Mike said.

"And wouldn't they be terrible eegits if they didn't plant them?" Tom agreed. "They're just as interested as we are. After all, isn't the Six Counties still officially part of the United Kingdom?"

"And what about all the people that gave evidence in private session?" Mike asked.

"They were soft in the head if they thought it was going to remain secret. Not only did the Brits get copies of it, but half of Dublin had copies the day after the evidence was given," Tom declared.

"I don't believe you" McCaffrey was incredulous.

"It's true, Johny. Sure, no less a person than Mr. O'Brien himself, and he gave evidence in private session, told the Inquiry straight that he believed that anything he might say would be communicated outside the room in a matter of hours."

"It's hard to credit it all the same."

"Well, that's the way it was, Johny."

"For God's sake, Johny. Will you have a titter of wit?" Mike turned to him. "How many politicians were on that Inquiry, a round dozen, and all with their own angle to play? Do you think they could keep their mouths shut? Apart from the typists and the rest of them, anyone that gave secret evidence to that Inquiry and thought it would remain secret, was a fool. He would need to have his head examined."

"The whole thing was a disgrace, a complete waste of public money to find out what we know already, that arms were bought and paid for in Hamburg," Tom said.

35

I suppose you're going to the big gathering in the Clare Manor on Sunday?" Johny McCaffrey enquired of Mike in the September of 1971.

"Yes, Tom and I are going, and Willie McGinty has booked a seat."

"Since when did you become the great Republican,?" McCaffrey bantered.

"The same time as you," Mike replied, as two men entered the bar.

"Howya, men, long time no see," Tom said, recognising them.

"Did you find out the truth yet?" he addressed the burly white haired man, who, with his tall, gaunt companion, had been in the bar on the evening of Toler's and McWilliam's disclosures in the Dail.

"Aye, we had a few words the last day I was here, but that's over a year ago and ... and I'm back," the man stood grinning, his two hands on the edge of the counter top.

"That's Peetie Cosgrave's way of apologising, and he doesn't often do that," the gaunt man said, "I go by the name Thomas Maguire. That's when the people are being polite. You wouldn't know what they'd call me at other times. But we all know what to call you, Mister Thomas Burke."

"That's right," Tom said, with an edge of wariness in his voice. "But less of the mister, my friends call me Tom."

"Fair enough, son, Tom it is. Tom, like a good man, would you give us a couple of drinks. A pair of half ones to clear the gullet and two stouts to foregather with it below."

"You're from round this part of the country by the sound of you," McCaffrey said.

"You were always fairly quick on the uptake, Johny McCaffrey," Maguire said, rubbing the back of his head gleefully, shoving the cap forward over his eyes.

"Hold it, hold it, I know you. I remember you, a snotty-nosed gasson, you were hired out the Kingscourt road," McGinty closed an eye in a knowing wink.

"It's in your head you want it, McGinty, in your feet for dancing," Maguire sipped his drink.

"I know you now. Your father was Thomas too, a long lath of a man like yourself. And your mother was a grand wee woman. The Lord have mercy on them, the both of them went off shocking young," McCaffrey lifted his hat.

"God be good to them that's gone, they were all fine people," Maguire said. "Unfortunately," he gave a pull to his cap, "you can't say the same for some of the scamps that are round nowadays. I suppose you're all going up on Sunday?"

"Here, tell us something before we get off it. Where are you living now?" McCaffrey asked.

"Away over beyant Carrick, out Eniskeen way. That's why you don't see too much of us round these parts. It's a bit far to come to see friends even, that's if you have friends," Maguire showed stained teeth in a deprecatory grin.

"Aye, I suppose half the town is heading for Dublin?" Cosgrave looked directly at Tom.

"Are you not?" Tom asked.

"No danger. Only for Toler stood up to them, Slaney, McAtavey, O'Donnell and your friend, the great Captain Roche, would have walked the country into civil war," Cosgrave declared.

"That's a very definite statement, but I don't think you were reading the same papers as me," Tom said.

"We haven't all time to read the papers. Some of us have to work, you know. The cows don't milk themselves and they don't clane up after themselves either. See that, " he stood, pointing down at his dung encrusted wellingtons.

"A drop of water would remedy that and do away with some of the smell too," Mike said quietly.

"Never mind that," Tom added quickly as Cosgrave stiffened. "If you don't read, you must watch a lot of television to be so well informed."

"I wouldn't have it about the place, but I know what I know."

"But where do you get your knowledge from?"

286

"That's none of your business."

"Are you a Party man?"

"I am, and so are all belonging to me, and proud of it."

"And you're not concerned with truth?"

"McAdoo told the truth."

"How do you know?"

"Because the T.D. in this county is a friend of mine and didn't he bring McAdoo down to Cavan to address the Party convention? That was enough for me. No one needs to tell me anything after that."

"And the same T.D. went to Dublin and chaired the Ard Fheis there and applauded when the same McAdoo stood with his hands above his head swearing to God that he never told a lie. He forgot that he also swore to God in the High Court as he lied through his teeth," Mike said.

"You're right, amhic, but if you listened to McAdoo above in Dublin, Washington was only in the halfpenny place with him. He has a brass neck, yon fellah," Maguire asserted.

"Whose side are you on, Maguire?" Cosgrave demanded.

"You don't have to ask that, Peetie. You know damn well that I'll be above in the Clare Manor with the rest of them on Sunday."

"Aach," Cosgrave half-turned away in disgust.

"Don't get me wrong, Peetie. I don't want to fall out with you after thirty years over bloody politics. As far as I'm concerned, we came together and we're going home together."

"You better drink up then, because I'm getting out of here."

"One tick," Maguire swallowed the end of his stout.

"Up the Party and McAdoo," Cosgrave shouted as he swung open the bar door.

"I'll see you on Sunday, lads," Maguire said in a stage whisper round the halfclosed door, as he followed.

"That's the quare boy," McCaffrey said, "that Cosgrave fellow, I'd say he's not too bright."

"No more than myself, he only met the scholars coming home from school," McGinty laughed.

"He's well indoctrinated. It's obvious that the party hacks have been working on him. I've heard the same old rubbish in this town," Mike said.

"Aye, and you know who's behind it, that old whited sepulchre at the top of town? He's out whispering and coggering on the street every day in the week," McCaffrey signalled to Tom for another drink for McGinty and himself.

"Old Knobby Knees Kissane, old Klu Klux Klan himself, the master of character assassination, whispering the word from on high," Mike said. "You can excuse poor old eejits like Cosgrave. He's illiterate. He must believe what he hears from the top man. But there's no excuse for Knobby Knees. He can read only too well. Making a mockery of his own intelligence, he believes only what he wants to believe, takes his gospel from above and propagates it without compunction. Get out the Party line and to hell with honesty and truth."

"God, Mike, I didn't know you felt that strongly about it," Tom said.

"I do and the reason is very simple. I've read every word of the arms trials and I know for certain that Captain Roche told the truth. Kissane is every bit as capable as me of finding out what really took place, yet he chooses not to do so. I'd even accept that, but when he goes round using his position of so-called superior knowledge to mislead the public, I find him contemptible. And, then, when I go to Mass on Sunday morning and find him in front of me, parading up and down to the altar, and, then coming out whispering his message to some poor fool like Cosgrave, who stands open-mouthed and nods his head wisely, as though he is the recipient of nothing less than revealed truth, the disgust wells up in me, because I know that the gospel of perjury has again got an airing. As far as I'm concerned the whole exercise is the antithesis of religion, truth and democracy, all concepts that old Knobby Knees pretends to hold dear. It's enough to make one vomit."

There was silence in the bar when he finished, his listeners embarrassed by the intensity of his feelings.

"You suggested that I was not a Republican earlier on, Johny," Mike continued. "You're right, but wild horses wouldn't stop me going to the meeting next Sunday and Sylvia feels the same way as I do. We are both firmly convinced that the arms trial was a negation of truth perpetrated by the Government for base political advantage at the expense of justice, and of democracy itself.

If democracy is based on anything it is based on truth. That is why Sylvia and I are travelling on Sunday."

"When you put it like that, Mike," McCaffrey said after a pause, "I think I'll travel myself. Captain Roche is a man I admire. I told him that myself in this very pub. I might be a dyed-in-the-wool Fine Gael man, but I'll stand with an honest man any day."

"I won't tell anyone you wore a blueshirt in your day," Mc Ginty said.

"Tell them whatever you damn well like, McGinty. I was proud to wear the blueshirt, just as I'll be proud to support the Captain on Sunday, and Kevin O'Donnell, another honest man."

The group travelled to Dublin in two cars for the inaugural meeting of the new political party, Aontacht Eireann, with Tom, Maisie and McGinty in one car and the Houlihans and McCaffrey in the second. When they reached the meeting place on the northern outskirts of the city, the car-park was filling up rapidly and the question on everyone's lips was whether McAtavey and Slaney were coming.

"I can put your mind at rest about Danny McAtavey straight away," Captain Roche said, when he greeted them in the forecourt of the hotel. "I was talking to him earlier in the year and he told me quite clearly that he had made up his mind to stay in the Party. He believes the Party's heart is in the right place and, as he sees it, the organisational structures are there also. Give me ten years, he told me, and I'll be back as Taoiseach."

"What about Slaney then?" Tom asked.

"A lot of people are expecting him to turn up, but he won't be here. He talks about the Party leaving him and him not leaving the Party."

"Isn't he still a member?" Tom asked.

"But not for much longer, I'd say. Toler will see to that."

"What's stopping him then? Why's he hanging on where he's not wanted?" Mike demanded.

"He still believes in the Party, that as a party it will come right, and he wants to be there to take his rightful place when that time comes. That's why he won't touch us, that he'll have nothing to do with the formation of a new party."

"That means we're ruined before we start," Tom said with disgust.

"I wouldn't say that," Roche said.

In the event, over one thousand people crowded into the hotel ballroom, with the hotel staff ferrying in extra seating as latecomers arrived. Kevin O'Donnell was joined on the platform by only one other politician, the young John Moran, who had resigned his seat in protest at the Party's policy in relation to Northern Ireland.

In his address, O'Donell stated that the deaths of combatants and non-combatants and the terror and brutality inflicted by the British soldiery in the Six Counties were the personal responsibility of the Taoiseach, Mr. Toler.

"Prior to May 1970," he thundered, "the Citizens' Defence Committees had obtained the confidence of the people and had placed their confidence in the Dublin Government. They made the tragic mistake of relying on the many promises of support they received and of relying on the formally adopted policy of the Government, which led to the making by the Army of a contingency plan for what Mr. McAdoo described as a Doomsday situation. The Taoiseach's treacherous *volte face* in May 1970, had two particular effects which place it in a category of its own in the long list of actions by Irishmen against their own country. In the first place, the people who were relying on the support of Dublin to protect their lives and property were betrayed and thrown on their own pitifully inadequate resources. Secondly, the Taoiseach's action in arresting Billy Jackson, who was a key figure in the defensive and peacekeeping arrangements in Belfast, gave the signal to the British to go in and get them with the approval of the Dublin Government; this they promptly did and have been doing since. It is these two direct consequences of the Taoiseach's action in May 1970 that have created the present Six County situation."

O'Donnell continued: "It is just two months short of a year ago that a proposal to express confidence in Mr. Toler, the Taoiseach and the members of his Government came before Dail Eireann, just after the verdict in the arms conspiracy trial, and that verdict established as definitely as it is possible to establish such a thing, that at least two members who were included in that motion were not worthy to hold the positions they then held and they still hold, namely, the Taoiseach and his present Minister for Agriculture, Mr. McAdoo. It is important," O'Donnell concluded, "that the people should know that a lack of integrity, to say the very least, has been established not only in the Minister for Agriculture, but more so in the Taoiseach himself."

Captain Roche, as vice-Chairperson of the party, set the Irish claim to nationhood in its historical context.

"This is like a bloody history lesson," McCaffrey exclaimed, "we heard it all before."

"Now, where has all that led us?" Roche's voice became more strident. "It has led us to August 9th last, when 342 men were arrested under the Special Powers Act and internment and imprisonment without trial became the current reality. It is a negation of democracy. It is a negation of the concept of freedom of the individual. It sets at naught the belief, central to the process of Irish Justice, that a man is innocent until proven guilty. Central to our system of Justice also is the right to *habeas corpus*, the right of a person to be brought before the courts, to have the lawfulness of his or her restraint tested in open court according to the tenets of the law. Consequently, internment is inimical to justice, to any system of law and order based on justice, and to the very basis of democracy itself. It is nothing more than a weapon of repression ."

"Good man, Captain, now you're threshing," McCaffrey was on his feet.

"It is nothing more than a weapon of repression," Roche continued, " but when one takes into consideration the brutality associated with internment, one gets some indication of its debasing and dehumanising effect. Soldiers burst in the door at three or four o'clock in the morning, that is the best time, when man is at his lowest ebb. Search the house and when I say search, I mean search, pull out the fireplace, rip out under the sink and cut open the family couch in the living room, and then drag off the son, father or brother. You probably heard of the obstacle course, strewn with stones and rabble, over which the men were forced to run, the Alsatian guard dogs snapping at them. And, then, on August 17th last, just a month ago, 11 men were selected for special treatment. With hoods over their head, they were removed to a secret destination, where, for days, still hooded, they were subjected to very definite brutality. Standing spreadeagled against the wall, their torturers nearby to force compliance, their feet were constantly kicked apart. Deprived of sleep and toilet facilities, they were subjected to a high whining noise which literally drove them out of their minds. Fed only on bread and water, this interrogation in depth, where a man is driven out of his senses, is the reality for fellow-Irishmen in the North of our country today. The men are dragged off to interrogation centres to be subjected to systematic ill treatment. Some of what went on at places like Ballkykinlar, for example, may not sound much, but try holding your hands out in front of you for 10 or 20 minutes, then holding arms behind your head, then above your head, and performing these actions standing, kneeling, sitting and lying on the floor in succession. Imagine having to perform these exercises continually for 12 to 24 or 30 hours. Several men broke down under this torture and consider the case of the young man who objected. He was tied hand and foot and trussed up like a chicken and left hanging from the roof beams.

"At Girdwood Park, men were put into moving helicopters and thrown out. They were made to sit blindfolded in the helicopters with their backs to the door, the engine running and the machine lifting. The helicopter could have been a foot from the ground, or a hundred feet, as far as the prisoners were concerned.

"Why? Kevin O'Donnell has told you. Quite simply because our Dublin Government has thrown the nationalists of the Six Counties to the wolves. It has stood back, and like a collection of Pontius Pilates, it has washed its hands of responsibility for fellow Irishmen.

"Within weeks of Mr Toler having signalled his change of policy to Britain, by the bizarre expedient of bringing false charges against those concerned with the undercover arms importation, the British went into action. Constrained until then by the knowledge, gleaned through its Intelligence services, that the Dublin Government was making arrangements to defend Six County nationalists in the event of attack, Britain, in July of last year, decided to use military means to sustain the Stormont regime.

"The result is over 100 dead this year already, with the death toll certain to increase as Britain seeks to sustain the *status quo* by means of internment and the obscenity of the associated brutality.

"Because of what I have outlined, in conjunction with what Kevin O'Donnell has already said, I call on you to assist in the formation of a new republican party dedicated to the ideals of Pearse, Connolly and Tone."

In the bar afterwards, the concensus was that it was a successful meeting.

"But it would have been a great meeting if Slaney had turned up," a man at the next table shouted across to the Tunnygee group.

"Or McAtavey or, better still, both of them," Tom said. "But as far as I'm concerned it's off the ground now. We've two good men in O'Donnell and Roche and, by the sound of him, young Moran is no bad one either."

"No point in waiting for Godot," Mike laughed.

"I never heard of that fellow," the man said, looking doubtfully at Mike.

"Neither did I, whoever he is," Johny McCaffrey said, "but Captain Roche is good enough for me any day in the week."

36

A branch of Aontacht Eireann was formed in Tunnygee in November with Tom as Chairman. Johny McCaffrey proposed Olga as Secretary.

"I am a member of Sinn Fein," Olga stood erect in a toggled duffle coat, shoulders imperiously squared, "and so also is my son, Patrick," she tapped the shoulder of the fair haired youth beside her, already almost as bulky and as broad-shouldered as herself. "In the circumstances, I do not see why Mr. McCaffrey should suggest me for membership or officership or any other ship of this organisation."

"Why did you come then?" McCaffrey asked.

"I came . . . I came out of courtesy, because I respect Kevin O'Donnell and Captain Roche and the stand they've taken, but I've no intention of joining another talking shop, a carbon copy of the party that betrayed the north."

"Hear, hear," a stoop-shouldered, balding young man called from the back of the room. "I don't agree with all you say, Mrs. Kennedy, but tell us one thing, Chairman, what's an old blueshirt doing at a meeting to form a so-called Republican party?"

"Hold it, hold it for a minute, Johny," Tom waved his hand at McCaffrey, who was getting to his feet. "Olga, Mrs. Kennedy, is in Sinn Fein and so is young Patrick. I'm sure all of us here respect their right to be a member of that organisation, but we're here tonight to form a branch of Aontacht Eireann, a constitutional Republican party, and I must ask members of other parties to leave."

"I'm proud to be in Sinn Fein," Patrick said, as he pushed after his mother towards the door.

"I know that, Patrick," Tom told him.

The stoop-shouldered man squeezed forward from the back of the room and stood at the door.

"I'm not a member of Sinn Fein," he said, "I'm a member of the Party, the real Republican party, and you can form any party you damned well like, Mr. Thomas Burke, but it won't be a Republican party with blueshirts like Johny McCaffrey in it."

"No, you won't stop me this time, Tom," McCaffrey was on his feet. "I wore the blueshirt, what about it? Does that mean I'm not as good an Irishman as you, young fella? Was Michael Collins not as good an Irishman as you? I supported Collins."

"So did the British," the man rejoined.

"Sit down," Willie McGinty called from the floor. "Johny did his bit before you were pupped."

"We'll have order here," Tom rapped the table. "Johnny McCaffrey has the floor."

"I was about twenty the time of the Truce," Johny began, "when we were all paraded at Dundalk Barracks. Like a lot of them, I wasn't too sure which way to go. What way are you going Paddy, one of the lads asked the man in charge. 'I'm sticking with Collins,' he said, 'he's good enough for me.' Most of us followed him. That's how I came to join the Free Staters, it was as simple as that."

"So, you didn't know what you were doing," the Party man jeered.

"Maybe, I didn't that day, son, but I was soon shocking glad that I went the way I did. Collins was right. We should have used the Treaty as a stepping stone. I am a Collins man and proud of it. And I'll tell you something for nothing, Collins was training men in the Curragh to go back into the North before he was shot."

"Who are you trying to bluff with that rubbish?" the Party man asked contemptuously.

"I'm not trying to bluff anyone," McCaffrey straightened up, his mouth tightening in anger. "I'm nearly eighty and I never bluffed anyone in my life, you young whelp..."

"Shush, Johny. You don't have to explain yourself to anyone," Tom interrupted. "Perhaps, our young friend would leave and let us get on with the meeting."

"Tom, you know what Johny is going to say, and so do I," Mike was on his feet. "I propose that we listen to it because I think that it has some relevance to the formation of this new party."

"Alright, keep it as short as you can, Johny," Tom said.

"It won't take me long, Tom. Frank Davis of Longford was one of Sean McEoin's men, a grand wee soldier. Collins arranged for a meeting beyant in Clones in February 1922 to form a brigade to carry on the fight in the North. O'Duffy was there and so was Frank Aiken, Dan Hogan, Sean McEoin and Joe Sweeney, all OCs of divisions in the border area. The only Divisional OC in the area missing was Billy Pilkington of the 1st Western. Anyway, brigade officers were appointed that day, with Frank Aiken in charge, Joe McKelvey as adjutant, and Frank Davis as quartermaster. I was with Davis that day and I was with him after when he collected arms at Gormanston and brought them to Dublin. The headquarters of the new brigade were at Burke's Distillery in Brunswick Street, now Pearse Street. At the same time, the I.R.A. lads from the north were training in the Curragh to go back and lead the fight. The start of the civil war put paid to that and then Collins died."

"It's all bullshit. Collins sold out in London. Didn't Lady Lavery twist him round her wee finger?" the Party man objected.

"Ah, shut up and you might learn something," Tom told him.

"Throw the wee fart out," McGinty demanded. "If I was twenty years younger I wouldn't listen to him for five seconds."

"Are you finished, Johny?" Tom asked.

"There's just one more thing I want to say. Collins' teeth were pulled by the crowd around him, but who pulled Toler's teeth? No one pulled them. He was like the old ruster of a threequarter that the Tracker, God rest him, had at the time of the Economic War. There was a bit of a slope on the few fields Tracker had that time and if you put a graipeful more of dung on the cart, the horse would stop dead in his tracks when he came to the slope. Once he took that notion, you could light a ditch of whins under him and it would do no good. He'd dance sideways or let the cart back, but damn the up he'd go. Collins was blocked by his own, but Toler was a ruster like Tracker's threequarter, the worst type of animal you could put between the shafts, always sure to let you down when the pressure was on. Toler was only a ruster. That's why I'm here tonight. I know that O'Donnell and Captain Roche are no rusters."

There was a burst of applause when Johny sat down. The Party man stood dry - spitting with anger, obviously waiting to get in the last word.

"I'm going for a piss," he said contemptuously. "Where's the jacks?"

"First on the right. Gents on the door but don't let that stop you," Tom called after him.

Aontacht Eireann's first big test came at the by-election in mid-Cork on August 2, 1972. Paddy O'Sullivan of Mallow was selected as candidate and Captain Roche was appointed as Director of Election. On a Friday in mid-July, Tom and Maisie and the ten year old Tom Pat joined Kevin O'Donnell in Dublin for the journey to Cork. Olga, still a member of Sinn Fein, and Peadar volunteered to mind the bar until the election was over.

On the journey to Macroom, Tom suggested that they should stop and canvass a small village at a T-junction on the way in.

"I'll do the pub," Tom said, "you and Tom Pat do the houses, Maisie, and Kevin here can give the sermon."

There were about a dozen customers in the pub, straggling along the counter and Tom felt the cold draught of hostility as soon as he entered.

"Do you mind if I canvass?" he asked the man behind the bar.

"It's a free country," the man said gruffly, rubbing hard on the counter top.

"You might give this man a vote," Tom pointed to O'Sullivan's picture on his canvass cards.

"I wouldn't give him a stroke if he was the last man in Ireland," a big-handed farmer, sitting sideways on a stool, spoke out of the side of his mouth.

"What about yourself?" Tom asked another man.

"You're far from home," the man said.

"I'm from Cavan."

"And you're down to put us poor Cork fools on the right track?"

"It's him that's the fool," the barman said, throwing the cloth in under the counter. "Listen, Mr. Whatever your name from Cavan," he addressed Tom, "this is Toler country and we don't want any outsiders coming in here telling us what to do."

"I wouldn't get too excited about it if I were you. Here, study one of these and calm yourself," Tom handed the barman an O'Sullivan card.

"Here's one for you," he handed a card to the big handed farmer, who crumpled it slowly, staring Tom straight in the eye.

Slowly and deliberately, Tom handed a card to each man in the bar, only one of whom grunted, "Thanks". Three of them threw the cards on the floor.

"Don't forget now, do the best you can for him," Tom said as he left.

"Fuck off," someone muttered as the door closed behind him. There were three men in a Volkswagen parked outside.

"One a piece," Tom handed in three cards through the open window. "Give Paddy a number one if you can. He's a good candidate."

"Fuck off," a burly man in the back seat said.

"That's the second time I heard that in the last few minutes. It must be a common salute in Cork" Tom said.

"Fuck off, you're not wanted here," the man in the front passenger seat said.

"What about you?" Tom asked the driver.

"Just fuck off," he spat out the words, staring straight to his front.

"You'd want to watch your language, lads, or an outsider like me might get a wrong impression. Maybe it's because you all support perjury," Tom grinned in at them.

Maisie and Tom Pat had finished the few houses in the village when Tom arrived back at the car.

"How did you get on?" he asked.

"Great," Maisie said. "They're all very friendly."

"Probably all Fine Gael," O'Donnell said.

"No," Tom Pat pointed down the street. "There was one house down there where mammy and I got three number ones."

"More than I got," Tom looked back towards the Volkswagen. "Toler supporters to a man in that pub, and see the three buckos in the car. Three Tolerites, bought and paid for, redneck to the core."

"I'll give them a blast," O'Donnell said, pressing the button on his hand mike.

"Hello . . . . Hello . . ., " he tested.

"That's grand, Kevin, let her rip," Tom said.

"I wish to thank you . . . great reception to canvassers . . . Vote for O'Sullivan. . . . Aontacht Eireann . . . Vote for integrity . . . Irish unity . . . The common good . . . Wolfe Tone's dictum of Protestant, Catholic and Dissenter united under the common name of Irishmen . . . Show your disgust, distaste, abhorrence for perjury and corruption as arms of government . . . Show by your vote that you believe in one Ireland and not the partition which Toler and his Government now underwrites . . . And if there are Party men listening to me, be they sulking in pubs or cringing in cars, let them hang their heads in shame . . ."

Captain Roche had established his headquarters in a caravan in the centre of Macroom with the walls of the old castle in the background.

"That appointment with General Tom Barry is fixed for to-morrow morning in Cork, eleven o'clock, myself and yourself," Roche told them.

Tom drove the car into Cork next morning and parked at an entrance to the park on the Western Road.

"There he is," O'Donnell pointed to a tall figure on the footpath about fifty yards away.

As they approached, Tom realised that the General was not as tall as he appeared from a distance, his upright military bearing and shock of thick grey hair giving an impression of greater height. Tom found himself somewhat in awe of the legendary figure from the past - the guerrilla leader who had fought the British and won, a Chief-Of-Staff of the I.R.A. in the thirties - as he was introduced.

"Cavan, it's a county with which I am not over familiar, but I had the honour of unveiling a memorial there a few years ago. I can't remember the name of the place, but it was about four or five miles from Cavan town."

"Ballinagh!" Tom suggested.

"That's it, Ballinagh with a *nagh* at the end. A Captain Sheridan killed in an encounter with the R.I.C. during the War of Independence. Another brother was wounded on the same day."

"That's right, yet another brother, Commandant Sean Sheridan, is in Aontacht Eireann. He should be down here. No sign of him yet?" Tom asked Roche.

"He's here. He was one of the first to arrive. He made arrangements to stay in Kanturk last night. A couple of them were canvassing out that way."

"He's something the same cut as yourself, General," Tom said.

"I know him," the General smiled, "but I think he was a bit slimmer than me, not much, but a bit. He was like a whippet when I met him in Ballinagh. He was our host that day and no more hospitable man could you wish to meet."

"Now, Kevin, down to business," he turned to O'Donnell. "I admire your stand and you have my wholehearted support for what it's worth. You'll get a thousand votes in mid-Cork."

"A thousand!" O'Donnell looked at him.

"A thousand, that's what I said. You may shout and sing about rebel Cork, but real Republicans are scarce on the ground in it. They were always scarce."

"What about 1920?" Roche asked.

"We had some great supporters and some great families and great fighters came out of West Cork, but the bulk of the population took no sides. As for the rest of them, those we didn't intimidate, we terrorised."

"That's the way a guerrilla operation works," Roche said. "But electoral support is another matter."

"You'll get a thousand votes. I'm sorry, Captain, but I must say what I believe. Have you opened a subscription list yet?"

"We have."

"Here," he took a five pound note from his breast pocket. "Just a gesture. I'm not a rich man, you know, but it's one way of showing my support. I'm past the canvassing stage and, anyway, I might say the wrong thing. I was never the best man to pull in votes."

"We'll put your name at the head of the list," O'Donnell said.

"You don't mind if we used your name from the platform?" Roche asked.

"I don't give my support lightly, but when I do it's wholehearted. Use my name any way you like, Captain."

Back at Macroom, several carloads of supporters had arrived from various parts of the country. Roche allotted them tasks for the weekend.

"The big meeting is in Millstreet tonight," he told them. "Get your live bodies there around nine o'clock and we'll do a canvassing blitz on the town while the meeting's in progress."

At Millstreet, the local pipe band, white gaiters flashing and kilts swinging, marched down the street to the rattle of the kettledrum and the shriek of the pipes.

"There's O'Donnell," a man at a street corner pointed."You're in the wrong place," he jeered, "the Party meeting's in Kanturk tonight."

"That explains the band," O'Donnell said to Tom. "They're on the way to Kanturk too."

The music stopped on a rising crescendo of sound and the band piled into a bus as Tom and the rest of them mounted the platform. Slowly, people drifted down towards them, and when O'Sullivan the candidate spoke, about two hundred stood listening, applauding politely when he was finished. "Another friendly enough town," Roche said on the way back to Macroom, "but I don't think that there are many votes in it."

"Keep your hearts up, boys," O'Sullivan said cheerfully from the back seat. "No matter what Tom Barry says, Cork is still the rebel county."

On the eve of the election, Tom and O'Donnell, accompanied by Maisie and Ciss O'Donnell, canvassed a small village. As they finished, a car skidded to a halt beside them and a youth stuck his head out.

"McAdoo's coming . . . McAdoo's coming," he shouted. "He'll be coming in below at the cross."

"Here he comes, come to visit your village and seek your votes, McAdoo himself," O'Donnell's voice blared out from the loudspeaker. "The great McAdoo fresh from his performance in the High Court, a performance for which he gained little applause; a performance for which he deserved no applause; a performance which was rejected in the court, rejected because it was a false performance, a performance based on lies and half-truths. . .Will he stop. He will. No, he won't. He's still driving. He's going to the take the coward's way out. No, he's slowing. Maybe, he has no loudspeaker. He may have mine if he is willing to explain his High Court performance. He's speeding up again. See the tyres skidding on the gravel, leaving a yellow streak behind him and the hot smell of shame, a whiff of sulphur."

That night, the Party had its pre-election rally in Macroom. The platform stretched fifty feet and more along the old castle wall and the square was packed. Minister vied with Minister for a place in the spotlight as they stood shoulder-to-shoulder with Toler. The public thoroughfare was blocked as Tom sought to drive the car through the crowd to the Aontacht Eireann caravan .

"I wonder could you give us a hand here," he called to a Garda Sergeant.

The Sergeant and two guards attempted to clear a way.

"It's O'Donnell," someone shouted pounding on the car.

Soon, several people were pounding on the car, crowding around it. O'Donnell attempted to open the door, but the crowd were pressing against it. Two more guards arrived and cleared some space at the car door. Ignoring the advice of the Sergeant, O'Donnell jumped out and stood foursquare to the crowd, a solid block of a man on slightly bowed legs, his hands hanging loose in fists.

"If anyone has anything to say to me, come out here and say it. Come out and stand up like a man," he pointed to the ground in front of him. "No, you'd all rather cringe in the anonymous safety of the crowd. Like piranha fish, you only work in shoals. Turn round and listen to your leader and let him explain McAdoo's performance in the High Court; let him explain why he betrayed the North; let him explain Operation Motorman, the new sell-out of Nationalist Derry and the Falls in Belfast to the British; let him tell you how glad he is that every inch of the Six Counties is once again under the jackbooted heel of the British stormtrooper. Let him tell you how he connived to achieve that happy situation . . ."

As O'Donnell talked, the space around him increased, the crowd imperceptively fading back.

"Now, Kevin, get into the car," the Sergeant said.

"Yes, Kevin, come on, it's not worth wasting your breath on them," someone called from the back seat.

"The way's clear now, Kevin," the Sergeant held open the door of the car.

"I was afraid you were for the high jump there for a minute," Tom said as O'Donnell got in.

"But the way they faded away, I could hardly believe it."

"You were great, Kevin," Maisie laughed, "standing there on your own. You were like Cuchulainn in the Gap of the North."

"I wouldn't go that far, Maisie," O'Donnell laughed also.

On the following day, the black and white posters of Aontacht Eireann were lost amidst the garish superfluity of the abundant posters of the major parties. Also Aontacht Eireann could not match the caravans which gave shelter to party workers and doubled as hospitality suites. At the count, which took place in Macroom, Aontacht Eireann got close to twelve hundred votes. When O'Sullivan was eliminated, O'Donnell, Roche and Tom left the hall. The yard outside was crowded with people who had come by train from Cork city to celebrate another victory for the Party under Toler's leadership. The hubbub of conversation died down when O'Donnell appeared, one nudging the other until silence reigned. O'Donnell, flanked by Roche and Tom, pushed forward, the silent crowd reluctantly clearing a path.

"God, that was like walking on eggs," Roche said when they got back to the hotel. "One wrong word and we were done for."

"The atmosphere was certainly tense. You could feel the animosity. There was naked hatred there," O'Donnell agreed.

"Naked hatred, you're right, Kevin. They put naked fear in me. We deserve a drink after that," Tom said.

"Some of your crowd are in the front room above," the proprietor told them.

"Grand, we'll join them," O'Donnell said.

O'Sullivan arrived shortly afterwards.

"Three cheers for Paddy, the best candidate in the field," Roche shouted.

"Even if he was last," O'Sullivan rejoined to cheers and general laughter. "What do you think, Kevin?" he asked O'Donnell.

"To tell you the truth, Paddy, I'm disappointed. With the canvass that we did and the response that we got I thought we'd do better."

"Didn't he do rightly for a first time? Remember what Tom Barry said. Don't be too pessimistic, Kevin," Tom advised.

"I'd like to agree with you, Tom, but I can't. Maybe you're right. Maybe I am a pessimist."

"Shake out of it, Kevin," O'Sullivan clapped O'Donnell on the back, "We got two hundred more than General Tom Barry forecast. You can't do much better than that."

37

Tom and Mike stood in the foyer of Tunnygee's Community Hall.

"God, it looked bad at the start," Mike said.

"Who're you telling, but it's filling up a bit now," Tom said. "There are nearly a hundred inside at the moment."

"How she's motoring, lads?" McGinty came in, shrugging under the too wide shoulders of his overcoat.

"He's coming," Olga appeared at the outside door.

"Who?"

"Slaney," she mouthed the name and ran back down to the gate. Holding him firmly by the elbow, she escorted Slaney up the path, but at the door, he stood back and insisted that she go in in front of him.

"This is Mr. Slaney," she announced, taller than the square thick set man with the thinning hair, who stood behind her, grinning round a big bowled crooked-stemmed pipe.

"You have some fine big women in this part of the country," he winked at the men, "and good looking women too."

"You're welcome, Mr. Slaney," Tom held out his hand. "I'm Tom Burke."

"Glad to meet you, Tom. You made a good showing in the election."

"I didn't get in and that's what counts."

"I met you before someplace, Tom. Was it above in Sligo last year. You were there with Kevin O'Donnell and Ned Roche."

"That's right. I didn't think you'd remember that. I was only talking to you for a few minutes."

"I'm a politician, don't forget," Slaney grinned, taking the pipe from his mouth.

"And if I'm not mistaken, you hurled a bit in your time," he turned to Mike.

"That shook you," he chortled, before the surprised Mike could reply. "Don't worry, apart from the fact that I saw you playing in Croke Park once, I've a brother-in-law in the bank above in Newry. He told me you were here. I think you know him, Johny Hamill?"

"That's right. He was at the regional outing in Dundalk last year. Even though I'm retired I still get an invitation."

"Well, here's one man you don't know," Olga shoved McGinty forward.

"You have me there, Olga," Slaney admitted graciously.

"This is Willie McGinty. He's a great supporter of yours, Mr. Slaney," she introduced McGinty.

"Now, hold on for a minute there," Slaney held up his hand. "I'm Mick to my friends. No more of this old Mr. Slaney nonsense. And it's Mick to you too, Willie," he shook hands with

McGinty.

"You're Mick to me anyway and you the son of Mick Slaney. I met him during the Civil War and him hiding without in Coote's hayshed."

"Right enough, he spent a while around here in the civil war. I'm more than glad to meet an old comrade of my father's, Willie."

"And I'm glad to meet a son of my old comrade, and to welcome him to Tunnygee. There's only a few of us left, you know."

"Willie was one of the old brigade," Tom said.

"Aye, and there's the proof," Willie pulled his overcoat to show the Black and Tan medal pinned on the lapel of his jacket.

"I suppose you're all with O'Donnell and the Captain, all members of Aontacht Eireann?" Slaney asked.

"That's right," Tom said.

"It's not right," Olga tossed her head.

"Sorry, I forgot. Olga's a Sinn Feiner," Tom explained.

"And none the worse for that," Slaney said equably.

The meeting got under way half-an-hour later. There were over three hundred people present, many of whom had worked for Tom's candidature in the general election of a month previously.

"We didn't win, but we didn't do badly either. At least, we gave the others a fright," Mike, who chaired the meeting, told the crowd. "It was a good effort for a first time. Two thousand, it was a respectable enough vote."

"And it'll be a helluva let more respectable the next time," a black-haired, sallow-faced youth shouted from the body of the hall.

"That's the spirit, Mickey ," Mike called back. "But you didn't come here to listen to me, or to Mickey Clarke either for that matter, so I'll call upon the first speaker, a man whom we're all proud and happy to welcome to Tunnygee, a man who needs no introduction, Mick Slaney . . . He has to hit another meeting in Monaghan tonight. So he goes first at his own request."

Slaney put the pipe in his pocket and adjusted the height of the microphone, before waving a dismissive hand in acknowledgement of the applause.

"You'd know he was used to it," McGinty nudged Olga.

"People of Tunnygee, people of Cavan. I'm delighted to be here tonight," Slaney's voice boomed out, the sharp Northern accent taking on a rasping tone as it grated through ill-adjusted loudspeakers. "I'm particularly glad to stand here on the same platform as my good friend here, Tom Burke."

"You didn't stand with him in the Clare Manor," a gruff voice came from the back.

Slaney stopped and looked down the hall.

"You're right, my friend, dead right. But I'll tell you something. I would have loved to have been there. Nothing would have pleased me more. I know that I would have been among friends, but I had reasons, and they seemed to me to be good reasons, why I was not there. Quite simply, I did not believe that a new political party would get off the ground . . ."

"You don't agree with Burke then?" the voice at the back shouted.

"I didn't say that. I couldn't agree more with him. I just didn't think that a new political party was on then, or that it is on now."

"What about the Party, the party you left?"

"I didn't leave the Party. The Party left me. It's no longer the party I joined."

"A bloody traitor."

"Stand up there till we see who you are. I don't like responding to a voice coming from a person skulking in the anonymity of the crowd. Stand up till we get a look at you."

"Well, here I am then, a Party man and proud of it," the man jumped to his feet and Mike recognised Peetie Cosgrave, the burly white haired man from the pub.

"Ignore him, ignore him, he's not right in the head," Mike came forward and whispered to Slaney, the microphone picking up what he said.

"I heard that. I heard that." Cosgrave burst out into the aisle, nearly knocking two or three people from their chairs. "Come down here and I'll show you who's mad. If you're a man at all, come down here, Houlihan," he waved his fist above his head, saliva oozing from the corner of his mouth."Traitors, a platform of traitors . . . traitors , the whole lot of you . . ." he lapsed into incoherence and stood slack-mouthed, arms hanging by his sides, fists clenching and unclenching.

Two men, one on either side of him, were talking quietly to Cosgrave. He looked at them blankly, before turning and walking slowly to the door. The two men followed him outside. Slaney stood on stage, one hand in pocket, head down, as the embarrassed crowd sat in silence. Finally, he turned to Mike, who nodded.

"I feel sorry, extremely sorry for that poor man," Slaney resumed quietly. "We all feel sorry for him. Like many another he has the wrong end of the stick, but he's not to blame. Someone else made the balls for him to throw. The faceless muckrakers in the background, I know who they are, you know who they are, we all know who they are. We have them in every town, we have them in every parish. One could go on, but I did not come here tonight to talk about such people, flies buzzing around, feeding on a diet of horse manure and letting their excreta fall where it will, contaminating everything and everyone. I came to talk about something much more important. I came to talk about this," he held up a pamphlet. "This, another British production, the latest White Paper from the Westminster paper factory telling us poor simple Irishmen, aye, and Irishwomen too, how to run our country. Anything new in this British production, you may well ask? Damn all, is the simple answer," he declared, leafing through the White paper. "Baugh," he threw it from him, "It talks about peace and reconciliation, yet it sustains partition, the cause of Ireland's woes for the last sixty years. Here we are in 1973. We've seen the violence of the last three, four years, up the road a few miles from this hall. We've seen its effect down here in the Twenty Six Counties. . . "A solution . . get the British out is the solution. Let Britain make a declaration of intent to withdraw from Ireland and give Irishmen, Protestant, Catholic and Dissenter, a chance to get together and negotiate a future on this island." Slaney finished, mopping perspiration from his brow with a folded white hankerchief. He then shook hands quickly with the platform party, before nimbly skipping down the three steps from the stage and striding up the hall, shaking hands here and there without breaking stride. The crowd gave him a standing ovation. At the door, he waved and was gone.

"At least some of you voted for the next speaker, last month," Mike began to introduce Tom.

"We all voted for him," someoneshouted.

"I certainly hope you did; but whether you did or not, you are going to have to listen to him now. It is my great pleasure to call on Tom Burke," Mike waved Tom to the microphone.

"Now, we have a new Government," Tom began, "with Oscar McWilliams as Taoiseach and Labour's Jackson as his deputy. An unlikely alliance of capitalism and socialism, you may well say and you would be right, but they are agreed on one thing and that is the Six Counties. No change is the cry. It's Britain's mess and let Britain solve it. We have no interest, we agree with Toler, maintain the *status quo,* is the McWilliams cry. Toler and he made their bargain in May, 1970, their foul bargain to hide McAdoo's name in an attempt to create an impression in the public mind that, as Minister for Defence, McAdoo had not authorised the arms importation.

"The latest manifestation of that bargain was in December last before Toler was rejectted by the electorate. In the previous months, Darragh O'Looney, Toler's Minister for Justice, introduced an Act to amend and extend the Offences Against the State Acts. This was such an undemocratic and repressive piece of proposed legislation, that Mr. McWilliams' Fine Gael party opposed it in the most unequivocal terms, classifying it as immoral and unjust and as an abnegation of any democratic concept. Despite his party's stand, McWilliams was ready to vote in favour of the amendment. On foot of the 1970 bargain, he was still willing to work hand-in-glove with Mr. Toler. Yet, on the last day of November of 1972, just a few short months ago, it looked as if the Toler Government, even with the support of McWilliams, would be defeated on the Bill. Something had to be done to ensure the passage of the Bill and it had to be done quickly. And it was Britain that acted.

"Britain wanted, what it termed the anti-I.R.A. Bill put into effect and a recalcitrant Dublin parliament was not going to stand in its way. Consequently, on the following day, December 1, two bombs exploded in Dublin's city centre, killing two passers-by and injuring over one hundred. Who else to blame for such a nefarious deed, but the I.R.A., at least as far as the gullible Dublin politicians were concerned? To the sound of exploding bombs, the Bill became law, but they were not I.R.A. bombs. They were British bombs, the Bill became law,

"That the Dublin Government had become a mere British puppet by the end of 1972 was emphasised by the bombs, but there was more to come in the saga of collaboration. On December 21st last, John Wyman, a British MI6 agent, was arrested in Dublin. His main contact was Patrick Crinnion, the chief confidential clerk in C3, the headquarters branch of the Garda Siochana concerned with subversion. Crinnion was arrested on the same day. Both were charged under the Official Secrets Act, but early this year both were freed and allowed to leave the country. When the case came to court, the extraordinary position arose that the prosecution refused to bring forward evidence on the basis that the information which Crinnion was handling was too top secret to be put before the court, even to the extent of conveying it to the trial judge. Yet Crinnion, a veritable repository of information, both *top secret* and otherwise, on all aspects of security matters, was sent out of the country into the arms of the British to be debriefed by them at their leisure. It is inconceivable that this could have happened except in the most extraordinary circumstances, in circumstances so extraordinary that the security of the State itself did not matter; that some other factor took precedence over Stae security. The other factor was the credibility of the Toler Government.

"Because of his work, Crinnion was in the position to expose the full extent of official cooperation between the British and Irish security forces, including the RUC, if he was forced to defend himself. Further, the chichanery involved at various levels from the cabinet down when Toler mounted the arms trial of 1970 would also have been brought to light. Crinnion had to be got out of the way and the sooner the better, and, as with O'Looney's repressive legislation, the British were only too glad to come to the rescue.

"Britain did not resort to anything as crude as bombs on this occasion. They had an ace up their sleeve. They were in a position to do a trade. They had the Littlejohn brothers, who had carried out a major bank robbery in Dublin and sought refuge in Britain. They were also British agents, recruited on an ad hoc basis to gather information on the I.R.A. in Ireland. Their Irish contact was a man whom they knew as Douglas Smythe, who was, in fact, Wyman. When Wyman and Crinnion were arrested, the British Government indicated to Dublin that, although the Littlejohns were British agents, Britain was not accepting responsibility for the bank robbery, the clear inference being that they could be extradited to Ireland for such criminal activity.

"A few days later, the British Director of Prosecutions came to Dublin, where he met the Attorney-General and the Minister for Justice, Mr. O'Looney. The purpose of his visit was to secure a sworn affidavit from the Attorney-General that the Littlejohns would not be prosecurted for political offences if extradited. The affidavit was readily forthcoming and the swop was made, Crinnion and Wyman released to make their way to England in return for the extradition of the Littlejohns.

"Dublin had got rid of Crinnion, a potentially explosive witness from the Toler Government's point of view. His release to Britain and the return of the MI6 operative, Wyman, was a feather in Britain's cap, while the Littlejohns, an embarrassment to Britain, were effectively silenced by being branded as criminals, maybe rightly, but that is another question.

"Such was the state of Government in this state of ours in the run-up to the election, with repressive legislation being bombed through parliament by British bombs and the executive playing musical chairs with British spies, while we awaited the next British move. We now await it no longer. The White Paper is with us and it states quite bluntly that it is the responsibility of the United Kingdom Parliament to determine how Northern Ireland shall be governed as part of the United Kingdom. This means nothing more or less than that partition will be copper-fastened, as Mick Slaney said.

"As our newly-elected Taoiseach, Mr. McWilliams, prepares for the conference envisaged in the White Paper, he will do so secure in the knowledge that he can rely on the support of Mr. Toler, as leader of the opposition, not to rock the boat. The short outline of the activities of the Toler Government over the past six months clearly indicates that. Meanwhile, the violence will continue and more Irishmen will die as long as the Dublin Government accepts that part of Ireland is part of the United Kingdom."

The crowd had listened attentively to every word and, when Tom finished, they sat in apparently stunned silence for a moment. Then the clapping started, sustained and prolonged, impressive in its solemn intensity. Outside, the crowd was slow to drift away, many shaking hands with Tom..

"I never heard you speak like that before. You were word perfect. You spoke with...with authority," Mike congratulated him.

They walked to the pub together.

"I would like to tell you something Tom," Mike said, "it's something I've been meaning to tell you for a long while."

"Fire away !"

"Maybe now is the best time to do it...but...don't get me wrong, Tom, you gave a great speech tonight and I was proud to be Chairman, but, I have to tell you this, I'm leaving the party."

"What on earth for?"

"I think you know as well as I do, Tom. I only joined because I'm opposed to hypocrisy in public life. I joined Aontacht Eireann and I worked for you in the election, because I saw O'Donnell and Roche as two honest men, as two men of principle. I'm also a friend of yours and I know that you're a man of principle too, but the truth is, I'm not a Republican, Tom."

"I know that, Mike."

"I'll always work for you and vote for you if you ever run for election again, but I won't do so as a member of Aontacht Eireann, Tom, because....because, and I don't want to sound pompous when I say this, because, to put it bluntly, I'm not machiavellian enough to pretend to be what I'm not. And if I remained in the party, I'd have to pretend that I am a Republican."

"Yes, Mike, I appreciate that."

"Well,"Mike shrugged, "that's that I suppose.....no...no hard feelings?"

"None at all, Mike, I understand your position perfectly. I'd do the same myself, if the shoe was on the other foot."

38

I n March 1973, the people of Northern Ireland went to the polls in a referendum on the border question. Generally, nationalists declined to vote. On the day of the poll, three car bombs exploded in Central London. One man died and about two hundred were injured. In Belfast, there were six bomb explosions and in Derry there were five. In Belfast, a British soldier was shot dead outside a polling booth, while another was injured by a booby-trap near Forkhill, Co. Armagh. Dolores and Marion Price, Belfast sisters, were convicted of causing the London explosions. A campaign was mounted to have the girls, and others convicted with them, transferred to Irish jails. For over two hundred days, the hunger-striking sisters were forcibly fed, before eventually being moved to Armagh jail in June 1974. Through the late winter and spring of that year, protest marches were held on several Sundays, from Sandyford village in the foothills of the Dublin mountains to the residence of the British Ambassador about a mile away. The marches halted at the main entrance to the residence, where the speeches were delivered as a large force of gardai stood by. On the first Sunday, Maisie and Olga were there. Earlier in the week, Tom had declared his intention of travelling, but, as it turned out, Maisie and Olga had other ideas.

"One of you has to stay at home to mind the pub," Olga opened the subject, "and I don't see why it always has to be Maisie."

"That's right," Maisie agreed, "but don't worry, Olga, Maisie is not staying at home this time. As far as I'm concerned, women should march on behalf of women. I'm afraid you'll have to take over the shop on Sunday, Tom."

"A woman's place is in the home, or in the pub in this case,"

Tom winked at Josie Tynan to whom he was serving a pint.

Burly in an old tweed overcoat, Josie sat, leaning forward, elbows flat on the counter-top, a ragged hole in the right sleeve of the coat showing a lesser hole in the jacket underneath.

"Jasus, that's a great looking pint, a lovely white collar on it," Josie showed his nicotine-stained teeth in a contented grin, as Tom placed the pint before him.

"Are you not having one yourself?" without taking his eyes from the pint, he addressed himself to Willie McGinty, who stood at his left elbow.

"I've Willie's medicine here," Tom said, pouring a bottle of stout.

"By God," Josie sat back on his stool, gleefully rubbing the palms of his hands together.

"There's a fair old collar on that pint all the same," McGinty said.

" A bit of bishop's collar right enough, but I'll soon tell you what it's like," Josie lifted the glass and took a deep slug.

"Mother's milk," he put the half-empty glass down carefully. "Look at that, the froth sticking to the sides there, a sure sign of a good pint."

"Did you hear what Tom said, Josie?" Olga asked.

"Aye, I heard, about the women, you mean?" Josie glided his glass in a half circle through the spillage on the counter-top.

"What do you think, Josie?" Olga persisted.

"I've nothing against women," Josie laughed. "You wouldn't have a fag on you, Olga, would you? I hadn't a smoke since dinner time."

"Here, give him a package of fags and take it out of that," McGinty gave Tom a tenner as Olga fumbled in her bag for cigarettes. "You know I don't smoke much, Josie," she said.

"I know, Olga, but I love the black Russian ones you have sometimes."

"I'm afraid you're out of luck this evening, Josie. I don't seem to have any cigarettes, Russian or otherwise, with me."

"Don't worry about him, Olga," Tom threw a twenty packet of cigarettes on the counter in front of Josie.

"He can smoke his own now," he said handing the change to McGinty.

"Here," McGinty gave Josie a fiver. "Does that satisfy you?"

"That's grand, Willie, sure, it wasn't that big a job."

"Did he do the job for you at last?" Tom asked.

"Aye, and when he was at it, he fixed the old electric fire that hadn't worked for the last five years," Willie said.

"No better man at the electricity even though I say it myself," Josie fingered his empty glass.

"You might as well blow your own coal, I suppose. No one else will do it for you. Give us two more drinks there and then maybe Josie'll change his fiver," McGinty said.

"Good man, Willie, I always knew you had it in you," Josie rubbed his hands again.

"You still didn't tell us about the women, Josie," Olga said. "Do you agree with Tom that their place is in the home?"

"No, I don't."

"Jasus, Tynan, whose side are you on anyway?" McGinty asked.

"Well, women have their place, Willie . . ."

"What do you mean, have their place?" Olga demanded.

"What I mean is, there's nothing wrong with them. They . . . they should be allowed to enjoy themselves. A few drinks never did a woman any harm. It only tunes them up and that's not a bad thing. They're easier to handle after," Josie laughed, throwing back his head to show his bad teeth.

"You're a terror, Josie, you're a holy terror," a farmer in wellingtons, who sat listening at the end of the counter, spluttered into his bottle of stout.

"He's just another male chauvinist pig, the same as most men," Olga said.

"I'd say that's a quare sort of baste," the farmer grinned.

"It's a very common kind of beast around Tunnygee," Olga said shortly, glaring at the farmer, who, still grinning, busied himself pouring the end of his bottle into the glass.

"Since when did you join the women's lib, Olga?" Josie asked. "They're only a crowd of man haters."

"Man eaters is more like it," McGinty cackled into his stout.

"I'd say it's a long time since anyone ate you, Mr. McGinty," Olga said, putting her bag under her arm and turning towards the door.

"Don't go off in a huff now, Olga. Tell us what's biting you before you go?" McGinty asked.

"There's nothing biting me, Mr. McGinty. It's just that men like you and Josie Tynan make me sick, too self-centred and selfish for their own good."

"I always thought you were fond of the men, if you know what I mean. That you were a man's woman sort of thing," McGinty said, averting his face and winking towards the wall .

"You're a sly little shit, Willie McGinty, a miserable little shit," Olga told him.

"You're a bit hard on Willie," Josie said.

"You're another shit, Tynan, all a crowd of shits," Olga snapped at Josie.

"Where does that leave woman then? Are they shits too?" Josie asked.

"No, it's men are the shits, the shits who have exploited women for generations. That's why we have to stand on our own, stand for the rights of women everywhere. That's why we're marching next Sunday, for justice for the Price sisters, for justice for women."

"There'll be a good few men marching too," Josie said. "I bet you what you like that there'll be more men than women there."

"You won't be one of them."

"I might surprise you now, Miss Olga. I'll probably be driving Johny McCaffrey's car on Sunday."

"Johnny didn't leave his bed for the last fortnight," Olga said.

"But that doesn't stop him giving his car. Willie here went out and asked him yesterday. The three of us are going, Willie, Mike Houlihan and myself. Isn't that right, Willie?" Josie turned to McGinty.

"That's right, Josie."

"Now, Olga, who're the shits?" Josie asked.

"Maybe, you're not so bad if you're going to march on Sunday," Olga relented slightly.

"That's good. I thought you were serious there for a while. You were in a bit of a temper there for a minute."

"What if I was? Hadn't I every right to be? Women have been and are treated disgracefully by men. That's why I make no apologies for supporting Women's Lib."

"I'd be afraid of that crowd," the farmer at the end of the counter said. "Did you see the big fat Yankee on the TV the other night? She was vicious. She'd think nothing of castrating a fella, that wan."

"Jasus, that would be a sore thing," Josie laughed.

"Not half sore enough for some of the men that are around," Olga said, glaring at the farmer.

"Still, it's no joking matter. You would destroy a fella altogether that way," Josie continued.

"What the hell do you know about it anyway, Tynan?" McGinty asked.

"Damn all, but you wouldn't want that much imagination. You'd even shrivel up thinking about it. Do you remember the pigs above in the market, Willie ?"

"I do, Josie. You could never forget. You'd hear the screams of them a mile away. Your man, what's his name, he was at it as long as I can remember. He was like lightning with the wee butty penknife. He was a long fellow with a cap and brown boots..."

"He was from Leitrim, over from the Mohill direction. The name's on the tip of my tongue. Mac....Mac something...Mac, Mac Shane, that was it !"

"You're right, Josie, long Jackie MacShane. He castrated the *suckers* as quick as they were handed to him. I'll never forget the screams of the poor little bastards."

"It was savage work, but no one thought anything of it and that was only twenty years ago or less," Josie said.

"Yes, it was savagery," Maisie said quietly, "but it is also savagery to force-feed two young girls in a British jail, as is happening to the Price sisters at the moment."

***

On Sunday, the Tunnygee group huddled in a corner of the Sandyford pub car park, seeking some shelter from the heavy rain.

"Come on," Patrick Dwyer, Olga's son, came running, "the parade's forming up on the road."

Patrick and Tom Pat, Maisie's son, had travelled up with Maisie and Olga. Patrick had been drafted as a parade marshal and, as the march moved off, he, with the much smaller Tom Pat by his side, walked up and down, obviously taking his duties seriously.

At the entrance to the ambassadorial residence, the Gardai Siochana stood hunched, their blue trench coats apparently black in the lashing rain. There were three speakers, including Captain Roche, who spoke last. As Roche was speaking, a man, his anorak hood pulled well forward over his face, stepped forward and challenged his right to speak.

"Once a Free Stater always a Free Stater," the wild-eyed man declared. "Once an Intelligence officer, still an Intelligence officer. He's a British agent, an M16 man. . . "

"He's a CIA man too," Patrick Dwyer shouted.

"He's a bloody eejit," a Dublin man behind him declared.

"Who?" Patrick turned on him

"Jasus, son, take it easy. It's your man I'm talking about, not the Captain. It's your man that's doing the mouthing, the guy that's interrupting, it's him that's the bleeding eejit. Not Captain Roche, ah no, not Captain Roche."

"I'm sorry," an embarrassed Patrick muttered.

"Don't worry, son," the Dublin man assured him. "We all make bleeding mistakes."

"Listen, friend, if you want to speak you're free to do so," Roche told the heckler. "Give me two or three more minutes and you can blather away as much as you like."

"Who's he?" a man asked Maisie.

"I don't know," Maisie looked at him, "but I think I know you. I . . . I must have met you somewhere before."

"You did, Mrs. Burke, you met me before. Remember that day in Buswell's Hotel in May 1970? Remember the lad who got you into Dail Eireann?"

"I do indeed. You're a friend of Slaney's. You're Padraig Sweeney, Padraig Sweeney from Monaghan."

"The very man and how's Tom. I don't see him here today."

"No, I left him at home to mind the pub. It's great to meet you again, Padraig. I often think about that day in Dail Eireann."

"So do I. I can still see Billy Jackson hitting the man below in Leinster House. I didn't see Billy this long time."

"We don't see that much of him either," Maisie said, "he only comes down to Tunnygee an odd time."

"By the way, this is a friend of mine, Ger McIntosh," Sweeney introduced the man who was with him. "This is Mrs. Burke, came up all the way from Tunnygee, away in the wilds of Cavan," he introduced Maisie.

"Now, we'll let our friend have his say," Roche finished and handed the microphone to the objector.

"I protest against the platform here today," the man began. "I know Roche's family well. He's an anti-Republican breed. His people are all Free Staters. One of the Capitalist Class, an establishment man, he's still working for the establishment. . . "

"The man's a bloody nutcase," McIntosh said, as someone cut off the microphone.

"We might see you in the pub after," Sweeney told Maisie.

Back at Sandyford, most of the marchers went home, but some, including the Tunnygee contingent, crowded into the pub. It was half an hour later before Sweeney and McIntosh arrived.

"I had given up hope. I thought you were not coming," Maisie said, as she introduced Olga.

"We were held up. We gave your man a lift," Sweeney explained.

"Who?"

"Your man, the objector."

"What did you do that for?"

"We tried to throw him in the river."

"You what?"

"Blame McIntosh here. It was his suggestion that we throw him in the Dodder."

"And we nearly succeeded too," McIntosh grinned. "It was only at the last minute that he copped on."

"What happened?" Maisie asked.

"We offered him a lift into town," McIntosh said. "At the bridge at Rathfarnham, I told Padraig to stop, that I wanted to see if the swan was still trapped. I hopped out and leaned over the parapet. I was trying to lure your man out of the car, you see. He fell for it. Next thing, he was beside me. Lean over further and you'll see it, I said. Padraig was coming up behind and your man must have sensed something. Suddenly, he sprang back, nearly knocking Padraig here. There was fright in his face, I tell you. He stood for a split second staring at us, before turning and belting up Rathfarnham Road.I tell you one thing, we frightened the wits out of him."

"You were going to drown him," Maisie said.

"Ah, not at all," McIntosh assured her. "We were only going to give him a look at the water. It's a pity he got away."

"Ach, he got enough of a fright as it was," Sweeney said.

"Maybe you're right, Padraig," McIntosh agreed. "It'll be a while before we see him again, I'd say."

On the way home, Josie Tynan stopped McCaffrey's car in front of Smith's pub in Navan. Olga pulled in behind him. Josie rushed back as she wound down the window.

"I have to go in for a leak," he said.

"I don't believe it," Olga replied.

"Ah, Jasus, Olga, I'm bursting."

"We'll wait here for you," Maisie nudged Olga.

"The lads are talking of having a drink," Josie nodded towards Mike and McGinty, who were standing on the footpath.

"And what about you, Josie?" Maisie asked.

"I'd never have thought of it, only I wanted to go for a piss. That's as true as God is my judge," he assured her.

"If I didn't know you better, Josie, I'd say you were serious, Maisie said.

""Now you're talking Maisie. Anyway, now that we've stopped, we can't leave with the curse of the town on us."

Two drinks later, Maisie stood up.

"Where's Mike and Olga?" she asked, looking around the lounge.

"They're in the bar," Patrick said.

"Go out and tell them we're going," she told him.

"You can't go now. The news will be on in a few minutes," Josie nodded towards the television in the corner. "There might be something about the march on it."

"I doubt it, but you win as usual, Josie," Maisie sat down again.

A few minutes later, Josie was vindicated when there was a quick shot of the marchers on the Nine O'Clock News.

"There we are, up there near the front," he shouted, pointing on the screen.

"A crowd of I.R.A. bastards," a man who was passing said contemptuously.

"Who's a bastard?" Josie jumped up. "I'm no bastard."

"You're the two ends of a bastard and what's worse, an I.R.A. bastard," the man, bleary eyed and swaying on his feet, turned to face Josie.

"I'm no I.R.A. bastard," a red-faced Josie reiterated, emphasising the words.

"Sit down, Josie," Maisie ordered sharply. "Can't you see that the man is drunk?"

"I don't care whether he's drunk or not, he's not going to call me a bastard," Josie shouted glaring at the man.

"Sit down," Maisie pulled sharply at the tail of Josie's coat, knocking him back on his seat.

"You shouldn't have done that, Maisie," he remonstrated, as a friend took his protagonist by the arm and led him away.

"Tell Mike and your mother we're going," Maisie told Patrick.

"They are thinking of going to the dance," Patrick said.

"What dance?"

"The dance out at Greenfields. The Green Shadows are playing there tonight. Tom Pat and I are thinking of going too."

"Who started all this anyway?" Maisie demanded.

"Well, to tell you the truth, it was Tom Pat. He told me to ask my mother. She said no at the first. But when Mike said he wouldn't mind hearing the Green Shadows, she agreed to go."

"So, it's all arranged then?"

"That's right," Patrick said. "They said you could go home with Josie and Willie."

"That's very nice of them. Could they not come and tell me themselves?"

I don't know," Patrick hesitated, "but...but may we go, Tom Pat and me?"

"If Mike and Olga are going, I don't see why you two shouldn't."

"Thanks, Mrs. Burke," Patrick grinned at her and went back to the bar, side-stepping round the tables in the lounge.

"He's a shocking fine looking fellow this minute," McGinty said, "and he's growing more like the bold Olga every day."

"Yes, Willie . . . I didn't think she was that fond of dancing."

"God bless your wit, daughter. It's not today or yesterday that Olga set her cap at Mike, you know that yourself. It's easy to kindle a burnt stick, you know."

"I don't believe you, Willie. Anyway, Mike won't get involved. Sylvia would have his life."

"Aye, maybe you're right. Anyway, it's time we went home," McGinty stood up, shrugging his shoulders in the overcoat.

"God, you'll never get wit, Josie, letting that amadhaun rise you in the pub," McGinty teased Josie from the back seat of the car.

"He wasn't going to call me an I.R.A. bastard and get away with it. I'm no bastard."

"And you're no I.R.A. man either, Josie."

"I know I'm not. But that's all a bloody eegit like him can do, blame the I.R.A. for everything."

"That reminds me. Did you ever hear the story about Mickey Carolan?" McGinty enquired.

"Which Mickey Carolan?"

"Mickey that lives up the lane out at the back of the wood yonder."

'That Mickey?"

"That's right, Josie, that Mickey. It's nearly twenty years ago now, the time of the I.R.A. campaign in the fifties You know this artificial insemination for cows, that was fairly new that time. Anyway, Mickey had an old skinny cow, a bag of bones that he bought in the fair of Shercock, and she wouldn't hold to the bull. Someone told him about the artificial insemination and he sent for the A.I. man. A couple of months later, he was driving the cow down the road. Jack Doherty caught up with him on the bike and stopped to walk a bit of the way with him. 'She looks a bit light for a baste supposed to be in calf,' Jack said. 'She's in calf alright,'

Mickey told him. 'How do you know?' 'I know well,' Mickey grinned, ' because she was bulled by the I.R.A.' "

"You're a holy terror, Willie," Josie spluttered with laughter.

When they arrived back in Tunnygee, the bar was wide open even though it was an hour after closing-time. The Garda Sergeant was standing at the door.

"Jasus, there's a raid on," Josie said, as the Sergeant approached the car.

"I'm sorry, Mrs. Burke, I'm afraid I have bad news for you," the Sergeant opened the passenger door. "Tom's in hospital. He collapsed behind the counter. No, he's not too bad. He recovered after a few minutes, but Carroll sent him in as a precaution."

39

I hesitate to say it, but there is a possibility that he may have cancer," the hospital physician told Maisie.

"I'm arranging to get him a bed in the Mater in Dublin," he continued. "Further tests will have to be carried out before a definite diagnosis is possible. I'm afraid, in...in fact, I'd be less than honest, Mrs. Burke, if I did not tell you that the prognosis is not good."

Maisie left the hospital and went across the street to where Olga and Tom Pat sat waiting in the car. She did not cry, but she walked with a straight-backed stiffness. Her high colour gone, she was pale-faced under the golden-blonde hair. Olga's grip tightened on the steering wheel and her knuckles showed white, but she said nothing as Maisie got into the passenger seat and sat staring blankly at the dark Cavan street, flanked by the terrace of three-storey houses on the right and the wall of the Protestant cathedral on the left.

On the back seat, Tom Pat stared at the back of his mother's head. He had his father's good looks and the same dark curly hair. He had the dark complexion of the Burkes also, but his olive skin only partially concealed his pallor and his lips were pinched and blue as he sat watching his mother.

"He's going to die," he said in a strangled voice.

"No, he's not," Maisie half-shouted, without turning her head.

"Of course, he's not," Olga reached back and patted the distraught boy's knee.

"Get into the front and sit beside your mother," she told him.

Maisie embraced him as he got in beside her, and he lay against her, gulping sobs racking his twelve year old body.

Two months later, Tom was home with a kidney removed. He seemed well, but Maisie was still worried. It was Josie Tynan who reassured her.

"It's only a diseased kidney, ma'am," he told her. "Sure, I had mine taken out years ago, long before I came about the place."

"I don't believe you, Josie."

"As true as God is my judge."

"And there's not a bother on you?"

"Not a bother, ma'am."

"Any man that can put away as much drink as Josie can't have much wrong with his kidneys," Peadar Kennedy, who was washing glasses behing the bar, said.

During Tom's illness, Peadar had offered to help Maisie run the pub. She had rejected his offer, but he arrived one morning and announced that he was going to help despite her.

"You're letting the place go to pot," he told her. "Tom Pat may be your son, but he's my grandson. We have to keep the business going for him and well... well I'm not going to stand idly by and let it go to rack and ruin."

"It's not going to rack and ruin. Myself and the barman will be able to manage," Maisie told him.

"Look at you, you're worn out. I'm a business man. And an extra pair of hands won't go astray," Peadar insisted.

Despite his years, Peadar with the assistance of the apprentice barman, Sean Maguire, was soon running the pub, leaving Maisie free to spend more time attending to Tom.

By Christmas, Tom had recovered fully, but the arrangement with Peadar still stood. It had become a habit. Occasionally he stayed the night, sleeping in the second bed in Tom Pat's room but he went home most nights.

Months passed and sometime before the end of June, Peadar, having spent the night at home, arrived at the pub about ten o'clock one morning. Unusual for him, he looked bedraggled and was unshaven.

"Peadar, what happened? You look like a man who wasn't in bed at all," said Maisie.

"I wasn't."

"What happened?"

"I'm worn out, Maisie. I'm not fit to talk. I only want to go to bed," he stood, eyes red-rimmed, his white stubble making him look much older than his sixty-seven years.

"It's not a nice story," he said enigmatically, steadying himself with a hand on the wall, as he made his way down the hall towards the stairs.

Maisie had not to wait until Peadar reappeared to hear what had taken place. Shortly after eleven, Josie Tynan arrived, bursting with news:

"Christ, Mike Houlihan's after coming out of the doctor's and the head swelled up on him like a pot. With the big white bandages wrapped around him he looked like one of the Indian fellas you see on the buses in London. He went home in the car with the missus. Did you not see Peadar? It was him brought Mike into the doctor. He just dropped him and went off."

"Peadar's in bed. He just fell into it and went fast asleep."

"And he told you nothing?"

"He was hardly able to talk. What happened anyway?"

"I heard the guards are on the way out to the Kennedys'. And they say that Olga's in hospital, that the ambulance came and took her away."

"I don't believe you."

"I'm only telling you what I heard."

"I'll have to get out there. Would you go out to the yard, Josie, and tell Sean to come in. He's in the store, sorting empties."

"Where's Tom?" Josie asked.

"He's up the town. There's a vintners' meeting in the hotel. I'll give him a ring."

When Tom and Maisie arrived, the squad car was parked in front of the Kennedy house. Garda Martin was in the driver's seat, apparently dozing, the cap down over his eyes, but he looked up as the Burke car stopped, and waved his hand in a casual salute.

Sergeant Harty answered the ring on the front door.

"Hello, Tom and Mrs. Burke. The very people we want to see," the Sergeant greeted. "We were going to call on you. We want a word with Peadar. Did he stay in your place last night?"

"No, he stayed here," Maisie said.

"That explains why he brought Mike to the doctor. It looks to have been a serious enough row. Mrs. Kennedy's in hospital. There's no trace of Marie, or the Patrick fella either, and Mrs. Kennedy's car is missing too."

"You've no idea where they are, Patrick and Marie I mean?" Tom asked.

"Give us a chance, Tom. We only got here a few minutes before you. The doctor told us about Mike's injuries and we came out for a look-see. I just had time for a quick look round the house here before you arrived. There's nothing disturbed in here. This door wasn't locked, but, probably, that's not unusual."

"No, it's nearly always on the latch," Tom confirmed.

There was the crackle of a radio message from the squad car.

"Yes, okay, yes. Roger. Out," they heard Martin's acknowledgement.

"The lads in Cavan checked out the hospital," he called to the Sergeant. "Mrs. Kennedy has a broken arm, but otherwise she's A1. Aye, and there's no sign of the young Dwyers round Cavan, or of Mrs. Kennedy's car."

"Peadar is about the only one can give us further information. I think we'll head back to the town," the Sergeant said.

Peadar's story was straightforward. When he arrived home from the pub about one o'clock in the morning, Patrick and Marie were in the sitting room.

"Why are you two young people not in bed?" Peadar asked.

"We're waiting up until the lovers come home," Patrick announced. "We're going to settle this thing once and for all tonight. Running around, making fools of themselves and half the country laughing at them, and laughing at us too."

"It's not that bad," Peadar began.

"Listen, Peadar," Marie interrupted. "We don't want any more soft soap. We're not stirring out of here until they arrive."

"The age of them, making fools of themselves and of us. They're nearly fifty, the two of them," Patrick said in disgust.

Peadar dozed off several times during the night, but each time he awoke the young people sat opposite him at either end of the couch. It was eight o'clock on a bright Summer's morning when the car stopped in front of the house. Peadar awakened to find Patrick and Marie side by side at the window, the small, square figure of the girl, with dark hair and Butsy's snub-nosed good looks in contrast to her brother, blonde haired and tall, in appearance even more the stereotyped Scandinavian than his half Norwegian mother.

"Come on," Patrick nudged the girl and both of them left the room, moving silently on sneakered feet.

Outside, Mike stood with his arm around Olga, both of them looking down towards the lake, the sun glinting on its waters. Patrick came up behind them and tapped the unsuspecting Mike on the shoulder. As Mike turned, Patrick hit him. Mike staggered back, but held his feet. At that point, Peadar, who had moved to the window, rushed outside to find the two in grips wrestling across the tarmac. They fell and Mike hit his head on the bottom step. Still in grips, both struggled to their feet, the blood oozing from a cut over Mike's right ear. Olga grabbed her son from behind and tried to pinion his arms. As Patrick attempted to shake her loose, Mike hit him in the mouth with his fist. With a swing of his shoulders, Patrick threw his mother from him and, in practically the same movement, butted Mike in the face. Olga fell when she was thrown back and Peadar heard the snap of the bone breaking in her arm. Peadar ran to Olga, as Patrick threw punch after punch at Mike, who finally fell back across the steps, hitting the back of his head on the top one with a sickening thud. As Peadar led Olga into the house, Mike was unconscious.

"Get Patrick in here," she ordered, her right arm limp by her side and she grimacing with pain. "You killed him, you madman," she accused Patrick when he came into the house. "Get my handbag out of the car and take out the key of the safe."

"Open the safe and take out the money that's there," she told him when he came back with the key. "Then, I want you to take my car and get to the airport as fast as you can. I want you to take the first plane to London."

"Why?" Patrick asked.

"You fool, you fool, Patrick. If Mike should die I don't want my son arrested for his murder. Get some clothes together and get out of here as fast as you can."

"I'm going with him," Marie said, looking contemptuously at her mother.

"As you wish, " her mother said quietly. "But you were both very wrong. There was nothing between Mike and me only friendship and a mutual interest in golf. That's where we were last night, at a party in The Royal Dublin. We didn't leave the clubhouse until half past six this morning."

"I don't believe you, mother," Olga said.

"You may understand some day," her mother said. "Now, you'd better hurry if you want to go with Patrick. Just remember that you are always welcome back here."

When this discussion was going on, Peadar rang for an ambulance. He was told that it would be there within the hour. He then went out and placed a pillow under Mike's head and covered him with blankets. With another blanket and two chairs he erected a screen to keep off the sun.

"We should bring him in," Olga said.

"No, we should avoid moving him if at all possible. That is one of the lessons that was hammered into us in the Red Cross classes during the war."

Patrick, a bag in his hand, came into the sitting-room where his mother sat on the couch.

"I'm sorry, ma," he said, kissing her on the cheek.

"I'm sorry too, Patrick," she said as he left the room to join Marie who, ignoring her mother, waited in the hall.

"Ring your Aunt Diana, when you get to Heathrow," she called after them.

Ten minutes later, Mike recovered consciousness and when the ambulance arrived he was sitting at the side of the steps, his face puffed and swollen, a lump on the back of his head, with the blood still oozing from the wound over his right ear. His eyebrow was also gashed. The ambulance man wanted to bring him to hospital, but Mike was adamant in his refusal.

"You go, Olga, and get that arm set. I'll take my chances with Carroll," he told her quietly.

Jimmy Devine drove Mike to Dublin that evening. Afterwards, when questioned as to where he dropped him, Jimmy was very non-committal. Eventually, he admitted that he dropped Mike in Stephen's Green.

"But where in the Green?" his questioner persisted.

"Nowhere, just across the road from the Department of Justice."

"Did he say where he was going?"

"No."

"What did he say then?"

"Nothing, only he made a sort of a joke like. I didn't get it right."

"Tell us anyway."

"The Department of Justice, he said. We picked a good place to stop. That's poetic justice for you, he said with a half laugh."

"And that's all?"

"That's all. He paid and went off."

"Where did he go?"

"How do I know? The last I saw of him he was heading towards Leeson Street."

On the Saturday, Olga and Maisie called on Mike's wife, Sylvia. It was Maisie who suggested that they should do so.

"If what you say is true, Olga, and don't get me wrong, I believe you, we should go up and have a chat with Sylvia."

"It's true, Maybe, it was lack of opportunity, but it didn't happen. I'm not saying it couldn't happen, but the reality is that it did not happen. We did not sleep together. To convince Sylvia of that is another matter, espe-cially for a person with my reputation," Olga chortled.

"You've convinced me and maybe Sylvia might be glad to be convinced."

"Alright, Maisie, you are as wise as ever. Now, will you please light a cigarette for me. I'm incapable of performing the most simple action with this plaster on my arm."

Sylvia's reception was cool in the extreme. She stood with the door half open, obviously with no intention of inviting them in.

"It would be better if you let us in," Maisie said. "We can't talk here on the doorstep."

"I don't want that trollop in my house," Sylvia addressed Maisie from behind her gold-rimmed bifocals.

"That is precisely why we are here, Sylvia," Maisie spoke calmly. "Olga and Mike are . . . were just good friends. Maybe, they were not wise to be seen in each other's company so often, but, to put it bluntly, Sylvia, they did not sleep together."

"If you'd expect me to swallow that, you'd expect me to swallow anything."

"It's true, nevertheless," Maisie said quietly.

For the first time, Sylvia recognised Olga's presence, her blue eyes, a shade darker than Olga's, boring into her in a questioning look.

"Yes, it's true," Olga said.

Sylvia brought them into the front room where Peadar had attacked Maisie. Maisie had been in the room on various occasions since then, but it still brought back vivid memories. She thought of Peadar, an obsequious old man, whom she liked, and whom she now momentarily hated again for his frustrated arrogance of twenty years before.

"Please sit down," Sylvia said for a second time, her sharp tone breaking through Maisie's reverie.

The visitors took the two large armchairs on each side of the empty grate, while Sylvia stood stiffly in the centre of the room. Broad-hipped in a tweed skirt, her feet in flat-heeled casuals planted firmly twelve inches apart, she was heavy breasted under the white blouse. Her body showed her sixty years, Maisie thought , but the high-cheeked, finely boned face was that of a woman nearly twenty years younger.

"You are looking very well, Sylvia," Maisie said.

"Yes, I suppose I am, but . . . but where do we go from here?"

"Where's Mike?" Maisie asked.

"He's in the Royal Hotel in Bray. He rang me last night."

"I thought he was in a nursing home."

"Is that the story in the town? Maybe, it is just as well. The truth is that I told him to leave last Tuesday, that one of us had to go. He went off."

"I'm sorry, Sylvia," Olga said.

"And so you should be. The Mackens could always hold their heads up in this county and then you come along to steal my husband. I know what you think of me. You think of me as a snob, as a cold person, but I have feelings and they run deep. How do you think I felt this past year? I held my head high, but I knew that they were whispering, whispering and sniggering behind my back. My children felt it too. Mary Rose is now fifteen, you know. How do you think she felt? How do you think we all felt?" Sylvia removed her glasses and dabbed at her eyes.

"Excuse me," she replaced her glasses. "You see, I have emotions just like everyone else."

"Oh, Sylvia," Maisie went over and embraced her and held her as she cried quietly, large tears running down her pale face.

Maisie accompanied Sylvia to Bray next day, arriving in time to catch twelve o'clock Mass in the church on the Main Street. Afterwards, Mike, his face still showing the marks of the fight, and with a plaster on the back of his head, greeted them on the steps of the hotel. He kissed both of them.

"I've ordered lunch for the three of us," he said.

When he attempted to take Sylvia's arm, she pulled away from him and marched in front of him into the dining room. At the table she was politely reserved, repulsing Mike's initial attempts at conversation. Through the soup and the main course, the three of them sat ill at ease, with Maisie attempting to break the *impasse*. Eventually, she called the waiter and ordered three large brandies.

"I don't want brandy," Sylvia said.

"You're going to get it whether you want it or not and you're going to drink if I have to bottle it into you," Maisie was purposely aggressive.

The coffee was served and Sylvia sipped her brandy.

"I thought for awhile that I might have to put my threat into effect," Maisie said grimly. "Alright, now listen to me," she continued, "you're husband and wife and you've three teenage children. Mike made a bit of an eejit of himself over a woman called Olga and what happened? They went to a few dances together and to a few golf club hops and Olga's son waylaid Mike one morning and nearly killed him. Are you not glad he wasn't killed, Sylvia?"

"I suppose. . . I suppose I am."

"Are you glad the affair is over, that's if you could call it an affair?"

"I am, of course, I am."

"And why the hell don't you take that puss off you and smile at your husband?"

Sylvia looked at Maisie for a moment.

"I think I might need another brandy first," she said.

* * *

In London, Patrick and Marie were staying with Olga's half-sister, Diana. Diana lived with her parents, Alex and Elizabeth Aldbridge, in Hampstead, in a quiet suburban street across the main road from the Art College. Elizabeth, from the English Midlands was Olga's natural mother. She had met Olga's Norwegian father in London when she had come to work there as a sixteen-year old shop assistant at the end of the twenties. The father had disappeared when Olga was a year old. Elizabeth joined the British forces when the war started, and Olga was evacuated to a farm on the Welsh border, where she spent the war years. Meanwhile, Elizabeth had married Alex. Olga accompanied them to Bray on a holiday the year after the war came to an end. She stayed in Ireland when they returned to London. She was known as Olga Pike then, having been given her mother's maiden name, but in 1949, when she was twenty-one, she legally changed her name to Rasmussen, her father's family name. In Dublin, she emphasised her Norwegian ancestry, even to the extent of speaking a form of halting English on occasions. She had broken with her family and it was only when she went to England with Butsy that she learned that Diana, who had been born in 1948, existed. They exchanged Christmas cards after that.

The Oldbridges could not have shown greater hospitality to the visitors. Alex insisted that Patrick accompany him to the pub on the night he arrived. They came back talking and laughing as though they were old friends.

"You two seem to have hit it off," Diana said.

"Yes, we had a wonderful night," Alex agreed. "But, unfortunately, I found it difficult to understand Pat. That brogue of his was too much for me."

"That's funny," Patrick laughed, "your London accent stymied me. I hadn't a clue what you were talking about most of the time."

Next day, Patrick signed on as a labourer with a building firm erecting an extension to the Art College. Marie did not fit in so easily to her new surroundings, despite the undoubted kindness of the Aldbridges. She found the accents difficult, but without her defining it, it was the ambience of the urban scene with which she was at odds. Unlike the more extrovert Patrick, she was reserved to the point of appearing sullen on occasions, and from her first arrival in London, she knew that she had made a mistake.

Her heart was in Tunnygee. She loved the land and especially the little fields among the high hawthorn hedges that ran up from the lake to the Burkes' old place. She could see the two ponies in the well field, running across the brow of the hill, heads and tails up and manes flying, as they came to the gate to meet her. The night her mother telephoned, the loneliness was in Marie's voice.

"You don't sound very happy," her mother said.

"You don't expect me to be happy, do you?"

"No, but you're wrong, Marie. You should not have left. Patrick should not have attacked Mike, but I don't blame him. I blame the crawthumping scandalmongers in this town."

"I heard the stories too, mama. They were talking about the two of you at the school."

"But the stories were not true, Marie."

"But everyone said they were."

"No, Mike and I were friends, good friends, that was all. And we're still friends."

"Then, I'm not going home, mama, and that's final."

"Just listen to me for a moment, Marie."

"No, I don't want to listen. I don't want to talk about it anymore."

"Marie, please listen to me for a moment. Listen carefully. It is important that you should understand exactly what I'm saying."

332

There was silence at the other end of the phone.

"Are you still there, Marie?"

"Yes, mama, I'm still here. I'm listening."

"We are having a party tonight in the hotel. Mike and Sylvia have invited Peadar and me to dinner. Maisie and Tom are coming too. What do you think of that?"

"I don't know," Marie said uncertainly.

"Do you not think it strange that we are all having dinner together if the stories were true?"

"I suppose so."

"You suppose what?"

"I don't know. Maybe . . . maybe that the stories were not true."

"Are you glad?"

"I am, mama, I am."

"Perhaps, you should come home?"

"Should I?"

"Of course, you should."

"But, mama, Patrick wants to stay. He says he won't come home. He loves it here."

"He would, but you don't. I'd love to have you home again and so would Peadar. Maisie was asking for you and told me to tell you to take the first plane home."

"I could probably get a flight tomorrow, mama."

"That's my girl. I'm delighted, Marie. Ring me when you know the time of the flight and I'll meet you at the airport in Dublin."

40

I'm now the last of a dying breed," Willie McGinty announced to Peadar Kennedy on the evening Johny McCaffrey died.

"What's troubling you now, Willie?" Peadar asked.

"Johny McCaffrey died an hour ago."

"The Lord have mercy on him," Peadar blessed himself.

"Amen to that," Josie Tynan, sitting at the end of the counter said, taking off his hat and blessing himself also.

"For a man that's after losing an old comrade, you look very happy," Peadar said to Willie.

"God, now Peadar don't get me wrong. There's no one sorrier than me that poor old Johny is gone. There was no one like him. He had a heart of gold, but I'm the last of them now. That's why I'm proud. I'm proud to be the last of that gallant band of men in Tunnygee who went out and fought to give us the bit of freedom that we have today."

"Hear, hear," Josie laughed. "They'll put you up for the Dail if you keep that up."

"Shut up, Tynan," McGinty said sharply.

"Yes, sir," Josie jumped to his feet and stood rigidly to attention.

"Cut it out, Tynan. This is no time for acting the fool. There's work to be done. My old Captain has to get a military funeral."

"No better man than myself, Willie. Wasn't I a machine-gun instructor in the *F.C.A.?"

"Sit down and shut up. I won't tell you again."

"Jasus, Willie, you're a hard man. Maybe you'd buy us a pint if I sit down," Josie hopped up on his stool.

"Give us a bottle there, Peadar," McGinty ordered," and I suppose you better give Tynan a pint. I want him to do a wee job for me, anyway."

"No better man," Josie grinned and dry-washed his palms

*Forsa Cosanta Aitiúil - Local Defence Force

between his knees.

"Right, get up that telephone book beside you and get the number of Dundalk Military Barracks."

"I wouldn't be able to read that small print," Josie said, handing the book across to Willie.

"If you can't read it, what do you expect an old man like me to do?" Willie demanded, ignoring the proffered directory.

"Here, give it to me," Peadar held out his hand, "I might be an old man, but I can read, not like the pair of you."

Peadar thumbed through the directory for a few minutes.

"I can't find it," he said eventually. "I wonder what it's under?"

"Army. Try army. What else would it be under?" Josie replied with a laugh.

"You're a genius, Josie. I'm after trying D, M and B and never thought of that," Peadar riffled through the book again.

"Yes, here it is. Have any of you a pencil?"

"There's one behind you there," Josie told him.

"I suppose I'll have to make the call too," Peadar said, when he had the number written down. "You better tell us the message, Willie."

"Ask for the Commanding Officer when you get on and tell him that you want a firing party for Captain John McCaffrey of Tunnygee Company of the Old I.R.A. Today's Tuesday. Tell him that the funeral will be Thursday after eleven o'clock Mass."

"Grand, Willie, that's grand. I'll certainly phone in that message. There's just one thing bothers me. Do the family agree?"

"Agree to what?"

"Agree to a military funeral."

"It's Johny's funeral, isn't it, and it's him that's entitled to the firing party. That's the way I see it, Peadar."

"Still, Alice is entitled to a say and what about Father Eddie? Where's he now anyway?"

"The last I heard of him he was in England somewhere," Josie said.

"And there won't be a stir till he comes home," Peadar nodded sagely. "They'll be waiting on him to do the funeral Mass and he'll be the man that will decide about the military funeral too, if I am not mistaken. We can make no arrangements until he arrives."

"I'll just say one thing." McGinty declared. "He's not his father's son if he doesn't give Johny a military funeral."

Father Eddie arrived home on Thursday and the funeral took place on the following day. There was no military involvement at Eddie's express request. McGinty did not get an opportunity of speaking to him until the ceremony was over, when, although not invited, he made his way to the reception for friends of the family in the hotel.

"My sound man, Willie, I'm delighted to see you," Eddie came forward in the pathway of the hotel, his hand out.

"I wasn't invited, you know," Willie kept his hands in his overcoat pockets and his cap on his head.

"Standing on your dignity, Willie, are you? Well, we'll soon set that right. I'm inviting you here and now."

"I'm not looking for any invitation. I came to see you about something more important."

"What is that, Willie?"

"I'm a disappointed man, Father Eddie, that's what I am, that you saw fit to bury your father without doing him the honour that was his due."

"You mean that nonsense of firing shots over him? That's what's wrong with this country, there are too many people firing too many shots. It's the same in too many parts of the world . Violence is not the answer. I took a calculated decision not to have a military funeral, just because it might encourage violence; because it might drive another young man into the arms of the I.R.A."

"Do you know that the last words your father said to me when I went to see him in the hospital less than a month ago. I want to be buried, he said, with a firing party and a bugler."

"We're in changed times, Willie. The days of the men with the gun are over."

"Are you not proud of the part your father played in the fight for freedom?"

"God knows, Willie, but I'm not too sure whether I am or not."

"I never thought I'd see the day, Father Eddie, when I'd hear the son of Johny McCaffrey deny his father."

"For God's sake, Willie, have a bit of sense. Come in and I'll

336

buy you a drink."

"Keep your drink, Father. I'll go down to Burke's and buy my own."

Johny was buried at the end of January 1976. A month later, Mrs. Burke, Tom's grandmother, died.

"She must have been a fierce age," Josie Tynan said in Burke's after the funeral.

"She wasn't that old. Wasn't I at the wedding in 1910?" McGinty said.

"Get away out of that, Willie. Pull the other one."

"I was only a whelp of a gasson at the time. I don't remember much about it. I was only six, but my father brought me. He often talked about it after. And old Jeannie was only sixteen when she got married. So now you can work out her age, Mr. Tynan."

"She was still a brave age. Sixteen from 1910, that's 1894. She was eighty-two. We'll do rightly if we see it."

"Now, you're talking, Josie," Willie agreed.

"I saw Captain Roche there too." Josie said. "I'll be down. There'll be a night in this yet."

Peadar was the first back from the hotel.

"That fire's nearly out, Tom Pat," he bustled up to the counter. "Go out and get a few sticks and a bucket of coal and get it going."

"He has a few in him," Josie said in an aside to McGinty.

"It's a disgrace," Peadar poked at the fire. "Half the country coming down here and the fire out." `

"Give us a drink there, young Maguire," he addressed the barman, "a bottle of stout for me, give Josie and Willie whatever they're having. Give the lads at the end of the counter their pleasure too."

"They're coming," Josie said. "That's Olga's voice I hear outside."

Olga came in and held the door open for Pat and Mary Dempsey, Maisie's parents. Pat was bent over, his back hooped. His work-hard hand, with the oversized knuckles, supported him on a stick, as he shuffled to the counter. Mary's wispy white hair still had the yellow tinge of the redhead. Lively and alert, she stood up straight, still ready to meet the world on her own terms, but she looked her age, close to sixty.

"Come over to the fire, granddad," Tom Pat called to his eighty-four year old grandfather. "It's blazing nicely now."

The old man obeyed, holding out his left hand to Tom Pat, who took it and settled him in a chair. Mary came and sat across the fire from her husband.

"What's your grandfather and grandmother having, Tom Pat?" Peadar shouted.

"I'll have a half one," Pat muttered from behind his pipe.

"You're getting more like your father every day. If you're half as good a man you'll do rightly," Mary smiled up at her grandson.

"What are you having, grandma?" he asked her.

"A drop of sherry, Tom Pat, please."

"The others are walking down. They'll be here in a minute," Olga told Peadar.

"Ha, ha, Captain Roche, welcome back to Tunnygee," Josie saluted when Roche entered the bar with Maisie.

"The two warriors," Roche went over to Josie and McGinty and shook hands warmly with both, while Maisie joined the group at the fire.

"When's the next election? We had great crack the last time," Josie said with his characteristic laugh.

"I don't forget either of you, the way you worked for Tom," Roche said. "In answer to your question, Josie, I'd say you could have an election at any stage."

"The sooner the better is what I say. It's time we had a bit of excitement again," Josie rubbed his hands in anticipation.

"Give the lads two whiskies here," Roche told the barman.

"Ah, not at all, Captain, we didn't expect that," McGinty shrugged his shoulders.

"I hear your old sidekick, Johny McCaffrey, died. He gave Tom a hand the last election too," Roche said to McGinty.

"That's right, Captain, he did, but did you hear what happened?"
"No."

"The family wouldn't let him have a military funeral."

"Oh, Mike mentioned something about that up at the hotel. I was surprised to hear it I must say."

"Father Eddie shot it down. It was a shocking thing to do on poor Johny. I'd say he's turning in his grave this minute,"

McGinty declared.

"Another twirlin' Charlie," Josie said.

"Another what?" Roche asked.

"Ach, it was only a man who lived out the road a bit," Josie explained. "He was shocking fond of his wife, you know. It was a brave lock of years ago now but on the day he died, the wife knelt at the bedside and taking the dying man's hand, swore she would never look at another man as long as she lived. Bridgie, if you did, I'd turn in my grave, he told her. They say those were the last words he ever spoke before he passed away. From that day to this he's known as Twirlin' Charlie."

"That's what causes earthquakes, all the twirling Charlies tumbling away down below," Roche grinned at Josie.

"I suppose you'll be shoving Tom forward again in the next election," McGinty said.

"I won't be shoving anyone forward, Aontacht Eireann's almost dead, you know. When O'Donnell left, I got out too," Roche told him.

"Tom will probably give it a go all the same, he could run as an Independent," McGinty suggested.

"I hope he does. We had great crack the last time. Will you run yourself this time, Captain?" Josie asked.

"No, when I didn't run the last time, there's not much point in going this time. But I'll be around to give Tom a hand the same as before."

"Good man, Captain, the sooner the better, "Josie rubbed his palms.

When the election came in 1977, Tom stood as an Independent, with Josie, as in '73, his self-appointed chauffeur. In general, the response was reasonable, but there was a voice of dissent also. Canvassing close to Tunnygee one afternoon, Tom and Josie called to a farmer's house.

"You better talk to himself, he's out in the yard," the woman of the house said.

"You lads are for a united Ireland," the farmer, who was out in the cow byre, said. "Do you not think we're too small on our own?"

"But we'd be bigger if we were united," Tom suggested.

"We'd still be too small."

"What about Israel, then?"

"I wouldn't know about that."

"And Switzerland and Luxembourg?"

"I wouldn't know about them either."

At the very next house, a woman answered the door also.

"You better talk to himself, he's out in the yard," her message was exactly the same as that of the woman in the previous house.

Tom walked round the back to find the owner digging a trench in the farmyard.

"Hello, how are you? I'm canvassing," Tom said.

"Are you any good to dig a trench?" the man asked ill-manneredly, not stopping in his work.

At that moment, Josie, open shower coat flapping at his knees, hat on the back of his head, came dashing around the corner. Without breaking his stride, he went straight to the edge of the trench, stopping with the toes of his boots inches from the man's chest.

"Give us that shovel and I won't be long showing you how to dig," he said.

"No, it's alright," the man leaned back against the side of the trench, a look of fear on his face.

"That's no way to win votes," Tom told him when they were back in the car.

"You weren't going to get any votes there anyway, or in the house before it either," Josie assured him. "They couldn't get back under the Queen quick enough."

Tom spoke at various meetings in both Cavan and Monaghan, including one in West Cavan, where, inspired by the presence of the opposition parties, he made his best speech of the campaign. Claiming that the difference between the two parties was that between Tweedledum and Tweedledee, he reserved most of his contumely for Toler and the Party, which he described as being corrupt and accused of buying votes.

"I do not make this claim of buying votes lightly," he said. "No later than yesterday I canvassed a house. How much are you paying for votes, the woman of the house demanded. I looked at her. Hold on a minute, she said, running back into the kitchen.

340

She came back waving a piece of paper in her hand. It was a rates demand. That's for £70, she exulted, and that's the price of my vote. And, then, a few miles up the road, a family with three young men in it. Three battered cars, old jalopies, in the yard. See them, one of the young men said, we don't have to tax them any more. Drive where we like, when we like, and not a guard can say a word to us. Toler is the man who fixed that. Who else would we vote for? No rates and no tax on these old buggies, he clapped the palm of his hand flat on the roof of one of the cars.

"We'll pay for it yet," Tom continued, "but what matter? To-morrow is another day and the vote will be counted then, bought and paid for by the prospect of the gravy train of promise, live horse and you'll get grass economics . . .On the north the policy of both main political parties is the same. Bipartisanship is the word, the new in-word, a policy of do-nothing. Forget about the north, we've enough problems down here. Put a barbed-wire fence around it. Let them stew in their own juice. A plague on both their houses up there."

He continued: "Not good enough . . . We cannot desert our fellow Irishmen in their hour of need. We must put the blame squarely where it belongs. Britain partitioned this country and the responsibility for the present violence rests squarely with Britain. Britain must take a decision to disengage . . .To conclude, integrity in public life is the very basis of democracy. It is essential to democracy, any claim to which Mr. Toler forfeited not only for himself but also for a large segment of his party in 1970. He did this when he entered False Evidence, ridden by McAdoo, and trained by O'Looney in the Arms Trial Stakes. That the horse did not win was not the fault of the rider or the trainer, or owner Toler for that matter. Quite simply, the false evidence of McAdoo was shown to be just that when produced in open court. It did not need to be challenged. It tripped over its own obvious falseness. Yet Toler still talks about integrity in public life. It is enough to make a dog sick," Tom finished.

One week later, Tom got three or four per cent of the vote and Toler led his party back into government with the greatest majority ever achieved in the State.

41

T here's only one way that Britain will leave Ireland and that's when forced to do so through the barrel of a gun," Olga declared one evening shortly after Easter 1979.

"With all due respects, Olga, I think that is a bit simplistic," Tom said. "After all the Irish claim to unity is based on the wishes of all the people, as opposed to a dissident one-fifth gathered primarily on the North-East of the country where they form an unreal majority in an unreal Six County statelet. Under the circumstances, it will be hard to shift Britain until the Dublin Government asks her to go."

"Talk and more talk. The Vietcong did not beat the Americans by talking...."

"Hold it, Olga, hold it right there. On the contrary, it was talking won for the Vietnamese..."

"Ah, Tom, please. You're being simplistic now. The Vietcong fought. They fought like demons."

"I know. I know, I accept that, but the Vietnamese won the propaganda battle. They won the talking war hands down. The Americans could blow ships out of Haiphong harbour and...and blast the Ho Chi Minh trail until the cows come home, and defoliate the land by the square mile, but in this age of communications, Ho won where it counted, when he swung world opinion to his side. He won the battle for the world's minds and hearts, against which overwhelming American military superiority was largely a waste of effort. Talking was the major factor in Ho's victory. Vietnam was a media war which Ho won hands down."

"That's because he had right on his side, just like the Republicans here."

"But Olga, that's precisely the point. We have a Government under Toler and we've an opposition led by O'Grady. They have an agreed policy, a bipartisan approach, which recognises that part of Ireland is a British area of responsibility and will remain so for the foreseeable future. Thus, Irish unity is on the back boiler, put there by the majority of the Irish people..."

"What do you expect the I.R.A. to do then, give up the fight too?" Olga demanded, agitatedly rubbing her hand through her hair, which she was cutting short again.

"No, that won't happen, but I do believe that if the Dublin Government, as a sovereign government, exercised its muscle on the international scene in the interests of Irish unity, that it could possibly obviate the necessity for violence."

"And when do you think that's going to happen, Tom?"

"Not as long as the Toler-O'Grady alliance lasts, that's for certain."

"It'll never happen and even if it did, I believe we'd still have to fight. I believe what my late husband, Butsy, believed, that the British won't get their imperialistic arses out of Ireland until they're blown out of it. That's my real opinion," Olga declared.

"Maybe, but I don't agree with you, Olga. It's not the only way, and maybe not the best way."

Later in the year, Tom ran as a candidate in the local authority elections. He stood as an Independent Republican, finding himself in opposition to Olga, who was nominated by Sinn Fein. Shortly after handing in his nomination papers, Tom was asked if he would consider withdrawing from the contest as his candidature could only split the Republican vote. He did not do so, claiming that he would only maximise the Republican vote. This was accepted by the majority, including many Sinn Fein supporters, but Olga was far from happy and two days later she called on Tom, flanked by the two people who had asked him to consider withdrawal. Maisie, fully supporting her husband's decision to stay in the election race, was present for the interview. It soon became obvious that Olga's two supporters had taken some counsel since their previous visit. They made it clear that it would only be to the advantage of the two main parties if Tom did not run, and merely requested that Tom do all in his power to obtain number two votes for Olga. At this point, Olga exploded, accusing the two men of selling out and ordering them to leave the bar. When they were gone, she turned to Tom:

"You are a conniving bastard, Burke," she shouted, thumping the counter. "You arranged all that."

"Come now, Olga, how could I arrange it? I thought you had more sense than that, girl."

"Don't girl me, Burke, and don't try to tell me you were not involved," she said and stormed out.

"I suppose I'd better go too," said Peadar, following her out.

"What's wrong with her ?" Tom asked.

"What do you think?" Maisie looked at him. "Did you see the flushed face of her? It's her age."

"You could be right. She must be fifty or over it, come to think of it."

Next morning, Peadar, who still assisted in the bar two or three days a week, arrived as usual.

"I thought you might have gone absent this morning, Peadar," Tom said.

"I'm too long in the tooth to let a wee upset like last night put me off. Anyway, Olga doesn't know the crowd around here as well as I do. She'll be lucky to get a hundred votes. She hasn't a chance and when I told her that this morning she nearly hit me. So you're not the only one that's getting the sharp end of her tongue," Peadar laughed as he moved slowly to clear the tables of the debris of the night before.

Peadar's forecast proved to be correct, with Olga getting less than one hundred votes. Tom missed winning a seat by a handful of votes. In fact, on the day of the count it was announced on radio that he was practically certain to be elected. That night, when he arrived home, the pub was packed with well-wishers who had assumed that he was in. Mike and Sylvia were among them. They were disappointed when he told them that he was not successful. The others were only slightly deflated. They were intent on enjoying the night at that stage.

Olga was a late arrival. She looked strained and her eyes were slightly red-rimmed under a freshly made-up face.

"I'm delighted you came," Tom hugged her bulk as the crowd cheered.

"I'm sorry about the row," she whispered in his ear.

***

In the overall, the election had not been a great success for the Government and with the result of the elections to the European Parliament, which had taken place on the same day, it emerged that the Toler electoral high of over 50% in the 1977 general election had dropped to 34%.

Such a drop in electoral support in such a short space of time did not augur well for the future of the Party and there were many backbenchers who saw themselves losing their seats if Toler was to continue as leader. They saw McAtavey as the man most likely to save them. When, in November, Toler lost two by-elections in his home area, he had to go, and by December, McAtavey was both leader of the Party and Taoiseach. On the day after the take-over, Captain Roche was in Tunnygee, where he joined in the celebrations in Maisie's pub.

"There are some long faces around this town the day," Willie McGinty announced. "I went into O'Keeffe's for a quick one this morning. I was in the back when Knobby-Knees Kissane came in for his paper. He thought there was no one there only Mrs. O'Keeffe and he said to her, you know that quiet way he has of talking, I think the party has made a wrong decision. McAtavey will be the ruination of it."

"A lot more think the same way around this town. Most of the Party members around here would cut McAtavey's throat," Maisie said.

"He'll get it tight to survive," Tom said.

"Why?"

"Apart from the crowd trying to knife him down here, the blanket men could put him to the test."

Several hundred Republican prisoners in Northern Ireland had gone "on the blanket" in September 1976, refusing to wear prison clothes and wearing a blanket instead. This protest arose because the British authorities denied them political status, classifying them as terrorists and criminals. In March 1978, the prisoners escalated their protest by adopting a "no-wash" policy. In October 1980, less than a year after McAtavey had come to power, a number of them went on hunger-strike, which came to an uncertain end on the basis of a negotiated agreement. When the British Government did not meet the terms of the agreement, it caused discontent and mistrust among the prisoners, who came to the conclusion that once again they had been tricked by the British.

Consequently, another hunger-strike was undertaken, with Bobby Sands refusing food for the first time on March 1, 1981.

In Tunnygee, Tom was the first to raise a voice on behalf of the hunger-strikers, when he held a meeting in their support.

"You all know why we're here," Tom told the ten people at the meeting. "We're here to do what we can to assist the hunger-strikers in the H-Blocks in Long Kesh. First we need a Chairman."

"A Chairperson," Olga murmured.

"What about yourself, Olga?" Joe Mitchell asked.

"No, thanks all the same, Joe, but I don't see myself as a Chairperson."

"I propose Tom, then," Mitchell said.

"I second that," said McGinty to a general nod of agreement.

On the following Wednesday, a drummer giving the beat, Tom, flanked by two men with black flags, led two hundred people down the main street of Tunnygee and across by the police barracks to the Market Square where Tom and Olga addressed the crowd. It was announced that a similar parade would take place each Wednesday until the hunger-strike issue was resolved.

Tom was asked to attend the next meeting of the Chamber of Commerce, where the parades were to be discussed. It emerged that some members of the Chamber were concerned because shops closed their doors during the parades. It was suggested by one particular individual that there was intimidation involved. Tom denied this, but when asked what shopkeepers should do, he implied that the most sensible approach would be to close the doors as the parade passed, advice which was accepted. The local parades continued, while Tom hired buses to bring protestors to parades in places such as Armagh and Dublin. In Armagh, a police cordon blocked off the approaches to the Women's Prison. There was a strong British army presence also. The crowd pressed up to the police lines with some of the Tunnygee contingent to the forefront. Tom was with Joe Mitchell and they found themselves squeezed forward.

"We better move out of this, Joe," Tom advised. "If the police charge you won't be able to get out of the way. They'll just belt you to the ground and run across you."

"They won't belt me and, anyway, I'm not that stiff."

"You're nearly seventy, Joe."

"Maybe, you're right, we'll move over to the side."

"Two brave men, getting out of the line of fire," they heard Olga's voice when they reached the side of the road.

"Ah, there you are, "Joe spotted her. "You're fairly out of the line of fire yourself."

"If you were carrying my weight you would be too," she chortled. "Hey, there's Bernadette Devlin," she called, clapping her hands above her head, as the small, familiar figure appeared in the middle of the road.

"Sit down, all sit down," Bernadette instructed.

Eventually the crowd obeyed and Bernadette spoke in her usual no-nonsense style, describing the plight of the H-Block hunger-strikers and of the women prisoners in the jail, four or five hundred yards distant, behind the lines of police. She advised the crowd to disperse quietly, but for awhile it was touch and go, as stones and missiles continued to be thrown, but gradually people began to move away towards the buses and confrontation was avoided.

It was in Dublin that the major battle of the H-Block campaign was fought between protestors and the Garda Siochana. As the parade formed up on Stephen's Green, Tom joined Captain Roche and Kevin O'Donnell. Tom's old I.R.A. friend, Sean Sheridan, and Mick Slaney were also there. They were moved up towards the front to lead the parade.

"That's it, get the cannon-fodder up to the front," Tom heard someone say .

Passing the American Embassy, a few ritual stones were thrown at the gardai to shouts of "Pigs" and "R.U.C. bastards". At the Anglesea Road corner of the R.D.S. grounds in Ballsbridge, a large force of gardai blocked the road to prevent the march reaching the British Embassy further out.

"There's going to be trouble here," Tom said to Tom Pat, who was marching beside him.

As the first onslaught was mounted on the police lines, they took shelter in a garden to the left of the road. The hand-to-hand fighting in the street increased in intensity and the police lines wavered, but, gradually, the momentum of the marchers' attack was weakened.

"It's time we were getting out of here," Slaney said.

"Where's Tom Pat?" Tom asked, looking around.

"Come on," Slaney said, going down a passageway at the side of the house.

Out on the road, about fifty yards from where the battle was still going on, men and women and whole families ran and walked to get away.

"It's time to start moving," Captain Roche came running up. "The police will come charging down this road any minute."

"I've lost Tom Pat," Tom said.

"You won't find him now and you'll get your head hammered in if you stay here," Roche told him.

They walked down the road swinging round to the left to get back to Jury's Hotel. On the way, they were joined by two other Tunnygee men, Jack O'Neill and Tom Smith, who had escaped through another garden. At a bridge over a dried-up stream they stopped to watch, as police chased a group of young men along a road at the other side of some waste ground. One boy hid behind a wall. He put his head up to look over the wall as a policeman was passing. He was chopped down with a baton. Obviously dazed, he struggled to his feet, to be set upon by two baton-wielding policemen; they battered him into a slumped heap behind the wall where he lay, with blood pouring from his head.

"Bejasus, if I had a rifle with me, I'd blow the heads of those bastards of guards, a right pair of fuckin' savages," Jack O'Neill declared with feeling.

There was a sudden scream from the bushes down under the bridge, like that of an animal in pain. A wild-eyed youth came running from the bushes. He ran in under the bridge.

"Me and my pal, we only came out for a walk, and now they're beating the shit out of him in there," he shouted back, as he ran to safety on the other side of the bridge.

A blue van, with the passenger door swinging open, pulled up with a screech of brakes, skidding sideways on the road about thirty yards away. Several policemen jumped out, most of them running off down the road, while one of them approached the group on the bridge.

"What the fuck are you doing here. Get moving or we'll soon shift you," the policemen glanced back towards the van in which three or four of his comrades still lurked.

"Get to fuck out of here," he shouldered up against Slaney.

"Do you know who you're talking to?" Slaney stood his ground, his shoulder nudging the policeman's chest.

"No, and I don't give a fuck."

"And where's your number?" Slaney demanded. "You should have it on your tunic. Here," he pulled his identification from his pocket. "See that? M.E.P., Member of the European Parliament. I'm Mick Slaney, a member of the European Parliament."

"Jasus, see the glazed eyes of the hoor, the man's beyond reasoning," O'Neill nudged Tom.

"Come on, Mick, let's get out of here, the man's past it," Tom caught Slaney's elbow.

"God knows, I think you're right, Tom," Slaney put his identification card back in his pocket.

"And the boys beyant have left the van," Tom said.

Three policemen were already ten yards from the van, walking slowly, batons gripped tightly in their hands. Slaney moved, walking steadily after the group, while the policemen stood in indecision.

"You were as well to move, Mr Slaney. He's like a mad bull, yon fellow, you wouldn't know what he'd do next," O'Neill told Slaney, looking back from the corner.

"Be God, lads, you may get a move on. He's coming after us," he called suddenly.

As they passed the next junction, the policeman was coming round the corner.

"Is it far to the hotel?" O'Neill asked.

"Only a couple of hundred yards," Slaney answered.

"Thanks be to God," O'Neill said.

That night back in Tunnygee, Tom Pat was still missing. Close to midnight, Maisie answered the phone. It was Tom Pat.

"Where are you?" she asked.

"I'm out at Kevin O'Donnell's."

"What are you doing there? What happened?"

349

"Here, Kevin wants to talk to you."

"It's alright, Maisie," Kevin assured her. "The guards gave him a bit of a hammering..."

"What?"

"He's alright. There's not a bother on him, except for a few bruises. I brought him home with me. I'll drive him down tomorrow."

"He's alright, Kevin?"

"I give you my word, Maisie," O'Donnell laughed, "except for a few bruises, there's not a bother on him."

Tom Pat had left the garden in which he and Tom had taken refuge for a few minutes. When he returned, Tom and the rest of them had gone. Uncertain what to do and worried about Tom, he remained where he was until the battle was over. He sat on the high wall bordering the side road as the police cleared the streets. When a garda officer appeared, he pretended to be assisting a cameraman who had been photographing from a tree in the garden. The officer ordered the cameraman down out of the tree and made a swipe at Tom Pat with his stick. He then herded Tom Pat out of the garden still swinging his stick. He shouted at the policemen returning from their baton charge up the road:

"Here's another of the bastards."

Tom Pat then had to run a gauntlet of punching, kicking and baton-wielding policemen. He managed to get across the road before being beaten to the ground at the R.D.S. railings, where he lay, semi-conscious, his face against the railings. A policemen inside the grounds came running across and kicked him in the face through the railings. As he attempted to get up, two girls came to his assistance and the police attacked them, knocking one of them to the ground with a baton. Eventually, with the two girls supporting him, Tom Pat made his way up the road, where he was brought into a house that had opened its doors to succour the frightened and the injured.

Marauding policemen still scoured the streets, clearing out gardens and bursting into houses where they thought people might be hiding. It was an hour before a shaken Tim Pat felt fit to leave the house, from which he made his way to Stephen's Green, where Kevin O'Donnell, who was collecting his car, recognised him.

42

Bobby Sands died on May 5, 1981, having been elected as a Westminster M.P. during his sixty-five day period on hunger strike. Francis Hughes died seven days later and Raymond McCreesh and Patsy O'Hara died on the twenty first of the month. In the following month, Charlie McAtavey called a general election. Slaney's Independent Fianna Fail organisation decided to run candidates in the border constituencies on a Constitutional Republican ticket. Tom was selected as the Slaney candidate for Cavan-Monaghan. Sinn Fein indicated that they were going to put up hunger-strikers as candidates in selected constituencies in the Republic. At a Slaney Convention in Sligo to ratify candidates, Tom proposed that Slaney candidates should withdraw if opposed by hunger-strikers. This proposal was unanimously accepted and, when a hungerstriker, Kieran Doherty, was nominated in Cavan-Monaghan, Tom withdrew.

"Are you still in the race?" Olga demanded of Tom on the final day for nominations.

"I am."

"Don't you know that we have Kieran Doherty up?"

"I do."

"And you're not going to withdraw?"

"Who told you that?"

"You're leaving it very late, then."

"I have until twelve noon tomorrow. I said I was withdrawing and that's what I intend doing. Do you not trust me?"

"I didn't say that, but . . . but you're leaving it late."

"I've arrangements made to meet the County Registrar tomorrow at eleven o'clock, to go through the formalities of withdrawing. Does that satisfy you?"

"But today's the last day."

"The last for nominations maybe, but not for withdrawals. Noon tomorrow is the final time for that."

"A lot of our people were worried," she said. "They don't trust politicians."

"Whether they do or not, I'm withdrawing tomorrow morning. I'm doing so because I'm on the side of the hunger-strikers, because I believe that they are political prisoners and that they and the vast majority of other prisoners in Northern Ireland would never see the inside of a jail if Britain did not insist on maintaining that part of Ireland is part of the United Kingdom. That's the precise reason why I'm withdrawing, but I have very serious reservations."

"I know that, Tom."

"You know I'm opposed to the Sein Fein policy of absentionism and . . . and . . ." .

"I know, Tom, but the hunger-strikers are a different case. Look at the publicity Bobby Sands gave our cause when he was elected to Westminster and now we have a good chance of getting three or four in down here. It will be a great propaganda victory for us."

"That's a short term view. You remember what happened in 1957 ? Sinn Fein got four seats in that year's general election, but refused to enter Dail Eireann. It was a great breakthrough at the time, giving a national platform to the Sinn Fein organisation, but it was wasted. It will be the same again with the hunger-strikers.

"Come off it, Tom. They're hunger-strikers. They'll get the sympathy of the world."

"For a short while, Olga. The reality, as I see it, is this. Assume two hunger-strikers are successful. There are 166 Dail seats. The Dail will meet and carry on with 164 members, the same as if the absentee members did not exist. A government will be formed and that will be that."

"What difference does it make what government gets in? Neither of them is going to do much for Republicanism."

"On the contrary, if Sinn Fein threw its weight behind the Slaney candidates and got three or four of them elected, it might achieve something. Three or four, or maybe five Slaney candidates, equally committed to British withdrawal as any Sinn Feiner, could hold the balance of power in the new Dail."

"They'd be supporting McAtavey then?"

"That's fairly obvious, I'd say. I don't see the other shower meeting Slaney's demands. Anyway, apart from demands, McAtavey has a Republican outlook himself. He'd have no objection to paying our price and his party, with five years in Government staring it in the face, would go along with it. What I'm saying, Olga, is that if Slaney had the balance of power, it would only strengthen McAtavey's hand in having his party accept the Republican philosophy as the basis of future government policy."

"That would never happen, Tom."

"God, you're stubborn, Olga. Well, put it this way. With Slaney and Roche and one or two others in Dail Eireann, there might be some chance of making it happen, but with Sinn Fein's policy of abstentionism, there isn't a hope. Further, the plight of the hunger-strikers, and I'll put it no higher than this, Olga, would not be worsened, if Slaney and his supporters held the balance of power in Dail Eireann. In fact, it would increase the likelihood of an equable settlement."

"I don't know about that, Tom. Anyway, Kieran Doherty is standing."

"And I'm withdrawing."

On election day, Tom, accompanied by Tom Pat, went to assist a Slaney candidate in a neighbouring constituency. In the afternoon, he called at the polling station, where he had left Tom Pat that morning, to find him missing. When he arrived home that night, Tom Pat was having his supper.

"Why did you leave? At least, you could have told me before you ran off," Tom complained.

"I didn't know where you were, dad. You said yourself you'd be travelling around the constituency.

"You still should have waited."

"But it was a waste of time, dad. There was no one supporting your man and, anyway, he had three or four canvassers there. I got a lift back to Tunnygee and worked for Kieran Doherty."

Next morning, Olga called for Tom Pat.

"I promised to bring him to the count," she told Maisie.

That night, Tom Pat burst through the bar door, followed by Olga and two or three others.

353

"We won, dad, we won, mammy," he shouted to his mother and father, serving behind the bar.

"We walked it. We got ten thousand votes, ten thousand votes for the hunger-striker," Olga danced around the bar.

"And little Willie," she hugged McGinty.

"A drink here for Willie," she called. "No one worked harder for Kieran Doherty yesterday. And a drink for Long Joe, another Doherty man not afraid to pin his colours to the mast. And one for Tober and one for Martin and John here, and don't forget young Tom Pat. Here, a drink for the house, and where's Peadar?"

"He's upstairs having a cup of tea," Maisie said.

"Charge the drink up to him," Olga ordered. "I spent my last pound in the Lavey Inn on my way home."

The overall result of the election was defeat for McAtavey and his party. He was only a few hundred votes short but it was enough to permit McWilliam's successor, O'Grady, to form a government.

"I must admit that I would have preferred McAtavey to O'Grady," Olga told Tom.

"What effect have the hunger-striker T.Ds now?" Tom asked.

"They won and isn't that enough?"

In the following weeks, Olga marshalled several cavalcades of cars through the town, horns triumphantly blaring. Speeches were delivered, but the general air of triumphalism did not please all the hunger-strike supporters. The neighbouring woman who came in to the bar each day for her cigarettes, was one of them.

"Like yourself, I had a hand in stirring the pot," she told Maisie.

"What do you mean?" Maisie asked,

"I voted for the hunger-striker this time too, but I'm going back to where I came from next time, back to Fine Gael."

"Why?"

"I voted for Kieran Doherty, the hunger-striker. That doesn't mean that I gave Sinn Fein the right to take over the country."

"You're exaggerating," Maisie said.

"Maybe I am, but someone should tell that friend of yours, Olga, to cool it."

"That's Olga's way. She's never half-hearted about anything. By the way, Tom and I are off on holidays next week," Maisie changed the subject.

"Where are you going?"

"We're going to London. My sister, Betty, is married over there. She lives in Ealing."

"You'll be there for the Royal Wedding."

"So it seems."

***

When Tom and Maisie arrived in London, Betty and her husband, Eddie Timmons, were, somewhat to the surprise of the visitors, in the throes of preparations for the wedding of Prince Charles and Diana Spencer. The street on which they lived was a *cul de sac* and the residents had decided to have a street party on the evening of the wedding. The idea was to stage a play illustrating some aspects of the history of royalty, which was to be followed by dancing and merry-making. The evening was perfect for an outdoor party and, when Tom and Maisie returned from a day in the city centre, Eddie was dressed as Henry VIII and Betty as Anne Boleyn for their parts in the play. Tom and Maisie were, of course, invited to participate in the merriment. Tom asked to be excused on the basis of tiredness after a long day in town, but when Betty persisted, he told her:

"I don't want to be awkward, Betty, but I don't want to celebrate the wedding of Prince Charles. First he's Colonel-in-Chief of the Parachute Regiment that murdered the thirteen in Derry. Secondly, he epitomises the British establishment which persists in remaining in Ireland as a result of which Irish men are dying on hunger-strike at this very moment. I'm sorry, Betty. I don't want to spoil anyone's enjoyment, but I support the hunger-strikers in opposition to the regime that forced men to adopt such measures."

"That's crap, Tom, and you know it."

"Maybe it's crap, Betty, but it's my way of making a very minor stand, a protest, if you like."

"It is also discourteous, Tom, discourteous to me as your hostess and to Eddie as your host."

"I'm sorry you feel that way, Betty, but I think my discourtesy is of little consequence when balanced against the life of Kieran Doherty which is ebbing away at this very moment."

"Don't be so dramatic, for God's sake. Celebrating Charlie's wedding is not going to save Doherty's life."

"No, but if every Irish person in Britain made it clear that he or she was not celebrating the Royal Wedding because of the hunger-strike, it might . . . . it might just make Mrs. Thatcher reconsider and grant the minor concessions that would bring the hunger-strike to an end."

"Have a titter of wit, Tom. You obviously don't know Mrs. Thatcher."

"I know she's a politician and I know that if all the Irish vote was harnessed against her that it might at least give her food for thought. In the meantime the Irish could show their abhorrence to and rejection of Mrs. Thatcher's attitude by boycotting the wedding. After all, your friend, Charlie, is one of the titular heads of the establishment of which Thatcher is chief executive."

"You're impossible, Tom."

"No, Betty, not impossible, just realistic. How much better to make the type of peaceful protest I advocate than to blithely stand by and then wring our hands in horror when the further violence and death, which Mrs. Thatcher's obduracy is certain to ensure, takes place."

"Do you agree with all this?" Betty asked Maisie.

"Yes, I do."

"Well, if both you objectors don't mind, I'll excuse myself. All my guests are out in the street," Betty bowed facetiously and left.

"Excuse me," a woman's voice said from the corner of the room, "Bert and I couldn't help overhearing what you said to Betty."

"I'm sorry, I didn't see you there," Tom peered at the couple, who stood out of range of the light from the table lamp.

"No, we came in through the french window as you were talking and we didn't want to intrude. So we just stood here as quiet as two mice. Isn't that right, Bert?"

"That's right, Lizzie."

"We're friends of Betty and Eddie, you know," Lizzie said.

"Join us," Tom invited.

"Or maybe you'd prefer to join the party outside?" Maisie said.

"We'd prefer to stay with you, if you don't mind," Lizzie said.

"Bert is an old soldier," she added. "That's why he agrees with you. He understands these things. He says you're right to object. Isn't that right, Bert?"

"That's right, Lizzie."

Bert was a Liverpudlian, who, having left the British army in 1946, spent thirty-five years as a milkman, and, later, as a supervisor with the milk firm up the road.

"And I'm from Wales. I worked with the same firm. Both of us retired in March and we're just back from a holiday in Dublin. That's why we know all about the hunger-strike," Lizzie said.

"I always keep in touch with what's happening in Ireland," Bert said. "And there's no reason why we should be there. We should get out, that's what I say."

"How many Englishmen think like you?" Tom asked.

"You'd be surprised. I was talking to a mate of mine last evening and he said, that if Germany occupied part of this country, he'd try to bomb them out too. I wouldn't go that far, but I still think we should leave Ireland. It's our last colony and it's time we gave it up."

"That's why we're sitting here with you. We think you're right. Isn't that right, Bert?"

"That's right, Lizzie."

On the boat train North a few days later, Tom bought an evening paper.

"Hey," he shouted to Maisie, "someone burned the Orange Hall in Tunnygee last night."

43

I n October, over two months after the event, four young men were arrested under the Offences Against the State Act and questioned about the burning of the Orange Hall. The one thing that they had in common was that the four of them had been active campaigners on behalf of the hunger-strikers. Eventually, they were charged with burning the hall on the basis of alleged confessions given under questioning. They were remanded on bail. On release, the four of them vehemently protested their innocence, but there were many in Tunnygee who did not believe them.

"There's no smoke without fire," was the conventional wisdom of some, while others shook their heads and said: "The guards know what they're about. Them fellas don't make mistakes."

"Tom Burke has a lot to answer for," Jack Mahoney, a local political hack was quick to place the blame. "They organised the H-Block parades that led the young lads astray," he announced to all who cared to listen, and there were some who believed him.

"Never mind the bastards. They'll have to eat their words yet," Olga told Maisie.

"Yes, but the gossip-mongers are having their effect. I've noticed that some people don't come in here any more," Maisie said.

"They're not worth having if they're that easily influenced."

"That's all right for you, Olga, but they're our customers."

"And Tom Pat is certain it was the night of the fire O'Toole was in the bar?" Olga queried.

"Didn't I ring him from England on the night before we came home? It was after midnight by the time I got through. Tom Pat remembers taking the call. O'Toole was in the bar at the time. And for a considerable time afterwards."

"It was unfortunate I wasn't in that night," Olga said. "It was the one night I missed, the night of the fire. But the phone call ties it down."

"Of course. Anyhow, there were other witnesses. Mrs. Dempsey remembers O'Toole tripping across her as he staggered up to get cigarettes out of the machine. And she remembers Tom Pat taking my phone call and saying that we were coming home on the following day. There were nine or ten others who were here, who are willing to swear the same."

"They'll swear to it?"

"Four or five of them have been up with the solicitor already to make statements."

"Did you tell the guards about O'Toole?"

"I didn't. Tom did. He went up to see the Sergeant, but he got nowhere. The Sergeant said it was as much as his job was worth to interfere, that it was out of his hands."

"In the hands of the Heavy Gang?"

"I suppose so."

On Wednesday January 21, 1982, the trial of the four men on a charge of maliciously setting fire to the Orange Hall on the night of July 31-August 1, opened in Dublin's Criminal Court. O'Toole was called to the witness-box on the Friday. He insisted that he made and signed a confession under duress, claiming that he was hit by a detective and knocked to the floor during an interview in Monaghan Garda Station after his October arrest. He stated that he was struck several more times and that, when he refused to sign the statement, he received a karate chop on the back of his neck.

One morning, in the middle of the following week, Olga arrived early in the bar. She was on her way to the trial, which she had attended every day.

"Where's Tom?" she demanded.

"He's still in bed," Maisie told her. "I'll call him. It's time he was up anyhow."

"No, leave him there. I haven't time. I want to get to Dublin, but he should be up there too. Nearly every detective mentioned Burke's bar when giving evidence. It's the same old rubbish as Mahoney goes on with, putting it over that Tom was trying to subvert young lads during the H-Block marches. It's quite obvious that they're trying to create the impression that Tom is some sort of an evil genius, corrupting young people, as Mahoney puts it, and that in some way Tom was involved in hatching the conspiracy to burn the hall."

"You're not serious, Olga?"

" Well, that's the impression they created on me, Maisie. Tom should be there."

That afternoon, Tom verified from one of the defending solicitors that the name of the bar had been gratuitously bartered around by detectives in evidence.

"It's fairly obvious," the solicitor told them, "they're trying to drag in your name, Tom, as often as they can. What they're trying to convey or suggest to the court, without putting it in so many words, is that because you organised the H-Block protests, you have some responsibility for the burning of the hall too."

"It was the bloody opposite," Tom said. "I warned everyone when Bobby Sands died and feelings ran high. I overheard some talk one night and I stopped a group taking wild action. In fact, I did more than any person in Tunnygee to keep the situation under control. I'd like you to call me as a defence witness," he told the solicitor.

"I don't think that's necessary," the solicitor advised, "All mention of you is completely irrelevant in the context of the trial."

The evidence of the three other defendants was in line with that of O'Toole. They had all been beaten, but it seemed that the last man to give evidence had suffered most grievously. He was a good witness, as to how he received his injuries during interrogation, as was his mother to his physical state afterwards. It was the medical evidence in relation to his injuries that did most to undermine the State case.

"Watching this young man giving evidence," the doctor said, "I could scarcely believe that he was the person I examined in the Garda Station. He is obviously an intelligent, alert young man, as he demonstrated here while giving evidence, but when I met him in the station, I thought he was subnormal, he was so distressed and disorientated."

"Was this distress and disorientation caused by pressure, either physical or mental?" counsel asked.

"Both."

"During interrogation?"

"Yes."

Despite this evidence and other medical evidence, which showed that all of the accused showed signs of injury to varying degrees, detective after detective told the court that not a hand was laid on any of them, and that no undue pressure, psychological or otherwise, was exerted to obtain the statements. At the end of the prosecution evidence, the court accepted the defence contention that the statements were not voluntary, and threw out the case, thus rejecting the police evidence as to the manner in which the statements were obtained.

The delighted defendants left the court to stand chatting and laughing with friends in the watery sunshine outside the historic Green Street building, from where Irish patriots of the past had gone out either to face long prison sentences or the hangman's rope. Unaware of the history that surrounded them in the barricaded, rundown Dublin street, the four clapped each other on the back and shook hands with their friends and the twenty or thirty people who had come to give evidence on their behalf.

"In a way, it's a pity the case didn't go on," Tom Pat said, "It would have vindicated the lads more, if the defence witnesses had given evidence."

"Maybe, maybe," his father demurred, "but if the statements had been admitted, it would have been very difficult to counteract them."

"It's ridiculous," Tom Pat declared. "The guards can do what they like. They hammered the shit out of me because an old geriatric of an officer ran me out like a hare to the hounds and then they can go in there and swear they never lifted a hand to anyone. I bet you they won't be charged with anything."

"If you're thinking of false evidence, that's very hard to prove, Tom Pat," his father said.

"I don't know about that, but anyway, the State doesn't want to prove it. Justice doesn't matter. It's more important to protect the police. The whole thing would make you sick. It's no wonder people are losing respect for the guards."

"You shouldn't talk like that, Tom Pat," Tom said. "You have to have a police force. Anyway, there are bad apples in every organisation."

"There were a hell of a lot of bad apples in that court, dad, and you know that."

"Aye, but you still have to have a police force."

"But not a bunch of thugs, dad. See the way they talked about you, throwing the name of the pub around, trying to drag you into it. What was that only badness, just because you're not afraid to stand up for something? They're more subversive than the so-called subversives."

"That's not true,Tom Pat."

"Only I know you, dad, I'd nearly believe you. But you don't fool me. They act the way they do, because the politicians let them, because it suits the politicians, and then...then, they excuse themselves because they're doing their duty, doing what they're told, just like the Nazis at Nuremberg attempted to excuse themselves. But a good few of the Nazis found themselves with a noose around their necks."

"I'm not going to argue with you, Tom Pat."

"That's right, cut me off. Well, I'll tell you one thing. I'm honest with myself. I see what went on in that court and it turns me off. It would drive a fellow into the I.R.A."

"That is not going to solve anything."

"Maybe it's not, but it's worth a try."

"Don't be foolish, son..... Are you ready to come home?"

"Patrick's flying in at ten."

"Oh, I forgot. Is Olga going to meet him?"

"She is. I'll travel with her.."

* * *

Two days after his arrival home, Patrick called to the bar shortly after it had opened.

"Peadar's not coming in today," he told Maisie.

"I expected that. He wasn't in the best of form yesterday."

"Is Tom Pat in?"

"Yes. I think I hear him moving about upstairs. Go up if you like."

"Thanks Mrs. Burke, I'll do that."

"You got very polite, Patrick. It used to be Maisie before you went to England. There's something very strange going on. What trickery are you up to?" she grinned up into the open smiling face of the big man.

"I'm up to no trickery, Maisie."

"I hope not," Maisie said, as he grinned down at her.

"I'm going for a spin with Patrick," Tom Pat said when he came down a few minutes later.

He did not arrive home that night and was still missing next morning.

"I don't want to create a furore, but I'm worried, Tom. You've no idea where he is?" Maisie persisted.

"As I told you already, I've the same idea as you have. That Patrick fella's probably in the I.R.A. in England. Did you not ring Olga yet? She might know something."

Olga was matter of fact when she answered the phone: "Yes, they're in Belfast. They should be home today sometime. Did Patrick not tell you?"

"No, he didn't."

"He's too well trained," Olga laughed.

"What do you mean?"

"Nothing Maisie, only a joke, that's all it is, a joke, Maisie."

"Is he in the I.R.A.?"

"If he is, he didn't tell me. Anyway, if he was, he'd keep his mouth shut."

"Olga, will you answer me straight? What are they really doing in Belfast?"

"I can't answer for Tom Pat, but Patrick went up to see his girlfriend."

"His girlfriend?"

"Yes, Mary Rose Houlihan, Mike's daughter.

"I know who she is,"Maisie cut her short.

"And you probably know also that Mary Rose is nursing in the Royal Victoria in Belfast now. She's there since she finished her training in London. You knew they were seeing each other in England?"

"But I thought it was all off since Mary Rose came back to Belfast."

"So did I, but she rang the night before last and off he went yesterday morning. He said he'd be home today. So, there's no need to worry, Maisie."

"That's a relief, Olga. I admit I was worried. All sorts of ideas ran through my head."

"It's only love, Maisie. Patrick is like me. He is a good lover and when Miss Houlihan calls, he, like Sir Galahad, goes to the rescue."

"What are Mike and Sylvia going to say when they hear they are back together again?"

"I don't think they'll be too happy, but it is strange, isn't it?" Olga asked.

"I suppose you could say that, but Patrick and Mary Rose were together for three years in England."

"Yes, but that's not what I meant. I left Mike and went off with Butsy. He swept me off my feet the very first night. You remember, of course, Maisie?" Olga laughed into the phone .

How could I ever forget? You and Butsy in the kitchen and Mike, at the end of the bed, staring into his bottle of stout. How could I forget?" Maisie laughed at the memory also.

"And then the row and, now, Mary Rose calls me when she's in trouble."

"Trouble?" Maisie was alert again.

"Yes, she wanted me to go up. I thought that strange. Why not call your parents, I asked. Not under any circumstances, she said. When I mentioned that Patrick was home she was delighted. Anyway, she left a number and Patrick rang her when he came in. And Tom Pat and himself headed off yesterday."

"Is she pregnant?"

"No, I don't think so. It's something else."

"It can't be that serious?"

"I don't know. Anyhow, we haven't much longer to wait to solve the mystery. They should be here today sometime."

Josie Tynan brought the first definite news.

"Young Patrick Dwyer is above in the barracks. He was arrested below in the wood an hour ago," he told Tom.

A few minutes later, Tom's Aunt Bernadette arrived. Tom was very surprised to see her. She only came to Tunnygee rarely and, then, on very special occasions.

"Tom Pat is outside," she whispered across the counter.

"Outside? Where?" Tom looked at her.

"He's out in the car. He hurt his leg, but he's alright. It's only a bit stiff and sore. Paul's in the car with him. If you open the halldoor, we'll bring him in and up the stairs."

Tom went to open the halldoor. When Bernadette went out, Josie followed her.

"I thought you might want a hand," he said, when he reached the car, where Tom Pat sat on the back seat, dwarfed by the big frame of Paul Comiskey, who sat beside him, a protective arm around his shoulders.

"What's wrong with him?" Josie asked.

"Never mind what's wrong with him. Just give us a hand to get him inside," Comiskey muttered.

Obviously weak, Tom Pat made an attempt to hop on one foot as the two men half-lifted him into the hall.

"It'll be awkward going up the stairs," Josie said.

"Leave him to me and we'll manage alright," Comiskey assured him.

There was sweat on Tom Pat's forehead, accentuated by the pallor of his normally tanned skin, as Comiskey laid him gently on the bed.

"He's as cold as death," Maisie said, putting a hand on his forehead.

"You go and get a couple of hotwater bottles, Maisie, and I'll get him under the clothes," Comiskey said in his quiet practical voice.

"I'd go for the doctor," he told Tom.

The wound on Tom Pat's leg was ugly looking, but not too deep.

"He won't die this time," the doctor said, putting a final knot on the bandage. "I don't know what happened him and I don't want to know, but he's exhausted. He needs about twenty-four hours sleep and there won't be a bother on him."

Peadar went bail for Patrick, and the two of them and Olga were in the bar, when Tom and the doctor arrived downstairs.

"What do you think of this young reprobate?" Peadar asked, when the doctor left. "Going off and nearly getting himself killed, crashing into a tree in the wood and, worse, writing off my brand new Granada. That's what I call adding insult to injury."

"You've no injuries?" Tom asked Patrick.

"Only a scratch over the eye here," Patrick pointed to sticking plaster over his left eye.

"He was a very lucky boy," said Olga.

"What did the guards say?" Tom asked.

"They had plenty to say," Olga laughed. "He's charged with failing to stop at a checkpoint, speeding and dangerous driving and several other small charges, including not having a driving licence."

"He won't swing for any of them," Tom said drily.

"Tom Pat got safely away," Olga said, half statement, half question.

"Well, something happened him in the meantime then. He's upstairs in bed, out to the world, and a fair old tear in his leg."

"It happened after he left me," Patrick said cryptically, as Maisie called Tom from the end of the bar.

He followed her out to the hall, where Paul and Bernadette Comiskey waited.

"Mary Rose Houlihan is out in Comiskey's house," Maisie said, "She was in the car too along with Tim Pat and Patrick, when it arrived in the wood. Young Dwyer let them out a few minutes before the crash."

"We'll be on our way, Tom," Bernadette said. "Mary Rose will stay with us until the dust settles a bit."

"What dust?"

"Maisie will tell you all. We told Mary Rose we wouldn't delay," Bernadette smiled, showing her good, white teeth.

It emerged that Mary Rose had attended the occasional Sinn Fein meeting with Patrick in London. Back in Belfast, Philip Raftery, another Sinn Fein sympathiser from London, recognised her and asked if she would assist in nursing a man who had been wounded in an ambush. She agreed to do so. Afterwards, she helped move weapons from one house to another in preparation for an attack on a police patrol. Later, she helped move the weapons back to the original dump. Several weeks after that, a man called to the hospital.

"One of the lads is below in Castlereagh and he's a regular blackbird," he told her. "He mentioned your name, but he made a mistake in the hospital. He told them you worked in the Mater. They're probably checking the Mater at this stage. Philip told me to tell you to get offside as fast as you can."

That evening, she went to a house off the Falls Road, from where she rang Olga. Next day, Patrick and Tom Pat arrived and, after some discussion, it was decided that they should leave Belfast at daybreak on the following morning and cross the border at Aughnacloy. All went well, until safely across the border, about a mile outside of Monaghan, they ran into a garda checkpoint.

"You can't stop. The word might be out about Mary Rose," Tom Pat said as Patrick slowed down.

"Don't worry, here goes," Patrick revved and shot forward, sending a stop sign shooting into the hedge.

Almost immediately, a squad car was on his tail, but Patrick stayed ahead of it easily enough. A few miles further on, two other cars joined the chase and attempts were made to cut him off at two crossroads, but he got away on by-roads on both occasions. At first, he was pushed eastwards and went through Inniskeen at ninety miles an hour, closely followed by two screaming squad cars. He went south of Carrickmacross and on to Shercock. Ten minutes later he shot into Tunnygee wood, hotly pursued by one car. Round by the lake he went, bucketing through the pot-holes, the Garda car remaining on his back bumper.

"Hold tight, I'm going to swing it left over the bridge," he shouted.

He swung round, the body of the car scraping along the low parapet on the right and the wheels skidding in the soft margin, before he straightened out and picked up speed again. Meanwhile, the squad car had overshot the mouth of the bridge and was having difficulty in reversing on the soft river bank. It gave Patrick the vital few seconds he required.

"When I turn to the right at the top of the wee brae here, I'll slow down. That'll be the chance for the two of you to jump out," he shouted.

Both jumped, Tom Pat pulling Mary Rose after him. Mary Rose came to rest in a clump of willows, but Tom Pat went

367

plummeting down into a drain tearing his leg on a jagged root. Patrick continued on to the main roadway through the wood and swung right. A mile further on, he turned up towards the old castle and, then, back down to the lake again. At the end of the shore road his way was blocked by a squad car, with the following car close behind. He swung hard over a small bridge on to the far shore road. He knew it was a *cul de sac*, but he kept going to the end, where, misjudging the speed of the car, he shot over the edge. The car somersaulted twice before coming to rest close to the lake shore. The doors were jammed but he crawled out through the broken rear window. He ran off into the trees and when the guards came upon him five minutes later, he was sitting on a tree stump, an unlighted cigarette in his mouth.

"You haven't a match," he said to the guard who found him.

"It's not a match I'd like to give you," the guard said, pulling him to his feet.

In the squad car, he sat between two guards.

"Where to now?" the driver asked.

"Where do you think, Tunnygee Barracks," the arresting guard said. "By the way, is that cigarette lighter working there? This fella wants a light."

Meanwhile, Tim Pat and Mary Rose had left the wood, Tim Pat leaning heavily on Mary Rose initially, but as he walked the stiffness left his leg, although more blood seeped through the bandage Mary Rose had made from his shirt. Two hours later, an exhausted Tim Pat, and an equally exhausted Mary Rose, knocked on the Comiskey backdoor.

44

The district justice was adamant. There was absolutely no possibility that he would suspend the three months sentence that he had imposed on Patrick.

"My client wishes to appeal," Michael Kilbride, the defending solicitor, said.

"That is your client's right and privilege Mr. Kilbride," the justice was at his grandiose, most gracious best.

"There is no question of Mary Rose marrying a jailbird," Sylvia asserted that evening.

"He's not a jailbird yet," Mike told her.

"Well, he's Olga's son and that's nearly worse. Olga's son marrying our daughter. There's an irony there somewhere,"

"Maybe, there is, but there's not much either of us can do about it. Patrick is nearly thirty and Mary Rose twenty-five. They're both well past the age of reason."

"That doesn't mean that either of them have sense. Mary Rose, our daughter, associating with the I.R.A. and Fangio himself, as the judged called him, driving like a lunatic. The judge was right. He could have killed innocent bystanders going about their lawful business."

"Cut the crap, Sylvia. All you have against him is that he's Olga's son."

"It's enough, isn't it, apart from the fact that he half killed my husband for associating with his precious mother."

"There's nothing wrong with Patrick."

"Except Olga."

"You're just prejudiced, Sylvia."

"At least, I'm honest about it. I may have to accept the marriage, but I don't have to like it."

"Maisie has no objection to her as a mother-in-law for Tom Pat."

"That's Maisie's business. And that's another thing. Did you hear Olga last night? Not a word about today, or that Patrick might go to jail. That possibility was ignored, while she expounded on her plans for the double wedding. A tent on Peadar Kennedy's front lawn, if you don't mind, and, then, a ceremony by the lake shore. It's only a foreigner like her would think of it. I wonder would Fr. Tierney agree? He's such a sweet man, the way she says it, in that simpering voice she puts on sometimes. I wonder would Fr. Tierney agree and she not even a Catholic."

"Still, she drives Peadar to Mass every Sunday and attends the Mass too."

"You still have a soft spot for her, Mike. She can still wrap you round her little finger."

"I'm not too sure about that, Sylvia. The fact is that I am willing to accept the inevitable. Anyway, despite what happened in the past I like Patrick. He's one of the finest young men around. I think our daughter made a good choice."

"And Olga?"

"To blazes with Olga," he reached out and pulled her towards him. "You're getting more stubborn as you get older."

She lay against him, arms around his waist and he kissed her gently on the forehead.

"Do you know, that I am sixty-five next week?" she asked, looking up at him.

"Yes, a fully certified old age pensioner and you not even a grandmother yet," he grinned down at her.

"You should have seen Sylvia's face when I suggested a lakeside ceremony," Olga told Maisie that same evening. "You'd think I was talking about some pagan ritual, involving headless cockerels and dead sheep."

"Well, you have an overpowering personality, Olga."

"Do you know, Maisie, I think that woman still doesn't like me?"

"You hardly expect her to throw her arms about you," Maisie said tartly. "After all you nearly stole her husband a few years ago."

"No matter, that is now in the past. Now we must plan for the future, for the future of our children, of your Tom Pat, of Mary Rose, and of my children and Butsy's, Patrick and Marie."

"Aren't you getting to be the right old matriarch.?"

"Yes, that's right, Maisie. I feel like the earth mother. It must be my Scandinavian blood. That is why I want to make this wedding of my son and daughter a big occasion. That is why I think a big tent for the reception would be a good idea."

"I fully agree, Olga. It would be ideal. Even if it were to rain, the weather will be warm enough in June."

"You don't agree with a lakeside ceremony?"

"What I think doesn't matter. It's Fr. Tierney you have to talk to about that," Maisie told her.

The double wedding took place in Tunnygee parish church in the last week in June, with the reception in a tent on Peadar Kennedy's front lawn.

Under the heading, "Three Tunnygee Families Unite", a double column photograph appeared in the following week's issue of *The News*. Against the background of the lake, with Tom's old home nestling in the hills behind, the two brides sat with the three mothers in front. The five men stood behind.

On Sunday night after the two couples returned from their honeymoon, Tom hosted a party in the hotel to welcome them home. It was a small family gathering and Father Edward McCaffrey, who was home on a short holiday from his parish in the north of England, was among the guests. At the end of the meal, Tom made a speech, in which he jocosely referred to Mary Rose's Republican sympathies which, "like the flower in the desert seemed to spring from the most barren soil". It was an obvious jibe at Mike, whose anti-Republican feelings were well known, and when Mike shook his fist in mock anger at the smiling Tom, there was a general titter. At that point, Tom suggested that Father Edward might like to say a few words.

The priest got to his feet and stood staring over the heads of his audience, apparently lost in thought. His serious mien gradually impressed itself upon and silenced the diners, who watched him as he continued to stare at a seemingly imaginary spot on the opposite wall.

"I came here on a celebratory occasion, invited by my good and lifelong friend, Tom Burke. It is a happy occasion. It should be a happy occasion, but . . ." the priest paused, before continuing in a stronger voice. "I left my parish on Wednesday last, but I left in the afternoon, not in the morning as I had originally planned. Despite my previous arrangements, I did not leave on Wednesday morning because it was my painful duty to officiate at the burial of one of my parishioners, a young man of eighteen years. Tom here spoke of a flower blooming in the desert, or in barren soil, or in some such place, but I want to speak of another flower, the flower of life that bloomed in my young parishioner, but that was cut off all too soon. I speak of a man, a youth, who less than a year ago stood at the street corner, unemployed like his two elder brothers, like his father and his mother. An unemployed member of an unemployed family in an unemployed area, he decided to do something about it and he took the only course, the only means of escape open to him. He joined the army of his country, he joined the British army. Last week, they picked up his scattered remains from a Belfast street and wrapped them in a plastic bag. He had been blown to pieces by an I.R.A. bomb. Why? Why, and I ask you this, my good friend," he looked down at Tom, 'why, Tom, should the son of an Irishman, who, like you, Tom, went to England in the fifties because he could not get a job at home, why should the son, an unemployed youth like his father before him, be blown to bits by another Irishman in the name of Irish freedom?"

"He died because he was a British soldier, not because he was unemployed," Tom Pat said quietly from his seat two chairs away.

"Not good enough, not acceptable, young man. The British army is only in the Six Counties to keep the peace. If it wasn't there, we'd have another Irish civil war."

"What do you think we have now, if it's not war?" Tom Pat persisted.

"Well, if it's war as you say, Tom Pat, it's an immoral war, an unjust war. It's allegedly a war to achieve a united Ireland, but the majority in the Six Counties don't want that. If we want a united Ireland, that majority must be won over. It's not a question of uniting pieces of territory, it's a question of uniting people and you do not unite people by violence. Kill another eighteen-year-old

British youth tomorrow and what will you achieve? It won't unite anything or anybody."

"No, but it might drive the British out, just as you're driving me out," Olga could contain herself no longer. "I'm leaving now and I'm leaving in protest,"

Patrick and Mary Rose followed her from the room.

"So much for the welcome home party," Tom said, half to himself.

"I'm sorry, Tom, but in all conscience I had to say what I did," Father Edward apologised.

"Don't worry about it, Eddie, but you better say Grace before we break up," Tom told him.

Mike accompanied Tom back to the pub. On the way, they caught up with Willie McGinty, moving slowly on a stick.

"Is the old knee still at you, Willie?" Tom asked.

"When you're as old as I am, the old knee might be at you too," Willie said shortly. "But tell me, what do you think of the bold Father McCaffrey now?"

"He's a bit upset because of the young lad he buried," Tom excused the priest.

"Bullshit, Tom, and no one knows it better than you. Eddie's a wrong one. I knew he was a wrong one since the time he wouldn't let us fire the few shots over poor Johny's grave. Anyone that would do that on his own father could only be wrong."

"You're a hard man, Willie. Are you coming down with us?"

"No, thanks, Tom. I can't drink at all this last lock of months. I'm bet. I'm not the man I was, bloody stiff knee and all. I'll head for home, Tom, thanks all the same."

Olga, Patrick and Mary Rose were in the bar when Tom and Mike arrived.

"It's a wonder you didn't bring the Reverend Father with you," Olga said sourly.

"No, he went home," Tom told her.

"Just as well. We'd only have a row. He doesn't know what he's talking about, that fella."

"I don't agree with you, Olga. Edward was right," Mike said. "As far as I'm concerned the I.R.A. are all a crowd of gangsters."

"Will you tell him, or will I tell him, Mary Rose?" Patrick

spoke loudly to catch Mike's attention at the other end of the counter. "It's time he knew the truth. It's time someone told him."

"Shut up, Patrick, you're drunk," Mary Rose warned.

"I'm not drunk, but even if I was, it's time your father knew the truth. I'm in the Movement, did you hear me, Mike? I'm in the Movement. Call us gangsters if you like, Mike, but I'm an I.R.A. man and proud of it. What do you think of that, Mike, your son-in-law an I.R.A. man?"

"I suppose I shouldn't be surprised," Mike said quietly.

"No, Mike, you shouldn't. I'm not surprised either, but unlike you, Mike, I'm proud," Olga said.

"You're a fool, Olga," there was disgust in Mike's voice.

"Yes, Mike, I'm a fool, but, if I am, I'm in good company. Maybe Padraig Pearse was a fool also. He had an English parent too and he knew something about fools. He had something to say about them at Rossa's grave," Olga was contemptuous.

"It doesn't matter what he said. It's in the past. It has no relevance today. It's nearly seventy years ago, you know, since Pearse spoke at the O'Donovan Rossa funeral."

"Maybe you don't want to hear what he said, Mike, but I'll tell you anyway. I, the daughter of an Englishman, will tell you what Pearse, the son of another Englishman, said at the graveside of the old Fenian. *The fools, the fools, the fools! They have left us our Fenian dead, and while Ireland holds these graves, Ireland unfree shall never be at peace.* That's what Pearse said in the months before 1916. Ponder those words well, Mike, and then ask yourself who's the fool."

"You're living in a dream world, Olga. Face facts, for God's sake. We're not able to run the truncated bit of a country we have and you talk about a united Ireland. Forget about it, Olga. Forget about Pearse. Henry Ford said that history is bunk and he was a more practicable Irishman than Pearse any day in the week."

"How dare you insult Pearse in my presence," Olga stood to her full height and stared menacingly at Mike.

Patrick moved down and stood behind her.

"I should have finished the job the last time," he said over her shoulder.

"Calm everyone, everyone calm. Let me handle this, Olga. Let me handle it, Patrick."

Tom took Olga's arms and guided her to her stool, while Mary Rose pulled Patrick back to his seat.

"Now," Tom said, moving in behind the counter "it's two o'clock in the morning and you have a few drinks, so maybe it's time you went home, but before you go, I think Mike should apologise to Olga."

"Why?" Mike demanded.

"Because you were wrong. You were wrong on two counts. You were wrong to denigrate Pearse and, like Henry Ford, you are wrong about history. To say that history is bunk, is too simple. There's a Russian proverb that I heard one time. It tells about the warders tightening the handcuffs and, then, excusing themselves by begging the prisoner, don't dig up the past, forget about the past, just like you, Mike.

"Dwell on the past! The warders warned, and you'll lose an eye! But the warders never finished the proverb, which continued; forget the past and you'll lose both eyes. As I see it, Mike, you're in danger of losing both eyes."

"He's in danger of losing his head too," Patrick growled from the end of the counter.

"Quit that, Patrick, I've the floor," Tom said, "and I've only a few more words to say. A few facts! First, Ireland was partitioned by a British Act of Parliament in 1920. Since then, there have been periodic outbreaks of violence, with young men and women dying on both sides of the border, with bombings in England, while British soldiers, like Eddie's young parishioner, lose their lives in a cause they don't understand, all lending credence to Pearse's claim that Ireland unfree shall never be at peace."

"God, Tom, you never lost it. You were always a great man to give a lecture, speaking down from that high moral plane that you adopt by times. Remember thirty years ago, when I saw you to the boat train at Westland Row, you gave me a lecture that time too. It is long past time you put a sock in it," he glared at Tom. "Well let me tell you something, I'm damned if I'm going to apologise to Olga or anyone else for my beliefs. As far as I'm concerned, it's obscene to encourage young men, or young women either, to go out and kill or be killed to achieve a united Ireland. Answer me something, Olga, and you too, Patrick, what are you going to do with the million Unionists? A united Ireland! Regardless of Pearse, Rossa, Tone and the rest of them, the whole pantheon of Irish heroes from Brian Boru down, this God-forsaken country is not worth the shedding of one single drop of blood. At one stage I might have believed otherwise but no longer. Having said that, I am now going home," Mike declared and walked towards the street door.

"Ireland unfree shall never be at peace," Patrick shouted after him.

45

I n September, Patrick's appeal against his jail sentence was successful. One of the grounds put forward on his behalf was that he was a newly married man and that his wife was expecting a baby.

On the following night, Tom Pat rang him at home and told him that he and a friend would be at the house in about ten minutes.

"That was Tom Pat. I'll probably have to go out. We won't be home until late," he told Mary Rose, who was in bed.

"Tony Dempsey again, I suppose?" she muttered, half asleep.

"With two revolvers and three rounds of ammo, I suppose. He kept us out all night the last time with fifty rounds of nine millimetre. Some quartermaster, that fella," he was derisive.

"Be back as soon as you can, Patrick."

"Don't worry. I won't waste any time."

Two hours later, with Tom Pat driving and Tony in the passenger seat, they were north of Monaghan town.

"Are you nearly there?" Patrick asked, from where he lay sprawled across the back seat.

"Not too far now," Tony answered.

"Slow here a bit now, Tom Pat," he instructed a couple of minutes later. "It's the next lane to the right. We'll have to foot it from there, I'm afraid."

When Tom Pat stopped the car in the overgrown laneway, they removed six sub machine-guns and twelve magazines of ammunition from the boot.

"You brought something worthwhile this time," Patrick said.

"We have to cross the border, so it's not a sound from here on," Tony ignored the comment. "Get a gun on each shoulder and make sure they don't clatter against each other, or against anything else. Four mags apiece. Put them in separate pockets. No noise and no talking from here on. Just follow me."

They crossed two fields and jumped a small stream.

"That was the border," Tony whispered. "The house is over to the right. The moon won't break through till we get there. We're in luck."

They approached the deserted house through an overgrown garden, the damp grass wetting them to the knees. The front door opened straight into the farmhouse kitchen, where they placed the guns and magazines on an old table.

"I'd love a cigarette," Patrick said.

"Don't attempt it," Tony warned. "There are Brits in a hide on the hill not two hundred yards behind us."

"Quiet, there's someone outside," Tom Pat whispered some minutes later, picking up one of the machine guns and slipping a magazine into it.

"It's probably the two lads," Tony said, loading another weapon.

"I don't think so," Tom Pat was at the window. "Two figures crossed the gap into the field and there's three more. There's a bit of a moon now and they're silhouetted against it. And there's a sixth man. It's a patrol and they're taking cover behind the ditch."

"Christ, it's an ambush. They must be on to us. Someone gave the game away," Tony was at the window also.

"I'll go upstairs and have a look," Patrick clicked a magazine into place.

"Watch the noise," Tony warned in a hoarse whisper.

"Fire," the order rang out from behind the ditch, and, almost simultaneously, a fusillade of heavy machine gun fire drowned the fire of the smaller weapons.

"They got the two lads in the yard," Patrick called down the stairs. "The bastards, I'll fix them," he shouted, as he opened fire.

"You fool, Patrick, you haven't a chance," Tony roared up at him.

Bullets battered the front of the house and screamed off into the night. Shattered glass, pieces of window frame and stone chips showered Tom Pat and Tony, as they cowered on the kitchen floor. Ricochets shrieked and tore at the stone walls and floor in the confined space of the kitchen, and the heavy front door was blasted in before the firing ceased.

"If you're alive in there, come out with your hands up," a Yorkshire voice broke the sudden silence.

"What will we do? We're trapped. We'll have to surrender," Tony crawled across the floor.

"Stay where you are for a minute. I'm going upstairs," Tom Pat said.

He was back within seconds.

"He's dead. They nearly blew his head off," he told Tony.

"We'll have to surrender. We'll have to surrender," a frightened Tony murmured.

"Pull yourself together, Tony," Tom Pat half shouted at him. "There's still a chance. There's a ditch to the right of the door. If we charged out, we might make it before they opened fire."

"We hear you. We know you're there!" The Yorkshireman shouted again. "Listen to me and listen carefully, this is your last chance to come out alive. I'm going to count down from ten and on zero we'll blast the house down around your ears. The count starts now. Ten ... Nine... Eight..."

"Follow me," Tom Pat thumped Tony and ran crouching through the door.

He reached the safety of the ditch and threw himself into it, but Tony hesitated too long. He was riddled in the doorway. Tom Pat fired a burst and the ditch erupted in front of him in a volcano of clods and stones. He dropped his gun and ran, his face torn and bloody, but otherwise uninjured. When he reached the field, he instinctively sought the cover of the thick September hedge. He jumped the border stream and, as he crossed the next field, the sound of firing died down. This galvanised him further and he tore through two whitethorn hedges, scarcely slackening his pace. At

378

the car, instinct still guiding him, he reversed out on the road and headed for Monaghan. As he entered the town, he met an armoured car and two loads of soldiers speeding towards the border. At the turn for Cootehill, he saw the police road block was already in position. He turned to the right and went back to the centre of town, where he parked at the Westenra Hotel. Sitting in the car, he took stock of the situation. Suddenly, it came to him. Stay in the hotel. He jumped out of the car, but his clothes were torn and there was blood on his face. He went over to the public toilets, where he washed himself and straightened his clothes as best as he could. He then went back to the hotel and booked in.

He spent the night at the bedroom window, watching for the movements of the security forces. At five, all seemed quiet, but he waited until eight, and was home within an hour. When he entered the kitchen, his father was there, sitting at the table, the radio in front of him.

"Were you there?" Tom asked.

"I was."

"There are four dead. I heard it on the eight o'clock news. Was Patrick with you?"

"He was."

"Is he one of the dead?"

"Yes."

On the following day, the authorities released the bodies from the mortuary at Newry's Daisy Hill Hospital. As Patrick's coffin was put in the hearse, Olga placed the Tricolour on it. An R.U.C. man rushed forward and whipped it off, rolled it in a ball and handed it back to her.

"Don't produce that again until you're back in your own country, back in the Free State," he told her.

"I wonder will Father Thomas come to the funeral?" Olga asked that evening, "I'd love to have him there."

"He doesn't miss many Republican funerals. I suppose we could give him a ring," Tom suggested.

"Do that, Tom. I'd appreciate it very much."

"But where's he based now? I've lost track of him since the H-Block marches."

"What about Charlie Daniels?" Olga asked.

"The very man! He's no longer active, but I'd say he's still in touch with Father Thomas."

"Yes, I'll be there myself," Daniels told Tom when he rang, "and I don't see any reason why Thomas won't be there. We're burying Tony Dempsey on Saturday and the Tunnygee funeral is the next day."

"That's right, after eleven o'clock Mass on Sunday."

"Leave it to me, Tom. I'll have Thomas there. It's the least I could for the son of my old sparring partner, Butsy. How's Olga taking it by the way?"

"I don't know. It's hard to explain. Patrick was the apple of her eye, you know. She feels the loss. Yet, she's proud at the same time, proud of the manner of his death. Proud and defiant too. That's why she'd like Thomas to come. She met him at one of the H-Block marches and she's a great admirer of his. A true Republican, she says."

"Tell her he'll be there. Even if I have to kidnap him to ensure it, he'll be there."

"Thanks, Charlie, I appreciate that and . . . and Olga will appreciate it twice as much, I assure you."

The parish priest said the Mass and Father Thomas delivered the panegyric. Having extolled the virtues of the deceased and having sympathised with the relatives, he went on to speak of the manner of Patrick's death:

"Patrick and his companions died violent deaths in a confrontation with the British army," he told a hushed congregation. "For over seven hundred years, Irish men have died in confrontations with the forces of the Crown. And in the early decades of this century, Irishmen gave their lives to wrest from Britain the freedom we enjoy in this part of the country today. Since then, there has been a continuous stream of what can only be described as patriotically motivated young people in conflict with this State and with Britain because the job was not finished then. Today, our prisons, north and south, are full of such young people, and some not so young, the overwhelming majority of whom would never even have been arrested, if Ireland was not in dispute with Britain over partition. Also there are men and women in British jails serving long sentences who are not guilty of any crime. Wise men tell us that they, whether at home or abroad, are not political prisoners, but the wise men are out of touch with reality. If there was not a political problem, there would be few if any of them in jail, that is the reality.

"Having outlined the case for the defence, as it were, or is it the case for the prosecution? - anyhow, having touched upon the problem, I want to make it clear that I am opposed to violence as a means of solving it. So, like many Irishmen, I'm torn and pulled in two ways. My ideal, my hope, my ambition, my desire, is for a united country, but I do not accept that violence is the best way of achieving it. There must be a better way.

"Coming down in the car this morning, I thought about what I was going to say here today, and I thought of the poet, Yeats. Prior to 1916, he despised Nationalists for lack of action, eulogising Edward Fitzgerald, Robert Emmet and Wolfe Tone, all that delirium of the brave, in his poem, *September 1913*. He told us that romantic Ireland was with the old Fenian, John O'Leary, in the grave.

"Obviously, Yeats espoused violence prior to 1916, yet, when it came, it was too much for him. He regretted it afterwards, wondering if words of his had sent men out to die. I think that in this, Yeats gives expression to the dichotomy of the Irish people in relation to political violence. There's an ambivalence towards it, but it is that very ambivalence that promotes it. And the ambivalence exists because, as prior to 1916, our leaders have not the political will to seek out and eliminate the causes of the political unrest, which sends brave and idealistic young men like Patrick to their deaths.

"In fairness, I and all who condemn violence, be we churchmen or politicians or others, must plead guilty to an element of self-exculpation in our condemnation of political violence, if we leave any stone unturned in our efforts to eliminate the cause of that violence. In that sense, it could be said that we all bear some responsibility for Patrick's death.

"Maybe, it was to us that Yeats referred, when in *September 1913*, he wrote:

What need you, being come to sense,
But fumble in a greasy till
And add the halfpence to the pence
And prayer to shivering prayer, until
You have dried the marrow from the bone.

"If that is so, we, the wisemen of this generation, like the wisemen of 1913, have written Patrick's epitaph: "We have not dried the marrow from the bone. Let us pray."